GOLDEN VENGEANCE

Also by Simon Gandolfi

ALISTAIR MACLEAN'S GOLDEN GIRL

GOLDEN WEB

GOLDEN VENGEANCE

SIMON GANDOLFI

CHAPMANS

First published in Great Britain in 1994 by
Chapmans
An imprint of Orion Books Ltd
Orion House, 5 Upper St Martin's Lane, London WC2H 9EA

A CIP catalogue record for this book is available
from the British Library

ISBN 1 85592 821 3

Printed in Great Britain by
Clays Ltd, St Ives plc.

In memory of Baron Frederick van Pallandt and Susannah, beloved friends, murdered by robbers on board their yacht at Puerto Galera, the Philippines – May, 1994.

ACKNOWLEDGMENTS

My gratitude, in the Philippines, to Maria Nielson for her research, enthusiasm, and extraordinary patience; in Mexico City, to Beldon Butterfield for his hospitality and encouragement during the preparation of the second draft; and to American Airlines for their support and to their staff for having shepherded me through the bewildering jungle of innumerable international airports.

PROLOGUE

He held the Manlicher 9mm sniper rifle cradled against his side. He was a small man. Some reports said he was Spanish or Latin American and he was known as *Sin* in the trade, an abbreviation of *sin error*, Spanish for *without mistake*. It was true that he had never missed a target.

His transport was an ancient open-sided hearse and he lay hidden on a pad of foam inside the ebony coffin plinth.

The back of the hearse resembled a Victorian four-poster bed with chrome crosses crowning the varnished mahogany posts. The engine had overheated in the Hong Kong traffic and he could hear steam escaping from the radiator as they turned in through the wrought iron cemetery gates. The hearse shuddered as the driver eased the wheels over the curb onto the clipped grass.

Sin folded back the two panels in the rear of the plinth. An old wreath of cream plastic lilies camouflaged the opening. He looked out through the centre of the wreath at the grass slope planted with neat rows of stone and granite tombstones. He tapped twice to let the driver know when the freshly dug grave was perfectly centred. The grave was midway up the rise and at a range of one hundred yards. Two cemetery workers were arranging a carpet of plastic grass over the earth which was red and crumbly and shone moist in the fierce sunlight.

The hearse rocked and its springs groaned as the portly Chinese driver clambered out of the cab. Opening a Swiss army knife, he dug the spike into the front left tyre. The jack and wheel brace were stowed in a sunken tray behind the coffin plinth and he raised a stubby thumb at Sin before lifting the lid. Having jacked up the hearse, he removed the wheel and trundled it away to the main road.

*

The funeral of Sir Philip Li's granddaughter, Miss Mai'sin Jasmine Li, took place three hours later on that humid Friday early in the typhoon season. The Episcopalian bishop of Hong Kong conducted the service. Journalists were unsure in their reports as to whether the service marked the end of the most savage of the Colony's financial battles, or merely a truce. The two opposing commanders in the battle attended at the church; Sir Philip Li, naturally, but there was much surprise at Wong Fu's inclusion in this select band of mourners. The two opponents were very different in background and in the reputed conduct of their affairs.

Sir Philip Li was the doyen of old-money Chinese and believed that his immense wealth carried responsibilities to the community. He chaired a dozen major charitable trusts, had sat on official enquiries into the Colony's future, and was party to the British Government's negotiations with the People's Republic of China. He had been invited to give evidence before the Foreign Relations Committee of the US Senate and was a member of the Supervisory Committee on regional aid at the World Bank.

In business he took a paternalistic interest in every part of his empire, while the legend of his kindness came from many small acts rather than from his contributions to formal charities. Thus the mountain of small wreaths came more in gratitude for hospital bills paid or the supporting of an intelligent child through school and university than in memory of the deceased.

Then there was his culture. Having read French literature at Kings College, Oxford, he took his Masters at Princeton in Business Studies and had endowed Chairs of Chinese studies at both universities. He was a trustee of the Royal Opera House, a life benefactor of the Metropolitan; his private collection of glass and of silk prayer mats were reputed to be unique.

Fluent in French and Spanish, he travelled widely and enjoyed the company of presidents, diplomats, and academics. He also enjoyed the confidence of his fellow financiers – at his granddaughter's funeral, Sir Euan Wiley, Chairman of Cairns Oliver, stood at his shoulder, a reminder of Sir Philip's alliance with the great foreign *hong*.

In contrast to Sir Philip Li, the reclusive Wong Fu was new money and spoke a blunt Shanghaiese that hinted at humble beginnings, though this was conjecture, as were most scraps of personal information such as his customary wearing of an old-fashioned skull cap and that he spoke through an interpreter at business meetings. He was reputed to control his empire by telephone and through intermediaries and seldom to leave the fastness of his quarters at the top of the Wong Fu building on Connaught Road. The one certainty proven through a score of cameras smashed by his bodyguards was his hatred of photographers. None of the agencies had photographs of him, nor did photographs exist in the newspaper archives, so that he could walk through Hong Kong without fear of recognition. Yet here he was at the funeral of his rival's granddaughter, and people craned to see into his Mercedes limousine as the funeral cortege left for the cemetery.

For the sidewalk crowds this cavalcade of the great and the good – or at least the great and powerful – was much like the arrivals at the Oscar ceremonies. The crowds responded to the living stars. Perhaps they had sympathy for Sir Philip in his grief, but there.was little interest in the dead girl. Born and educated in the United States of America, she was foreign to local society, nor was the car accident that had killed her sufficiently unusual to arouse comment. However the truth was far more curious and vicious than even the most knowledgeable and imaginative could have guessed.

1

The seven thousand islands of the Philippines archipelago spill like drops of water across the South China Sea. To the south lies the Malaysian province of Sabah and the channel which separates the two nations is one of the busiest shipping lanes in the world. It is also one of the most constricted; at its narrowest point a bare twelve miles across. The International Maritime Bureau warn of piracy in the area.

On this night the soft light of a half-moon touched with pale yellow the strip of coral and sand that marked the southern tip of the archipelago. Two boats waited within the reef. Their black hulls were narrow Vs, sixty feet in length, and five feet in beam. The boats were held from capsizing by outriggers lashed to bamboo poles that arched out fifteen feet from each side of the hulls. Massive petrol engines powered the boats which, fully crewed, could knife over the surface of a calm sea at more than forty knots.

Protected by the island from the faint breeze and from any movement of the sea beyond the reef, the surface of the water was almost invisible and the *baslig*, as the boats are called, appeared to float on arched wings, slender birds of prey, beautiful but deadly.

There were eighteen Filipinos to each boat. Small and neat-bodied, these Muslims of the *Badjao* tribe continued to smile and joke and giggle amongst themselves in these last minutes before they fell on their prey. The four Chinese were very different. They were serious men, professionals in violence, and retainers tied by blood debt to Wong Fu, richest of the new-money Chinese to have settled in Hong Kong in the post-Kuomintang era. Rather than cutlasses, these modern-day pirates carried AK-47s with a fire rate of two hundred rounds per minute. The pirates also carried sidearms and leaf-shaped *barong* knives honed razor sharp. And two of the Chinese bore grenades on their belts.

The senior Chinese squatted over a direction finder. No expression betrayed his thoughts as he watched the pinpoint of light creep out from the edge of the screen. The light was their target, a three thousand ton freighter on its maiden voyage from the ship-yards of South Korea to Davao in the Southern Philippines, then onward to Singapore.

Three hundred feet in length, sixty feet in beam, the MV *Ts'ai Yen* had been designed to carry two thousand tons of mixed cargo at a cruising speed of eighteen knots. However this was the *Ts'ai Yen*'s maiden voyage and the chief engineer kept the MAN diesel down to three-fifths of its designated cruising revolutions. The *Ts'ai Yen* sailed under the Philippines flag with the South Asia Sail & Steam Ship Company as registered owners and Manila as her home port. In fact the freighter was the latest addition to the merchant and passenger fleet of Sir Philip Li.

The *Ts'ai Yen* carried a Filipino crew of eight men, a Croatian skipper, Seychelleois first officer, Hong Kong Chinese second officer, and two Taiwanese engineers. Thirty-two ships showed on the freighter's radar screen as she pushed westward up the channel and both the skipper and first officer were on watch in the wheelhouse with the helmsman. Meanwhile, from the shadows of a lifeboat, the tall young Chinese second officer watched the ship's only passenger, Miss Jasmine Li.

Twenty-two years old, Jasmine, or Jay as she was known, was the only daughter of Sir Philip's younger son, Peter, a naturalised US citizen, as was her mother. Her parents had been killed by muggers in Washington, and her grandfather had wanted her brought to Hong Kong. Her mother's family, strongly supported by Sir Philip's wife, had argued that she be educated in the United States. As a result, Jay had attended an East-Coast prep school before majoring in creative writing. Jay would have preferred the Idaho State programme but her grandfather had stipulated one of the prestigious women's universities, Wellesley or Bennington. Not daring to argue, Jay chose Wellesley where most of her school friends had enrolled. Now Sir Philip wanted her safely married, preferably to a Chinese descendant of one of Hong Kong's founding houses. Jay's grandmother had presented, through continual allusion in conversation, a short-list of candidates. Jay wanted none of them.

Leaning against the rail, she looked down on the curtain of phosphorescence tossed aside by the ship's bows. She had imagined the sea as freedom but, as always, the second officer watched from the shadows, one more bar in the cage constructed to protect her from any error of behaviour.

Briefly she considered demanding to be left alone. But it was pointless. The second officer would be polite, apologetic, a little embarrassed. To disguise his vigilance, he would bow in pretended obedience, and seem to look at his feet while his eyes never ceased for an instant their patrol of Jay's surroundings. Unconsciously, he would clench and relax his hands, an exercise that corded his arms and transformed his gently sloping shoulders into hills of muscle.

The anger tasted suddenly sour in her mouth. She turned away from the sea and, without acknowledging the watcher, ducked in through the steel companionway that led to the officers' accommodation. The second officer's cabin was hers for the voyage while this fake second officer who had been set to protect her slept, if he slept, on a couch in the saloon.

In Jay's small cabin the bunk ran fore and aft below the single porthole. A narrow tabletop supported by two sets of drawers served as a desk or dressing table. There were also a folding chair and a hanging locker. The head contained a marine toilet, shower, and handbasin.

Jay's laptop computer waited open on the tabletop. The cargo-handling machinery on the *Ts'ai Yen* was the most modern available and Jay had contracted under a pen name to write three separate articles on the freighter's maiden voyage. She had set herself a goal of two thousand words a day. At a guess, she had written two hundred opening paragraphs and she stood now, confronting herself in the mirror screwed to the bulkhead above the table top.

At school and at university she had possessed a very clear concept of who she was and her friends had envied her certainty. But in her first week home in Hong Kong, her grandmother had warned over lunch at Gaddi's restaurant in the Peninsular Hotel that her every action reflected on her family; her clothes, of course; how much she showed of her body, whether on the tennis court, at the pool, or on the Sunday outings that were called sailing by her grandfather's generation; two or three motor yachts rafted up in a bay, each yacht with a ten-man crew in starched whites, *mah jong* played with tiles that would have graced a museum.

For Jay, sailing was weekends at Martha's Vineyard and the long beat back into a head wind on an eighteen-foot open sloop, spray soaked, and with nothing but a mug of hot chicken soup from a thermos for reward as they rounded the point and eased the sheets for the final three-mile reach south to the yacht club. There were barbecues on the beach, moonlight swims, races down the hard sand at the tide edge, sometimes a lover.

This was the Massachusetts she remembered and she recalled the parents of her school friends who had summer houses on the beach with driveways that could as well have had signs on them, *No Jews*. But Jay was Sir Philip Li's granddaughter and an Episcopalian – ships, property, cattle ranches, a couple of banks.

That was the society she had belonged to and she hadn't thought of herself as special. She could have been Richard Smith's daughter; banks, steel.

Or banks and coal.

Or banks and any other raw material or industry.

Banks were the passport. Proper banks. Old Money. There wasn't a proper banker on the beach who didn't know that Sir Philip Li's great-great-grandfather had banked two Scots traders in Macau against the Company, Jack Cairns and Matthew Oliver, and after the destruction of their opium by the Chinese Emperor's Special Commissioner, Lin Tse-hsu, in 1839, provided fresh finance, and later financed their relocation on Hong Kong.

Cairns Oliver, Jardine Matheson, Swires: these were the original great European *hongs* or trading houses. Now they had mushroomed into vast multi-nationals with their billions of dollars in shares traded on the world's stock markets. There was only one shareholder in the house of Li, Sir Philip.

As she confronted herself in the mirror, Jay acknowledged that there would be a single shareholder in Jay Li as long as she remained a member of the House of Li. Even were she to marry in Hong Kong, she would remain Sir Philip Li's granddaughter. She was a possession. She always had been. Any belief she had of being her own person was self-deception.

She drew down the zip on her raw silk boilersuit to reveal a slim, small-breasted, and almost boyish figure. Hours on the tennis court had given her strong thighs and she had played two-handed from

13

the start so that there was no difference in musculature between one arm and the other. She wore her hair clipped short, neat ears, small nose, ebony eyes spaced well apart, clean jawline – attractive to men, Chinese or otherwise – but even this she owed to her genes.

During her last months in the States, she had overheard rumours that her grandfather had expected an up-turn after the past two years of world recession and had speculated in the London property market. The amounts whispered were in billions. Though her grandfather had bought cheaply, he had borrowed at high interest and was overextended. There were snippets in the financial pages that he was expected to ask the banks to renegotiate his loans or roll over the debt. He had been criticised for being old-fashioned and too set in his ways while, at the same time, linked with other big players who had fallen over the past years.

Jay knew her grandfather better. He never played. During the day he wore a grey suit. In the evenings, either dark blue or a dinner jacket, black of course. White dinner jackets were for waiters and musicians. No; her grandfather never played. Jay smiled at the thought.

She wondered whether she loved him but it was the wrong question. He was more a power than a human being. In general a benevolent power, she thought, and to be admired and respected, but to be feared, too, like the distant volcano she had seen from the deck, which could be harnessed to produce thermal power but with its power unleashed, became a massive force of destruction.

The moon had set and the *Ts'ai Yen*'s navigation lights shone against the deep matt darkness so that the leader of Wong Fu's Chinese had no further need for the direction finder. The leader had ordered the black-hulled pirate ships out from behind the island and they waited now in the path of the freighter. Sound travels far across the sea and even the Filipino *Badjaos* were silent. They could hear, through the gentle slap of the sea against the hulls, the low grumble of the *Ts'ai Yen*'s diesel. The soft orange glow of an active volcano showed to the north and a faint trace of sulphur scented the warm salt air while the boats had their own smell of dead fish and coconut oil.

As the pirate *baslig* rose to the slight swell, their outriggers dripped minute trails of phosphorescence. Each boat carried an eighty-five-metre coil of nylon warp. The two ropes were knotted to each other and the weight of the loop held their bows together. The *Badjaos* fidgeted to ease their muscles. The spread V of the freighter's bow wave was clearly visible. The Chinese leader gave the command and men in the bows paid out the two warps as the pirate craft leapt apart.

The *Ts'ai Yen* drove between the two *baslig*. Her bow caught the rope so that she snatched and held the pirate boats against her sides aft of the wheelhouse where they were hidden from the three men on watch. Muffled grappling hooks on light lines curled over the freighter's rails. In seconds the first pirates reached the after deck. Dressed in black and on bare feet, they were almost invisible. The Chinese led in the race to the twin external companionways that led up from the cargo deck to the wheelhouse. A low whistle signalled the moment. Feet smashed open the port and starboard doors.

The skipper held a steaming mug of coffee. He was a tall man, grey-haired, and with a sternly upright carriage. The leader of the Chinese put three bullets through his heart. A single bullet smashed through the first officer's forehead. With the automatic pilot steering the ship, the helmsman had been keeping watch to starboard. Fear made him dribble as he dropped to his knees. His prayers were Christian and one of the Muslin *Badjao* giggled as he shot him first in the back of the legs and then six times more in the spine before finally firing a burst into his skull. The Chinese were already gone from the wheelhouse.

The second officer had been resting on the couch in the saloon. There was hardly a measurable lag between the shots in the wheelhouse and his feet hitting the deck, a 9mm Colt automatic drawn from a spring ankle holster. He opened the door to the corridor and saw two Chinese armed with AK-47s. The lead pirate kicked open the door to the skipper's cabin while the second man hosed the corridor. Had Lu tried to reach Jay, he would have died inside his first step.

Lu slammed the saloon door and shot the bolt. He had ten seconds at the most. The attackers must have boarded aft of the wheelhouse. He spun loose the brass fasteners on the forward of the saloon's three portholes. The porthole opened on to a narrow side deck enclosed by a vertical extension of the ship's hull. The attackers would have left at least one sentry covering the side deck.

Lu gripped the trigger guard of the Colt automatic between his teeth. He grabbed an overhead pipe that fed the fire sprinklers, swung away from the porthole, then forward, and shot through the porthole feet first. The Colt was already back in his hand as he hit the deck. A burst of automatic rifle fire spattered the bulkheads as he somersaulted on his left shoulder and he returned fire, not at a target, but to distract the pirate's aim. One more somersault took him out onto the forward deck. He grabbed the top rail with his left hand and fired again as he kicked off with his left foot. It was a gymnast's move that sent him arcing over the rail on one arm. He saw the bows of a *baslig* below. The hull was painted black inside and out with four grey ribs between the engine compartment and a second bulkhead midway between the engine and the decked bow section. Tucked into a ball, he fell with his arms round his head. His right shoulder smashed down on the bamboo pole that held the forward end of the outrigger and he pitched forward into the water. He dived immediately and kicked desperately to escape the deadly whirlpool that swirled above the huge propellor. The *Ts'ai Yen*'s lights disappeared into the distance. Then he was alone in the ocean.

The shots that killed the men in the wheelhouse jerked Jay out of deep sleep. For a moment she was undecided as to what she had heard and, if she had heard shots, whether they were in a dream or were real. Then came the hammer blows and thunderous echo of automatic fire out in the corridor that had sent the second officer diving back into the saloon. More shooting came from other parts of the ship. She heard the door of the first officer's cabin next door smash open. She sat squeezed into the angle of the bulkheads at the head of her bunk with the sheet clutched to her chin. She wasn't able to think and didn't seem to be a part of herself but had become more an abstract recorder supported in some sort of vacuum. The vacuum was intensely vulnerable. Even the slightest movement would shatter it so she held her body immobile in the bunk even when the door to the cabin slammed open and she saw the two Chinese dressed in black cotton roll-necks and loose-fitting black pants.

The leader of the Chinese grabbed the sheet back: 'It's her.'

'She looks like a boy,' his companion said, and the leader chuckled deep in his throat:

'Then use her like a boy.' He grabbed Jay by the hair. The

vacuum that had held her burst and she screamed and clawed at his face.

He hit her once on the side of the jaw and she collapsed, unconscious. The two men bundled her in the sheet and carried her out onto the deck. The other two Chinese reported that one man had escaped from the officer's saloon. Two *Badjao* had been left to guard the deck against escape and the leader of the Chinese ordered them to the ship's rail, faces to the sea. He shot them in the back of the head and pitched them into the water.

'Let this be a warning,' he told the remained *Badjao*: 'We pay you well but neither God nor Prophet will save you from mistakes.'

The leader ran to the wheelhouse while his Chinese companions lowered Jay into the port side *baslig*. He smashed the ship's radio and changed the course on the automatic pilot to take the freighter clear of the shipping lane. Next he brought the engine up to full speed and switched off the navigation lights. Taking a miniature radio beacon from his belt, he unscrewed the plastic cap that protected the activating switch.

2

The resident director of the Clean Construction Timber Company
had returned soon after dusk to the Company's top-floor office in
Davao City on Mindanao Island in the southern Philippines. The
radio receiver beside him was fixed in frequency by a crystal
identical to that of the beacon activated on the *Ts'ai Yen*. The
transmission came at 04.21 hours. The Director fed the following
week's schedule for his logging teams to the fax machine and
transmitted it to the Clean Construction office in Hong Kong
together with a cash flow projection of the logging operation for the
following month.

In Hong Kong the Clean Construction office stood at the rear of
the company's private wharf and timber-yard. The manager had
watched, for the past couple of hours, logs of Philippine mahogany
swing ashore from the Wong Fu freighters that had docked that
evening. All managerial staff in the Fu combine were relatives and
this nephew had been bought out of Shanghai in the final year of
the Cultural Revolution.

He took a photocopy of each fax before filing the originals. The
photocopies he slid into a transparent cover. He flinched as he
stepped out of the air-conditioned office into the yard, the air an
almost solid barrier of humidity thickened with warm diesel oil, sea
salt and the stink of rotting fish, pine tar and fresh sawdust. The
pale yellow light of a dozen arc lamps shone on the sweat-drenched
chests and biceps of the dockworkers, small, pale-skinned men with
bow legs and tight bunches of muscle. A stevedore yelled instructions above the whine of the freighter's derricks. A circular saw
shrieked. The manager dodged a fork-lift truck.

A narrow side door opened to an alley that led up the wall of the
timber-yard to the main road. At this hour the bicycles and

motorcycles of night workers, heavy lorries, and delivery trucks made up the bulk of Hong Kong's never-ceasing traffic and a car would have attracted more notice than a passer-by on foot.

The manager's path led through a half-dozen blocks of go-downs and warehouses, doors open in forlorn hope of a breeze shifting the muggy air. Tired, sweaty faces peered at him from the food stalls that lined the sidewalk, soup bubbling over charcoal, heaps of thread-thin noodles, shrimp, duck, chicken.

As the manager scurried along the sidewalk, he glimpsed men and women and children hunched over work benches in the go-downs. The hiss of soldering irons and shrill of lathes filled his ears, and, over all, came the continual suck and belch of injection moulds allied to the stench of heated plastic.

As he crossed Connaught Road, stock and money brokers were already driving down for the close on Wall Street. The Fu building was a three-sided crystal of blue glass drawn to a point thirty storeys high. A uniformed security guard let the manager in through the service entrance and he inserted his card into the slot by the private elevator to his employer's penthouse. Once within the elevator, a video camera inspected him and Wong Fu's personal bodyguard met him in the narrow lobby from which a single flight of marble steps led to carved doors that had come from a mainland fortress of the thirteenth century. Wong Fu's decorator had discovered the doors and his security consultant had ordered them transformed into a sandwich filled with thirty millimetres of steel armour.

The door opened at the touch of a button. Wong Fu stood behind a thick crescent of rose-tinted marble twenty feet long by four deep. The desk, with its five sunken VDUs, was an anchorman's fantasy but Wong Fu dominated it as he did the vast glass three-sided pyramid of a room. He was tall, his face square and thrust forward on a short neck, broad-shouldered, and with the barrel chest of an all-in wrestler.

He wore his scalp shaved and seemingly polished to confront the world with the white scar that ran from a point three inches above his right eyebrow diagonally back over his skull to end a little to the rear of his left ear. The two centre knuckles of his right hand were crushed. They were heavy hands with thick fingers still webbed with the muscles of his childhood servitude to a blacksmith's forge and he wore a workman's suit of washable blue cotton. The unpadded jacket hung open to disclose a monogrammed Jermyn Street shirt of dark primrose silk and a paler pink tie with diamond shapes patterned in the weave. His shoes were bespoke Florentian wafers of the finest leather; silk socks, and for jewellery a heavy signet ring set with a green jade *chop* and a *Patek Philippe* watch on a woven gold band.

Even had he wished, there could have been no concealment of the power behind his eyes which were almost black and set far apart. And there was something of the jungle cat in him as he accepted the photocopies, something threatening and arbitrarily cruel.

Dismissing his nephew, he crossed to the triangular wall of tinted window that looked out across the city toward the Li compound. Wong Fu hated the old-money mandarins of Hong Kong. He hated them for their polite language, and their education; but, most of all, he hated them for their culture. Their culture had trapped him. Sir Philip Li's culture.

Born under the Japanese occupation, physical strength had made Wong Fu leader on his block but his intelligence led him to the opportunities offered by civil war between Kuomintang and Communists. There was no law so crime became unpunishable while inflation made cash worthless. Wong Fu led five companions in pillage of the rich. Antique objects d'art were their booty, more prized than gold or jewels, worth more in weight, and untraceable, so Wong Fu thought.

He learnt values with a knife to the throat of his victims. The fences belonged to one or other of the *triads*, the criminal fraternities who were part of China's establishment and might offer protection and restitution to his victims. Wong Fu wanted no part of them. He intended flight to Hong Kong with his booty as investment capital.

He and his companions pirated a small junk and forced the crew to take them to the colony. Wong Fu was the lone survivor of the voyage and came ashore in the junk's sampan. He bought residency and work permits with gold and worked in his old trade as a blacksmith for six months while acclimatising himself. Then he approached the owner of an antique shop with the least valuable of his pieces. Through the antiquarian he came to his first dealer and so on up the ladder until finally the best of his glass was exhibited to Sir Philip Li.

Wong Fu expected to be shown immediately into Sir Philip's

presence and had rehearsed remarks that would found his business connection with the colony's aristocracy. However he had failed to comprehend the encyclopaedic knowledge of the great collectors. A majordomo ordered him round to the servants' entrance. From there he was shown across to a windowless concrete lean-to where Sir Philip waited.

Wong Fu's pieces had been arranged on plum-coloured velvet spread on a trestle table. The long hooded light left the rest of the room in gloom and Wong Fu had been unable to see Sir Philip's face as the mandarin indicated the delicate glass with the tip of an ivory wand. Voice quiet and cultured, Sir Philip had recounted the history of each piece, its owner, and the circumstances of the robbery.

'You are a murderer and a thief,' Sir Philip finished without apparent emotion; he was simply stating the obvious: 'Scum. Take your stolen goods and get out.'

From that moment the respected old money of Chinese Hong Kong was closed to Wong Fu. Worse, Sir Philip had traced the relations of Wong Fu's victims so that they should know against whom to seek vengeance. Thus the steel doors, the bullet-proof cars, and the bodyguards.

As always, thoughts of Sir Philip Li made the scar across Wong Fu's scalp throb and become tinged with crimson. But now, finally, the mandarin had made a mistake and Wong Fu could taste the sweetness of revenge as he turned away from the window to review his troops ready marshalled on the battle ground of the computer screens.

The screens showed Sir Philip's exposure to the banks at 2.8 billion pounds Sterling. Twice already he had delayed repayments – true, for only a matter of days. Now he was thirty-six hours late with payment of interest on a twelve-million-dollar loan at Hong Kong City Trust. For months Wong Fu's agents had fed rumours into the markets; Sir Philip's reputation had withstood the attacks.

Now Wong Fu had attacked from a fresh direction, a play in four acts. First came the attack by pirates; then the mental and physical destruction of the girl; her theatrical rescue by Wong Fu's own men; and finally the press conference at which Wong Fu would present her to the cameras.

Driven insane by rape and torture, she would stand dribbling on the stage, symbol of Sir Philip's failing strength. What faith could

21

people place in a man incapable of protecting his own granddaughter? What greater loss of *face* could Sir Philip suffer? *Face*, that fragile amalgam of dignity and pride in conduct and position, was all important in the East. The run on the Li investments would begin; first the banks in which Wong Fu held large stakes; then the final panic as every petty financier ran for shelter. Wong Fu would swallow up the pieces at ten cents in the dollar. However the profit was unimportant. It was the taste of vengeance that he longed for as he imagined the freighter *Ts'ai Yen* surge toward the rocks.

With the light north-west breeze on her stern, the sloop-rigged fifty-foot MacAlpine Downey catamaran, *Golden Girl*, slipped through the first light of dawn toward the southern tip of the Palawan islands in the western Philippines.

There was sufficient breeze to fill her spinnaker. Twin aluminium poles held the great balloon of featherweight nylon square across the bows. Connecting the two rudders, a varnished tiller bar ran athwart-ships at the after end of the cockpit. Both dagger boards were down and rubber bungees held the tillers steady while the owner entered a plot on the chart.

The owner had been christened Patrick Mahoney. He had been employed for eighteen years by a department of the British Government's SIS. A brilliant linguist, the combating of terrorism through infiltration had been his expertise. He had operated undercover in Ireland for three years near the end of his service. Supposedly for his future security, his death had been faked in an ambush in South Armagh and a body had been buried there one rainy morning in a small cemetery behind a grey stone village church. Now he answered to Trent, a name confirmed both by his British passport and by the ship's papers.

Trent's Control in the Department had leased him frequently to the American cousins for the 'wet work' forbidden by Congress. With the end of the Cold War, he had been subpoenaed by a Senate Committee. His evidence had earned him the enmity of the conservatives in the intelligence community in both London and Washington. Others considered him a maverick. There were also terrorist groups who had marked him 'seek and destroy', so he was watchful, and thought of himself as careful – an attribute unbelievable to erstwhile colleagues.

A full beard and mop of loosely curling black hair disguised his features and made his age difficult to guess, but he was in his late thirties, supple, and well muscled. A loose smock of light cotton and matching trousers cut midway down his calves hid the scars that hinted at his past employment. A string of coral beads held a small throwing knife to the nape of his neck.

As Patrick Mahoney, he had owned a cottage on the Hamble river. Now the *Golden Girl* was his home and the Caribbean was his usual sailing ground. He had shipped the yacht deck cargo to Manila at the invitation of an Australian friend who had been determined to explore the wreckage of the Japanese fleet sunk off the northern tip of Palawan in 1944. With Puerto Galera as their base, the two men had spent a month scuba diving on the ships. Now Trent was sailing for Singapore and onward passage to the Mediterranean with the same shipping line.

His present course would take him round Balabac Island off the southern tip of the Palawans. The chart table lay to port of the cockpit companionway. A Magellan GPS gave his position within fifty feet and Trent used a brass parallel rule to enter the plot.

He returned to the cockpit armed with a mug of coffee. The wind had lifted with the approach of dawn and swung round a couple of degrees. Trent made a small adjustment to the spinnaker sheets and watched the Brooks and Gatehouse repeater on the cockpit bulkhead. The *Golden Girl* had been designed as an ocean racer. She drew two feet with her blades up and had no need to fight the sea as would a mono hull of the same length with tons of lead to force through the water. Now she stretched into her stride on the freshening breeze and the needle on the speed indicator rose to fifteen knots.

The hulls left two dark tracks pressed on the smooth sea and rather than the crash and slam of a conventional yacht, there came from her bows only a crisp whisper that reminded Trent of skis speeding over the early morning crust of ice crystals that covered spring snow.

Suddenly a huge white curl of a bow wave charged out of the dawn. Trent smashed open the cleats holding the sheets and rammed the helm hard to starboard. The spinnaker flew free and the mainsail slammed over as the bow wave hurled the catamaran away. A black hull drove past, vast as a cliff and menacing, no lights. Then came the suction of the huge propeller and foam drenched the *Golden Girl*'s cockpit. Driving on, the ship left the catamaran rocking in her wake. The mainsail slapped and the spinnaker fluttered pale as a sheeted ghost.

First there had been shock and a fear, familiar, as was the surge of adrenalin and the rage. Trent shivered in the aftermath and cursed as he watched the freighter's stern disappear into the shreds of dawn mist.

Dropping the mainsail, he made his way forward to capture and stow the vast footage of featherweight spinnaker. He worked carefully and with concentration, his movements sure and strong. However thoughts of the ship preyed on his mind. No lights but a freshly painted hull. And the ship had been on a course miles out of the normal shipping lanes. . .

The incongruities nagged. Abandoning the half-bagged spinnaker, he checked the compass before swinging into the saloon. He adjusted the rule across the compass rose on the chart to give the freighter's course and rolled the rule across to his present position.

Puerto Princesa was the nearest harbour but the freighter was on a heading way to the south. Either she changed course or she drove onto the rocks. He judged her speed at eighteen knots. No lights. He hesitated for a moment but the ship was none of his business.

Back on deck he completed the bagging of the spinnaker, set the large jib and sheeted the main, drawing the catamaran back onto her original heading. Streaks of gold tinged the eastern sky, pale at the horizon and darkening above to a deep umber. Then came the lip of the sun to transform the underside of a cloud into shivering waves of fire.

Trent shuddered in sudden memory of another dawn and the sun lifting above the track where it crossed a desert ridge a couple of miles away. The cream Range Rover appeared on the crest. Outlined against the sun, it looked like a melted marshmallow. He had closed his eyes to protect his vision and waited, listening for the engine.

His position overlooked the desert track from a distance of two hundred yards. He used a rifle. Explosives would have been certain and immediate but would have destroyed the briefcase and the Range Rover's radio. The radio was essential to his escape.

He kept his breathing deep and steady while he waited, counting to eight as he inhaled and eight as he exhaled. It was a method of building a barrier against the fear – fear, not for himself, but for what he had to do. Lying there on the dune he had known exactly

24

how it would be: first the driver, then the two bodyguards, lastly the target. He had to confirm the men were dead. He had to disarm the target's briefcase, retrieve the documents that detailed the Russian-designed air defences, remove the radio, then use the explosives in the briefcase to make a pyre of the vehicle. Reporting in on the radio to the target's base would give him an hour's grace.

That had been the first time, and seated now in the *Golden Girl's* cockpit he recalled the feel of the sharp grains of sand pressing against his wrists and the first trickles of warmth seeping into muscles stiff from two days in the saddle.

The first time, and he had wanted to walk back to the waiting camels and ride away as if none of it had happened, none of the training and the months of detailed preparation. It had nothing to do with him. It, of course, was the target and the three other men. Five minutes to wait, and lying there on the dune he had remembered running, as an eight year old boy, along the wooden verandah at the Gulf Sheik's racing stables to his father's office. His father was at his desk. A big old-fashioned revolver lay on the green Morocco bound blotter. His father looked up and Trent had seen the despair and the pleading in his eyes. He had stood frozen in the doorway. He had known what he had to do. He had to cross the few feet to the desk. He had to fling himself into his father's arms and make him feel his love. That was all. Instead he had fled, and for that he could never forgive himself. He fled to the stables and squatted in a corner of the furthest loosebox, hugging his knees to his chest to stop himself disintegrating beneath the weight of misery and guilt.

A groom discovered him there a half-hour after the shot and Trent hadn't cried, not then, nor at the death of his mother three months later at the wheel of her old two seater Jaguar. Trent had driven the same desert road fifteen years after his mother's death. A five mile straight ended with a curve. The concrete wall that she had hit was still there twenty yards back from the road's edge. The Jaguar had been travelling at over a hundred miles an hour.

Trent had been eight years old when his mother died and already in London at the big gloomy house of his adoptive uncle and guardian, Colonel Smith. The Colonel had judged the boy a cold fish for his lack of tears. There had been no affection between them, however the Colonel had paid for Trent's privileged education and recruited him into the SIS, where he had acted as Trent's Control.

Trent hadn't run from his duty that first time on the dune. Years later, as he increasingly questioned the goals set by his Control and by the men in Washington, he had recognised how well he had been programmed. His service in Ireland had been the final turning point. The Colonel had sensed it and, nervous of his giving evidence before the Senate Committee, set him up to be killed in the SAS ambush. Trent had survived only to be set up again in Central America. But Trent had become the hunter, trapping the Colonel, and bargaining his own retreat from the Department into civilian life.

He had thought himself clear of it only to be manoeuvred again, this time by a senior officer of the United States Drug Enforcement Agency. The target was a Cuban Admiral in the drug trade.

But Trent was free now, free for the first time in his adult life. It was this recognition that made him hesitate as he thought again of the unlit freighter. These were pirate waters. It seemed so unlikely in these modern times but he had heard tales from his fellow yachtsmen in Puerto Galera, read newspaper reports of the attacks, and studied the warnings issued to shipping.

Half an hour had passed since the near collision. The freighter must be ten miles away. He knew, even as he dropped the sails and climbed the mast steps, that the ship would be hidden within the last strands of mist to the west above which the dark mauve peaks of Palawan and Balabac floated. There was neither need nor purpose, Trent told himself as, seated on the top spreaders, he searched the horizon through his binoculars. The rising sun slid sheets of gold between the pale strands of mist and the slight swell eased gently under the *Golden Girl*'s twin hulls. Cooled by the night, the sea scent was fresh on the breeze. Only the lap of water between the hulls disturbed the silence.

Rougher sea and wind conditions would have allowed him an escape into action but the peace held him trapped in thoughts of the years in which he had avoided responsibility for his missions because he was under orders.

Now, with freedom, there were no excuses.

Even with the mist gone, the distance to the coast would remain too great for him to spot the freighter against the land and he descended the mast. Dropping into the saloon, he studied the chart for a moment. He considered calling the coastguard, however habit made him reluctant to broadcast his name and the name and position of his ship. He had a week in hand and the coast was little more than an hour away. He returned to the deck, still irresolute. Again he told himself that the ship was none of his concern, that the chances of anything being wrong were slim, and that anyway there was nothing he could do. He was undecided as he raised the sails; however one hour was a small sacrifice with which to pacify his conscience. The sails filled and he drew the *Golden Girl* onto her new course.

3

The repetitive shrill of the telephone woke Sir Philip Li. The telephone was in his study – he considered it immodest to conduct business from his bed. He fumbled at the bedside table for his spectacles and his pocket watch – 06.20 hours. He slipped his feet into brocade slippers and reached for a silk dressing gown. He was five foot four in height, of upright carriage and had retained a trim figure; nor did his face betray the burden of his seventy years. On the way through to his study, he stopped briefly at the adjoining bathroom to rinse his eyes in cold water and run a comb through his hair.

An old-fashioned black Bakelite telephone and a fax machine stood on a low table in his study. Only a dozen senior executives knew the unlisted numbers. The news must be urgent for any one of them to call at this hour and the financier seated himself before picking up the receiver.

His Marine Superintendent announced himself as: 'Mr Ching, Sir Philip. The *Ts'ai Yen* failed to radio her position at 06.00. We are unable to contact her.'

Six hours since the last contact at fourteen knots gave a circle of search with a radius of eighty-four nautical miles. A further half-hour until the aerial hunt could begin. The initial actions were detailed in a company instruction and the report would be on Sir Philip's desk at 09.00.

The financier imagined the mounting anxiety at the marine office and the final decision to wake the elderly superintendent. Execution had been the favoured treatment for bearers of ill tidings to the Manchu court and Sir Philip wondered if Mrs Ching had squeezed her husband's hand or perhaps patted his thigh while he put through the call.

'Thank you, Mr Ching,' he said: 'Most kind of you to call. We must have disturbed your wife's sleep.'

Replacing the receiver, he reached for a legal pad and propelling pencil. He adjusted the lead carefully but there was nothing to write. He knew what had happened to the *Ts'ai Yen* and his granddaughter. Not the details, of course, but the reasons, and who was responsible.

Pressure on a floor switch lit a sixteenth-century Florentine panel depicting a young girl. Normally a few minutes' meditation would have charged the financier's batteries but today he required stronger meat. He crossed to the French windows, stepped out onto the balcony, and looked across to his warehouses. In the beginning they had been called factories, but that was back in Macao.

Family records showed that Sir Philip's great-great-grandfather, the merchant moneylender, Quang Ji Li, first sailed across from Macao to the unimportant offshore island of Hong Kong on the 22nd November, 1840. There he bought one hundred and thirty-two perches of land with two hundred metres of foreshore. The Royal Navy took possession of Hong Kong on the 26th January, 1841, and the Scots traders, Euan Cairns and Matthew Oliver, registered ownership of the same land on the 25th June. With their property thus protected under both Chinese and British rule, the houses of Li and of Cairns Oliver sowed the seeds of empire. Now, a century and a half later, the House of Li was under attack and Sir Philip gathered his roots about him, the smell of the air and of the sea, the bustle down on the wharf, a tanker lying at anchor out in the roads.

His valet brought in a tray set with a cup of hot chocolate and a freshly baked *brioche*. Such had been the financier's breakfast for thirty years but today, like the painting, it seemed insufficient and he left the tray untouched. A half-hour later he appeared on the waterfront, bathed and dressed in a lightweight grey flannel suit. He was seen to roll a ball of rice and fish from a tin plate as he chatted quietly with a group of his dockers. He greeted the captain of a house tug by name and asked after his daughter, called a mason over to examine a short stretch of loose stonework on the wharf, and looked into the warehouses. He entered the House of Li's offices at 07.20.

Completed in 1886 and built on three floors, the brick building stood at the head of the main wharf. The counting house continued occupation of the ground floor. The massive desks of solid mahogany were original, as was the carved ceiling divided into fifteen foot squares by beams supported on three rows of marble pillars. A fan turned slowly in each square – with thick cloistered walls on the ground floor, there was no need for air conditioning but the computers demanded dehumidifiers.

Sir Philip's own desk was one of seven arranged behind a wooden rail on a dais at the back of the counting house. Already a dozen of the desks in the pit were occupied by slick-haired young Chinese focused on their computer terminals. With nine minutes to wait for his secretary, Sir Philip spoke briefly with a market analyst.

He mounted the three steps to the raised floor area and sat down at his desk at 07.25 hours. Every employee in the pit knew that this was the time to present a problem or special interest. The financier searched the bowed heads but there was no response and he turned to greet his secretary as she stepped out of the birdcage elevator. Miss James had been in his employ for thirty-five years. She placed before him six Morocco folders that carried the morning reports which he would read before his young assistants reached their desks shortly before 08.00 hours. Today five would be present: banking, ships, property, manufacturing, and agriculture – energy was away at a conference in the Philippines.

At 08.05 hours, the in-house security expert would report the conference room secure and, by tradition, they climbed the wide wooden stairs that led up from the pit to the first floor. For the next four hours they would discuss the various parts of Sir Philip's global empire. These daily brainstorms between youthful experts kept his businesses young and interactive. Sir Philip was often absent and, when present, listened more than he spoke.

He skimmed the reports and noted concern as to the rumours of financial trouble threatening the House of Li. Banking reported the market nervous as to the outcome of Sir Philip's meeting with the bank scheduled for 10.00 hours and Property reported further mark-downs in London office space with two new buildings dumped on the market.

Property was Rudi Beckenberg and he was the first of the financier's *kindergarten* to arrive. A report on creative valuations in company accounts written by the young German while studying at the Harvard Business School's Brussels campus had brought him to Sir Philip's notice. Next came Tommy Li, a distant cousin and a graduate of the London School of Economics; banking was his field. Peter Cameron was part Cairns through his maternal grandmother. Sir Philip had recruited him because of the controversies he had stirred while attached to the agricultural development branch of the World Bank. A great-niece of the Marine Superintendent, Sheila Ching had written her doctoral thesis on hidden subsidies in the shipping industry. The absent Miki Tarma was from Madras in the Indian state of Tamil Nadu and expert in forecasting Third World energy needs.

As Sir Philip had done, so each of his assistants stopped at one or two desks en route to the dais. Sir Philip rose to greet them and they chatted quietly while waiting for the security expert.

A skin-and-bones American with red hair and incipient acne, the security expert looked to be in his late teens. He came from Nebraska State via MIT and had joined them through an American agency. At first he had protested at having to wear a suit. The suit he wore now was a charity shop wash-and-wear blue-stripe too wide across the shoulders and too long in the leg. His white T-shirt bore the slogan *LOVE SUCKS* and his trainers were a disaster area. Sir Philip was alone in calling him Timothy rather than Timmy.

Already the rumours had made Sir Philip's employees anxious and he felt every eye in the pit watch as he led his *kindergarten* upstairs. With the first shots fired, he found himself wondering dispassionately whether or not he would prove too old for the battle, because it would be rough, very rough indeed.

Timmy unlocked the conference room to them with a bob of the head to Sir Philip that was midway between a bow and a nervous tic. The financier waited for his assistants to settle at the rosewood table. He sat neatly upright, hands clasped loosely on top of the morning reports. His accent was that of the English upper class, though he selected his words with greater precision.

'Your morning reports display anxiety concerning the effect of rumour on our business,' he began quietly: 'Remember that your usefulness is in creative thinking. Leave the nuts and bolts to the mechanics upstairs.'

The German, Rudi Beckenberg, was about to interrupt but Sir Philip stopped him:

'Wait, Rudi. There are ground rules that must be understood. You all know that I am under attack. People say that I am too old, that I am out of touch. In a quoted company there would be moves

31

to unseat me and you would have duties to the stockholders. There are no stockholders in the House of Li. However I am indebted to various banks; most of these are public companies and you must make up your own minds as to where your responsibilities lie. In doing so, and in considering your futures, you should remember that you are employed as catalysts. Ideas men – or should I say ideas persons, Shirley?' he suggested to the young expert in shipping to his left who seemed engrossed in her hands: 'I was educated to consider calling someone a person was to insult them – so perhaps I am too old, or old-fashioned. There is a difference, of course.'

He smiled at them, not prying, nor even wondering yet if one of them would play the Judas. The curly-haired Rudi Beckenberg; Tommy Li with his gymnast's body; the superficially placid Shirley Ching; Peter Cameron, pugnacious as a Border Terrier.

Sir Philip sighed and closed his eyes for a second, then deliberately straightened his shoulders. It was to Shirley Ching that he began his explanation: 'I understand my relationship to the House of Li as a trusteeship. Therefore my decisions may be influenced by matters of history and of family as much as by financial imperative. You, on the other hand, should remember that this is merely a stage in your careers. Only the stupid make enemies unnecessarily and only the vainglorious seek credit for decisions that are not their own.'

Again he looked round the table, searching their faces. They seemed so young.

'Remain outside the fray, all of you,' he warned. 'Consider the battle an academic exercise of which I am the examiner. I expect daily analysis accompanied by advice on policy for each protagonist. Thank you. . .' And he bowed to then, knowing how he must seem: an old man, neat and punctilious, but frail, and well beyond the *use by* date.

Leaving them to their discussions, he rode the birdcage elevator up to the top floor. A corridor separated his own and his secretary's offices from those of the accountants whose duty lay in control of cash flow. These men and women he dispatched to all corners of the world, confident that they would fall on their subject like vultures, tearing until the bones lay naked.

The financier's office faced the sea. The square partners' desk had been made in Edinburgh in the early 1870s for Euan Cairns and Matthew Oliver, while the leather-upholstered captain's chair was a relic from the House of Li's first steamship launched on the Clyde in the spring of 1876. The lacquered cabinets left and right of the windows were Ming dynasty, the china in them from the 14th-century period. Two plain glass shelves supported dark, almost black pottery moulded two thousand years before the birth of Christ. Model ships were displayed in a glass case. The Compaq 2000 laptop was state of the art.

Sir Philip switched on and keyed through the security programme that led into his private situation report. A single sheet of paper showed his US holdings at close of market and he fed the figures to the computer.

In the next room, his secretary, Miss James, answered the telephone. Born in Hong Kong of a Cantonese mother and a Scottish engineer, she had led a peripatetic childhood and was a skilled linguist. She was a tall thin woman, impervious to either heat or humidity, and dressed severely in a high-collared white blouse and blue linen skirt. When travelling, and in a colder climate than Hong Kong, she changed linen for wool and added a matching jacket, but neither colour nor cut had altered in the thirty-five years of her employment.

From the beginning, they had worked as a team – the soft and the hard faces of capitalism – her sarcasm had taught Sir Philip's employees to be concise and accurate. She listened to the telephone now for less than a minute before knocking on the financier's door: 'The planes are up, Sir Philip.'

4

The Palawan chain of islands stretches south-west from the western tip of Mindoro toward Malaysia and divides the Sulu Sea from the South China Sea. Though there are more than a thousand islands in the group, Palawan is by far the largest, four hundred kilometres long by forty wide. Palawan is mountainous and forested, the highest peak rising in excess of two thousand metres. Balabac Island lies some forty kilometres to the south of Palawan and marks the end of the chain. The gap between Palawan and Balabac is strewn with reefs and islets.

The *Ts'ai Yen* hit the reef almost exactly midway between Palawan and Balabac at 07.37 hours. The laden freighter weighed six thousand tons and she had been travelling at eighteen knots. Latent energy equivalent to the explosion of three tons of gelignite drove her bows into the coral at an angle of forty five degrees. The wedge of South Korean steel gouged a trench in the limestone fourteen feet deep at the point of impact and ten feet wide. Her propellor thrashed the water as she drove up out of the trench and sea water poured into the engine-room through a gash in the hull twelve feet long.

The MAN engine breathed through the funnel which remained forty feet above sea level and the fuel tanks were safe from flooding. However the sea no longer supported the forward part of the freighter's hull. The strain increased with every cubic foot of water that poured into her after-section. Her spine broke at 08.09 hours. Her stern dipped a further twenty-eight inches before her propellor dug into a rock and snapped. The shaft buckled and tore loose from its mounting. Water seeped into the engine sump through the damaged shaft seal. The piston in the number three cylinder seized, the connecting rod broke at the bearing and smashed through the side of the block. Imbalanced, the crankshaft ground the white metal from the remaining bearings and the engine locked solid. With the ship dead, only the surf disturbed the silence.

The *Golden Girl* raced in toward the coast. Up on the coach roof, Trent stood supporting himself against the mast. His binoculars were rock steady as he swayed with the surge of the big catamaran. He had found the freighter. Her accommodation and bridge rose like a rifle's foresight above a white line of broken water. He eased the binoculars smoothly, searching for a ship's boat or a liferaft.

The surf ground a white powder of coral from the reef. The powder reflected the early morning sun, dying the currents pale blue between the greens and browns of the shallows. Sand blazed white gold below a fringe of palm trees on the main islands north and south of the gap. The islands were mountains and forested. There were no signs of life.

Dropping into the cockpit, Trent checked the catamaran's speed – twelve knots. He could be alongside the freighter in ten minutes. The alternative was to wait for a navy or coastguard helicopter to fly out from Puerto Princesa, capital of Palawan. But that was a hundred miles to the north-east – three-quarters of an hour even if an aircraft was immediately available.

The attack must have happened hours ago. The lives of any wounded were unlikely to be endangered by a further fifteen minutes' delay. Trent doubted if any of the attackers had remained on board but he couldn't be sure. He didn't doubt the courage of the Philippines armed forces. However, given a tight situation, inexperienced men were as likely to shoot the innocent as the guilty. He had seen it happen. A lone yachtsman making a casual approach would seem innocent enough.

A horseshoe couch half encircled a table mounted on the mast at the forward end of the *Golden Girl*'s saloon. Trent lifted the centre section of the couch and removed a stack of blankets from the locker beneath. Loading the shotguns, he laid them under a beach towel on the cockpit seat.

He dropped and bagged the jib when still half a mile from the *Ts'ai Yen*. The curl of spray at the stern of the wreck showed the flow of the seas. Stowing his binoculars, he went forward and looped a small buoy on light line through the eye on the head of the main Danforth anchor so that he could retrieve the anchor easily from the coral. Next he readied the small anchor from the Zodiac inflatable that hung in davits aft of the cockpit. He kept an eye on the freighter's deck as he worked. A Kevlar flak jacket under his cotton smock would have been nice and he smiled, a small wry smile directed at himself.

He dropped anchor fifty metres out from the ship and paid out sixty metres of warp before letting the catamaran swing stern-on to the *Ts'ai Yen*. With the mainsail backed, he slid the catamaran under the freighter's stern, hurled the Zodiac's anchor over the rail, and eased the catamaran away from the ship. At sixty metres he dropped the *Golden Girl*'s second anchor and led the warp aft to the cockpit.

The two main anchor warps formed a wide V that held the big cat off the ship. With the mainsail furled, Trent looped the line to the freighter round the sheet winch and edged the cat alongside.

He slung a loaded twelve-gauge down his back and climbed over the rail. Three men dead on the deck looked to be Filipino crew. He found the captain, first officer, and coxswain in the wheelhouse. The officers had been shot to kill while the coxswain had been killed brutally and for the fun of it. The damage to the ship's radio had been done with a fire axe.

The steel door down to the engine-room was blasted off its hinges. A stink of hydrochloric acid came up the companionway and Trent wrapped his shirt over his mouth and nose before clambering down the ladder. The engineers had hurled tools at the attackers and these were scattered over the moulded steel deck plates. The two men lay face to face with their necks looped together with electric flex. They had been shot in the stomach. Battery acid had been poured over their heads.

Trent had to raise the shirt from his mouth so that he could spit. Rage wouldn't bring the men back to life and he counted silently to calm himself, then climbed the ladder out of the engine-room in search of the rest of the crew. He found two shot dead in their foc's'le bunks – eight bunks in use but only six crew found. There was a chance that the remaining two were alive and hiding so he searched again from the bows, calling as he moved aft, and he checked off the cabins by their blue enamel nameplates against the dead: captain, chief engineer, first officer, second engineer.

The last cabin was labelled Second Officer. Trent smelt perfume as he opened the door. A Compaq laptop computer had tumbled from the table and been crushed. He stepped over it to the basin in the small head and sniffed the soap. The top sheet was missing from the bunk. A raw silk boilersuit hung on the back of the chair. Three pairs of faded chinos and half a dozen short-sleeved cotton shirts hung in the wardrobe. A loose dress in something special hung behind the casual wear – *Isse Miyake, New York* – an odd label to find in the second officer's cabin aboard a small freighter.

The dress was a dry clean only and Trent cupped the folds to his nose and breathed in the owner's perfume. He thought that it was Chanel and she was a non-smoker. The three-zipper travel bag folded in the cupboard was blue tapestry with a rabbit design he recognised from the Cluny museum. It had the Yardby label inside and was of the same cost and quality bracket as the dress. He wanted more time to search the cabin but, with the woman missing, time counted. He looked into the saloon and saw the bed made up on the couch and a uniform shirt with a second officer's single gold bar. Back on deck, he dropped the ship's ladder.

As he went down the ladder, he saw bullet holes and a dark stain in the bottom of the port-side lifeboat. He climbed back and lifted the boat cover. The last two members of the crew had been friends and had died in each other's arms.

Ducking into the *Golden Girl*'s saloon, he switched on the Sailor radio and slid the Admiralty Pilot from the bookshelf. Raising the coastguards at Puerto Princesa, he reported the piracy and gave the freighter's name and port of registration, and its position.

The wireless operator ordered him to stand by. Ten minutes passed before a new and authoritative voice came on the air – a helicopter was on its way and he was to remain at his radio. Still with the SIS, Trent might have disobeyed, but his days of official protection were over and he was new to the Philippines. With electrical generation by solar panel, he couldn't pretend that his batteries had gone flat.

Having stowed the twelve-gauge, he made himself a fresh pot of coffee and concentrated on the chart. An intersection of the shipping lane south of the Sulu archipelago with a back projection of the course that had brought the *Ts'ai Yen* onto the reef gave the approximate position of the piracy. A distance of 60 nautical miles at 20 knots gave the local time as 03.00.

The pirate boats would have a speed of at least thirty knots and need to be hidden by first light, a distance of ninety nautical miles.

37

The circle of probability enclosed much of the Sulu archipelago, North Palawan and Balabac, San Miguel, and sixty miles of the Malaysian coast. There were a thousand islands and uninhabited creeks in the area and a thousand boats sailed there daily on lawful business.

He had been trained to search for incongruities and his thoughts went to the missing top sheet in the woman's cabin. The pirates must have used it for something – perhaps for the woman. If so, and if she was alive, only inside information or a miracle could lead to her rescue. He shuddered as he thought of the wanton cruelty in the engine-room. The woman would be better dead. Trent wondered who she was. In all probability there was little that could be done for her or for the missing second officer.

The man who had passed for second officer on the *Ts'ai Yen* had been renamed Lu at the school that had trained him in his profession. Bodyguards are taught protection. Lu had been trained to kill. For five hours he had swum steadily north toward the Sulu archipelago. Only death would stop him, and he had no fear of death. His fear was of failing in his duty. To live with failure was unthinkable and he held in his mind a picture of the Li granddaughter as she had stood in the moonlight.

Robert Li was Sir Philip Li's only living son. Like his father and his grandfather, Robert had been educated at the Dragon School and at Eton. He read history at Trinity College, Cambridge, and met his wife while they were both studying at the Courtauld Institute. Descended from pre-Empire French provincial nobility, Jeannine Li had already completed her studies at the Louvre.

The Lis had chosen their four-bedroom Pimlico house for its convenience to the Tate Gallery. Summers they spent in the Champagne where Jeannine Li had inherited a small property and fortified manor house. The Lis visited Hong Kong twice a year for two weeks.

Despite their wealth, they were unassuming and a popular couple amongst both the academics and the collectors of the art world. The Hong Kong Chinese considered them foreigners and thought of Robert as a foolish dilettante.

With a time difference of eight hours, Sir Philip called his son at his Pimlico home at 01.30 hours London time. He used the plain phone, no scrambler. Without preamble, he said: 'The *Ts'ai Yen* is missing, Robert. You'll see it in the morning papers.'

No exclamation came, and Sir Philip imagined Robert sitting up in bed, calm as he threaded his spectacles behind his ears. There was so much in Robert of the early Florentine portraits he admired. Perfection of technique had enabled the portraits to survive. So it must be with the House of Li. Sir Philip's granddaughter was a piece on the chess board. Let judgment be hurried or influenced by emotion and the game was lost.

Switching to business, he said, 'Two buildings came on the market last night, your time. We need them, Robert. Try UBS first. Offer three-eighths of a point over. They don't take it, try the clearing banks.'

Replacing the receiver he buzzed his secretary and they took the elevator down together to the ground floor. Miss James carried a slim leather Cartier envelope that contained the few documents necessary for his meeting at the bank. Every member of Hong Kong's business community knew of the meeting and the financier took his time crossing the floor of the counting house, stopping at a desk here and there to boost morale with murmured advice or commendation.

The forty-year-old Phantom Five Rolls Royce had been built by Mulliner for Sir Philip's father with a secretary's seat and folding desktop built into the rear of the driver's partition. Air conditioning had been added in the 60s and updated frequently and there were two telephones and a fax. Sir Philip's chauffeur kept the door shut until the financier and his secretary reached the sidewalk. The *Hong Kong Standard* and the *South China Morning Post* lay on the seat. Miss James poured the financier's tea from a monogrammed silver vacuum flask. Out on the main road a truck driver braked as he recognised the giant car. The chauffeur eased into the gap.

Less than three miles separated the Li compound and the bank. In Hong Kong's traffic, the journey took half an hour and Miss James answered the telephone twice in the first few minutes. A third caller spoke at length and she took notes which she passed to Sir Philip: an English yachtsman had found the *Ts'ai Yen*, no survivors. The coastguard would board within the next quarter hour with Sir Philip's team less than ten minutes behind.

Sir Philip thought for a moment, then wrote detailed instructions in the neat script he had learnt at preparatory school. Last came a request to Sir Euan Wiley, chairman of Cairns Oliver, to have his security consultant check the yachtsman's background.

Trent climbed back onto the freighter as the coastguard helicopter hovered over the cargo deck. The pilot was clearly nervous and held the aircraft in the lee of the accommodation, broadside to the slight breeze, dropping a foot at a time. A passenger eased out through the open side door and stood on the landing skid. The drop was more than ten feet and he yelled angrily at the pilot. The helicopter dropped another six feet and the man jumped. Catching his foot on the hatch cover, he tumbled sideways onto the deck and crawled clear of the downdraft. Two more men followed. The pilot lifted clear and swept away to a flat beach.

Already the dead on the deck had begun to swell in the heat. Trent had expected the coastguards to go below into the comparative cool of the ship's saloon but they moved, instead, into the shade of the after deck. The three men wore khaki, a commander and two enlisted men. The officer faced into the breeze and mopped his face on a handkerchief before producing a ballpoint and note book. He wasn't in a hurry and he left Trent at the approach of a second helicopter.

This pilot was highly proficient and put the helicopter down on the hatch cover without preamble. Two Chinese were out first. The older of the two wore a hand-embroidered *barong tagalog* that must have cost a couple of hundred dollars and a pair of leather loafers of the same quality; a good tailor had cut his slacks to hide a deskbound executive's belly. In contrast, the younger one's sports shirt covered a chest that would have been at home in the ring.

The third passenger was a Japanese hiding behind mirror lenses in round frames. Though in his early forties, he wore his hair long and tied back in a pony tail. The jacket of his Paul Smith suit threatened to slip off his sloping shoulders. He accompanied the suit with a denim shirt, flowered tie, and Doc Marten boots. Trent wondered whether he was in disguise. And, if so, as what. Owner of a fringe gallery exhibiting minimalist art? Or on the jury of a minor Latin American film festival?

The coastguard commander barely restrained himself from saluting the lead Chinese. The two men went into a huddle on the far side of the after deck while the younger Chinese ducked into the officer's accommodation. Meanwhile the Japanese leant his back against the rail and pretended to be asleep. He hadn't even nodded to Trent. None of them had. But now the lead Chinese came over. The card he took from a slim billfold said that he was Ricardo Ling, President of the South Asia Sail & Steam Ship Company, offices in Manila. He thanked Trent in excellent English for his cooperation and bravery in boarding the vessel: 'The killers could have remained on board.'

'I couldn't see anyone,' Trent said.

'Nothing unusual?'

'The crew were dead.'

The Chinese smiled despite himself: 'Nothing else?'

Trent was sure that he was referring to the woman. The Chinese's obliqueness made him wary and he kept his own counsel.

Perhaps satisfied, the Chinese took the coastguard commander by the elbow and led him to the wheelhouse.

Pushing himself off the rail, the Japanese yawned and stretched before wandering forward to the bows. He stood there a while looking out over the broken rocks and islets but it was too hot out in the sun and he came back along the same side of the deck.

Trent thought that he had hesitated at the rail a few metres forward of the ladder on his way to the bow and was certain that he hesitated on the way back.

The coastguard commander reappeared with the Chinese executive. The shipping executive beckoned the Japanese and they went into a huddle. The coastguard joined Trent in the shade. Embarrassed, the commander said: 'There will be an inquest Mr Trent. Your presence is necessary.'

Trent had expected as much and asked how soon the inquest would take place.

'Two or three days.' The commander nodded to himself: 'Yes, four at the most, Mr Trent. Definitely the most.' He glanced round at the Chinese as if for confirmation, then back to Trent: 'One of my men can assist you to Puerto Princesa, Mr Trent. Of course you can stay here,' he added doubtfully and peered over at the *Golden Girl*, then looked towards the reef strewn gap: 'There will be guards on the freighter so you will be quite safe.'

For Trent, Puerto Princesa was a hundred miles in the wrong direction. 'I don't suppose the *Ts'ai Yen*'s the first ship to run aground on these reefs,' he said. 'I'll stay here and take a look.'

5

Wong Fu's number one bodyguard checked the sidewalk outside the side entrance to the bank before he opened the door of the bullet-proof Cadillac. A second bodyguard kept the bank door open while a third held the elevator. Wong Fu had dressed in his usual workman's denim suit with silk shirt and tie, and bespoke Italian shoes. An embroidered skull cap hid the scar that dissected his scalp. He crossed the sidewalk rapidly and strode down the corridor to the elevator where his number one bodyguard pressed the button for the conference floor.

Four of the bank's major stockholders waited in an anteroom. Two were Chinese. Wong Fu smelt their fear as he had smelt fear in those he had robbed and killed in the distant days of his Shanghai beginnings. Fear had brought the stockholders to his side and it would finally defeat the House of Li; as he crossed the room to accept the greetings of the two European stockholders, he thought of the girl.

She had screamed when they first dropped her into the boat and one of the men had silenced her with curses and his foot. She had lain at the bottom of the boat for three hours. The roar of the engine drummed in her ears while the vibration shook her body through the thin cotton of the sheet in which they had bundled her. Blindfolded by the cotton, she existed in a limbo in which there was only her fear of what would follow the voyage; she prayed for the voyage to continue for eternity.

Now the engine had stopped and the keel slithered over sand. The scraping was loud and threatening in the sudden silence. She tried to make herself small so they would forget her but she was grabbed and thrown high. She struck the sea. She hadn't expected water and, terrified of drowning, fought desperately within the sheet while the men laughed. She thought of her grandfather. Cried to him for help. Prayed for the shelter of his power.

Alighting from the Phantom Five, Sir Philip gave the waiting photographers a slight smile and calmed the journalists with a promise to answer questions after the meeting. Then he was gone into the lobby where the bank's English chairman waited.

The two men shook hands for the photographers but the Englishman seemed uncomfortable as he turned Sir Philip towards the elevators.

'We thought the main conference room,' he said for Sir Philip's ear only: 'We'll be less crowded.'

Sir Philip had turned to Miss James for the Cartier cover. Momentarily bewildered, he said: 'Crowd? Surely you and I?' He saw in the chairman's embarrassment that there was more to their meeting and, clumsy, fumbled and dropped the papers.

'Thank you, my dear,' he murmured to Miss James as she retrieved the cover from the floor. He held her arm: 'Perhaps you would come with me? You know? In case there's something I've forgotten.'

Miss James glared at the chairman over Sir Philip's head. There too was a sign of the financier's age – that he was in need of protection. The chairman knew that he had been sensible in switching allegiance. The financial pages were correct, Sir Philip was too old and set in his ways while the son was a dabbler in the arts, not the sort to direct an empire. The empire would be lost of course.

Few outsiders appreciated the toughness and determination required of a leader in the financial world. But the banker knew. His wife might belittle him in the privacy of their bedroom, but, by God, one of these days he'd teach her. Yes indeed, he thought, and smiled thinly as he steered Sir Philip into the elevator.

Freeform chunks of black marble supported the bevelled glass table top in the bank's conference room. Twenty feet in length and six wide, there was ample space on one side for the four stockholders and their advisers. Sir Philip faced them with only Miss James in attendance. The chairman had taken his place at the head of the table.

As he fumbled through his documents, Sir Philip was conscious of the liver spots that marked the backs of his hands. Miss James leant across to straighten the papers and he thanked her. Then he looked to the chairman.

The chairman gained further courage from the presence of the other four. He opened with an assurance that no one doubted the strength of the House of Li but the rumours reported in the financial pages together with the late payment to the bank of six million in interest caused concern. Nothing that couldn't be sorted out, of course.

'We are all friends here,' he assured Sir Philip and smiled round the table.

One of the British stockholders said: 'Absolutely,' and the two Chinese nodded. A lawyer interjected that the House of Li had always refused to disclose its assets and this posed a legal problem for the bank.

The chairman said, 'Banking regulations, Phil.' It was the first time that he had dropped the honorific let alone dared shorten the financier's name and he finished confidently: 'That's something we have to deal with at this meeting.'

An accountant had the figures of the loan: 'One hundred and thirty million dollars represents four percent of the bank's capital.'

'Unwisely exposed,' a lawyer said.

The chairman said: 'That's with hindsight, of course.'

A financial adviser drew attention to a clause in the loan agreement that gave late payment of interest as grounds for return of the principal.

The chairman nodded: 'That's certainly our understanding, Phil. I've taken soundings with the board. You know, the way one does? Nothing official, but there's a definite feeling that we'd be happier. . .' He left the sentence hanging in the air.

The chairman shifted in his chair and Sir Philip, hearing the door open to his left, knew that he had pressed a bell.

A clerk slipped a note to Miss James who read it quickly before passing it to her employer – a Lloyd's notification that the MV *Ts'ai Yen* was missing in the Sulu Sea.

Sir Philip looked up. Wong Fu watched from the doorway.

The chairman said, 'Phil, you must know each other. Mr Fu has recently become one of our major shareholders.'

Apparently oblivious to Wong Fu's presence, Sir Philip sifted his papers again. Onto the table he dropped an agreement of sale between a Bahamian registered holding company and the House of Li. The properties sold were a Florida meat processing facility, three giant feet lots, and forty thousand head of beef cattle at a price of one hundred and thirty seven million dollars. Payment was due in thirty days with the Morgan Trust as guarantors of payment and the Bank as bank of receipt.

One of the lawyers was first to reach for the document but Sir Philip was halfway to the door. Gripping the crystal doorknob, he looked back at the chairman. They had lunched together every three or four months, but had never been close. He found himself incapable of uttering the man's name. Nor did he bother to hide his contempt as he switched his attention from the banker to Wong Fu. 'Gutter scum,' he said in Mandarin. As if afraid of contagion, he dabbed a white handkerchief to his lips: 'Miss James will wait for your signatures.'

'The House of Li has no further business with the bank,' he told the journalists and stepped into the Rolls.

The commandant, the Japanese, and the Chinese shipowner had lifted away by helicopter. Later a launch from Puerto Princesa, capital of Palawan, delivered four extra men and supplies to the *Ts'ai Yen* so now there were six guards on board.

Light cloud had turned the sea a pale green. The flanks of the distant mountains looked bare in the filtered sunlight. The breeze had dropped and the heat and humidity seemed to hold the catamaran motionless. She lay to three anchors within the reef above a basin of sand the size of a tennis court. Trent had spotted the sand at low tide and had moved the *Golden Girl* on the flood, easing her between the coral heads and rocks that now formed a fortress.

The missing woman obsessed him; the woman and the engineers with the acid poured over their faces; the viciousness of the pirates. The woman was in their hands or dead. Trent didn't believe in her death. Had she been killed in her cabin he would have seen blood. There was the missing sheet. There was his own feeling that she had been taken – he had learnt to trust his instincts.

Again his thoughts returned to the murdered engineers. He had witnessed the same deliberate cruelty in villages punished by terrorists and by anti-terrorist forces; the men executed, women raped and slaughtered, dead children discarded like bits of rag against the walls of the shattered huts.

He worried that he should have mentioned the woman to the coastguard commander. The Chinese shipping manager hadn't mentioned her – deliberately, Trent was sure. What could they do? Any of them? Search? Where?

Though further calculations were pointless, impotence drove him back to the chart. Then, irritated with himself, he sat in the cockpit and watched the sea suck at the freighter's bows. He needed information. A name and a background might tell him whether she had been kidnapped for pleasure or for ransom.

To occupy himself, he began sorting the photographs he had taken of the Japanese fleet. The hulls appeared green and ghostly underwater. One series of pictures concentrated on the holes blasted in the buckled armour. Others followed a shark as it glided past a turret. Trent thought again of the engineers on the *Ts'ai Yen* and of the woman. He had to do something. There were no excuses that he could live with.

Golden Girl carried a big sail-board on the webbing between the two hulls forward of the saloon. Trent had painted the board matt black and had converted it to carry a conventional mast sail. He waited for darkness before lowering the board into the water. He wrapped an electronic detector in a plastic bag and packed it into a small waterproof backpack. He added a pair of pen lights, a set of lock picks, a heavy dive knife. Pulling on the black nylon scuba suit with a hood, he wrapped a length of light line round his waist and muffled the small grappling anchor.

With the tide still on the run, the water sucked and slurped over the reef and the board scraped over the coral. Had Trent been swimming, he would have been cut and bloody within the first hundred yards.

The wheelhouse roof was the best lookout point on the *Ts'ai Yen* while boarding was simplest from the deep water aft so there would be a watch on the after deck.

Trent slipped the board's painter over a coral head twenty feet from the freighter's bows and let out slack so that the board drifted in under the overhang. He waited forty minutes for footsteps to disturb the sound-pattern of the sea and the ship. Finally he hurled the muffled grappling anchor, climbed quickly, and rolled under the rail.

A flame showed momentarily on the roof of the wheelhouse and the glow of a cigarette split in half as two men saved matches by lighting one cigarette from the other. Two more on the aft deck and two sleeping somewhere, probably on deck because, without power for the air-conditioning, the accommodation would be unbearably hot.

He looped his line over the freighter's anchor chain, eased the grappling anchor off the rail, and lowered it back down to the sea. Then he crawled aft towards the accommodation, halting every few feet until finally he distinguished the low whistling of two men asleep on the midships hatch.

Snaking past the men, he gained the deep shadows beneath the wheelhouse. Both port and starboard doors to the accommodation had been locked but the locks were new and the tumblers moved smoothly beneath the pressure of his picks. Once inside the accommodation, he re-locked the door. Taking a blanket from a locker in the corridor, he made for the second officer's cabin. The curtains were already drawn but he tucked the blanket over the brass curtain rail.

Someone had spread a top sheet over the bunk. A single uniform hung in the wardrobe where he had seen the women's clothes; a couple of drawers were stuffed with men's shirts and underwear; no laptop, no perfumed soap, no cosmetics; just a single Bic razor and a bar of carbolic soap.

Trent sat on the desktop facing the bunk. The hint of a woman's perfume lingered in the cabin. He stripped the top sheet. The lower sheet was uncreased at the foot of the bunk. He searched the pillow and found a couple of black head hairs. Pressing his face into the pillow and lower sheet, he breathed deeply. No sour trace of sweat so she was probably slim; say twenty-five years old given the perfume she used and the traces of cosmetic scent; the smooth bottom of the lower sheet gave a height between five foot two and five four; straight black hair worn short; the Isse Miyake dress and Yardby luggage showed taste and money and she was well enough educated to use a laptop.

He had her now, not a name yet, but her absence had to be hidden so she was important, and that would lead him to a name. He straightened the top sheet, replaced the blanket, and slipping back on the deck, re-locked the door. A boat was approaching from the north, twin V8s and fast.

His electronic detector operated only at short range. He climbed the companionway to the wheelhouse and crept aft along the deck to the foot of the ladder leading to the wheelhouse roof. The two guards talked urgently as the boat came closer. A sentry on the after deck called up, voice hoarse with anxiety. There came the metallic slither of weapons being readied. One of the men threw a coin at the guard asleep on the hatch and one of them woke with a curse.

The guards' concentration absorbed by the launch, Trent climbed quickly to the upper level and swept the detector in a half circle; there was an active radio beacon, probably on the radio mast; the attack had been deliberate; the woman had been the target – a target worth mass murder.

A searchlight from the launch pierced the darkness. Trent ducked and dropped as the coxswain shut the throttles. The guards recognised one of the newcomers by voice and there was an explosion of nervous laughter. The two groups shouted at each other in Tagalog, the accent of the guards softer than that of the new arrivals. The new arrivals seemed to have greater status. The two men who had been asleep lowered the rope ladder and grabbed the lines as the launch slipped alongside.

Trent crouched under the companionway as the two men on the wheelhouse roof clambered down to welcome the new arrivals. There were six of them, and they had brought bottles and food. There was a lot of back-slapping and coarse humour. The laughter swelled in volume but it was off key and Trent wanted to shout a warning to the guards but he thought of the woman held prisoner.

She was being erased piece by piece. Finally there would be nothing left, not even a memory, because all those who had known of her existence would be dead. The sudden bubbling scream from below bore out his belief. It was over in seconds. Six against six, but the drink must have been drugged and the newcomers were proficient with their knives.

Guards dead, they switched to Chinese. One of them entered the accommodation – either he had a key or was fast with a pick. Two others climbed the companionway to the wheelhouse. Trent ran in a low crouch to the stern, swung over the rail, and hung for a moment, timing the surge under the counter so that he dropped into the hollow of the retreating swell. The suck and gurgle of the water covered his splash and he turned and swam along the hull to the sail-board. Retrieving his anchor, he paddled slowly round the bow towards the launch. Black-hulled, thirty foot and beamy, she was more of a fast work boat than a pleasure craft. Perhaps a dive boat. There was no name or number on her.

Trent moored the sail-board between the *Golden Girl*'s hulls. Dropping into the saloon, he unshipped his shotguns from the back of the locker, loaded them, and zipped them into waterproof cases. He undid the hatch under the carpet in the saloon floor so that he could exit between the hulls. Then he sat at the chart table in the dark. He imagined the men on board the *Ts'ai Yen* meticulously scouring the accommodation for any sign of the woman. The tough young Chinese who had come on board with the shipowner would be one of them. The initial hurried camouflage of the woman's presence had been his work.

Once they were finished on the freighter, they would switch their attention to the *Golden Girl*. They would have to wait for daylight and high tide to cross the reef. They would ask what he had seen and whether he had talked on the radio to anyone other than the authorities. Then they would kill him. They wouldn't be concerned with the commandant or the Japanese, neither of whom had been below. Once Trent was dead, the woman ceased to exist.

The kidnapping was too complicated to have been the work of ordinary pirates. But the woman had been taken and the shipowners were hiding her capture. Trent wondered whose side the Japanese was on. And the commandant. Puerto Princesa was five hours away by coastguard launch. He switched the radio to the international emergency frequency. A German tanker answered first and Trent reported the *Ts'ai Yen* under attack.

The radio officer asked for his own situation and Trent answered that it wasn't good but that he would probably be safe until first light.

Twenty minutes later the German came back on the air to tell him the Filipino marines were on their way: 'Good luck.'

Trent said 'Thanks,' but he didn't trust to luck.

He clipped two water canteens to his belt, slung the gun cases over his back and, dropping down between the hulls onto the sail-board, paddled to a small islet capped by a half dozen palm trees. Away in the distance he could see the orange glow of the volcano.

49

6

With property values soaring to ten thousand dollars a square foot, Braemar Lodge was one of the very few great houses on the Peak to have withstood the ravages of the developer. Home to the Taipan of the Cairns Oliver *Hong* for the past one hundred and twenty-five years, the fierce grey granite mansion with its Victorian minarets was as much a symbol of Hong Kong as the Governor's residence or the Hong Kong and Shanghai bank.

Sir Euan Wiley was a quarter Cairns on his mother's side. Hard work and loyalty had earned him the support of Sir Philip Li in the recent battle for chairmanship of the *Hong*. A few months short of his sixtieth birday, he accepted that the banks and most of the family members considered him a stop-gap.

The fax machine in the first floor library was connected to a bell on his bedside table and he groaned as he rolled away from his wife. Dragging on a dressing gown, he stumped ill-temperedly across the wide double landing and fumbled at the row of brass light switches to the left of the door. The fax was a report on the yachtsman, Trent, from their security consultant in London and had passed through the automatic scrambler. Sir Euan read it and immediately dialled Sir Philip Li's private number:

'Philip, Euan here. I'll be over in twenty minutes.'

He pulled on slacks and a sports shirt and shuffled his feet into loafers. Down in the garage, the guard saluted sleepily and slid the big double doors back before jogging down the drive to open the gates. Euan preferred their English nanny's Mini to the company Rolls or his wife's drop-head Jaguar. He was a tall man, kept slim by a second marriage to a younger woman. He drove competently and without need for spectacles. The gates to the Li compound swung open as he turned off the main road and Sir Philip's valet opened the front door to him.

Usually the fifteen years difference in their ages made him feel young but the spring was missing from his legs as he mounted the stairs to the Chinese financier's study. The calm with which Sir Philip greeted him made him feel momentarily foolish as he proffered the fax:

'The yachtsman, Philip. He's ex-intelligence with a background in anti-terrorism. There's a dozen unauthorised assassinations he carried out for Washington.'

Sir Philip seemed unmoved as he absorbed the report but Euan Wiley had never been able to read the older man's mind. There were times when he felt that he was little more than a pawn in the Chinese financier's schemes. Not that he wasn't good at his job – Sir Philip would never have supported him had that been the case – however the older man thought in far longer terms than the few years of authority which Euan Wiley expected to exercise. They were like that, the old-money Chinese – long term, and no free rides on the gravy train. Nor any dilution of the family's sharehold-ing as there had been over the generations with Cairns Oliver. Great Uncle Charley in the South of France with his young mistresses had never bothered to visit Hong Kong. Tim at the Bank of England, Charley Junior practising architecture, a Member of Parliament, a QC, gentlemen farmers, Bertie breeding racehorses at Newmarket, even an academic. And there were five generations of daughters whose dowries had further diluted the family's control. Even his own divorce – and momentarily ashamed of what he recognised now to have been a middle-aged weakness for younger flesh, he said: 'Trent, he sounds more of a terrorist than the terrorists. Lucky, I mean, with the pirates, just what we need.'

Sir Philip tapped thoughtfully at the fax with a manicured finger tip. He was small and physically frail, but suffered neither weakness of mind nor of will. What did he feel for his granddaughter, Euan Wiley wondered. Pain? Rage? Despair?

'Trent. . .' The Chinese financier folded away the fax into his dressing-gown pocket and smiled: 'Yes, I have a feeling you're right. Convenient, Euan, very convenient.'

Across town one of Wong Fu's many relatives stood in front of the great marble desk while Wong Fu read a second report, identical to that which Euan Wiley had received. The source was the same retired member of British Military Intelligence who now listed a dozen major customers in the Far East as clients. The foreigner was worth his wage, Wong Fu thought as he read the message. He dismissed the young man who had brought it and summoned his war chief. The man who entered the penthouse apartment a half-hour later was small and very neat, a clerk perhaps, or a schoolteacher.

Wong Fu wrote on a single sheet of paper laid on the marble desktop: *The yachtsman, Trent, is dangerous. Kill him. Use the triads.*

His war chief nodded and Wong Fu dropped the note and the fax into the shredder beside his desk. Security ensured, he returned to thoughts of the girl. Already she would have suffered her first lesson in humility and the tall Chinese licked his lips.

There were twenty Filipino pirates and there were four Chinese. The Chinese were in command. They had made her kneel in the shade of a coconut palm and they had tied her wrists together so that she embraced the tree trunk. But they didn't touch her. Not yet. They were waiting.

'Lady Li,' the leader called her. 'Would you like a drink, Lady Li?' He held her by the jaw and tilted her face round so that he could pour water between her lips. 'Remember your manners, Lady Li,' he warned, and she whispered her thanks.

He held the back of his hand out and she pressed her lips to it because that was what he wished her to do. She prayed to him with her eyes. And she whispered, 'My grandfather, he'll pay you anything you ask.'

He chuckled deep in his throat.

With darkness she was bundled again in the sheet and dropped into the boat. She surrendered, as she had the first night, to the roar and vibration of the big engine. She was safe within the circle of noise. Sanctuary, she thought, and she thought of herself at the altar of a church. Then she remembered the right-wing death squads in El Salvador dragging people out of church by their hair and shooting them on the steps. She had marched against State Department support for the Salvadoran army. She and her friends from Wellesley had driven down to a pizza parlour after the march. Jay remembered ordering an American Hot with extra chili.

She was no longer an American. Somewhere between San Francisco and Hong Kong she had crossed a frontier and become Chinese. She had failed to recognise or feel the frontier but now she understood her grandmother's warnings over lunch, advice as to the clothes she should wear, who she should talk with, how she should conduct herself in public. Her grandmother had tried so hard to impress upon her the status she had inherited as a memeber of the House of Li, Sir Philip Li's granddaughter. Face, caste, power. Jay had refused to listen. Rather, she had determined to be her own woman. How could she have been so blind? She began to pray. Episcopalian prayers. At school and at college she had sneered at the Episcopalian Church for being little more than a Sunday wing of a WASP country club.

Her tears came and she thought of the second officer of the *Ts'ai Yen*, Lu, whom she had despised.

Lu had been in the sea for nine hours before finding the island. First he rested, then he climbed a coconut palm that sloped out over the beach. He drank from a young nut and ate the jelly, then dragged together a dozen dry palm fronds. Now he lay hidden beneath them in the dark. He had survived, as he had known he would. With dawn he would find a fisherman.

Trent listened to the launch creep along the edge of the reef. The last of the night breeze had died and even the sea seemed exhausted as it slapped at the tiny beach below his hiding place. A searchlight in the bows of the launch found the *Golden Girl* and men's voices carried across the water. Trent spoke no Chinese, however he recognised the metallic slither of an automatic rifle being cocked.

He expected bullets to cut into the catamaran but one of the men called in English: '*Golden Girl*. Ahoy there, *Golden Girl*.'

Of course they didn't know who he was – or what he was.

The six killers on the launch could take him at first light if they were equally professional. They would have to accept casualties so it was important to learn the degree of their commitment. As an opening, he shot out the searchlight.

A steady stream of curse-words signalled that he had hit one of the men. The twin V8s roared as the coxswain spun the launch round and out of range. A single shot from a unexpected direction was insufficient for them to pinpoint him. Nevertheless he shifted a few yards and waited for their next move. With luck they would wait for first light and be caught by the Filipino navy or coastguard. Instead, the engines reawoke and he listened to the launch drive away to the east. Forty knots, at a guess.

Six dead men sprawled in coagulated pools of blood across the *Ts'ai Yen*'s centre cargo hatch. A marine helicopter swept first out of the dawn. The pilot sped over the *Ts'ai Yen*, banked over the *Golden Girl* and flew back over the freighter. Heavy calibre machine guns poked out of the side doors. The gunners kept their sights on the freighter as the pilot flew six more passes.

The wheelhouse was like a fort, windows of armoured glass overlooking the cargo deck. Once that was captured, the marines could take their time clearing the accommodation.

The pilot lifted the nose hard on the sixth pass and a dozen men dropped to the wheelhouse roof. The men spread fast, two on their bellys to cover the cargo deck, two to cover port and starboard companionways down to the wheelhouse sidedecks. The helicopter hovered beyond the bows, guns ready, as the last two men slid over the edge of the wheelhouse roof and dropped to the decks to the rear of the wheelhouse doors. Their backs protected by the bulk-heads, they slapped quarter pound shaped charges on the side windows, three second fuses, BANG! The armoured glass collapsed inward followed by stun grenades. The marines swung round, M-1's covering the interior. Empty.

The helicopter dropped four more men onto the cargo deck and banked away towards the catamaran. A marine with a loud hailer called down for Trent to come on deck. Trent was four hundred yards away on his island hideout. This was the part that made him nervous – armed men high on adrenalin. They wouldn't hear him above the roar of the helicopter. Flat on his belly, he raised his T shirt on the surfboard paddle. One of the marines spotted it. As the helicopter backed away from the catamaran, a gunner put a dozen shots into the shallows close into the islet as a warning.

Trent didn't need warning. He spread his legs and stretched his arms out as far as he could reach. The helicopter engines thundered overhead and the down-draft blasted the sand. There came the thumps of men jumping to his rear and the helicopter swept away. He shouted into the sand that he was the Englishman, Trent, from the *Golden Girl* and a marine yelled at him to get to his feet. The

54

marine wore sergeant's stripes and spoke English with a dead pan American accent he'd perfected watching movies.

'The Commander wants you back on your boat,' he ordered.

Waiting in the cockpit, Trent watched a navy patrol boat speed out of the north followed by the coastguard launch from Puerto Princesa. The patrol boat lay off the stern of the *Ts'ai Yen* while sailors launched a fibreglass tender. The marines had searched the accommodation and soon the freighter looked like a cocktail party – coastguards, navy, marines.

A marine dropped into the patrol boat's tender and the coxswain ran in cautiously across the reef to the *Golden Girl*. The marine wore a commander's bars on his epaulets. A few years younger than Trent, he was broad-shouldered for a Filipino, tough, compact, and light on his feet. He smiled without mirth as he boarded the catamaran between the twin transoms and dropped into the cockpit.

Trent nodded at the *Ts'ai Yen*: 'You've been practising. Nice operation.'

The commander wasn't interested in the compliment and he didn't bother introducing himself. He wanted Trent's story.

Trent told of having heard the launch approach the *Ts'ai Yen*. He had listened to revelry for perhaps half an hour, then silence. The silence had made him nervous and he had slipped overboard and hidden amongst the rocks within the reef. The launch had come hunting for him.

'You were armed?' the young marine commander asked.

Trent said, 'Shotgun,' and fetched it for him.

The marine commander spoke fluent English with an American accent. He sniffed at the barrel of the twelve-gauge. 'One shot?'

'One,' Trent agreed.

The commander appeared to lose interest. Perhaps he was thinking. Over on the freighter men were taking pictures, measurements, filling body bags. A sliver of gold showed above the horizon.

Finally the commander found enough energy to yawn and scratch the back of his scalp before pushing the twelve-gauge back across the cockpit table at Trent. 'What did you do? Take out their light?'

Trent said, 'Yes,' and the commander grinned suddenly:

'Son of a bitch. They thought they were hunting pigeon. *Bang!* and they woke up.'

'Something like that. . .'

Trent dropped down into the galley and put the coffee pot on the stove. 'Eggs?' he called and the commander said, 'Yeah, why not. Mind if I look around?'

'Be my guest.'

The companionway leading into the saloon that bridged the twin hulls opened off the port side of the cockpit. Big windows opened forward onto the bridge deck with domed hatches port and starboard in the cabin roof. The chart table lay to port of the companionway with Brooks and Gatehouse electronic equipment above the chart table connected to repeaters on the cockpit bulkhead: speed through the water, wind speed, depth indicator, barometer, satellite navigation. The Sailor radio was to port of the navigation equipment.

At the forward end of the saloon the mast foot supported a table cupped by a horseshoe settee spread with handwoven Guatemala covers. Hip-high cupboards lined the after bulkhead. A pair of wide-based ship's decanters for white rum and dark and a row of cut-glass tumblers were held in place by a fiddle rail. Afghan rugs lay on the blue carpeting. The bookshelves were full. A pair of nineteenth-century oil paintings of shipping on the Thames hung opposite each other beside the steps leading to the hulls.

The galley lay amidships in the port hull with double bunked cabins fore and aft. The cabins had their own handbasins and a head. The lone cabin in the starboard hull lay aft and was longer than those to port and separated from the sail locker that opened to the foredeck by a head and shower. Mexican bedspreads covered the bunks and there were matching curtains and bright rugs on the white carpeting.

'Nice home,' the commander said as he took his place at the saloon table.

'Thanks.'

Trent slid a plate of bacon and eggs in front of the marine and sat so that they faced each other.

The Filipino mopped the yolk up on a piece of bread and grinned: 'Yeah, Norfolk, Virginia – but you're a few years older.'

'A few,' Trent agreed. The Filipino was telling him that they had been through the same selection process and the same training. Where they had done their training didn't matter, nor which Special Forces they belonged to. Once you'd done the training, you became one of the people that were called upon when things got nasty. *Things,*

Nasty – just two of the words employed as camouflage for what you really did. What you did was kill people for your Government.

Surviving the courses was a major victory let alone winning battles out in the field. Seated in the saloon, they were like a couple of dogs taking soundings of each other's territory. They recognised the little things; the laziness because it might be the last chance of a rest in the next six weeks; a desire to avoid involvement because you might act too rough for the circumstances; anger at being thought useful but a little dirty; not someone who was asked for dinner; certainly not a suitable date for a favourite daughter.

The commander pushed his plate aside and watched as Trent refilled their coffee mugs. He added cream and said, 'Great breakfast. You know what this thing is about?' Then he grinned: 'Yeah, like you'd tell me. Anyway, you need something, let me know. Manolo Ortega. . .' He offered Trent a hand on which a half-inch bar of muscle ran up from the V of the thumb to the first joint of the first finger.

'Thanks,' Trent said. He wanted to trust the man but he didn't know the local rules. Now that he was out of the Department, he no longer had access to information.

'How do I find you?' he asked.

The commander took a visiting card from a slim black leather case with gold corners. The card was good quality, engraved rather than printed, and introduced him as Lieutenant Commander Manuel J. Ortega, executive assistant to an Admiral Jose Abalardo, Director of Operations.

Executive assistant covered a lot of ground. So did Operations. Understanding the pecking order in countries like the Philippines was an art form but Manolo Ortega was probably close to where decisions were made.

Manolo Ortega clearly didn't give a damn what Trent thought but he wanted to be friendly because of their shared background. He said, 'They want you to make a statement in Manila. I'll leave a couple of my men on your boat so nothing gets touched.'

Trent thanked him and Ortega said: 'Just remember to watch your back. My advice would be to get the hell out of here.'

'The Philippines?'

'And the general area,' Ortega said.

Trent thought of the woman.

*

57

The hut was square. The floor was packed earth and coral. The walls were made of mud and bamboo. One hinged panel formed the door and there was a window. A central wooden post supported the thatch roof. They had locked an iron bracelet round her right ankle. A light chain connected the bracelet to the centre post. A bucket in one corner served as a toilet and a second bucket held water for drinking or washing. Two grubby palliasses were the only furniture.

The four Chinese ringleaders had stripped her and played cards to see who would start. They had played slowly for the pleasure of feeling her fear build. She had fought briefly but the leader had taken a thick leather belt from his trousers.

'Lady Li,' he called her so that she would know that he knew who she was and that her grandfather's power was unimportant here in the hut. He made her kneel and he hit her across the face so that she would understand that nothing that she did would affect her treatment. She could be obedient. She could struggle. She could scream. It was all the same to her captors. They had been instructed to break her. There was no great pleasure in it. It was a job.

7

Trent was taken by coastguard launch to Puerto Princesa and flown with Philippine Airlines to Manila. A marine sergeant met him at the airport and drove him to naval headquarters to face an investigative committee. There were four men dressed in plain clothes. One was a policeman who had been trained in the United States and preferred force. The other three were brighter.

They asked what he had seen on board the *Ts'ai Yen* the first morning and he told them that he had searched for survivors. Finding none, he had called the coastguard in the hope of their capturing the pirates.

Nothing more?

Nothing.

And that night? Had he boarded the *Ts'ai Yen*? Why had he shot at the men in the launch? Did he always shoot at people who hailed him? No doubt he had done the right thing but why had he done it? Was he so sure that the men on the launch had murdered the coastguards? He must have heard something. Or seen something.

He replied that he had acted by chance. That he hadn't been able to sleep. That he heard laughter and then silence and that the silence had made him nervous.

'You don't seem like a man who gets nervous,' one of them said with a wry smile. A fifty-year-old with Chinese blood and a face that wrinkled easily, he moved a pencil backwards and forwards across the table. 'There's no accusation here, Mr Trent. We are simply trying to understand why the men in the launch killed the guards.'

One of the others said: 'They were either hiding something or taking something. Would you agree, Mr Trent?'

Trent said that he hadn't really thought.

The policeman grunted angrily and demanded why he carried a gun on board the *Golden Girl*.

Trent said that he'd declared both his guns on entering Philippine waters. He'd brought his gun permit from the *Golden Girl* and he passed it across to the cop who looked disappointed.

The Chinese fifty-year-old said, 'With the amount of piracy we've had over the past few years, a yachtsman would be a fool not to carry a gun.'

The man who seemed to be in charge of the enquiry looked more Spanish than the other three. He said: 'You've been very helpful, Mr Trent. We'd be grateful if you would stay on in Manila until the morning in case we find there's something we've forgotten.'

Trent was happy to stay. He said that they could find him at the Manila Hotel. He thought that they might offer to pick up the tab but they had other matters on their minds. They shook hands with him – even the policeman, though with little grace – and he found himself out on the street.

He took a cab over to Robinson's shopping arcade and sat in the coffee house. For a while he felt safe, then the atmosphere altered. There was no change or action at which he could point or describe but he never doubted the reality of the danger. His instincts had been too well honed by years of living under cover. Men were on his trail. He needed time to spot them because he was on foreign territory and hadn't developed checks that worked. Faces helped: ear lobes, distance between the eyes, angle of a jawline – or it might be a knot on a burnous, the tilt of a hat or the way a man's hair fell forward over his forehead; jacket buttons, shirt collar, the knot in a tie, the set of the cloth across a man's shoulders.

Trent was too expert to be deceived for more than a short while but he could feel them closing in and he wasn't ready. He thought of running for a cab and the Manila Hotel but doubted whether he would reach the sidewalk. He catalogued carefully the tables of mostly young Filipinos dressed in two-hundred-dollar hand-embroidered shirts. Over to his left, a young girl with a shy smile gathered her courage and propositioned a German businessman. A table of male Australian tourists boasted to each other of their sexual prowess in loud ugly nasal voices and language that would have had a missionary teacher reach for a basin of soapy water. An overweight American in his mid-fifties clung to the hand of an eighteen-year-old bar girl as if she were a virgin – he was the one in need of protection. A happy young Chinese in grey chinos and a pale blue shirt waved to a friend at a table behind Trent.

Trent flicked fingers at a waiter and dropped a one hundred peso bill on the check. He had identified the opposition before he reached the glass doors out to the arcade. They were middle-aged businessmen. Their alertness betrayed them. One of them carried a newspaper. Two others remained arm-in-arm as they closed in on Trent's flank. Back at training school it was called a shooting party. The three men were the beaters. The guns waited outside. Trent thought that the weapon would be a knife slid through the back between the sixth and seventh ribs into the heart. The attack would be silent and the assailants would have time to ease clear before anyone noticed the killing.

A shooting party was tough because the target couldn't place the guns until the last moment. Trent went out through the glass doors and slid immediately to his right with his back to the plate glass. Someone yelled over to his left and he dropped flat and rolled under the shoppers' legs, men and women tumbling over him.

Whoever had yelled, did so a second time. Trent rose to his feet. The fallen shoppers formed a protective parameter which he leapt and skidded left in a crouch towards the exit from the arcade. He spotted the Japanese with the pony tail from the previous day scuttle out onto the sidewalk as a stretch Mercedes skidded to a halt. Two young Chinese hit the pavement and charged forward each side of Trent. A third Chinese yelled at him from the back of the Mercedes. The door was open and Trent slid onto the leather seat. He said, 'Thanks for the lift,' and the Chinese said, 'My pleasure, Mr Trent.'

The chauffeur pulled into the curb beyond a traffic light and the Chinese slipped out onto the sidewalk. Trent didn't bother to ask where he was being taken. If they had wanted him to know they would have told him. The direction was south through suburbs that no one had planned. Finally the suburbs thinned and there were dusty fields patched with the shade of jackfruit trees and mango. Banana and papaya grew around the shacks at the roadside. Pigs and chickens; countless children, snotty nosed, their eyes leaking and fly-infested.

The occasional unpainted concrete building with a tin roof gave evidence of a Filipino having worked abroad. The trucks had twisted chassis and bare patches in their tyres. Stretch jeepneys with more chrome than engine gasped up the low hills. Only the trees seemed unmarked by poverty.

After an hour the chauffeur turned off the main road and immediately the country changed for the better. They drove into a small town and through a central square of Spanish colonial houses shaded by mango and avocado trees, town hall at one end, church at the other, a monument in the middle, and a half dozen stone benches.

Beyond the town, the road ran between fields of sugar cane. There were cattle paddocks, whitewashed stone boundary walls, fences that weren't in need of repair. The chauffeur turned in between stone gateposts and up a long avenue of jacaranda trees. In the distance Trent saw guards on horseback, shotguns slung over their shoulders. Irrigation sprinklers rained on fields of emerald green alfalfa and there were neat rows of fruit trees. They passed a helicopter on a concrete pad outside the boundary walls of an ochre washed hacienda that would have been equally familiar in southern Spain or Latin America just so long as the Spanish or Latin American landowner had the wealth of a Croesus.

Massive plane trees offered shade and there were fountains and drinking troughs and a triangular mounting block for horsemen, three steps on each side and a tethering post in the centre. Branches of red and white and pink hibiscus had been grafted to a single trunk; oleander bloomed where the spray drifted from the fountains; bougainvillea tumbled over the garden walls.

A majordomo in a starched white cotton suit opened the door of the Mercedes and led Trent across a flagstoned courtyard into the shade of a vast entrance hall with carved wooden beams and painted ceiling.

A glass bowl of roses stood in the middle of a refectory table in the centre of the room. Chairs with carved leather backs and leather seats stood against the walls. The paintings were a strange dark amalgam of Chinese and western art from the same early colonial period as the furniture; bars of hand-wrought black iron protected the narrow windows.

The majordomo pushed open double doors at the far end of the entrada and bowed Trent into a drawing room. One side was open to a patio in which a bronze sculpture of entwined young lovers poured water out of a cornucopia into a lily pond. The room was an almost perfect square, forty feet to a side, and over twenty feet high. An arched gallery ran along one side of the room. Four massive canvasses by Van Gogh glowed on the walls. Iron candlesticks stood on two big colonial tables against the walls and glass shelves had been led into one wall to support a collection of deep green jade. Chains supported an electric-powered *tunka* that slowly stirred the air. The only other furniture were four big straight-edged sofas arranged in a square and upholstered in rough, pale beige silk.

A tall European in cream slacks and a Lacoste sports shirt came to meet Trent while an elderly Chinese remained seated on one of the sofas.

'Wiley,' the European said, holding out his hand: 'Euan Wiley. Kind of you to accept our invitation, Mr Trent. I'm chairman of a company based in Hong Kong called Cairns Oliver. You may have heard of us?'

Trent said: 'Yes,' and Euan Wiley smiled, not from arrogance, but because Trent's knowledge eased matters.

'Sir Philip Li,' he said with a slight bow to the elderly Chinese in the grey suit. 'We're business associates, Mr Trent.'

'I know who Sir Philip is,' Trent said.

'Yes, of course.' Euan Wiley looked lost for a moment. Then he said, 'Won't you sit down?'

'Which one of you do I talk to?' Trent asked.

A slight and rather wintry smile touched Sir Philip's lips and he looked up at the chairman of Cairns Oliver: 'Euan, perhaps you should leave us for a while.'

Euan Wiley hesitated and Sir Philip said: 'It's not your affair, Euan.'

'I suppose not . . .' But Euan Wiley's loyalty to the older man made him reluctant to leave so that the Chinese financier was forced to rise and take him by the elbow, shepherding him to the door. He closed the door on the tall Scotsman and stood facing Trent across the big room:

'Tea, Mr Trent?'

Trent said, 'Thank you.' Finally he was close to the core of whatever had happened on the *Ts'ai Yen*. He had been up all night and he was tired and he didn't want to play games. Neither did he want the Chinese financier to know how much or how little he knew – knowledge of the woman's existence had proved lethal.

Sir Philip pressed a bell beside the door. When the majordomo reappeared, he ordered tea. Then he crossed to the patio and stood watching the flow of water out of the cornucopia.

Trent followed him out and stood at his shoulder. He wondered if the water was an accident or a precaution against electronic surveillance. He couldn't see into the elderly man's mind nor could he sense any emotion in Sir Philip.

Sir Philip stooped and picked a dead leaf out of the pool. The leaf was shaped like an open boat and he said, 'The *Ts'ai Yen* was my ship, Mr Trent. She was on her maiden voyage.'

'I'm sorry,' Trent said.

The financier gave a slight lift to his perfectly clothed shoulders and beckoned the majordomo to unfold a table beside the pool. The tray was dark lacquer and Sir Philip poured tea into cups of translucent bone china. 'I hope you don't take milk or sugar, Mr Trent?'

The tea was green and faintly smoky. No doubt that it was special and would have impressed a tea taster. Trent wondered if the financier ever became bored with always having the best. He smiled to himself because he knew that he had been the best at what he did – and probably remained the best – which was almost certainly why he had been brought here. He said: 'At least one lot of people have tried to kill me so I'd like to know what's going on.'

The financier shrugged: 'There's a war on, Mr Trent. The men who attacked the *Ts'ai Yen* are employed by one of my competitors, a man who hates me with all his being. When Europeans think of hate, they think of something sharp and fierce and short-lived, while, for us Chinese, hate is the deepest of all emotions.' He paused, lost for a moment in thought. Then he continued: 'I can't prove that this man is responsible for the loss of the *Ts'ai Yen*, Mr Trent, but it is true and everyone knows that it is true. I have lost a great deal of face. Face is extremely important in this part of the world. Find the pirates, Mr Trent.'

'I'm not a detective,' Trent said.

The elderly Chinese turned away from the pool. His eyes were pure black and there was a hardness to him that was common to men of great power. Trent wondered how long it had been since anyone had refused him a request. He recalled his years of service and the senior official in Washington who had named his targets as if enjoying the power to condemn a man to death.

Death. He hated the stench of it.

'And despite what you may have heard, Sir Philip, I am not an executioner,' he said.

The financier said, 'I know what you are, Mr Trent. We have a man in London who has supplied us with a very thorough profile.'

Trent had presumed as much. Sir Philip's source had to be Military Intelligence. The source would have sold the information and Trent fought to keep the rage and disgust out of his voice: 'Is that a threat, Sir Philip?'

For a moment the financier seemed surprised. Then he said quietly, 'I never threaten. You accede to my request, or I make the request an order. Those are your options, Mr Trent. Kindly drink you tea while it's hot.' He rang and a male secretary, part Chinese and part Filipino, appeared and hovered at the door while Trent drained his cup.

'Very pleasant,' Trent said to the financier and Sir Philip said, 'We must organise a tasting once this business is finished.' He walked Trent to the door as he had walked Sir Euan Wiley, full of friendship and courtesy. 'Good day, Mr Trent. Mr Chung will give you all necessary help.'

Chung was in his mid-forties, smooth and careful and considerate as a male nurse in a private home for the mentally handicapped. He led Trent down a long quarry-tiled corridor to a high-ceilinged office furnished with a Spanish colonial work table, two high-backed chairs, a big old-fashioned Chubb safe, and a wall of fireproof filing cabinets. A column of sunlight slanted down from the single window high up in the wall. A ceiling fan turned at about a revolution a minute.

Chung seemed relieved to be safely back in his own territory. Sitting down at his work table, he nodded Trent to the second chair and produced a letter printed with a carbon ribbon on thick writing paper that authorised Trent to act on behalf of the South China Sail & Steam Ship Company in all matters concerning the MV *Ts'ai Yen*. Chung supplied a crew list and he gave Trent a miniaturised radio beacon. Once Trent found the pirate base, he was to activate the beacon and help would be available within the hour.

'Don't try and do everything yourself,' Chung warned earnestly and Trent knew that the secretary had read the report from London – the report must have dwelt heavily on Trent's reputation for acting on his own and without respect for departmental orders and regulations.

Chung busily polished his spectacle lenses which were large and round and set in thin gold-plated metal frames with sprung ear-grips. He was a thin man with a slight stoop and bald on the top of his head so that he looked like a tonsured monk in civilian clothes. He threaded the spectacles back behind his ears and looked even more earnest: 'These man are dangerous and you'll get hurt, Mr Trent. That would never do and is quite unnecessary.'

Trent said that he had seen the evidence of the pirates' propensity for violence and would use the beacon if he came within long-distance sniffing range of the pirate base.

'I didn't ask for this job and I'm not a hero,' he assured the secretary.

'I am glad about that,' Chung said with a little smile that uncovered two gold teeth.

Trent asked for the ship's paper and Chung seemed surprised. 'Those will be with Mr Tanaka Kazuko,' he said after a moment's thought. 'I believe you met him on board the *Ts'ai Yen*. A Japanese gentleman.'

Trent said, 'Oh,' and pretended to lose interest.

Relieved not to be at fault, Chung took a heavyweight envelope from a file cover on the desk and handed it to Trent with a slight bow. 'Your remuneration, Mr Trent. I hope you will find it sufficient. Unfortunately I don't have much experience of this sort of work, but it did seem to come under the general heading of legal expenses so I gave you parity with outside legal advisers plus ten percent for, uhm, uh . . .'

Embarrassed, he came to a halt and Trent said: 'Danger.'

Chung dipped his head: 'Precisely. Precisely. Oh, and there was the matter of a weapon, Mr Trent. Again I wasn't quite sure but I thought that they might be a little like fountain pens. You know? Very much a matter of personal taste. So I had these prepared. Three?' he asked as he slid three firearm permits across the table. 'I hope that will be ample, Mr Trent? The Chief of Police here has already signed them. All you need do is fill in the details.'

Trent wasn't sure of the protocol. Did he thank the secretary for his trouble? He said that he wanted to inspect the dead and Chung immediately telephoned a police officer in Manila.

'The bodies are at the city morgue. The pathologist will be

expecting you,' he told Trent as he replaced the receiver. 'Inspector Martino will help you in any way he can.' He wrote the Inspector's number on a sheet of paper. 'Of course I'm not very experienced, but if there is anything,' he said and added his own name and number in neat capital letters. 'A car will take you back to Manila. Please do try and keep in touch. We don't want Sir Philip to become anxious, Mr Trent.'

There was the threat, politely stated by Chung in his softly accentuated and rather old-fashioned English.

'That would never do,' Trent agreed and Chung smiled, pleased that he had been understood.

8

The young man had difficulty in breathing as the private elevator shot him to the penthouse floor. He followed Wong Fu's personal bodyguard up the final flight of stairs and stood beneath the surveillance camera. The lock clicked, the door swung open, and a bell summoned him into the presence. He barely dared look at Wong Fu, who stood barricaded behind his vast marble desk. The tightness around the young man's chest threatened to make him vomit as he crossed the huge room and his knees nearly crumpled.

He took a sheet of paper from a pile on the left of the desk and wrote on it: *the yachtsman, Trent, escaped in Manila. He was rescued by men from the House of Li.*

He bowed and offered the message in hands cupped together to form a shallow tray. Wong Fu read it and dropped the paper into the shredder. The scar across his scalp throbbed and reddened. He smiled and licked the right corner of his upper lip. Then he hit the young man flat-handed across the face.

Lu knelt with one knee across the back of the fisherman's neck. He twisted his hand into the fisherman's hair so that he could hold the man's face in the sand. 'What boats came past in the last day?' he asked softly: 'Boats of fifty feet or more?' He lifted the fisherman's mouth clear of the sand so that the man could answer his question. 'Tell me the boats' colours,' he whispered. 'How many men were on board? What kind of men were they?'

But the fisherman had seen nothing and Lu let his weight fall on the man's neck. He took the fisherman's clothes and the man's machete. Dragging the fisherman's boat down the beach, he raised the sails and turned the bows towards the next island. It was only a matter of time before he crossed the path of the Chinese and the pirates. Then he would find the girl.

All morning they had used her. She wanted to be dead but she had nothing with which to kill herself. The pain came in waves. The pain, and the shame of what they had done to her, and the shame that she had allowed them to do whatever they wanted. She had begged to be allowed do what they wanted. She had implored them to tell her what they wanted. Begged to be their slave if only they would stop hurting her. But they enjoyed her pain. The leader laughed at her and told her that this was only the first day. That there would be many days. That she would become mad. And that only then would she be rescued. Rescued by Wong Fu and presented to the world in her imbecility, desecrated, the very symbol of her grandfather's loss of face, of his loss of power.

She beseeched them to tell her who he was, this Wong Fu who would rescue her, and they beat her again. They beat her because they could not imagine a Chinese ignorant of Wong Fu and his power, and his hatred for the House of Li. They presumed that she was casting a slight on the head of their clan and they punished her for her impertinence. They punished her, each in turn, then they used her again, and she wept to be allowed to die.

A standard Mercedes 190 dropped Trent off outside the morgue. As usual, Manila was suffering what the Filipinos call a brown-out and what anyone else would call a collapse of the city's electricity generating capacity. Brown-outs lasted for eight hours or more at a stretch. The poor and the middle classes were the chief sufferers. Five-star hotels and the houses of the rich were equipped with generators. So was the morgue.

The pathologist read Trent's letter of authorisation without much interest but he shouted for a clerk when Trent asked to see the reports on the crew. The clerk fetched the files and Trent read them down in the cold room.

The captain, first officer, and one sailor had been killed without any unnecessary force while the other men had been slaughtered. Trent asked to see the bodies and checked them against the pathologist's copy of the crew list. The second officer was missing. The crew list gave his name as Lu. He was male, and twenty-eight years old. There weren't any women amongst the crew.

69

The pathologist offered him a rum bottle and Trent took a swallow to be friendly. A man coughed while he had the bottle to his lips and he looked up to see the Japanese with the pony tail standing in the doorway. Mr Tanaka Kazuko, Chung had called him. He wore a different double-breasted Paul Smith suit, Prince of Wales check, that only a miracle kept from slipping off his shoulders. He wore a kipper tie with a button-down flowered shirt and two-tone Paul Smith shoes. Round spectacles with mirror-coated lenses hid his eyes and he carried a blue plastic briefcase.

'So you've got yourself a watching brief for the South China Sail & Steamship Company,' he said in English marked by a strong Liverpool accent.

He didn't bow which Japanese were meant to do. Instead, he nodded at the rum bottle: 'Next you'll be joining a lock-back.'

Lock-backs are the privileged drinkers at Liverpool pubs who are allowed to stay behind locked doors after closing hours. Trent said, 'What are you? The last Beatles fan?'

He hadn't intended to insult the Japanese but he had struck home and he wasn't ready to apologise. 'I might learn more if I had the ship's papers,' he said.

Tanaka Kazuko took the papers from his briefcase.

There weren't any passengers listed. Trent gave the papers back and said: 'I know your name – that's it.'

The Japanese dug a billfold out of his jacket pocket and handed Trent an engraved business card that named him Executive Vice President of the Abbey Road Investigative Unit with addresses and telephone numbers and fax numbers in Tokyo, Hong Kong, and Singapore. 'I represent the insurers,' he said and shrugged as if it wasn't important. His jacket slipped down his shoulders and he pushed it back. 'Where are you staying?'

'The Manila,' Trent said.

Tanaka Kazuko said: 'More comfortable than a morgue. Let's go.'

They took a cab across town, riding in silence because of the driver listening and because of the heat. Trent had asked for a room in the original part of the hotel rather than in the new wing. The lobby was only the size of a couple of tennis courts and the beams supporting the ceiling were black with the smoke of a million or so cigars. Raffles in Singapore, the Taj in Bombay, and the Manila, and Saigon's Continental, all shared the same scent of romance but you had to be inside to breathe the perfume, Trent thought, as he stood at the window of his room and looked down at the street and the traffic belching fumes into the already fetid air.

The Japanese took off his jacket and his shoes, loosened his tie, and made himself comfortable on the double bed. Head pillowed on folded arms, he looked as if he intended staying there a while.

Trent said, 'The *Ts'ai Yen* is a write-off, so what's your interest, Mr Kazuko?'

'The cargo.'

'Crap,' Trent said. 'The insurers want the cargo off-loaded, they don't need a private detective with offices everywhere that matters. Abbey Road! Next you'll ask me to believe you're the man who knows who to bribe to get the cargo off. Bagmen may wear Armani mirror shades but they don't wear Paul Smith suits and a ribbon in their hair. That's too public an image.'

Tanaka Kazuko yawned at him and Trent said: 'At the shopping arcade, were you warning me or warning the people who were trying to kill me?'

It was a stupid question and the Japanese didn't bother answering. Trent was tired and angry at being trapped into an operation which he didn't understand. He was concerned for the woman. He felt that her predicament was his fault if only because he wasn't doing anything. But he wasn't sure where to start. He thought that he could get started if only Tanaka Kazuko would leave. Or he could lie down which he couldn't do with Tanaka Kazuko on the bed. He said: 'What's the name of the man who hates Sir Philip Li?'

'Wong Fu.'

'Was he behind the attack on the *Ts'ai Yen*?'

'Probably.' Tanaka yawned again as if to prove his indifference.

'What does probably mean, for Chris sakes?'

'That I'll give you fifty percent of my fee if you produce the evidence,' Tanaka said: 'That's half of twenty percent of what I save the insurers and the claim's sixteen million Hong Kong so don't bitch that I'm on your bed.'

'I wasn't bitching,' Trent said.

'You wanted to,' Tanaka told him. 'What did Li pay you?'

Trent hadn't looked. He slit the envelope and found a bank draft on the Hong Kong and Shanghai Bank for three hundred and forty thousand dollars. Tanaka Kazuko reached for the draft and said:

'Hong Kong dollars. Chickenfeed. You should have thrown it in his face.'

'That wasn't an option,' Trent said and Tanaka said: 'A real warrior.'

Trent considered hitting him, or throwing him off the bed but, without his jacket, he could see that the slope in Tanaka's shoulders was solid muscle. An unarmed combat routine produced that sort of development and Trent thought that the hotel management might object to his finding out how good Tanaka was at it.

'I'm good, and if you want me to stop reading your mind, don't be so obvious,' Tanaka said. He took off his Armani shades, folded them, and put them away in their case. 'You're meant to be good too, according to what I've read. Mahoney. That's what you used to call yourself.'

Patrick Mahoney had been buried in an Irish cemetery on a rainy Saturday morning with only one witness other than the priest and the four men from the undertaker in their black boots and black gloves and blue serge suits. Trent sat down in a chair facing the bed and said: 'Where did you hear that name?'

Tanaka Kazuko shrugged as if it wasn't important: 'Li's people. Want my story?'

He had been a Detective Chief Superintendent in the Kyoto police force before he got bored with having crooked politicians tell him which of their friends he wasn't allowed to prosecute: 'Now I get rich and get laid and listen to Beatles records.'

'Yeah, yeah, yeah,' Trent said.

'So what do you do that's so great?' Tanaka swung his feet to the floor. He stood up, stretched, danced a soft shoe shuffle, and crooned into an imaginary microphone: 'Show me.' Then he grinned at Trent and said: 'In case you can't do the math, twenty percent of sixteen million Hong Kong is four hundred thousand US and you get half. For a Brit, that's good money.'

'What's good for a Jap?' Trent asked.

'You'd be jealous.'

Tanaka felt for his shoes, laced them, and draped his jacket over one shoulder. He didn't bother straightening his tie. 'What's your next move?'

'Find the pirates,' Trent said.

'They might eat you.'

Trent chucked him the radio beacon. 'Li's man says he'll bring on the cavalry.'

The Japanese dropped the beacon on the bed: 'Russian. It may work. It may not.'

'So now you're a Japanese trade delegation,' Trent said.

Tanaka Kazuko had been about to put his shades back on. He stood in the doorway. An observer untrained in how to look might have thought him a little ludicrous with his pony tail, and his suit, and two-tone shoes – probably an account executive in a minor advertising agency or a director of cheap TV commercials. The image was deliberate.

He said: 'What I am is the one man you can trust in this business and that is something that you had better believe, Mr Trent. You've studied terrorism which is pretty much the same any place in the world, but what we have here is serious wealth. Asian wealth, Mr Trent. Chinese, to be exact. And that's something you don't know a damn thing about. We're on the same flight back to Palawan in the morning. Make a list of what you think you know and give it to me. Then there's a chance I can watch your back long enough for you to collect your fee.'

He flashed a grin and, back straight, bowed a few inches: 'Felly plissed to meet you, Mistah Trent.'

Trent lay on the bed. He could feel the warmth left by Tanaka's body. He would have liked to have known whether Tanaka knew that there had been a woman on the *Ts'ai Yen* and, if so, whether the Japanese knew who she was. To ask would have betrayed Trent's own knowledge and he saw no reason why he should trust Tanaka.

The one person whom Trent had trusted had been his guardian and control, Colonel Smith – a near-fatal mistake.

Trent wondered what a retired Kyoto police superintendent considered a good fee and whether Tanaka always charged twenty percent. The Japanese had told him to make a list of what he knew, something Trent would have done anyway.

First, the radio beacon planted on the *Ts'ai Yen* proved that the attack had been planned. The pathology reports, and his own judgment of the wounds, indicated that the attack was led by one or more trained killers in command of run of the mill pirates, almost certainly Muslims from the Sulu archipelago. There had been a woman on board. She was missing. When they had first boarded the *Ts'ai Yen*, Li's man had tried to hide her existence. At least one team of killers, probably also in the employ of the House of Li, had committed murder to hide her existence. The second officer was also missing. The woman and the second officer could have been killed and thrown overboard. According to Li, and supported by Tanaka Kazuko, the Chinese financier, Wong Fu, was behind the attack. Wong Fu's aim was to destroy Sir Philip Li's face. From Li's and Tanaka's desire that Trent find the pirates there followed the probability that Wong Fu must wish to stop him. So Wong Fu's men had tried to kill him that morning. And Li's men would probably try to kill him if they discovered that he knew about the woman.

Trent walked down the stairs to the lobby and took a cab south. He paid the driver one hundred pesos and told him to run a light as it switched to red, then take a right and slow on the next corner. He ducked down an alley, walked a block, doubled back, and took a second cab over to the British Council reading room where he found a copy of *Who's Who* in the reference section.

Sir Philip Li had been knighted in 1976. He was married and there was a son, Robert, a French daughter-in-law who was a countess in her own right, and two grandsons of school age all resident in England. A younger son had married in the United States but both he and his wife were listed as deceased in the same year so they had probably been killed in an accident. There were no grandchildren listed under this marriage but that could be because they were American citizens – *Who's Who* was a British publication.

He replaced the book, found a payphone in a café round the corner, and called Commander Manuel Ortega at Navy Headquarters. A secretary told him that the Commander was back from Palawan but out of the office. If Trent would give her a contact number, she would try calling the Commander in his car and have him call Trent. Trent told her that his name was d'Oro and gave her the number of the café.

There were two street entrances and a doorway to the kitchen covered by a bead curtain. He sat with his back to the wall at the table closest to the bead curtain. He had no reason to believe that anyone at Navy Headquarters would give his name to Wong Fu's men but Wong Fu was rich and most Filipinos were poor. He thought that five minutes was probably too short a time for Wong Fu's men to get to the café and time enough for the secretary to contact Manolo Ortega. The phone rang with a minute to spare and the café owner signalled Trent.

'Ortega,' the commander said. 'There are some people who want to meet with you.'

'People I would want to meet with?'

'Not if you have any smarts,' the commander said: 'Where am I calling?'

Trent gave him the address of the café and handed the receiver back to the cashier. He paid for his coffee and crossed the road to a menswear shop where he bought a pair of short white socks while keeping an eye on the opposite sidewalk. Ortega drove up in a navy jeep and parked outside the cafe alongside a *No Parking* sign. He sounded his klaxon a couple of times. Trent couldn't spot anyone on Ortega's tail so he crossed the road and slid into the front passenger seat.

Ortega rammed the jeep into gear and drove round the block and down a narrow one-way street to be certain they were clean. Then he pulled into the curb and sat beating time on the wheel to a Filipino rendition of American rap that was on the radio. The muscles in his hands stood out like iron bars. There was none of the relaxed confidence that had marked him that morning at breakfast on board the *Golden Girl*. He didn't look at Trent.

Still beating time, he said: 'This is my country. Talk to Americans and they'll tell you it's a dump. What would they know? There's more tourists murdered in Miami than we have people killed in a year, and that's with a Muslim insurgency movement down south and the communists up north. Now we've got six coastguards dead. I get back from Palawan and a little bird tells me one of the Chinese *triads* has a price on your head. The price is ten thousand dollars US which is money in the Philippines. So I want to know what in the name of God is going down, Mr Trent.'

Trent said: 'A Japanese asked me the same question an hour ago. Tanaka Kazuko. He's a Beatles fan.'

'A real humorist,' Ortega said, but he stopped beating time and turned off the radio.

'Thanks,' Trent said. 'Is that what you do? Fight the insurgents?'

'I'm the one asking the questions,' Ortega said. Trent stayed silent. Ortega swore and finally turned to look at Trent: 'Yeah, that's what I do. I fight the insurgents. What's left of them.'

Mindanao was the largest of the Muslim islands and the centre of the insurgency. Basilan and the Sulu archipelago were to the southwest. Both were Muslim and pirates were active in the surrounding waters. Even the backpackers' guide books advised travellers to exercise extreme caution.

'The insurgents must have sympathisers throughout the Sulu islands,' Trent said.

'Terrorists,' Ortega said.

Trent shrugged: 'It's a question of where you're standing. Some of them must believe that piracy loses them potential support. Give me a name and a place I should look.'

Ortega punched the wheel boss. Then he glowered at Trent. Finally he made up his mind. 'Ishmael Muhammad. He's some sort of fundamentalist intellectual, Teheran University. He's always on the move which is why I haven't caught the son of a bitch but mostly he's round the Samales. That's the north-east end of the Sulu archipelago. The locals think he's some sort of goddamned Robin Hood which is another reason I haven't caught him. He's got twenty men, thirty at most. Some of them are real sweethearts so watch yourself.'

'Thanks,' Trent said.

Ortega swore and punched the wheel boss harder than he had before. This time he hurt himself. He sat shaking his hand and cursing. '*Thanks!*' he finally spluttered. '*Thanks!* Jesus goddamned Christ, is that all I get?'

Trent showed him the miniaturised radio transmitter: 'Do a deal with Sir Philip Li and you get the pirates.'

'If you find them.'

'I'll find them,' Trent said.

9

The surf gave them privacy. Sir Philip Li in his town shoes was so light-framed that he hardly marked the sand but Manolo Ortega was bigger and heavily built and his feet dragged. Sir Philip Li's Mercedes limousine accompanied them a hundred yards away on the shore road and the financier's bodyguard stalked fifty yards to their rear.

'All of them, Commander. That includes the leader and his woman. Is that understood?' Sir Philip asked.

Ortega studied the drawings of the couple. Trent's origins had been disguised by the artist but his beard was unmistakeable as was his hair, thick as thatch on a cottage. The girl was slim and boyish and probably Chinese. Not that it mattered. For the fee they all died. Ten thousand American dollars to whoever killed Trent and another ten for the girl. Then there was the team prize of fifty thousand split between his men and one hundred thousand for himself. But it was all or nothing.

Manolo Ortega understood.

Late evening in Manila and in Hong Kong, but only mid-afternoon in the City of London where Robert Li ducked out of a black cab and scurried through light drizzle across the sidewalk and up the steps into the Traders Funds Bank.

He had gone first to the Union Bank, and to three of the four big English clearing banks, to the Royal Bank and the Bank of Scotland, and to both Rothschild and Schroeder. The bankers had been polite, for there was no certainty yet in the rumours that concerned the House of Li's liquidity. But the rumours made them wary, as did Robert Li with his experience restricted to the management of charities and museums. Fortunately the points over base offered by the House of Li were insufficiently generous and the bankers could decline without offence.

The Traders Funds Bank was different. Dutch in background, it was new to London and rich in capital, much of it, so rumour reported, from Latin America and in need of disguise. However this was said of any institution that appeared overly fluid in a period of world recession. Robert Li was shown immediately into the office of the local managing director.

The managing director travelled on a Dutch passport. His English was immaculate, the accent almost imperceptible. His shoes were unmistakeably English as was his shirt; his dark grey flannel suit had been cut in Savile Row. Only a silk Italian tie in silver on silver ribs lightened the image of bourgeois respectability. His smile showed perfect teeth, their almost startling whiteness further exaggerated by a natural suntan. He agreed the terms of the loan to the House of Li with an almost indecent haste which he explained, with gushing sincerity, as a demonstration of the bank's commitment to long-term investment.

With Robert Li gone, he called Hong Kong on a scrambled line and reported his success to the Wong Fu relative who acted as intermediary between the bank and the Chinese financier. Robert Li, safe back in the ordered quiet of his Pimlico home, called his father at the counting house on an open line and reported his own success.

'Well done, Robert. Very well done indeed,' Sir Philip said and on the top floor of an office building two streets away Wong Fu's men listened via the microphone installed for them by Timmy Brown – they chuckled as Robert asked for news of the girl.

The sulphur stench was part of Jay's hell. She could hear the volcano cough and, at night, the cracks in the walls of her prison were filled with the glow from its crater.

Radio Philippines had broadcast instructions to the squatters at the foot of the volcano to abandon their patches of land and make for the flat land bordering the north coast from where, should the need arise, they would be rescued by landing craft. Meanwhile they would be fed by a kindly government.

The peasants were Muslim and had reason neither to love nor trust a largely Christian government hundreds of miles away across the sea. They had been betrayed too often with guarantees of land reform. Now they had their plots of land that none of the rich had bothered to claim because of the periodic eruptions. They had planted cassava and papaya and bananas and each family kept one or two goats and a few chickens penned behind their huts. Were they to obey the instructions of the geological department, how could they survive? What would they eat? Promises? They knew those promises for what they were, Christian lies.

The telephone rang and Trent reached for the receiver. Tanaka was on the line. The Japanese said, 'I've had a hard day's night so don't argue. You can get to the pool enclosure without going through the lobby. The wall on the left is about two metres high. I'll be there with a cab in fifteen minutes.'

The Japanese had saved him once. Trent looked at his watch. Seven fifteen in the morning – he had slept for eleven and a half hours. He pulled on a pair of swim-shorts and a T-shirt and packed the rest of his clothes into a hold-all. Leaving the hold-all on the bed, he crossed to the hotel's new wing and down the side stairs to the pool club. A pool attendant bade him a polite good morning and offered him a towel.

The pool was set in the middle of a tree-shaded garden. Trent walked along the side of the pool, dropped his T-shirt on to a sun bed, and dived into the deep end. Around twenty strokes took him across the width of the pool. A car klaxon peeped a couple of times from the far side of the garden compound. He pulled himself out of the water and jogged round to where he had left his T-shirt. He grabbed up the T-shirt and speeded up as he headed for the wall. He jumped, caught the top of the wall in both hands, swung over, and landed on his feet. The rear door of the cab was open. Tanaka beckoned him to hurry.

'What's going on?' Trent demanded as he slid in beside the Japanese.

Tanaka grinned. 'Not a lot. I wanted to know if you trusted me.'

'Never again,' Trent told him.

'Too bad. There's a price on your head.' The Japanese seemed pleased by his news: 'Ten thousand US. So you're still cheap, even for a Brit.' He told the driver to slow at the side door by the ballroom and circle the block while he paid Trent's check and fetched his bag.

'Two hundred and thirty dollars,' he told Trent as he dropped Trent's hold-all on the cab floor: 'Comes off your end of the fee.'

Trent and Tanaka flew Philippine Airlines back to Puerto Princesa on Palawan. A launch took them down the coast. With the tide high, the launch dropped Trent off on the *Golden Girl*. The first lighters were alongside the *Ts'ai Yen*. An engineer had set up a diesel generator on deck to power the twin derricks and stevedores were swinging the cargo up from the main hold.

Trent slipped the *Golden Girl* out over the reef under her working jib, dropped anchor again in eighty feet of water, and ran the Zodiac over to the freighter. Clambering on board, he inspected the area that had interested Tanaka the first morning and found specks of blood on the deck and a couple of streaks on the hull about a metre apart – as there would have been if a couple of bodies had been dropped overboard.

The door of the officers' accommodation was open and he checked the second officer's cabin. A man's shirts, socks and underwear were in the appropriate drawers, neatly folded and all marked in ink with the name Lu. Lu's uniforms and work clothes hung in the wardrobe. Two pairs of plain black shoes, a pair of trainers, and a pair of Japanese sandals stood on the bottom shelf of the wardrobe. Writing paper, a couple of postcards, and two technical manuals were arranged neatly in the top drawer of the desk. The bunk smelt of a male aftershave that Trent found on the shelf above the handbasin together with all the other standard male toiletries. The medicine cabinet contained a packet of Bic razors, a spare tube of Close-Up toothpaste, half a packet of condoms, a tube of haemorrhoid cream, and a bottle of Healthcrafts high potency multivitamins.

He wondered what reason the pirates or their leaders could have for executing Lu and the woman. If she was dead, why did Li's men need to hide her existence? There had to be a connection between the woman and Sir Philip Li. His mistress? And her lover, Lu? The elderly Chinese billionaire didn't look the type but types and sexual habits seldom conformed.

Looking round, he found Tanaka watching from the door. Trent said, 'Lu's clothes but no Lu, and a couple of people got shot on deck.'

'With Lu, you've accounted for the crew, so that leaves one of the pirates or the woman.' Tanaka grinned at Trent's discomfiture: 'Li's granddaughter home from the US. Did you know there was a granddaughter? The parents got murdered by a pack of Puerto Rican pre-teen crackheads playing Saturday night hoodlum instead of eating popcorn at the movies. A bird told me she was on board. Li's granddaughter and Lu – he's her bodyguard.'

So now the girl had a name. She must be worth millions in ransom. Surely no pirate would be idiot enough to kill her. The bodyguard, yes, but not the girl.

'Think Asia,' Tanaka urged: 'Old Man Li will lose a lot of face if news of the granddaughter gets out. That's what this piracy is about.'

Trent pictured the financier sipping tea beside the lily pond at his *hacienda*, quietly spoken and courteous, but his power barely sheathed. He would have brought in experts to negotiate the girl's release. A second set of specialists for revenge. And a bird dog . . .

A reef surrounded the island. The island was round and low and only a hundred metres in circumference. A few palm trees were the only vegetation. Lu drove the small sailboat ashore and dragged it up the beach into the shade. The three houses the far side of the small island were square, thatched with palm, their walls made of palm matting. They were built on wooden stilts in the shallow water within the lagoon and were protected by the reef that showed as a white curve of foam. Canoes stirred under the houses and at each house a fishing boat lay moored to the stilts by the steps so the men were home from the fishing grounds.

The islanders drew their water from a well in the centre of the island. Lu crawled to within twenty feet of the well and waited in a dip in the shade of the trees. A woman came first. Lu caught her by the throat. He whispered that she should call her husband but she was too frightened to understand so Lu killed her and waited. Ten minutes passed before the husband shouted for her from the step outside their hut door. She didn't answer so he paddled ashore.

Life on the little island might lack material advantages but it was safe and there was no real fear in the man as he strolled up the shore to the well. Anxiety, yes, and he called softly, perhaps worried that his wife had fallen asleep and might be harmed if he awoke her too abruptly. He looked back over his shoulder and shouted a caution to a child who had come out of the hut onto the step. He saw the crumpled shape of his wife on the sand beyond the well and ran the last few yards.

Lu chopped him on the neck with the side of his hand. It might as well have been a stone club. Lu caught the fishermen in his arms as he dropped, tumbled him into the shade, and slapped his face. The fisherman moaned as he regained consciousness and rolled his head, searching for his wife.

Lu struck him again flat handed across both cheeks and asked what fishing boats he had seen around fifty to sixty feet in length and outside their immediate home waters. The fishermen swore that he had seen nothing but he had heard from the crew of another boat that they had seen two big *baslig* hauled out of the water the previous day. Lu asked where and the fishermen said that it had been to the west.

Lu held him by the hair and made him draw a chart in the sand. He questioned the man on the distances and once they were firm in his head, snapped the man's neck and rolled the body down the slight slope so that it would be hidden from the huts.

He pushed his boat back into the water. Then he erased the track left by the hull, the chart, and his own footprints. The plaintive wail of a child floated across the water as he raised the sail and steered his stolen craft out through the surf.

Trent's Magellan GPS gave a position accurate to within fifty feet and he was able to navigate the reef-strewn waters under cover of darkness. The island was reported in the Admiralty Pilot to have no water and to be uninhabited. He approached under a small jib and reefed mainsail, dropping anchor three hundred yards from the shore. The tide was on the make so he let out a lot of scope, then dived down the anchor warp to check that the flukes were well imbedded.

The island was two hundred yards long and only fifty yards wide. He circled it first, then criss-crossed from east to west and again from west to east in a double Z pattern. There were no signs of visitors.

Unshipping the *Golden Girl*'s twin rudders, he withdrew the dagger plates from their slots. Then he lifted the anchor. As the big cat drifted into the shallows, he dropped overboard and drew her bows onto the beach.

There were no trees so he dragged his spare anchor and warp

across the island and set the flukes. Leading the warp back over the fairleed, he made it fast to a small hand winch made for lifting engines that had a sixty to one purchase. Rollers had to be eased under the bows and under the hull. He dragged the warp and winch back to the anchor. Five minutes on, the winch lever moved the bows clear of the water and he climbed back on board.

The twin spinnaker poles formed an upright V when slid into sockets in the bridge deck forward of the saloon. A socket on the beam connecting the bows held the boom at an angle so that it formed a tripod with the spinnaker poles. The mast foot sat in an open-ended steel shoe supported by a post that ran through the cabin top to the saloon sole. A steel pin allowed the mast foot to pivot fore and aft in the shoe and the removal of two bolts in the cabin top enabled him to swivel the shoe ten degrees to starboard.

Trent slackened the after-stays and carefully lowered the mast down the starboard side of the tripod. Disassembling the tripod, he lashed the rigging to the mast and lashed the mast fast to the forward beam. With rollers under her hull, a further hour on the winch shifted the *Golden Girl* well clear of the high water mark.

While sailing over from Palawan, he had prepared a list of the equipment he required on the sail-board:

> *Radio beacon.*
> *Dive knife in a leg scabbard.*
> *Sun cream in quantity.*
> *Jungle boots.*
> *Magellan GPS.*
> *Chart.*
> *Water.*
> *Food.*
> *Spear gun, fishing line and hooks.*
> *A coil of light line.*
> *Folding grappling hook as anchor.*
> *Paddle and spare paddle.*
> *Dive gear and one tank.*

He loaded the equipment into a foam box held by bungees to the deck of the sail-board and fitted the mast and sail to the board.

He washed a bowl of cereal down with a mug of strong coffee. Then he soaked the spinnaker in the sea, spread the sail over the catamaran, pegged it to the ground, and covered it with a layer of sand. He had to wait for first light to check the camouflage and he sat on the water's edge, waiting.

The breeze that had brought him across the Sulu Sea from Palawan had died with the approach of day and the small waves seemed to collapse from exhaustion. A slight scent of iodine and corruption rose from the line of dead seaweed at the tidemark while a hint of sulphur came from a volcano. Fresh eruptions in the crater of the volcano gave a soft glow of orange to the northern horizon while, to the east, a barely perceptible lightning of the sky presaged the dawn.

With first light, he paddled the sail-board out. The sky remained deep mauve to the west above the dark blue-grey of the water. Even against this background, the *Golden Girl* was difficult to spot at a hundred yards. From two hundred yards she was almost invisible. Later in the day the fierce sunlight would drain the colour out of the sky and sea and sand. There would be few shadows to betray the last hints of the yacht's shape. A passing fisherman might stumble upon her but otherwise she was safe.

Trent raised the sail and turned the sail-board toward the Samal islands. At the same time, twenty miles to the north west, Lu slid his sailboat onto the beach of another island.

Darkness had hidden the island when Lu first smelt wood smoke. Now the scent of the hunt was thick in his nostrils as he crept up through the palm trees. Four fishermen crouched over a fire of coconut husks. They were small men, thin of haunch. They held slices of fish on sharpened sticks to the coals. Their hunger made them see only the food so that Lu came within a foot of the nearest man before he was discovered – a faint shadow against the dark horizon. A ghost, a phantom – these men believed in such things as they believed in magic. Lu's speed must have seemed magical to the two men on the far side of the fire. The fisherman nearest to Lu and the one to his right both died ignorant of his presence. In each case a single blow snapped their necks and they pitched forward into the coals.

The third fisherman dropped his stick. He made no attempt to avoid his death. Rather he crouched lower and seemed to stretch his neck in obedience to the summons and he turned his head to hide from himself the moment, so making the manner of it simple.

The fourth fisherman fell to his knees and beseeched the phantom

84

to spare him. He had fathered seven children in nine years – starvation would take them . . .

Lu silenced him with a slap across the face and rescued the fallen fish slices from the coals. Other than coconut this was his first food since diving from the *Ts'ai Yen*, but he flicked away the embers from the white flesh with a twig before commencing his meal. He ate neatly and without haste and he watched the fisherman as a stoat watches a rabbit.

Finished, he wiped his lips on the back of his hand and wiped his hand on the ragged sarong worn by the nearest of the dead men. The fisherman proffered in both hands a brown-glazed water pot. Lu drank sparingly. He wiped his lips again. Then he asked about the two big *baslig*.

The fisherman had heard of two boats drawn up on the beach of an island over to the west. He drew a chart in the sand which agreed in sufficient details to that of Lu's previous informant but he knew nothing more and Lu killed him quickly.

Lu fetched and cleaned the night's catch from the men's boat and set the fish to grill. There were four *barong* in the boat and he took two of these also, sharpening one blade against the other while he waited for the fish to dry over the low coals. He laid the fish on a bed of folded palm fronds in the stern of his sailboat where they would be protected from the spray and further dried by the sun, and he filled an aluminium mug from the fisherman's boat with seawater and set it to evaporate so that he would have salt to spread on the fish.

The bodies he loaded into the fishermen's boat and lashed the helm so that the boat would drift out on the tide to the west. Then he swept their footprints from the sand and, as the sun rose clear of the horizon, lay down in the shade of his own small craft and slept, confident that he was getting closer to the girl. He wondered whether she was alive.

They had left her sprawled on the dirt floor of the hut. She lay inert and might easily have been mistaken for a corpse. But her mind was alive. She understood, now, the purpose of her kidnapping and she no longer prayed for death. Rather, she had built a wall of hate behind which she hid the tiny inner core of herself, dense as anti-matter and as invisible, a core warmed by her faith in her grand-father's omnipotence.

*

85

Sir Philip Li stood in the midst of his *kindergarten* on the raised enclosure above the floor of the counting house. Timmy Brown reported the conference room safe and they walked up the stairs. Miss James had laid out the day's papers and faxes of the main headlines and comments in the foreign press. As Sir Philip had expected, the financial pages led with his disposal of the House of Li's meat-packing interests and the Florida feed lots. Most of the articles calculated that the forced sale had lost the House of Li thirty to thirty-five percent of the true value of its investments.

FIRST STEP IN HOUSE OF LI DISPERSAL? was a reasonable headline. LI RUNS OUT OF ROOM was another.

Sir Philip watched the faces of his kindergarten as they read. The battle was on, yet none of them knew what forces he could deploy, and he imagined their guesses, and he wondered which one of them would play the traitor first.

'Charming,' Rudi Beckenberg said of a British tabloid that carried a photograph of Robert front page beneath the headline: CHINK IN DRUG FORTUNE ARMOUR.

'Clever,' Tommy Li corrected and Sir Philip nodded. He imagined Wong Fu's enjoyment of the attack – but there were tales that Wong Fu was illiterate and he found himself wondering whether these were true.

At twenty-three years old, Pete was the youngest of the Fu clan to have regular access to Wong Fu's penthouse. In childhood, his mother had been the financier's favourite cousin. Wong Fu had bought her out of China and Pete had been educated at St Joseph's in Hong Kong and Manchester University where he read business administration. He had earned his masters with a computer study of overnight currency fluctuations. Now he prepared a daily resumé of the press and radio news and read it to Wong Fu each morning.

Wong Fu sprawled by the east window in a chrome-framed chair upholstered in black leather. The girl who had shaved him was in her mid teens. Pete waited for her to wipe the last traces of lather from Wong Fu's face with a hot towel before showing the financier the fax of the British tabloid front page that bore the photograph of Robert Li. He explained the double meaning of the headline and Wong Fu roared with laughter. The great Li with his English suits would be taught many a lesson over the next weeks.

*

From his first day as Chairman, Sir Euan Wiley had been embarrassed by the daily descent from Braemar Lodge to the office in the chauffeured Rolls. The vast limousine was a grotesque anachronism, particularly within the context of the tiny island colony.

He would have enjoyed the walk, however his wife had mobilised his fellow directors' wives, each of whom desperately desired to be the next tenant of Braemar Lodge.

The wives yearned for the titles and trinkets that went with the position and there was much talk of loss of face and of letting the side down.

Euan knew that he was little more than an office manager. Power lay with the House of Li. It always had, right from the beginnings in Macau. Philip had been kindly in protecting him from his arrangements with Trent. However Euan had felt demeaned and alienated as the financier walked him to the door – feelings exacerbated that morning over breakfast by his wife's demand that he be careful not to get in too deep.

Her mother had telephoned from England at midnight English time. Robert Li was on the front page of the yellow press, accused of smuggling drugs. And had Euan heard this and that? And did he know what they were saying at the club? And that she had never quite liked the financier. After all, blood would out, and Li was Chinese while they were British – something that she would be grateful if Euan would remember. They had a position to uphold in the community as well as back home where the children would go to school. Euan should consider the children. Children picked up on things and it wasn't fun to be called Chinky because your father preferred the company of Chinese businessmen to that of his proper friends.

Disturbed by this barrage, Euan had looked up from his toast to warn against gossip, but a new cruelty in the narrow line of his wife's lips had unnerved him and he had scurried for the fastness of the limousine.

Now, as the Rolls ghosted past the Wong Fu building, he looked up at the glass pyramid and wondered if and when the approach would come.

10

Trent trawled the Samal Islands for the leader of the Muslim insurgents. The Spanish occupation of the Philippines lasted three hundred and fifty years – in the Samal islands they gained only a toe-hold. The Americans failed to occupy the islands; then came the Japanese, followed by the US-protected Marcos dictatorship; and now democracy, Manila democracy, Christian-dominated – to the islanders, as much a colonial administration as its predecessors.

The islands were small and mostly flat, with few trees to shade the barren soil. The inhabitants came from two major tribes: the Badjao, known for their ferocity, and the more kindly Samal. The villages seldom numbered more than twenty huts supported on stilts in the shallows within the reef. The houses of the Samal were more sophisticated than those of the Badjao who used only palm frond piled layer on layer while the Samal employed woven mat and patterned cane. Rather than village lanes, there were slatted walkways of split bamboo with boats moored beneath: *baslig* fifty or more feet in length, the smaller *bancos*, and tiny outrigger canoes so narrow that the crew were forced to sit on a plank laid across the gunwales with only their legs in the hull.

Muslim women could be seen crouched over open hearths and a thin layer of smoke clung to the thatch roofs. Men squatted on the walkways deep in conversation. Naked children played in the water, teeth brilliant white against skins blackened by the sun. Fish and seaweed dried on racks. Sea birds swooped and screeched overhead.

Trent cruised the islands for two days on the big converted sail-board. The Badjao were to be avoided but he asked for news of Ishmael Muhammad at each of the Samal settlements, only to be met always by closed faces and often by open hostility.

It was only a matter of time before the insurgents heard tell of his enquiries. They found him on the third day. He lay apparently asleep in the shade of a palm tree. He had pulled the sail-board up the beach, grilled fish over a fire of dry seaweed, and drunk water from a young coconut.

There were six insurgents. Their boat was some forty feet long and painted gold with the name FATIMA along the hull in big decorative letters edged with green. Rather than use the engine, they crossed the reef under sail so as to surprise him. They wore gaily coloured sarongs and carried long-bladed *kampilan* in their belts. Their AK-47s came probably from Vietnam or Cambodia. Five of them were young while the sixth was an old man with a pleated scar that ran diagonally from his right shoulder down the length of his back. He wasn't the leader. The leader was young and tough and ugly with hate – the hate made him unpredictable.

The leader kicked Trent in the legs to awaken him. Trent slowly raised his hands and shifted a yard to his left so they would see that he was unarmed. Then he lowered his hands behind his head so that his right hand rested on the hilt of his knife. He could kill the leader at any time – the other five were unprepared for violence. As the leader dropped his gun, Trent could sweep it up and have the others covered before they understood what had happened.

The insurgent screamed at him and dug the barrel of his AK-47 into his ribs. Knowing that he could kill him gave Trent patience.

He said: 'I am looking for Ishmael Muhammad. This is the third day that I have looked for him.'

The old man asked: 'What do you wish with Ishmael Muhammad?'

The leader struck Trent across the thigh before he could answer and Trent watched his eyes and knew that the Filipino longed to kill him.

Trent smiled with the confidence of a man who knows that he is safe: 'Perhaps I bring you support, even millions of dollars. Kill me and you will never know.'

Still smiling, he said: 'Or I could be a film director who intends making you famous. There are many possibilities.'

The old man said, 'Many,' and almost smiled at the leader's rage: 'White as you are, you could be an evil spirit. Or a tourist.'

'There is a difference?' Trent asked, and two others smiled with the old man but the leader lashed out with his gun. The foresight gouged Trent's thighs and his trousers ripped. He felt the blood trickle down between his legs and he said: 'Perhaps you have forgotten that the Holy Book instructs us to be hospitable to strangers.' He began to chant before the leader could interrupt.

Such quotations from the Koran had saved Trent's life more than once. The old man asked if he was a believer and Trent asked, in turn, if a man could know the Holy Book and not be a believer.

'True,' the old man said, but the leader had learnt from watching films on television and shouted that Trent was a spy and that they should shoot him before he discovered enough and betrayed them. He raised his gun but one of the young men who had smiled pushed the barrel aside. Their argument was loud and angry and too fast for Trent to catch even a word of the English or Spanish which lards most Filipino dialects.

Those against killing him won the debate. Tying his hands behind his back, they shoved him down the beach to their boat. He was made to lie on the floor boards with a fishing net over his head so that he would be unable to see what direction they steered. They towed the sail-board.

The weight of the sun on his back told Trent that they sailed north. A six-cylinder petrol engine drove them over the water within the reefs at fifteen to eighteen knots. The narrow hull hobby-horsed when hit by the slight lop out in deep water and they were forced to drop their speed.

They ran ashore soon after dark. There was much excitement amongst the main body of insurgents and again the leader argued angrily. Two men grabbed Trent by the elbows and dragged him out of the boat. To be thought weak was an advantage and he pretended collapse as they forced him up the sand. They shoved him into a cage that stank of goat. A fresh argument erupted when he demanded that they retie his hands in front of his body. A man brought him water and he sprinkled his feet and hands, then faced towards Mecca and began to chant the prayers which every Muslim must repeat six times each day.

As a boy he had prayed with the old Arab groom at the Gulf racing stables where his father was manager and trainer. He had prayed in the Libyan desert with instructors in terrorism who had believed that he was Palestinian. He had prayed in the Lebanon and in Jordan and in the Gaza strip in company with terrorists who knew him as their Iraqi accommplice or as a Libyan or an Egyptian from the Brotherhood; he had passed for a Jordanian when he prayed on the slopes above Mecca the first time that he made the Hajj – the second time he was from the Sudan. To pray in the Samal islands was easy. Like a good actor, he became the character he played and he believed in the prayers he chanted as deeply as he had believed in the prayers of his Roman Catholic childhood. There was little difference in the prayers.

The old man with the scarred back fed him dried fish and rice and refilled his water pot. A younger man escorted him down the beach to urinate. Then Trent was alone for the night.

He judged the strength of the insurgents at sixty men – there were only men. As always with freedom fighters or terrorists, this group comprised a few intellectuals motivated by belief, a few who were fanatics by nature, peasants forced by poverty into rebellion, and bandits with a lust for violence. Their encampment lay in a sand-fringed cove shaded by palms. A lone hut stood a little back from the beach and the men slept in homemade tents hand-painted with camouflage or in hammocks slung between the trees. The boat, FATIMA, with its gaudy paint-work, lay in the open but the other four *baslig* were grey and dragged into the shade where they were hidden beneath dirty sacks.

Trent had slept well and long during his sail-board cruise. With the point of his knife, he prised the knot loose in the rope that bound his hands. Then he dozed for a couple of hours in the centre of his cage and listened to the mosquitoes. He lay on his back with his hands behind his head so that he would appear helpless. The soft sand deadened footsteps but the touch of a sandal against a stone snapped him to full alert.

Palm fronds divided the moonlight into twisted patches that shifted in the soft breeze but he spotted a movement by the trees to his left which was foreign to the pattern. He rolled onto his side as if restless, then fell back so that his feet faced the movement. He thought that he heard a gasp and the heavy touch of a hand on a tree trunk – as if a man had slipped and grabbed to steady himself. These fresh sounds came from behind him. He was sure of the movement to his front.

He had used himself as bait to attract the insurgents but he had been conscious of his role and prepared. Now he lay sandwiched and blind to the intentions of whoever approached. He wondered if there could be an agent of the central government in the camp – or an agent of an outside power – an agent determined to contact him, or even save him perhaps, and a second man suspicious of the first.

A slight shift of shadow to his front betrayed the first man and he heard further movement to his rear. Were the two men in harmony? Or had an insurgent determined to kill him? Could the second man be a protector?

He had to know which way to face and he shouted suddenly, not words but a screech that drew a shot from his rear. The bullet struck inches to his left and blasted sand into his eyes. He was already rolling to his left as the second bullet smashed a wooden upright. He pivoted on his rump as a third bullet tore splinters from a stake. A burst of rapid fire from the other side of the cage drew a scream of rage and the man who had shot at him charged the prison.

The man behind Trent yelled a warning and Trent clutched his knife as the attacker fired a wild burst, but the stakes were close, deflecting the bullets, and only one found its target.

The muzzle flashes gave the second man his aim. He fired twice. There was a despairing shout of rage and the charging man tumbled, his grip gone so that his rifle spun away. His head smashed against the stakes with only a slight movement of one hand visible in the moonlight. Then that movement ceased.

A torch beam struck the man's face and Trent saw that he was the young leader of the band that had captured him that morning. The old man with the scar held the torch. He knelt beside the young man and felt his heart but his hand came away filled with blood and he shook his head in sadness or because he was exhausted by the drama and danger. He turned to look at Trent who had pushed himself into a sitting position against the cage wall.

'The will of God,' the old man said with fatalism. The rest of the insurgents had gathered now, and the old man looked up from the dead body. He shook his head again and asked Trent quietly and in front of these witnesses: 'Foreigner, are you a good man?'

Trent stayed silent under the old man's inspection and the old man said: 'He hated foreigners. Two of his sisters are tourists' prostitutes in Angeles City. Let us pray that God has given you strength to be a good man and that you will do good with your life.'

'I will try,' Trent said.

There were murmurs of *insh'Allah* from the men.

'Are you hurt?' the old man asked.

Trent said, 'In the leg.'

They opened the cage and an insurgent cut Trent's trousers. The blood welled thick as brown gravy from the side of his right thigh. The insurgent who cut the trouser made a pad of the cloth and held it firmly against the wound while another man returned to the camp for bandages and antibiotic ointment.

'It will heal quickly,' the man said and Trent said that the wound was not important.

Men carried away the dead body on a stretcher. Trent looked up to find the old man watching him. He had made a promise to the old man that he would do good and he thought of the woman. Five days had gone since her capture and he wondered if the ransom had been paid.

He said: 'Pirates attacked a ship out in the Sulu sea last week. They took a woman captive. A Chinese woman.'

'Sleep,' the old man said and one of the other men said: 'Ishmael will be here in the morning. He will decide.'

They freed his hands without heeding the looseness of the rope and they brought him a pillow of dried seaweed. The strike of the bullet had numbed the nerves. As the shock wore off, the pain came, deep and throbbing. Sleep evaded him and his head filled with pictures of the woman.

Her kidnappers had left her sprawled like an abandoned rag doll on the dirt floor. She was incapable of speech. Spit dribbled from the corner of her mouth, her nose ran with mucous and her eyes were hidden in bruised flesh.

The kidnappers thought of her as an imbecile, already mentally dead and dead to the pain of any new assaults, but they were incapable of seeing into the kernel of her being where the hate glowed like molten gold. Each fresh abuse was fuel for the hate and, though she was no longer capable of thought, she felt a happiness now that grew from the certainty of vengeance. She knew her grandfather's power.

Lu watched the fisherman beach his tiny outrigger. The fisherman was old and many years a widower. He had been abandoned by his children who had their own children and grandchildren to care for. Perhaps he was a little crazy. But he was capable still of sailing from island to island. This was his joy and because of his travels there were old men in many villages within the archipelago who greeted him with pleasure for the gossip he brought and fed him and gave him shelter in a corner of their huts.

Lu walked down the beach, skin darkened by the sun, muscles hidden beneath a stolen shirt and trousers. He greeted the fisherman with a hand clasp and gathered him into his arms with such power that the old man gasped and shuddered in sudden fear. But Lu was gentle with him now that he had the old man safe. He seated him in the shade and fetched him water and dried fish. Then he squatted facing him and watched as he sucked the flesh from the bone between the toothless gums.

The food gave the old man strength and Lu smiled at him and asked gently whether he knew of the pirate boats. The old man said that he knew every boat in the archipelago. These boats of which Lu inquired belonged to *Badjaos* from the north of the islands. He had seen the boats pass only four days ago. There were strangers on board, men of the same tribe as Lu. Lu should be careful for the *Badjaos* were dangerous. He could tell Lu stories of their doing stretching back for many years. The Christians were frightened of them and let them be. But all Christians were cowardly – even when they had huge boats that sprouted cannon bigger than the trunks of the palm tree under which he and Lu sat now. He had seen the cannon with his own eyes. And he had the Japanese put the Christians to flight. Both white and brown, there was no difference between the Christian tribes. Even their God was cowardly. Hadn't he surrendered to his enemies and been nailed by them to a cross of wood?

Lu nodded his agreement and offered the old fisherman water to drink so that his tongue would stay loose. There was no stopping the old man now and Lu had to hush him, pleading for further information regarding the matter of the two boats.

The fisherman insisted they return to the beach so that he could draw a chart in the wet sand with a stick. As he hobbled down the strand, he boasted to Lu of how fine he could draw the lines. He knew each bay and river, in what direction the trees lent, where there was sweet water, where crabs could be found in the mangrove . . . *Ayee*, he knew so much. Lu was fortunate indeed.

The old fisherman accompanied the drawing of the chart with stories of how he had sailed here and there and what had happened in each place. When he came to the hideout of the pirates, he drew a sand spit and, as he had promised, the trees leaning to the wind and, behind the spit, the mouth of the short river that led to the pirates' village stronghold. He drew a cliff behind the stronghold and, beyond the cliff, a volcano.

The fisherman was so proud of his work and of his memory. Lu questioned him carefully, then thanked him and snapped his neck with a single blow that the old man never saw.

11

The wound in Trent's leg made him appear vulnerable as he hobbled from his cage to the swept square of sand that served the insurgents as their mosque.

Ishmael Muhammad had come with the dawn. The insurgent leader sat cross-legged, his face to Mecca. He was in his mid-thirties, tall and slim. His followers were in awe of his presence. He bowed to Trent with a humility that spoke of the religious and God stood by his side as he posed his questions. Who was Trent? From what country? What reason guided his search for the insurgents? There was mention of a Chinese woman, was she his wife?

For Trent, Teheran and fundamentalist fervour were old acquaintances and he was careful in his answers. He was an English yachtsman. The woman had been kidnapped from a ship and the crew had been murdered. He had been told that Ishmael Muhammad knew of all that happened in the area surrounding the Samal Islands. He had come to him for help.

Was it his habit to rescue women? Ishmael asked, dark eyes curious but without humour. His eyelids opened and closed like shutters dependent on whether he was talking to Trent or to God.

Trent answered that it was his duty. He quoted from the Koran and Ishmael said: 'So it is true that you have studied the Holy Book.'

'Studied it, yes,' Trent said: 'One should try to understand what millions believe.'

'So you have studied Buddhism?'

Trent nodded.

'And the Hindus?'

The next question was already obvious and to inhibit it, Trent said: 'yes. And also the beliefs of the Jews. They are less numerous, but their influence is great.'

A slight hiss of breath marked mention of the enemy even here on a small island thousands of miles from the Eastern seaboard of the Mediterranean.

The deep brown eyes that had watched Trent so carefully turned inward as the insurgent leader communed with his God. The amber beads of an Iranian rosary slipped through his fingers one by one – beads the size of a table grape, *click, click.* 'And what do you now believe?'

'That I must try each day to be a little better at being me than I was yesterday,' Trent said.

'That is a belief?'

Trent shrugged. 'A way of living. One of your men died yesterday.' He looked to the old man with the scarred back for support: 'I was the catalyst. Poverty and unbridled male desire created the circumstance – men of every colour and every faith. Would you have me castrate or kill them? Or bomb the whore bars in Angeles city. Execute the owners?'

'So you do nothing.'

'I search for one woman,' Trent corrected: 'Pirates took her from a ship. You know which pirates or what pirates are capable of such an attack. Protect such men and you dirty your own reputation and that of your followers.'

Trent eased his leg and Ishmael asked: 'Forty or even fifty men? Armed with heavy machine guns bought from the army who report that they were lost in battle to the soldiers of Allah, and perhaps the small rockets – SAMs. What good could you do? Or is it enough to try?'

'To succeed is better,' Trent said, and some of the men smiled and nodded as Trent continued: 'These men are wicked, the enemies of God. Does it matter who punishes them? You will find in the mast of my small boat a radio beacon that I could have activated when your men found me.'

Again there was the hiss of indrawn breath and the men rocked forward on their toes like athletes ready to spring.

'You would all be dead,' Trent said into the silence. He searched the semi-circle of tense faces, the menace there like a cloud on every brow and in the curve of the men's lips. He looked back to their leader: 'This is your war. There must be some right on your side. Why else would you turn yourselves into exiles? But this is your struggle, not mine, and I have no side in it. I wish the woman to be safe. For this, I must have the pirates. They are as much your enemies as mine.'

Ishmael spoke to one of the men. The man rose and trotted down to Trent's sail-board.

'In the heel of the mast,' Trent said quietly and Ishmael called instructions.

The man found the radio beacon and brought it to his leader. Ishmael examined it with the accurate fingers of one who had been trained in illicit warfare: 'Russian.'

'Old friends of yours,' Trent said in memory of the Cold War years when the Soviets had armed both the Filipino Communists and Muslims in their struggle against the US-supported Marcos dictatorship.

'They are without belief but they were useful to us,' Ishmael admitted.

'Mutually useful. Commander Manuel Ortega will answer the beacon.'

Their breath hissed at the name of the director of special forces who had hunted their brothers in arms and in God out of the mountain fastnesses of Mindanao and of Basilan.

'War makes for strange bedfellows,' Trent said: 'Be rid of these pirates once and for all. Or are they your allies? Do you hide behind their guns?'

He had cast the die. Calm, he looked directly at Ishmael Muhammad with the challenge between them definite as a knight's gauntlet. He had nothing more to say. The insurgent leader would support his endeavour or command his execution – God's will or expediency. His thoughts returned to the woman. Had she been ransomed? Did she hope for rescue? Or was she already dead? Or so nearly dead as not to care? Or so abused that she prayed for death?

Voices rose amongst the men, arms waved. One of the insurgents stood to shout across the swept sand and Trent wondered whether he had overestimated the control Ishmael exercised. But the leader's voice cut through the argument, ordering the old man to escort Trent back to the cage.

The old man closed the padlock that held the door shut. He studied Trent for a moment then shambled off down the path only to return minutes later with a young coconut. He said that he must return to the meeting but he left his knife with Trent so that the Englishman could cut the top of the nut – or cut himself free of the cage which was already weakened on one side by bullets. Trent wondered whether the old man offered him this chance of escape from fear that he would lose the argument. It was useless conjecture and he drank from the nut and scooped out the thin jelly. Then he lay in the shade and dozed while waiting for the insurgents to reach their decision.

Ishmael came with three of his men to the cage an hour later. He unfastened the padlock and squatted beside the Englishman in the dust.

'We have talked,' he said, and drew from his sleeve the amber beaded rosary. *Click*, the beads went, *click, click*. 'There are those who believe that you are a spy. They wish to kill you.'

Trent pushed himself up into a sitting position against the stakes, wounded leg stretched out. The insurgent leader's dark brown eyes reminded him of a monk who had taught philosophy at his school, both to the older students and to the novices. Trent had spoken Italian with the monk for an hour three evenings a week, his last summer term, on the lawned terrace outside the monastery church. The monk had watched him as they conversed of architecture and books, watched him with a softness of despair and Trent wondered now, in the cage, whether the monk had known that he was already earmarked by the Department and that the exercise of his talent for languages was necessary to his Government's use of him as a trained killer.

He showed Ishmael the old man's knife. 'Had I been a spy, you would be dead. Had I used the beacon, you would all be dead.'

Ishmael nodded to his own thoughts: 'So I have said.' The beads clicked as he sought entry into Trent's mind or into his soul. His fingers were very clean, as were the hands of many terrorists whom Trent had known: terrorists, freedom fighters, executioners. Trent was suddenly deeply grateful that he was out of it – all those years as executioner for judges who considered a background of poverty, or prejudice, or abuse of power extraneous to the case.

He smiled at Ishmael Muhammad and asked quietly: 'Do I live or die? In the short term,' he added and one of the insurgents chuckled.

Click went the beads and the insurgent leader asked: 'Tell me first, are you here by accident?'

Ishmael's men were puzzled by the question but Trent understood. He had made no attempt to hide from Ishmael who he was or what he was. The woman mattered to him and he saw now that she mattered because she was unknown to him and that he acted simply from duty to the man he wished to become.

'*Confiteor omnipotens Deus,*' he murmured and for the first time there was light lift of the Iranian trained intellectual's lips.

'I'm my own man, no chiefs, no Indians,' Trent said, and because Ishmael's trust was important to him, he added: 'There was a time, but not any more.'

'There was no need to tell me that.'

'Between us there was a need,' Trent said. 'Can I ask for your trust without an explanation of what I am?'

The beads clicked: 'Manuel Ortega knows that you search for us?'

'He gave me your name.'

Ishmael nodded as if this were only natural and to be expected. 'We were at college together. Friends for a time,' he said with perhaps the faintest touch of regret for that other life and Trent thought again of the monks and their vows of chastity, poverty, and of obedience.

Ishmael said: 'You are safe with Manolo. He will think it unsporting to extract information from you. But there are men behind him of the old guard, Marcos men whom the Americans trained. Of those you should be careful. Once you have done your duty, you should leave the country. There are beaches and coral to be discovered as beautiful as ours but in less troubled waters.'

Ishmael unfolded a chart on the sand. 'The pirates have their base on a river,' he said and pointed to an island to the north. 'You will see the volcano. When there is an eruption, the lava flows away from their village to the east. There are said to be crocodiles in the river and the jungle is mined and sewn with traps so that only the path up the riverbank is possible and this is guarded.'

'There are other villages?' Trent asked.

Ishmael pointed east and west of the river mouth: 'Small settlements. The inhabitants may collude with the pirates, perhaps out of fear or because they are paid. But they are not part of them.'

'So I must go up the river.'

'Or put the other villagers in danger, yes,' Ishmael said, pleased with Trent for his decision: 'Or at least you must try, but success would be difficult even with two good legs.'

Trent said that it was only a flesh wound.

'Which will suppurate if not cared for. You will have to go up the river at night . . .'

The fires of the volcano glowed orange against the night and the stink of sulphur came thick to Lu's nostrils as he swam silently towards the sand spit that guarded the river mouth. Ten corpses marked his route to the spit, nine men and one woman. For five days he had thought only of the girl. Perhaps he had become unbalanced within the isolation of his obsession. Certainly there was a strange look to his eyes, both vacant and concentrated. The sun had burnt his skin dark as a chestnut. He had eaten fish, drunk water, and the milk of coconuts; he was used to stouter fare and had lost weight so that his muscles were uncamouflaged and stood out under the burnished skin like lengths of thick rope.

Heedful of discovery, he had abandoned his boat a mile from the island. Three miles of jungle lay between the coast and the pirate village. Nine hours of darkness remained. For weapons, he had strapped across his back the two *barong* that he had taken from the fishermen – the blades were honed sharp as razors. And his hands and feet had been transformed into lethal weapons by the tutelage of his master. There was no fear in him as he approached the beach, no thought for his own safety. Only his mission existed. The granddaughter . . .'

The four Chinese entered the hut. One of the four prised the naked body over onto its back with his foot. *It*, because there was too little of the human left. Wong Fu had ordered them to break her and they had obeyed. For a while she had spoken in whimpers but she had been dumb for the past day and a half. Spit dribbled from her mouth. Her eyes were empty and scummed with death like the eyes of a fish left on a market slab in the sun. She would never recover, not even with years of care in the finest sanatorium – this was the judgment of the four Chinese as they inspected their work. They were incapable of seeing into the core or even divining its existence.

The Chinese thought of the girl as mentally dead.

Jay saw the Chinese as victims of her revenge.

She saw her grandfather's competitor, Wong Fu, bound in an iron coffin with spikes in the lid. She had seen the coffin in a museum or in a comic book or in an old horror movie, but it was real to her now. Her fingertips rested on the wheel of a micrometer that lowered or raised the lid of the coffin in thousandths of a millimetre. The spikes touched Wong Fu's flesh and she saw his skin stretch beneath the pressure of the points. There was no need for hurry. She smiled as she looked into his eyes and licked her lips as he screamed.

The real Wong Fu lay in his black leather chair, motionless as a crocodile on a sandbank. The disappearance of the British yachtsman had enraged him but Wong Fu smiled now as he listened through earphones to the arguments in the House of Li conference room between the members of Old Man Li's kindergarten. The quality of sound was excellent; the American, Timmy Brown, had done well with his machines. Wong Fu's war chief had wanted him killed once he had served his purpose. Wong Fu preferred to wait for victory, then uncover him to the House of Li – as he would uncover those of Li's men who turned traitor. Let Li's men do the killing and let Old Man Li suffer the knowledge of betrayal and loss of face.

In Old Man Li's absence, the dissension and uncertainties in the conference room were obvious. The German, Beckenberg, would be the first. Greed and arrogance would bring him to the Fu camp – and Wong Fu scented in the Chinese woman's voice her fear of being tainted with Old Man Li's fall. Her Uncle Ching was the Li's shipping manager and must have told her of the kidnapping.

The girl . . .

On the distant surface of her body she felt one of Wong Fu's Chinese shift himself and she moved her enjoyment of Wong Fu's torture to enjoyment of the kidnapper's death. They would all die. She saw their blood spill across the floor. Its perfume was warm and thick and she rolled in it as if it were the most voluptuous of silk bedding.

The weight of the Chinese kidnapper was lifted from her in the moment of her enjoyment. She saw, as if through binoculars used in reverse, the second officer from the *Ts'ai Yen*. Lu stood tall against the pale light of dawn beyond the doorway. He was naked but for a loincloth and she saw the muscles swollen in his arms and across his shoulders and in his legs. He held a leaf-bladed cutlass in both hands. Blood spilled from the blade, spattering his body that was already filthy and polished with sweat.

She breathed the thick perfume of her vengeance now that he had come. She saw his teeth as he smiled. He stood with his feet planted each side of her chest and his muscles writhed as he raised the cutlass high. Blood dripped from the blade onto her face as she looked up into his eyes and saw in them only her own image.

She saw, behind Lu's shoulder, the pale figure of her grandfather in his grey suit. Behind her grandfather stood her Uncle Robert. Over by the wall her grandmother wept and wrung her hands and sobbed that she had told Jay that this must be her end. Hadn't she warned her to be properly dressed, to go out only with men on the list, to never be alone with them after six in the evening. Yet here she lay naked on the floor. Used like a slut by Wong Fu's men. How else could it end?

The cutlass swept down.

But suddenly Lu was gone.

She heard the blade clatter against the hut wall. She saw, through the reverse binoculars, the leader of her Chinese kidnappers way in the distance. He held a cudgel and he smiled down at her. And he said: 'We don't want you killed, Lady Li. Wong Fu would be very angry.'

She wept then, and scrabbled like a crab back into her core where she was safe and where she could wait and wait until the time was right. And now there were new faces on her list – faces to expose one day to the heat of her vengeance so that they would melt and flow like gold and fill her cup till it overflowed. Slow, she thought. It must be slow. She would sip their agony as she had seen her uncle sip wine on his property in France. Sip and roll it against her palate and spit it onto the dirt. They were the ones who were concerned with their precious Face. Ah, but what Face she would gain in enjoyment of their deaths.

12

A tiny atoll lay a mile south of the sand spit that obstructed the direct approach to the river mouth. Trent landed on the islet under cover of darkness and dragged the sail-board up the beach. The volcano marked the position of the pirate stronghold with striped fountains of gold and red against the night sky; a streak of molten lava coursed for a short distance down the east flank from the summit; the stench of sulphur spread thick on the humid air.

Dawn came and Trent studied the coast through his binoculars. A row of palm trees leant in the breeze along the spit. Beyond the spit lay the river mouth shrouded in thick jungle. Then came the cliff and the volcano. The breeze drifted the smoke from the top of the cone and every ten or fifteen minutes a fresh eruption spattered the sky.

Soon after first light a grey *baslig* approached under sail from the south. The boat turned in behind the spit and Trent watched the mast slide behind the trees before turning up-river into the jungle. Over to the west a couple of small outrigger canoes ventured into the breeze; the light improved and Trent located, against the dark green of the jungle, the outlines of a dozen or so huts raised on stilts. A curve of the coast hid the settlement to the east of the river mouth but a half-dozen fishing *baslig* appeared as the sun rose from the ocean.

Fourteen hours of daylight before Trent could move. High water that night would be at 21.00 hours.

Trent had spent much of his life waiting – he had waited on jungle tracks, in the curve of a *wadi*, shadowed by a doorway in an Arab *souk*, in the lee of a dry-stone wall that bisected the green of an Irish hillside. He had waited always in the past at some other man's command, his aims or target designated by whims of government policy. The exercise of his skills had increasingly frightened him. Finally he had been unable to continue, even under a new Control.

The sun rose to beat the colour out of the jungle. The fierce light shimmered on the water so that the fishing boats to the east seemed to hover above a grey mirror. The breeze dropped. There was a heaviness in the air, a heat and stillness into which the smoke rose straight above the lava cone. An absence of bird life wheeling against the bleached sky and the ghostly image of the boats floating apart from the sea built an illusion of suspended time.

Then a thick phlegmy cough barked across the water. As if wakened by the volcano, the first touch of wind trickled across Trent's shoulders and he turned to see a soft grey line low on the horizon. The tiny outriggers and the fishing *baslig* scurried shoreward and the line of coral that protected the settlement to the west grew whiter under a growing swell.

The oppressive heat seemed to trap the storm so that it was late afternoon before the bank of cloud rolled free of the islands to the south and spilled across the sea. The breeze strengthened and brought the scent of rain. Then came the silver curtain streaked with gold by the sunset. The rain whipped the sea into a light froth so that the foot of the curtain seemed made of lace. As the seas rose, white caps drove at Trent's back and charged on to burst on the spit.

With the wind behind him, Trent launched the sail-board into the lee of the atoll. Hidden in the dusk within the blanket of rain he sped under reefed sail across the narrow stretch of sea. He held the sheet tight against the force of the wind; the rudder shook under the strike of the waves which foamed under the light hull; the tiller trembled in his hand; the rain beat on his shoulders and flooded his eyes.

He steered for the spit and drove the sail-board up the shore on the foaming curl of a wave. Rolling the mast and sail, he dragged the board up the strand, than flat on his belly, looked across the water from the cover of the palm trees. The rain hid the river and even the trees showed only as a wavy line within the overall shadow of the island while the volcano had vanished within the storm shroud. Lightning lanced through the thickening dusk; seconds later, thunder broke across the spit; the gale tore at the palms.

Close at hand the rain had beaten the sand flat. With each second the pattern of pockmarks changed, the depth signalling the intensity of the downpour. Away on the flanks of the volcano hundreds of rivulets gathered to pour over the cliff and swell the river.

The tide would start its rise within the hour and dam the flood, spilling the river into the jungle. If the weather held, the rain would hide him and the wind drive him up river – three miles to the pirate village. The pirates might have cables stretched across the river or tripwires to signal a boat's approach – but there was no need to dive and he dragged the heavy dive gear up the crest and buried it at the foot of a tree.

The line of dead seaweed marking the previous high tide floated free as the waters rose against the shoreward bank of the spit. The gale held and, though the rain lessened, cloud hid the stars. A soft red glow in the cloud marked the summit of the volcano.

He waited until two hours before high water to launch the sailboard. The wind drove him across the narrows and into the river mouth. Lost in the dark, he hunted for trees to show the line of the river. Three bends had been marked on the chart, then a straight section, two further bends, and a final straight that led to the foot of the cliffs.

Finding the edge of the jungle, he dropped the sail and felt with his paddle for the river bank but the flood was too deep. The glow of the volcano enabled him to keep his bearings as he paddled into the dark, searching for the next tree and the next. He sought for the slightest change in sound through the background swirl of water against the tree trunks and the spatter of rain on the leaf canopy. The flood had stirred the rotting vegetation; the stench of corruption filled his nostrils, the heat and humidity stifling. An animal coughed to his left, perhaps a crocodile, and a parrot screeched.

Scrub scraped the underside of the hull as he crossed the inner point of the first bend. Then he was lost again in open water and had to drive the sail-board hard against a rip that threatened to fling him to the far bank. He regained the tree line but the rain slackened now and he heard the water swirl across the bow of the big board as he drove upriver.

As the storm lifted, the loom of the volcano spread on the underside of the clouds and a trickle of lava glowed on the mountain's eastern flank. The volcano coughed, frightening the monkeys huddled amongst the treetops so that they jabbered and shrieked at each other.

Now the river showed pale between its banks. Wind on his counter, Trent raised the mast and sail. Though weakened in its last hour, the tide continued its damming of the flood. Trees had been torn from the sodden earth by the gale. The shattered trunks jostled now at the junction of tide and flood, a massive blockade that, with the change of flow, would sweep down-river, smashing every obstacle in its path. Trent had seen loaded trucks tumbled like dry pine cones down *wadis* by such a flood, bridges snapped and torn from their mounts, highways ripped apart, dams shattered by the battering ram.

The first turn of the current would be his only warning. He watched the surface of the water carefully and, despite the need for speed, kept close to the trees. The volcano coughed and spilled fresh lava. The gibbering of monkeys betrayed their positions and one screamed as a serpent took it. Fruit bats screeched and the clatter of birds' wings beat through the leaves of the forest top; cicadas drummed their celebration of the rain lifting and the throb of a thousand frogs pulsated in the night.

The cloud curled on over the volcano and, as Trent reached the end of the straight stretch of river, the first stars shone to the south. In this pale light he saw the surface ahead heave and foam where the two currents struggled for supremacy. Trees rolled in the maelstrom like men lost to the quicksand, broken stumps grasping briefly at the sky before being tumbled into the depth.

Trent thrust the tiller-paddle hard over and shot the sail-board into the protection of the trees. Mast and sail furled, he paddled deeper into the jungle as the rival currents fought the last minutes of their battle. But the tide was on the turn and suddenly the massive raft of heaving logs spilled down stream. Huge trees snapped along the river bank; the thunder of their passing shook the forest. Over all stood the volcano, its sulphurous breath thick as the wind fell, its vomit burnt caramel against the sky.

Saplings emerged as the waters evacuated conquered territory. Then appeared the tops of bushes and Trent angled the bows of the sail-board back to the river bank. He heard the startled panting of an animal and a heavy body splashed away to his left, perhaps a wild boar. Through the background thrum of the jungle came the driving spout of a bathtub being filled by high-pressure taps – that would be the waterfall behind the pirate's base. Knowing he was close, Trent docked the sail-board alongside a tree that leant flat over the river.

Retrieving the radio beacon from the heel of the mast, he tied the light line to the sail-board, cut a short length from the other end, and looped the remainder over his shoulders. With the sail-board bobbing behind him, he clambered out along the trunk until he reached a branch that enabled him to cross to a more upright tree. The first limbs branched thirty feet above his head. He encircled the tree loosely with the short length of line, twisted the loop round his ankles, and went up the smooth trunk like a caterpillar to the first fork. Standing in the fork, he reached the next branch and climbed steadily until well hidden in the leaf canopy where he lashed the radio beacon to a branch and hauled the sail-board up. He was sweating and breathing hard by the time he had the big board securely hidden a hundred feet above the jungle floor. Switching on the beacon, he slid down and crossed back to the tree that angled out toward the river bank.

The combination of wind, tide and rain had caused the flood. Now that the wind and rain had ceased, and with the tide ebbing fast, the water was falling three inches every five minutes. Lowering himself into the water, he pushed himself down and, with his arms extended, reached the mud with his toes – seven feet and four inches. Three feet in an hour; six feet by 04.00 hours; mud and puddles by first light – and the village must be on higher ground. But there were the mines and traps to consider and he pushed off and swam to the next tree. He swam breast-stroke so as not to splash and every few minutes rested and listened. Half an hour and a man spoke softly a hundred yards ahead. A second man chuckled and Trent heard a stream of urine hit the water.

Footsteps squelched in the mud in proof that the ground was higher where the pirates stood. Only one person. A few minutes after 03.00 hours so probably one of the men had finished guard duty.

Trent pictured the territory ahead. There would be trees on the slope; tripwires between the trees; perhaps some kind of fortifications; either a trench or a wall protected by mines or pits hidden beneath brush wood. The sentry would be hidden by the fortifications. There might be a watchtower projecting above the jungle canopy to give a view down-river and another man up on the cliff spotting for aircraft.

He never considered waiting for Manolo Ortega and his men. In all probability the woman was already ransomed. He couldn't be sure. If she was still a captive, the pirates would kill her at the first shot. It was a risk he couldn't take.

The only approach to the pirate village was overland – the river current remained too strong. In dry conditions he could have felt with a stick for the patch of loose earth above a mine. In the mud and in the dark he would discover them with the weight of his body and his belly seemed to curl in on itself as he swam to the next tree.

He swam like an animal, head up and with short rapid strokes directed part downward to keep his body on the surface. The slightest noise would disclose his presence to the sentry now less than fifty yards ahead. He touched a branch and grabbed it, his body flat on the surface. Then he reached down, index finger fully extended. His fingertip touched bottom. The stink of the mud was thick with rotting vegetation.

He raised his hand slowly, feeling ahead for the thin tripwire that would betray him. Finding none, he searched for the outline of the next tree, drew his feet up and thrust himself away from the trunk. Too hard and he might set off an alarm or rustle a bush. But he pushed too gently and the retreating flood caught him and spun him round. His head cannoned against a tree stump and suddenly he was over the bank and into the river. He grabbed at an overhanging branch. The flood tore at him and forced his face down. He rolled onto his back and gasped for air; then edged shoreward along the branch until the current weakened in the small backwater behind the tree.

His lower foot struck a horizontal stake close to the surface. He felt down and found that he was outstretched above what seemed to be a ladder running parallel to the bank and only inches below the surface. Something butted him in the spine. He reached down and his hand met a hard lumpy object with a hole on one side. Whatever it was moved and he let go. A pale shape rose inches above the surface and gulped air. There were more of them, some pale, some dark; and everywhere the nightmare hiss and gasp of animals trapped and terrified of drowning. Crocodiles. A cage ran along the bank.

Only the largest of the reptiles could raise their heads between the stakes. The smaller had escaped through the bars. The remainder, too short to reach the surface at the height of the flood, had drowned. Trent pictured the cage. Under normal circumstances, it would stand some thirty-six inches clear of the water, a unique fortification. Soon the flood would fall below the level of the cage top. The cage was full of meat and every one of the crocodiles must be exhausted.

He had thought at first that the roof was a ladder – it could serve as such. Or he could crawl through the mud and pray that fortune kept him clear of mines and traps.

13

Less than an hour to first light and the volcano continued to cough and dribble. Already the stink of sulphur lay on the forest. Now, as the last of the flood water retreated, the gluey mulch of mud and rotting vegetation released a thick clammy stench of decay into the hot and humid air. The whine of mosquitoes pierced the deep throat-thrumming of the frogs and the crocodiles snuffled in their cage along the river bank like hogs at a trough. It was time to move and Trent rolled out of the shelter of the tree behind which he had been hiding and eased himself onto the cage roof.

The water had sunk a foot below the bars and Trent smelt the blood of the dead reptiles and the fetid breath of the living. He had cut and sharpened a branch with which to defend himself but the reptiles were busy at their cannibal feast.

The clouds dispersed, starlight giving a modicum of visibility. He counted the bars as he crossed them, one every twelve inches. Fifty yards, sixty. The river fell away as the ground sloped up to meet the deeper darkness of the cliff; the glow of the volcano showed him the crest. The trees thinned to his left. The lowered flame of a kerosene lantern lit the corner of a hut and threw a pale yellow V across a flat patch of mud.

The long snout of a crocodile surged up between the stakes only inches from Trent's right hand. He rammed the sharpened branch at it. The crocodile snuffled as it fell back. Trent froze as a dog barked. A half-dozen others joined in. A man, unseen in the shadows, cursed and hurled a rock at the first dog. The dog yelped. Finally there was renewed calm, but five minutes passed before Trent dared move.

The cage ended against the side of a wooden dock. Four boats, including the grey *baslig* that Trent had seen the previous morning, were moored alongside. The bamboo outriggers grated against each other in the urging of the current that swirled between the upright posts.

Trent rolled off the roof of the cage into the shadows and lay flat on his belly, watching. Both concentration and judgment were adversely affected by emotion, so he thought of the woman as a goal rather than a person. She would be under guard if she was in the village. The upper end of the clearing closest to the cliff would give him the best view.

Nothing moved and he inched forward, digging his toes and the tips of his fingers in the slippery mud. He needed to reach the vantage point by first light, thirty minutes, but a rapid movement might betray him. Surprise was the essence of attack and he had stripped naked while still in the trees. It was a trick he had been taught by a Yugoslav Scot in the SAS.

'Doesn't matter who they are, they'll look down at your perishables. Human nature,' the Yugoslav Scot had guaranteed: 'Gives you the edge – two seconds – that's not enough, you're in the wrong job.'

The village had grown without pattern round an open central area shaded by a pair of giant mango trees. The huts stood on stilts perhaps a metre or a metre and a half high. A few had tin roofs but most were thatched and had walls of woven palm framed in bamboo. Trent slithered under the huts between the stilts, watching always for a sentry or a dog. His movements were so slow as to be almost imperceptible. His toes supplied the power while he brushed the mud ahead in his search for sticks or perhaps a discarded can or a stone that might make a noise.

Low against the ground, he was able to see the outlines of the huts against the sky. He heard the scratch of a match ahead and for a moment a flame danced, cupped in a man's hands. The man's face was Chinese and he was sitting outside a hut. The flame shook and dropped but in that time Trent saw that the hut was built on a solid mound rather than on stilts.

The guard at the door suggested a prison. Or the armoury or perhaps the pirate leader's house? But the Philippines remained a highly tribal society so the guard would be of the same background as the chieftain and Ishmael Muhammed would have mentioned a Chinese.

Twenty feet of mud separated Trent from the sentry. He hesitated, knowing that he might have to kill the man. He had come a long way and it was always the same. First came total concentration on the approach as if it was the mission. Only at the very end did he allow the shift of his thoughts to the target. *Extraction*, the Americans called it. *Wet work. Take him out.*

Trent had learnt better in nights made sleepless by fear of nightmares and come to loath the hypocrisy of language behind which the man in Washington had hidden from his responsibility for assassination.

Trent's control, the Colonel, had been more direct: 'We want this man killed. Get in amongst them, Patrick. Learn what you can, but I want him dead before he does any further harm. Don't let me down.'

Harm comprised murders perpetrated by the opposition – car bombs, letter bombs, bombs set in passenger aircraft and in railway stations; AK-47s emptied into a crowded bar in a Belfast side-street; fathers shot in the gut while watching TV in the company of their wives and children in the front room. There were films to watch. Films of carnage and of police interviews with widows close to collapse and tearful children. The tears were important. It had been well done – in eighteen years of service never even the most oblique of references to his father's suicide.

He deliberately conjured the picture of the murdered engineers on the *Ts'ai Yen*, their faces burnt with acid. Then he thought of the woman and was sure of himself. He wiped his right thumb and first finger in his wet hair, drew his throwing knife, cleaned the blade, and rolled onto his back. Feet facing the sentry, he moved up the gentle slope like a caterpillar, pulling and pushing with his heels, his buttocks, elbows, and the back of his head. The last of the night protected him and the smooth slippery mud eased his advance.

He watched the sentry with the fixed intensity of a hawk. Once the man finished his cigarette, he would throw away the butt. Odds were on his flicking it downhill and watching to see where it landed. If he saw Trent he'd grab his gun and shout.

The butt spun by just as Trent reached the lee of the earth mound. The walls were made of bamboo staves cloaked with palm mat. He circled the hut and found a gap between the mats where the joins in the bamboo held two staves a little apart. Light leaked through the crack. As he rose to his knees, he heard a whimper and coarse laughter.

The muscled back of a man showed through the chink in the wall. The man hopped as he dragged up his trousers over powerful thighs and a second man laughed as the first cannoned against the wall. The stumbler lurched away and Trent saw that he and his companion were Chinese. The men were similar in physique, paratroopers, Special Forces, professional heavies. The light came from a lantern hooked on a wire to one of the roof beams. A pair of cotton palliasses covered part of the dirt floor. A young Chinese woman lay naked on her back across the palliasses. A chain led from a hinged iron cuff on the woman's left ankle to the centre post which supported the hut's roof trusses. Rivets had been hammered flat in the iron cuff; a heavy brass padlock fastened the loop of chain round the centre post.

The thing chained to the post was nothing to do with her. She knew that the pain it suffered was real but she herself was unable to feel it. She felt nothing of the surface world. She was too deep in her hiding place. And she was a spider.

She was a spider seated on the lid of the iron box in which her father's competitor, Wong Fu, lay bound. A single silk thread supported her weight and the spiked lid of the iron box was so perfectly balanced that each fraction of a millimetre of thread that she spun sunk the spikes a further fraction of a millimetre into Wong's Fu's flesh.

Now, added to the tortured and screaming Wong Fu, was the image of her grandfather, so immaculate in his fine grey flannel suit, and she sneered at him and watched with glee as he shrivelled beneath her contempt into something that resembled a dried and wizened walnut. Her grandmother wept and wrung her hands as Jay chuckled happily.

A strange gurgling came from the woman. One of the Chinese heavies booted her over onto her belly and lashed her twice across the shoulders with the buckle end of the belt which he had been about to thread through the loops in his trousers. Her back was already swollen and caked with blood but she made no effort to protect herself. Trent recalled other victims of torture lost inside themselves. For a moment rage and horror dulled his perceptions.

He didn't hear the footsteps. The cold line of a steel blade lay across the back of his neck. A voice whispered at him to turn and he faced the Chinese guard on the door who had come round the back of the hut to urinate.

The guard shouted to the men inside the hut. The three Chinese marched Trent down between the huts to the open space where the two mango trees grew. In the first light of a new day Trent saw a tall young Chinese pegged out on his back with a transparent plastic bowl taped to his belly. The bowl was filled with ants. The skin on the man's belly had been eaten away and the exposed flesh glistened red. One of the Chinese kicked the victim into consciousness.

The leader of the Chinese straddled the victim. Bending low, he spat in the man's face and laughed.

Trent longed to kill him. The desire began as a fire that spread from Trent's belly down into his loins. Only the certainty that he would die before he could kill the planner of this obscenity restrained him. He would kill the man. Of that Trent was certain. So he acted confused and helpless. Perhaps his nudity saved him. Because there were women now who had come from their huts. They and their children surrounded him and mocked him for the filth that cloaked his nakedness and for how puny he seemed to be, stooped and slack-shouldered to disguise his musculature. A European.

One of the women struck him with a stick. Another threw a stone that hit his collar bone. He bowed in humility as the leader of the Chinese grabbed his ear lobe, yanking him back up the slope to the hut where the woman lay incarcerated. The Chinese kicked Trent into the hut and smashed his legs out from under him with the butt of a rifle. Trent fell with his face against the woman's feet.

'Lady Li,' the leader of the Chinese called her. 'Oh look, Lady Li,' he crooned: 'Look at the new gift your munificent grandfather has sent to you.'

He hit Trent in the spine with his rifle and snarled at him to lick her feet. 'Pay homage to the great Lady Li,' he commanded and thrust Trent's head down: 'Don't you recognise your mistress?'

The woman hadn't stirred. Nor did she now as Trent ran his tongue through the grime that covered her instep. He felt the blade of a sword, sharp and heavy, rest on the nape of his neck. He waited for the sword to rise.

The pleasure in suspense was intense and, delaying the strike, the Chinese lifted the hair clear of Trent's neck with the point of the blade. He saw the hilt of the throwing knife, cursed and shouted a warning as much to himself as to his companions as he kicked Trent sideways into what became suddenly an inferno as the thunder of a jet engine shook the hut. Canon shells exploded in the clearing. Men and women screamed and the Chinese leader looked up for only a second. In that second Trent's knife flew straight as an arrow into his throat. He dropped his sword. His hands grasped the knife hilt and he looked down at Trent, his surprise as intense as had been his pleasure in contemplating Trent's death.

Already Trent was rolling for a rifle. He grabbed it with his right hand, firing one handed at the other two Chinese as the next jet screamed across the village. The two Chinese died almost unaware. Bombs burst on the clifftop. Trent heard the shriek of a rocket and the explosion seconds later. He rolled to his left and fired one long burst at the centre post. Chunks of wood spattered the far wall. Dragging the palliasses out from under the woman, he flung them over her and charged across the hut. He hit the centre post with his shoulder. The post snapped six inches above the floor. Trent grabbed the loop of chain free and fought his way back to the woman through a cascade of thatch released as the roof trusses and beams folded inward as if hinged at the top of the wall.

He slung the chain over his shoulder and, holding the girl in his arms, charged the wall of the hut closest to the cliff. The wall collapsed and he fell with the woman into the lee of the mound. The next wave of attacking planes screeched up the valley from the sea and he saw a sixty-yard length of the cliff snap and fall almost in slow motion. Then came thunder as the rock shattered on the last row of huts. Women and children screamed incessantly and he saw figures race for the trees. The helicopters came now, gunships that hovered back and forth spraying everything that moved. A hose job – Trent cursed Manolo Ortega for his effectiveness.

He lay on top of the woman, their bodies pressed tight against the mud foundations and covered by part of the roof that had broken outwards. A final sortie against the cliff blasted a fresh section down onto the huts below. Watching from between the thatch, Trent spotted a ladder of bamboo leading part way up an undamaged section of the cliff to the mouth of a cave about four feet wide by three feet in height.

The helicopters came again, three abreast. Cannon blasted what remained of the huts into kindling and Trent smelt smoke and heard the first crackle of flames. A dozen men and women and a half-dozen children had gathered to his left. They knelt in the mud, arms out to the helicopters, beseeching the air-crew for mercy. The helicopters rocked a moment as the pilots hesitated, perhaps confirming orders. Then the noses of the helicopters dipped and the men and women and children screamed.

Smoke drifted from the huts lower in the village and rifle ammunition burst like firecrackers in the heat. Trent pressed the woman hard into the ground, shouting at her not to move. He doubted if she could understand but he had nothing to tie her with. He slithered like an eel under the fallen roof that covered the remains of the hut and retrieved his knife from the throat of the Chinese leader. He found matches in the pocket of the smoker's polo shirt and struck a light to the dry inner thatch at the lower side of the house. He fanned the flames till they caught, then rolled back under the fallen roof.

The helicopters were down the far end of the village and he heard shots and fresh screams as they dug survivors from the wreckage.

Smoke billowed from the thatch and he took his chance, rolling with the woman tight in his arms uphill into the shelter of what remained of the next hut. He dragged her between the pilings, lit a match to the palm mat wall, and rolled uphill where he waited on the edge of the stilts for the fire to spread and the smoke to give them cover as they rolled to the next hut. The helicopters had landed now at the bottom end of the village. Manolo Ortega's Special Forces fanned out the moment they hit the ground and advanced up the village, driving the survivors against the cliff.

Trent set the next house alight and rolled again uphill between the stilts under the far wall. Fifty yards to the cliff and the ladder up to the cave. This close, and with the first of the sunlight brightening the cliff face, he could see that the cave mouth was covered by wire netting. Chickens beat at the netting with their wings but the howl of the helicopters drowned their cackling.

Smoke poured out of the hut as the thatch caught and smoke from the other huts had spread across the slope that separated them from the hunters. Trent looped the chain round the woman's free leg, grabbed her up in his arms and charged the ladder. A soldier stepped out of the shadows of the hut nearest to the cliff. He seemed to smile and Trent dropped the woman as the soldier raised his gun. Trent shouted at him and held his hands behind his neck in surrender but the smile didn't change so Trent brought his right hand over. The knife took the soldier in the jugular. He fired, spraying the air as he died. A second soldier appeared to Trent's right. Trent dived for the fallen M-16 and shot him. Then he snatched his knife back and fired three bullets into the first soldier to disguise the wound. Grabbing the woman up, he raced the last few yards to the cliff. He looked back down the slope at the curtain of smoke. The only people in sight were already dead.

With the chain looped over his shoulders, the woman hung by her feet down his back. He climbed with the full weight of her dragging him backwards. The bullet wound in his thigh burst under the strain and he hadn't much strength left. Forty-five rungs, forty feet. He began to count as he always counted under stress. One rung, two rungs, three, four, five . . .

The hunters were closing in, hunters at a turkey shoot, and as he climbed, Trent cursed Manolo Ortega again. Then, from directly below him, came a rifle shot.

14

Trent looked down. Outstretched on the ladder and with the sun blazing on their backs, he and the girl presented a perfect target. A pirate knelt in the mud fifty yards back from the cliff. He had missed with his first shot because he had been running. His chest pumped for air and rage and hatred twisted his face. Trent supposed that he had lost his family in the attack. The muzzle of the pirate's rifle became a black hole as he aimed but it shook a little with his exhaustion. Trent saw him hold his breath as he fought to steady the sights.

Trent twisted round to protect the girl with his own body. She would be killed in the fall but he didn't want the pirate to kill her. He was surprised to find tears in his eyes, he who had never wept, tears for the girl, and he blinked as he saw the rifle steady.

A short burst of automatic fire came from the jungle, not more than four shots. Mud spattered less than a foot from the pirate and he swung round, rifle already up, and spotted a marine on the jungle edge fumble as he tried to slap a fresh clip into his M-16. The pirate fired. The marine dropped his weapon and clasped his hands over his chest. He was young and Trent saw his surprise at dying.

The pirate turned back to aim at Trent and the girl. A dark stain blossomed on his shirt – the marine must have hit him at least once. He raised his rifle very slowly and closed his left eye. His finger tightened on the trigger. The bullet struck the cliff above Trent's head.

Helpless on the ladder, Trent watched him fight to control the rifle one more time. The Filipino's strength seeped out with his blood and he bent slowly backwards. Finally he groaned and tumbled sideways.

The lip of the cave was almost within Trent's reach. Two more rungs, and he tipped the girl onto the ledge. Prying the netting up, he rolled the girl under it while shooing the chickens back.

The cave stretched fifteen feet into the cliff and had been hacked into a chamber nearly six feet in height. The floor of the cave was slippery with water that dripped from the roof and from chicken droppings that reeked of ammonia. The fumes burnt his eyes and he dragged the woman only a short distance from the cave mouth. Then he lay close to the edge and looked down.

Because of the rain there were few flames but smoke billowed from the wreckage. The officer in command had divided his men in two, one squad closing off the forest while the rest acted as beaters.

The pirates were inexperienced in battle; the only gunshots now came from the military. A soldier halted by the young Chinese pinned under the container of ants – two shots in the head and he jogged on.

A woman carrying a child in her arms burst out of the smoke. She turned like a trapped animal but found nowhere to run and sank to her knees. Then came another woman and three men. The men had thrown away their weapons. Next a boy aged six or seven . . .

Trent's old control would have dubbed the operation a stockbroker's shoot – no gamekeeper to forbid the killing of hens or young birds. It was soon over and a whistle shrilled to the marines to gather on the river bank. A lieutenant was in command rather than Manolo Ortega. However Trent had signalled for the attack and he looked away in horror from the small bundle of rags that had been a child.

The ammonia in the chicken droppings had brought the woman back to consciousness. She coughed and dribbled and her eyes wept. She paid no attention to Trent as he wiped her mouth on his finger and eased her closer to the netting.

A minesweeper had anchored off the spit. A half-hour passed before a launch came up river and docked. The launch had a day-cabin amidships with cockpits fore and aft. Marines took the lines thrown by the sailors. Manolo Ortega ducked out of the cabin and blinked for a moment in the sunshine before returning the salute of the battle commander. Then he leapt ashore and the two officers shook hands.

The familiar sloping shoulders of Tanaka Kazuko emerged next from the louvred doors. A twist of red ribbon bound his pony tail and he wore a cream suit with ten-inch lapels. Rather than go ashore, he slouched over to the corner of the cockpit and stood with his backside propped on the teak coaming, shoulders drooped like a city teenager who believes that showing interest is out of fashion.

Next from the cabin came a square-looking Chinese in khaki chinos and a blue polo shirt. A heavy automatic protruded from his belt. The Chinese nodded coolly to the lieutenant but his eyes were busy and nothing escaped his notice as he stood on the river bank.

Even the air seemed to come to attention as the slight grey-suited figure of Sir Philip Li stepped out into the bright sunlight. He stood in the cockpit, one hand resting lightly on the varnished rail, very much at ease.

The lieutenant delivered a parade-ground salute and Trent, crouched in the mouth of the cave, was about to wave but the woman whimpered and he saw the terror in her as she scuttled back into the gloom. Not *the woman*, Trent reminded himself. This creature, so abused, chained and manacled, was Sir Philip Li's granddaughter.

She whimpered again and fear made her breathe in harsh strangled gasps so that he had to hold her, gentling her as he would a horse with whispered words of encouragement. He looked back at the party from the launch and saw Manolo Ortega pry a dead woman over onto her back with the toe of his shoe. Sir Philip shook his head and for a moment Trent refused to understand. Then the rage came cold and hard in his belly and he cursed as he watched Manolo turn to his lieutenant who directed the marines to fan out in pairs to collect the rest of the dead.

Ortega brought a canvas director's chair from the launch and set it in the shade of an avocado tree for Sir Philip Li. The financier accepted the courtesy with gratitude. Seating himself, he arranged his trousers to protect the creases, then folded his hands in his lap. The Chinese bodyguard stood behind the chair and even Tanaka stepped ashore and hunkered in the shade.

Ortega's men needed an hour to collect the dead into the clearing under the mango trees where Lu had been killed. They arranged the bodies in rows, face-up for inspection. The launch party strolled down through the smouldering remnants of the village. There would be no mention of a granddaughter here. She no longer existed. As

121

Trent held her, the ghastly scabs felt harsh against his fingertips and her lips had swollen from lack of water.

He watched the men check the corpses and walk back up the slope towards the launch. Sir Philip noticed the ladder. He spoke to Ortega but Tanaka was already jogging ahead. The sudden cackle of the chickens would have given them away so Trent waited until the Japanese was almost at the top of the ladder. Then he dragged the woman back into the darkness and sat face to the cave mouth, knife in hand, the rage in him absolute. He and the girl would die but first he would kill the traitorous son of a bitch.

The Japanese had drawn a heavy automatic from a shoulder holster. The birds were in his way and he raised the netting, whooshing them to freedom so that he could kneel in the mouth. He blinked into the darkness. Then he saw Trent and the knife and he smiled. The smile saved him. Trent hesitated and the detective fired twice directly down into the floor of the cave.

The explosions thundered in the enclosed space. The echoes faded and Tanaka whispered: 'Even for a Brit, you pick the weirdest places.'

He fired again and crawled forward, peering behind Trent in search of the girl hidden in the shadows. 'Jesus, the stink,' he complained: 'They'll have the south coast bottled up and they're serious. You'll have to traverse across the side of the volcano. Give me forty-eight hours.'

He reversed to the cave mouth and yelled down to the launch party that he'd found nothing but chicken shit.

Suspicious, Trent tried to divine the detective's motivation. However there was no one else for him to trust and he said: 'We need water.'

Tanaka grinned maliciously: 'So do the Arabs and they pay in oil wells.' He slid out of the cave onto the ladder and dropped from view. Trent heard Ortega joke at the state of Tanaka's suit and a marine laughed.

The helicopters quartered the forest while Ortega's soldiers beat the jungle back to the beach. A landmine thumped and there were quick bursts of rifle fire. The sun seemed to sit on the lip of the cave but within the cooler depth the ammonia fumes released by the chicken droppings were too strong for the woman.

Trent sat watching her, fearful that she would cry out. Sweat plastered her hair across her forehead and the tips curled into her eyes. He wanted to smooth it back but the gesture was too intimate and he sat thinking of his past and the women who had accused him of being incapable of emotion. They had meant incapable of love or affection but had avoided the words.

Service in the Department had imposed upon him an isolation more total than that of a monk in a closed and silent order who at least prayed in the company of his fellow believers. Trent, infiltrator of terrorist cells, had been cut off from all shared experience. Looking down at Li's granddaughter, he knew that they could only survive if she trusted him. For trust to exist, he must first resurrect her.

He recalled a diplomat whom he had brought out of a mountain village in the Lebanon – a man who had been famous for his intellect yet whom torture had so traumatised that he screamed at the slightest contact. Trent, unable to win his trust, had physically silenced him so that they might survive. Trent had known that each silencing only added to the man's terror. He had carried him in a fireman's lift for the last mile, jogging over the dunes to the sea. Exhausted, he had tipped the man off his shoulders into the inflatable at the beach rendezvous. The released captive had lain whimpering with terror on the floorboards and Trent recalled the look of disgust on the naval lieutenant's face, disgust that a man could so lose his self-respect.

Not even Trent's control had believed the rescue possible but Trent had known the captive and had insisted on the attempt. After debriefing, the diplomat had retreated into a world of shame from which the Department's psychiatrists had been unable to save him. He and Trent had never spoken again. Finally he had drowned himself one early morning in the Hamble River only a mile above Trent's cottage. The body must have floated by while Trent ate breakfast. Trent had understood the message.

And now? Knowing her name would help. He turned her wrist so that he could see the inside of the charm bracelet: *for Jay from Daddy with love*.

'Jay,' he whispered. It was easy with her eyes closed. 'Jay, you're going to be all right, I promise. We're going to make it. You're going to be all right. You have my word.'

He touched the hair from her eyes with the tip of his index finger. 'Jay,' he said again: 'Jay, we're going to make it. I'll fetch water as soon as it's dark.'

Her thirst was already dangerous and her lips had split so he crouched at the back of the cave and caught the drops of water that fell from the roof. There was insufficient for him to wash away the filth from his hands. Had he fed the water to her from his palms, she would have died of a dozen different bacteria.

Dragging her to the rear of the cave, he held her in his arms beneath the drip. The drops grew slowly, then hung quivering on the rocks before falling. Her mouth made a small target. Finally the sickly tip of her tongue appeared and ran over a spot of moisture caught in a crack on her upper lip. A fresh drop fell and she licked at it like a rattlesnake feeling at the desert air. Trent prayed that her eyes would remain closed. He couldn't have stood the emptiness or, worse, the return of life with all its pains and terrors.

She was content to remain in whatever private world she had created. The drips fell and he held her all afternoon, cramp in his arms a small price to pay for his incapacity to reach her. Dusk approached and he heard a man whistle Abbey Road along the foot of the cliff. He waited for a further two hours before venturing down.

Trent expected patrols and shuddered as the ladder squeaked. Mosquitoes whined above the thrum of frogs and cicadas. Fireflies darted across the clearing and embers glowed amongst the remnants of the huts. The stench of burnt wet wood and of smouldering thatch mixed with the sulphur thick in the air and the crest of the cliff quivered a pale rose in the glow of the volcano.

Once on the ground, he crouched low and searched for the outline of a sentry against the sky. His toes touched a stick that lay at right angles to the cliff. He brushed his finger tips beneath the stick and found a line drawn in the mud that led him to a water bottle tucked in a fissure.

He climbed back to the cave and held the bottle to Jay's lips. He called her Jay as he helped her drink. He found that he could talk to her more easily in the dark:

'Jay, my name's Trent. We're going to make it. That's a promise. Don't worry, I know what happened. I'm on your side, Jay.'

There was nothing else for her to understand and nothing more that he could tell her but he repeated her name again and again in the hope that it would penetrate. And he tried to explain to her, not because she would understand, but more as a mantra to guide him through the coming days.

'I'm on your side, Jay, because yours is the side I want to be on. I'm not for sale. And I don't give a damn how powerful your grandfather is. I'm on your side. That's a promise.'

She made no response but her lips moved and her throat accepted the water.

'I'm going to leave you,' he told her. 'It's just for tonight and maybe tomorrow. It depends how rough things get . . .' Easier to think in things rather than in specific risks.

With the opposition alerted, getting back was always the toughest part of a mission. Americans had been the best. Not the men from Washington, but the Good Ol' Boys of the pre-computer era, most of them ugly and overweight and prone to drink too much, but tough-minded and loyal to their own men. They hadn't given a damn for orders or committee decisions. They put a man in, they got him out and screw the consequences. Now all he had was Tanaka's word that he would be there for them – an ex-cop from the city, grown rich through serving the rich . . .

Trent would have headed across the volcano with or without Tanaka's promise of help; it was the longer and therefore more illogical route and probably under lighter surveillance. Their only hope was to steal a boat – sail at night, lie up during the day. Hunting them down amongst the hundreds of islands would take unconscionable luck. Once clear of pursuit, they could slip out of territorial waters into the shipping lane and get picked up by a freighter sailing under an American or European flag.

'We need to make believe we've escaped down-river. I'll draw a false trail, then we'll go up over the cliff. They won't be looking for us,' he told her.

He tipped the bottle again but allowed the woman only a few drops. The water had to be conserved. 'I'll be back,' he promised. 'Stay here. Don't move. And don't drink the water too fast.'

He closed the top loosely and hung the bottle on a corner of rock. Back on the ground he scouted towards the river. The launch had gone. Perhaps they were sleeping on the minesweeper. More probably a helicopter had carried them to Mindanao where there were five-star beach resorts with chefs, if not up to Sir Philip's normal standards, at least capable of grilling fresh fish and lobster over charcoal or serving local crab with ginger and chilis. Trent dwelled on the financier's meal as he slithered like a snake towards the river bank. He willed dysentery on the financier and almost laughed as he imagined Sir Philip desperate to get out of his suit pants.

His childishness was a symptom of exhaustion. He should have slept in the cave rather than hold the woman beneath the drips of water. No, not *the woman*. Her name was Jay Li and it was important that he should remember. Important because he was prepared to die for her. Only the why was unimportant – and what he would do after he had rescued her. With the Department, his official responsibilities in an operation had ended always with the writing of his report.

15

Starlight silvered the surface of the river. Along the bank, the rocket-shattered bars of the cage rose like the ribs of an immense skeleton. The stink of rotten meat mixed with the sulphur and the smoke and Trent thought of the crocodiles that had escaped and must be now in the river or in the jungle border. Already exhausted by near-drowning, the reptiles had then gorged themselves; with luck, they would remain somnolent for the next twenty-four hours. But the soldiers might be nervous of staying close to the river so Trent kept to the footpath that threaded the trees along the bank.

Wary of traps as much as of soldiers, he crawled on his belly, hands dancing like crabs over the path ahead. Sweat poured out of him and he brushed his forearm across his eyes. Already ticks and leeches were boring into his flesh in search of blood.

He loathed the jungle – the heat and the insects and the cloying stench of decay – but he was expert in its ways and moved silently as a snake along the path, nostrils flared to catch the scent of a man's sweat or of a cigarette; most male Filipinos were casualties of the tobacco companies' deadly propaganda that smoking was a mark of masculinity and sophistication.

He listened through the jungle orchestra for the movement of a boot or the brush of a twig across a man's shoulder or the sudden intake of breath. He listened for the shift in weight of a crocodile come ashore to doze beneath the dripping undergrowth and for the warning hiss of a snake awake in his path.

The frenzied squeal of a rodent shrilled under the strike of an owl's talons. The owl called to its mate, and wings beat, then came the scratch of claws on a branch and he heard the owls tear at the meat. The foot of a large or careless animal sucked at the mud. A trace of garlic drifted on a man's breath – perhaps a survivor of the massacre – more probably one of Manolo Ortega's men coming off sentry duty. The man stepped out of the jungle and turned up the path.

The broken cage cut Trent off from the river, a cage still inhabited by crocodiles. Nor had he time to feel his way silently into the undergrowth. He pressed down with his fingertips and drew his knees up and his feet in to his crotch. Crouched like a frog, he shifted mere inches to centre a patch of night sky above the path.

Boots squelched.

Then the head and shoulders of a marine were outlined against the stars.

Trent had no alternative. He drove up. The heel of his right hand struck the man under the chin while his knee slammed between the man's legs. The marine gasped and crumpled. Trent caught him and heaved him over a branch. The man would be unconscious for half an hour. Selected for Special Forces, he was big in frame for a Filipino and his camouflage blouse fitted Trent across the shoulders. The trousers were too tight and Trent cut them off at the knees and slit the crotch. He slung the soldier's M-16 over his shoulder and tucked the soldier's Colt into his belt.

The Filipino had come up the path for ten yards without getting blown up by a mine or caught in a trap and Trent took those ten paces fast. He found the tree that sloped out over the river bank. The soldier's shirt, sliced into strips, served as a lashing for his feet. He shimmied up the straight-trunked tree, retrieved the sail-board and manhandled it out over the water along the sloping tree trunk. There were four cans of rations left in the storage box. He stowed them under the tree, looped the rope over his shoulders, and stuffed the contents of the medicine box in his trouser pockets. Then he lowered the sail-board into the water and let it float away on the river current into the outgoing tide.

The sail-board on its own wasn't enough evidence that they had reached the coast but he was shaking after his climb and knew that he would make a mistake if he tried to do more without first resting. He ate from one of the cans and took three pills against dysentery, a malaria pill, and rubbed antibiotic ointment into his thigh. The tree where he had stowed the sail-board would be scuffed. Rather than advance into unknown territory, he retreated towards the village.

A *coapa* tree grew close to the path. He wiped his feet so as not to leave mud on the trunk and began the climb. His grip was greasy with sweat on the smooth bark and the looped rope that bound his feet slipped. The wound in his thigh leaked and throbbed. The throbbing spread up his spine and into his arms and deep into his neck muscles. Twice he had to stop. The tree shook in his arms as the volcano coughed. Exploding out of the crater, the lava threw its glow over the jungle and shadows shifted where there had been darkness. Again the volcano coughed, deep and heavy, and the tree shook again. Then there was quiet and Trent clambered the final stretch to a V formed by two branches hidden within the leaf canopy eighty feet above the ground.

Lashed securely into the V, he rested his head against the trunk. He had slept the same way many a night and in a worse state of health. He was older now and he had the woman to care for. Jay Li . . .

The ground shook her awake and a monster coughed and groaned close by. There was a burning in her sinuses and she wept. She was used to tears on her cheeks. She knew that she was alone because there was no fresh pain out on the distant surface of her body. The burning was inside and she was familiar with pain on the inside.

Thinking of the pain made her curl herself into a ball and she saw a circle of paler darkness rather than light. She expected pain to appear in the paleness but nothing came. After a long while she straightened her legs and eased herself across the slippery floor to the end of the chain. The chain dragged after her but it was longer than it had been. Reaching the paleness, she found that it was a hole. The night was outside, a night filled with another stink, thicker than the ammonia in which she had awakened, but less pungent.

Ammonia. At first she shied away from recognition of the word and of her capacity to name the stink that was outside her; everything that was outside her was dangerous.

She curled her legs and arms in quickly so that she became a ball again, small and difficult to find. She rolled to her hole and fell into it, back into the depth, back into safety.

There was something down there in her darkness. She sucked at it from a distance, drawing the taste in. There was no immediate pain so she uncurled and advanced a little, always prepared to retreat, and touched at it with the tips of her legs, felt at it carefully. A man's voice.

She wove a web round the voice quickly so that she could keep it and have time to investigate its content. It had been a long time ago. A man had called her by her given name and his voice had been softened by frailty rather than in mockery.

Then she saw her grandfather standing beside the man and she retreated quickly. But there was something wrong, and even as she retreated, she saw the picture change. Her grandfather had been there but the man had protected her. And he had promised. She was certain that he had promised. At first she couldn't recall what he had promised, only that he had done so.

Then she remembered. He had promised to strap Wong Fu in her iron box so that he wouldn't escape while she spun her thread above the lid. She watched as the man bent over the box to fasten the straps. Like his voice, he was weak and ineffectual. Wong Fu laughed and reached for the man's throat, squeezing until the man begged for mercy.

Jay hated him. Hated him as much as she hated Wong Fu, and as much as she hated her grandfather and his minions. She hated him for his weakness and for his promises that he would only attempt to keep if she drove him. She hated him because he was a man. All men were evil. She cradled the evidence within herself, the pain. She would never forget.

Slowly a name came to her, *Trent*. She tested the name and, as she felt around its edges, recalled that there was water. She was stronger than Trent, far stronger. She had no need for water or for food. The hate inside her was sustenance enough and it glowed suddenly gold around her as the earth shook. She rolled in its heat, relishing the sensuousness of her vengeance while firecrackers crackled in celebration.

The crackle of a light machine gun woke Trent. The shooting came from down river. He presumed that a soldier had spotted the sail-board. Rifle fire to the east was more probably a soldier shooting at shadows, though there could be a few survivors from the massacre. An outboard motor roared – soldiers checking the sail-board. A patrol jogged by below Trent's tree, heading toward the beach. A second patrol would advance up-river so as to

130

sandwich the quarry. They must find evidence or would suspect that the sail-board was a feint.

He listened to the soldiers' boots squelch in the mud along the path. The path was too dangerous. Traps waited inside the jungle. Two miles to the beach, the only possible route was the river.

He slid to the ground and out along the sloping tree. Undertow sucked at the surface so that the water boiled scarlet gold as lava fountained from the volcano. The current was swift on the tidal ebb and with the last of the flood. The crocodiles would stay in the slower water on the outside of the bends and in under the banks where they could wedge themselves between tree roots. He might have a chance if he kept to the centre of the river. The weapons he had taken from the soldier would have weighed him down so he wrapped them in the soldier's blouse and slid them into the water. Then he dived and swam out into the current.

The water was a thin gruel that stank of rotten leaves and of earth and he spat it away from his lips as he raised his head. Over on the mud bank, eyes glowed in the light of the volcano – eyes or fireflies – and he swam hard to keep in the flood. The river swept him into the straight. He lay on the surface, barely moving, while he watched and listened to soldiers shout to each other as they poked the bank with sticks.

Disturbed by the search, a crocodile smashed into the water and Trent searched anxiously for the direction taken by the ripples that veed back from its snout. The crocodile swam behind him, then turned downstream toward the mud flat on the outer edge of the next bend. The current sped Trent into the bend and again he was forced to swim, but with care because of the search parties. The last straight opened off the bend and he saw the pale gap in the trees. The sand spit beyond was a line of silver in the moonlight.

Head low in the water, he watched the surface and saw, suddenly outlined against the silver strip, the black triangle of a shark's fin. He cursed himself for a fool as he thought of the chunks of crocodile swept down, sharks and barracudas drawn to the scent of blood. He pictured the dark dribble oozing from his thigh and stayed very still in the water, letting the current do the work.

The water swirled to his left as a shark turned and he saw the darkness of its mouth and heard a snuffling grunt as it tore at the remains of a dead crocodile. He imagined his thigh between the shark's teeth, gripped and shaken, blood spurting as a calling card to other sharks that already circled; then the punch of a snout into his belly and the disgustingness of the pain as he was ripped open. Fear punched the pain up from his stomach into his lungs and was so thick and sour in his throat that he thought that he must vomit.

But he remained inert, inert as a corpse, while the fins slipped by on the moon-shimmer like the sails of model boats on the pond in Hyde Park where he had played as a child, his guardian's manservant waiting the other side of the pond for their model sloop to beach on the cement. Trent clung to that picture, clung to memories that were calm and free of fear until the sickness ebbed and the muscles in his stomach slackened so that he could breathe more easily.

The tide ripped round the tip of the point. It would slacken in half an hour and enable him to return from the open sea. As the current swept him out, he thought of the girl in the cave. Of the girl's grandfather. Of the soldiers who had committed massacre. And of his own dark deeds for the Department and for the Americans. Then again of the girl. He pictured her as he had first seen her outstretched in the hut and how she had lain curled in a ball up in the cave. He thought of her slight frame as a fragile container into which suffering and horror had been stuffed and he marvelled that she remained intact – she, who was untrained in infamy.

Fresh whitewash failed to hide the brown stains on the wall and Jay could see clearly the pit marks left by previous executions. Her family stood with their backs against the wall. Six generations. Fierce sunlight disclosed their features so that they were simply matched to their portraits and daguerreotypes and to old photographs. Jay had been told stories about them by both her Hong Kong grandparents. She had listened to gossip and folk tales. She had read histories of Hong Kong and works that camouflaged themselves as fiction while creeping bravely close to the fortress walls on which stood sentry the legion of lawyers armed with the laws of libel and unlimited finance.

A shuffle of boots in the dust heralded the approaching soldiers. The choice of whom to save was hers. Jay commenced a careful examination of their faces but the oppressive heat dulled her memories and why should she bother herself?

The fatigue was suddenly insupportable and she lay down. Shade covered her. She wriggled her shoulders against the slippery earth and smiled as she stretched her arms. 'Trent,' she called, remembering the name. She knew that he was at hand. 'Take care of it,' she told him. A burst of rifle fire reported his obedience.

Jay imagined her family crumpled at the foot of the wall. The bodies were a long way off and she would see them only if she lifted her head. The effort was too great. Rolling onto her side, she rested her cheek on folded hands and her nurse rocked her gently, crooning that she was safe now and that today was her birthday; she should unwrap her fine present.

Jay drew out the ends of the bow in the red ribbon and furled back the emerald wrapping paper from the iron box. She tried to open the box but the lid was too heavy so she summoned Trent once more and watched the muscles in his back swell under the weight of the iron.

Wong Fu lay in the box. Jay poked at him but he didn't move. She poked again, harder. Her nurse said that the batteries were old but Jay was used to white lies of comfort. The toy was broken. This was the truth. Desolation enveloped her and tears welled in her eyes. Her nurse cradled her in plump arms, the sweat between her breasts harsh and ammonic. From beyond, came a deep rumble and the stink of hot sulphur.

The deep growl of the volcano seemed to shiver the sea and Trent watched as vast chunks of molten rock fountained into the sky. He had fought to reach the sand spit but the current had been too strong and had swept him by. Finally he had been forced to await the turn of the tide. Now he swam carefully towards the beach.

The outgoing tide had washed the scent of dead crocodile out to sea and he imagined a fresh stream of sharks tempted into the narrow straits. He had swum eastward so as to land at the midway point on the spit that was furthest from the predators' path and close to where he had hidden his dive gear. He needed his dive gear if he was to recross the straits, needed it because no threat, however great, would make him swim again on the surface.

The moon dipped low in the west and dawn faintly stained the eastern horizon. The thin line of palm trees showed faintly above the crest of the dune. Ortega's men hid amongst the trees. Trent was certain of this as he was certain that he would fail without sleep and food.

Fearing that the marines would see the splash of his hands, he stopped swimming and let the gentle swell lift him towards the beach. His feet touched sand and he rolled sideways out of the sea as if dead and washed ashore. A sliver of gold touched the horizon and again the volcano coughed. Barely discernible within the stench of sulphur that drifted on the slight breeze came a hint of tobacco smoke. He listened for the slither of footsteps in the soft sand. Breathed shallowly so as not to move his chest. Waited for a bullet. The seconds passed and he began to count.

He counted slowly. He thought that two minutes was enough. The sea had washed clean the wound in his thigh but a dull throb of pain warned of infection and he was tired, desperately tired. He pictured the marine up on the crest of the dune, fit and rested and well fed. The Filipino would have seen him had he looked out to sea so he must be watching the straits and the edge of the jungle. Watching for escapees from the massacre but more importantly, for the girl. Sir Philip would have a price on her head.

Still counting, he rolled slowly onto his side. He had expected to see the marine's feet but the steep slope rose to a flat of dead ground so that even the trees were hidden. He eased his knife in its sheath, then snaked up the slope inch by inch, fingertips searching for stick or stone. He calculated the marine's position from the taint of tobacco smoke carried on the breeze. The sun warmed his left side as he crawled and his eyes stung with sea salt moistened by sweat.

He lost the scent of tobacco halfway up the slope; the smoker must have stubbed his cigarette out. A radio crackled suddenly to the right of where he had placed the Filipino – perhaps ten feet. Either he had miscalculated the breeze or two men lay in wait. They were Ortega's men and trained in hand-to-hand combat. He had neither the strength nor skill to combat both men. His only possibility was to kill one of them before the other moved.

He thought of the children and the women butchered by the marines. They had carried out orders as he had carried out orders. Now, if he killed, he would do so to save the girl, and he saw her again sprawled on the floor of the hut. If only he were less tired, but the fatigue lay on him like a thick cover of wet wool, heavy and deadening the anger on which he tried to feed.

16

The surf lapped gently on the beach and already the sun, though only a few degrees above the horizon, laid its warmth across the narrow spit of sand. A match scratched loud in the stillness of the early morning and Trent heard the marine above and a little to his right, draw deeply on a fresh cigarette.

The knife slipped easily from its sheath.

He couldn't do it.

The knowledge came without thought, but was absolute and crushed the last energy from his limbs. But he had to move, that was the rule of his profession, the old profession from which he had thought to escape.

Warped harsh by atmospherics, male voices sputtered at each other in Tagalo and the marine holding the radio grunted irritably. The second Filipino, the one with the cigarette, spat a shred of tobacco from his lip before commenting and Trent heard the first man smother his laughter. Trent had them both now, their exact positions. He pictured them sprawled beneath the palm trees, chins resting on the butts of their M-16s as they searched the straits and the jungle through powerful binoculars.

Binoculars! The rubber eye pieces would cut the two men's peripheral vision. He had to be certain that both men were watching and suddenly, as the breeze drifted the stench of sulphur, he saw what he should have seen earlier but for the fatigue. The risk was in having to wait but he slipped the knife back into its sheath and slithered to his left to be directly below the radio operator.

The minutes passed. The marine flicked his cigarette back over his shoulder and Trent watched the last trickle of smoke float away. The marine directly above him passed a remark and, rising out of the sand like a genie, stood fiddling below his belt with both hands.

In moments he would turn and come over the dune to urinate. Trent had nowhere to hide. He tried to gather himself, to think as he had been trained to think, of targets rather than of flesh and blood. It was too long ago.

Suddenly atmospherics crackled and a metallic voice barked orders or demanded a report. The marine grabbed impatiently at the radio and answered shortly. Then he picked up an M-16 and began to turn to face down the slope to where Trent lay unhidden on the open slope of the dune but the volcano roared and he looked back.

Chunks of molten rock hurtled hundreds of feet into the sky, rocks with tails of scarlet lace that disintegrated into droplets that spattered the golden outer lips of the cone. The marine propped his M-16 against his leg and raised his binoculars.

Trent rose to his feet.

Binoculars to their eyes, the two marines were blind to his approach. Eight steps to the radio operator. Trent walked on the balls of his feet.

There exists an instinct amongst professionals in the exercise of their profession that warns them of the unexpected and the marine suddenly glanced back and grabbed for his rifle. In so doing he opened his neck. Trent chopped him hard to the rear of his left ear, dived for the M-16 and swept it round to cover the second man.

The second marine already had a hand on his rifle. He had hate in his eyes more than fear. Trent had to prove his mastery or court disaster.

'Don't try,' he warned: 'Don't even think of trying. Get your hands behind your back like a good boy and there's a chance you'll live.'

The marine spat at him.

Trent hit him in the ribs with the rifle barrel, knelt on his spine, and hurled the man's M-16 and radio down the dune.

The marine he had chopped on the neck groaned as he regained consciousness. Trent ordered him to his knees with his hands out like a communicant. There was less hate in him than in his companion. Unsuccessful ventures in the boxing ring had left him with a squashed nose and scar tissue in his eyebrows. He was too intelligent to waste energy on curse-words. He was used to heat; it was the cooler night air that he didn't like and he wore a combat jacket zipped over a shirt and cotton undershirt. The butt of an army issue Colt automatic stuck out of a webbing holster that wasn't made for a quick draw and he wore a machete in a sheath laced to his right leg.

Trent ordered him to untie the lace with his left hand, unclasp his belt, and throw the whole tangle back down the slope. Next came his jacket, shirt, and undershirt. Last came combat boots and pants. That was one of them disarmed. 'On your belly, hands behind your back,' Trent ordered.

Too tired to work out how to deal with the other man, he cut the blood off from his brain long enough to black him out. He sliced the other marine's trousers into strips and tied his hands and feet before stripping the second marine and tying him up. Dragging the men to separate palm trees, he bound them so they faced away from the sun.

The marines had found his dive gear; the tank was leaning against the trunk of the tree close to where he had hidden it. Collecting the smoker's cigarettes from his combat jacket, Trent lit one and held the cigarette to the man's lips.

'Pure poison,' Trent said as the marine exhaled.

The marine told him to do something unpleasant to himself.

Trent grinned and left the butt between the man's lips. He thought that a lot of the man's anger came from loss of face and asked: 'Ortega warn you that I used to be a Special Forces instructor?'

The marine showed interest and Trent said: 'People say I'm one of the best so you should have been warned.'

The radio operator said, 'The Commander told us you had a boat.'

'A catamaran,' Trent said: 'You found the dive gear, why not the inflatable? Or didn't you search the beach?'

The men looked at each other and Trent grinned: 'If you'd slashed the hulls, we'd never have got back to the yacht. We're in luck.'

He slid his knife from its sheath and held it by the blade tip, springing it up and down like a diving board. The sun flashed on the blade. Then it was gone and the marine on Trent's left gasped as the blade dug into the tree an inch behind his head. 'Another danger Ortega didn't warn you against,' Trent said.

He retrieved the knife and squatted facing the radio operator: 'I like to know how many men I'm up against. If there's more than one in the same place, I'll kill them because that's easy, so tell the truth and you may save their lives. Lie and I'll cut your belly open so you bleed to death.'

The Filipino looked across at his companion and Trent said: 'I count to five . . .'

The smoker cursed again and said that there was a man on each point.

'One at each end? You're sure? Being wrong wins you a body bag.'

The radio operator said: 'It's the truth. The rest of the men are searching the jungle for you and your woman.'

So that was how Ortega had explained the operation. 'What makes us important? You killed the pirates and their families. Isn't that enough?'

'The pirates were a hundred dollars each, you and your woman are five thousand.'

'Each?'

The marine nodded: 'All or nothing – plus a ten thousand bonus for whoever finds either one of you.'

Trent grinned at him: 'Tough luck, but you may live, so it's not all bad.' The men each end of the point were too far off to hear his prisoners yell but he gagged them anyway.

A backpack contained water, biscuits, and a can of sardines. Having eaten and drunk sparingly, Trent jogged down the beach to the spot where he had landed and rolled back and forth on the sand till it was well marked. Then he scooped a hole sufficiently large to have hidden a deflated Zodiac.

Climbing back, he took the Filipinos' gags off, gave them water, and tied the gags back. He looked across at the coast through binoculars as if not much interested.

'Your friends are searching the wrong place. That's not a complaint,' Trent said and chuckled to himself. He took the bigger of the two men's trousers and combat jacket, shouldered the dive gear, and tipped an imaginary hat to the two marines: 'Take it easy.'

He kept to his old tracks for twenty yards, picking up the radio operator's machete on the way. Then, smoothing his new footmarks with the combat jacket, he returned to the crest east of the two men, lay flat, and searched the far side of the straits for soldiers.

08.15 hours and a helicopter came sweeping in from the east –

Ortega and Sir Philip Li. Had Trent been in charge, he would have taken his men back up to the village, spread them in a long line and beat the jungle down to the sea. He and Ortega came from the same school – the Filipino would act in the same way. Radio silence from the men he had tied up might bring a boat out from the coast. More probably the men on point duty would be ordered to close in. Once they had released the two marines, they would examine his footprints and the hole with the slide leading to the sea. Ortega would fly out. If he believed in the fake evidence, he would order a search for an inflatable and the *Golden Girl*. A mile to the nearest atoll – not finding the inflatable or catamaran, he might switch some of his men to check the beaches on the surrounding islands.

Trent thought that he had fifteen or twenty minutes at the most. There would be sharks in the channel and he didn't look at the water as he slid slowly down the slope, brushing away his tracks. Reaching the water's edge, he slipped into his dive harness, checked the regulator, fastened his weight belt, and dragged on his fins.

He eased out from the shore on his hands so that he could hide below the surface in an emergency. Clear of the shore, he spat into his mask and rinsed the saliva round to stop the glass misting. He wound the trousers and combat jacket round his left forearm and gripped the machete tightly in his right hand. Four hundred yards to the river mouth.

Fresh sea water, flushed into the straight by the incoming tide, had diluted the muddy gruel that flowed from the river. However visibility remained less than ten feet. Trent followed the bottom down, first pale sand then mud that lifted at the slightest movement so that a dark grainy curtain closed behind him.

Hardly stirring, the long silver bullet shape of a four-foot-long barracuda hung inches below the surface like part of a mobile in a draught-free room. Trent watched the dark gash of its mouth and the cold grey eye far back on the side of its head. He felt the sharks. They were there, hidden in the gauze cloud of jungle detritus, ceaselessly quartering their territory.

Dark, one came at him. No more than a shape at first, a fifties airliner, narrow in the tail, the tail fin split with the long upper section high and curving back. Tiger. Around seven foot long and weighing two hundred pounds. Viciously aggressive.

The shark turned towards him, black eyes wide apart, tail fin swaying. The crescent gash of its mouth smiled, or seemed to smile, as it eased closer – not in attack yet, but curious. It slipped by at a distance of ten feet, flanks sleek as anodised aluminium. Trent followed it with his eyes as it circled. Instinct made him want to turn with the shark, machete ready, but he was controlled by his air supply.

How many dive minutes he had left in the tank depended on his rate of breathing which depended on effort expended at what depth. He had forty-five minutes at most from the time he left the beach; forty-five minutes and four hundred yards; approximately nine yards a minute, so he had plenty of time – unless something went wrong. It was this uncertainty that forced him to keep the big pro-fins driving steadily through the water.

The shark eased parallel, head weaving like a Saturday night drunk in search of a fight. Round it came ahead of Trent and round behind again. Then back alongside so that there existed a visual illusion of companionship, two friends out for an aquatic stroll.

Fear and rage produced adrenalin to combat fatigue and Trent tasted the fear acid-sour in his throat and in his stomach. On he drove towards the island, the shark always circling. He thought that it must have already eaten. Breakfasted, he corrected and tried to smile to himself but the fear was too great, fear of the sudden swirl that telegraphed attack.

He had seen a fisherman snatched from a reef in the Persian Gulf. That was the year that his father shot himself at his desk so Trent had been eight years old. He had watched the fisherman cast his net. An old man, or so he had appeared to Trent – though anyone over forty seemed old when you were a child. The fisherman had been standing knee-deep on the edge of the reef. Trent saw the swirl in the waters and the sudden gash of white as the sun struck the under part of a shark's jaw as it spun away with the fisherman's leg in its jaws.

The fisherman grabbed at the coral. For a moment there was a tug of war. Then a second shark swept in and hit the man in the belly. The fisherman gave one despairing shriek as he disappeared. The waters turned red. A hand and forearm rose above the surface. For a brief instant Trent had seen clearly the end plate in his story book of King Arthur and the Knights of the Round Table. But the arm was unattached and a shark's snout snatched it out of the air. Trent screamed and ran blindly into the arms of the elderly groom who had brought him down to the sea from the Sheik's racing stables where Trent's father was employed as manager and trainer. Sharks! Trent feared and hated them and no amount of ecologists' propaganda could change his attitude.

Again he adjusted his course to the compass. He had been in the sea fifteen minutes. The shark accelerated effortlessly and vanished into the murk. Then there was a deeper darkness ahead that shifted and rolled. Brown threads drifted through the thin curtain of mud only to disintegrate as the current played with them. Threads of blood and the dark whirling mass was a dozen sharks and as many barracuda tearing at the remains of a crocodile and at each other.

As he back-paddled, a black torpedo hurtled past into the ghastly mass. One wrong move could make him the centre of the carnage. Belly in the mud, he eased to the east under the shadow of a second torpedo that flashed overhead.

Speed was both the temptation and the danger; any sudden movement would attract the carnivores; yet each delay cut into his air supply. Forced to the surface, he would be seen by the marines on the points and the laying of false trails would be wasted.

Clear now of the whirling sharks, he headed again towards the island but his confidence was damaged and he looked back frequently over his shoulder, and to his left and right, and above to where the surface of the sea shone pale silvery green.

Shadows showed momentarily through the mud curtain that thickened as he approached the river mouth – shadows, and now, near to the island, the visibility closed to less than six feet, a dark cave in which he swam without protection of walls or bars so that the slime over which he swam became his last contact with the outside world.

Finally the air came from the regulator in insufficient dribbles and he was forced to rise so as to lessen the atmospheric pressure, so releasing more air from the tank. The sea bottom had shielded his belly. Now, at the same level as the marauding sharks, he swam defenceless and uncertain of where he was. The fear was deep in him, fear and claustrophobia.

A shape burst through the curtain and slammed along his right side, then vanished into the murk. Again the shark came, this time from his left, and again slammed into his side. He saw the paler underneath of its belly as it spun into a tight turn. He saw the eyes, dark and shining. He saw the two dark slits like nostrils. He saw, in slow motion, the dark sickle open and the teeth show white in the swirling haze.

He plunged the machete down the throat but the shark was too powerful for him in the water and he jammed his left arm wrapped in the marine's clothing crosswise into the jaws to force them further open and lessen the leverage of the jaw muscles. The shark flung him back so that his legs spread each side of the thrashing body. He gave one last push at the machete, released it, and grabbed his throwing knife.

He fought, with great heaves of his lungs, for the last of the air in his tanks as he plunged the knife into the top of the shark's head. Again and again, so that blood streamed and he knew that it was only minutes before fresh aggressors were drawn to the fray. Yet, if he withdrew his arm from the jaws for even a second those teeth would sheer his stomach open.

Again he plunged the knife home. Again and again.

The fight whipped up the mud until there was nil visibility and he stabbed from instinct. The blade hit bone or flesh, perhaps an eye, as he stabbed repeatedly and in frenzy, a frenzy that projected, into that part of his mind that remained rational, the image of a crazed serial killer.

His lungs burnt with lack of oxygen and his strength ebbed. He had to fight to keep his arm in the shark's jaws as he buried the blade to the hilt. Through the desperate rage, he realised that victory was his. Still stabbing, he dragged his arm free and grabbed for the handle of the machete. He gathered all his remaining force and rammed the shark away, then swam without caring whether his fins would draw a fresh attack. He had to be clear of the blood, he had to surface. He freed the harness and rolled so that the tank sank away tugging the regulator from his lips. The last of the air dribbled from his lungs as he rose the last few feet. Dragging his lungs full as he broke surface, he felt for the mouthpiece of his snorkel and blasted the water out of the tube.

17

The river and tidal race had scoured a steep-edged channel east and west of the river mouth close in to the island. Mangrove trees flourished along the northern edge of the channel. Beyond lay the jungle.

The current had drifted Trent some way to the east of the river mouth but he had surfaced less than fifty feet from the mangrove. Behind him three shark fins slashed toward the carcase of his assailant. Instinct tempted him to swim fast on the surface for the protection of the undergrowth. Had he done so, the marine lookouts on the sand spit would have spotted the spume churned up by his fins. So he contained his fear.

He swam with only the back of his scalp and the tip of his snorkel breaking the surface. He kept his legs still and paddled with his hands like a dog. The swamp stench came to him through the tube and he could taste the sulphur.

The thick choking cough of the volcano seemed continuous. He would be taking Jay across the flank at night and he wondered how far the lava streams had reached down the cone. After the dangers of the past twenty-four hours, there would be vicious irony in the mountain delivering them to the enemy.

He touched mud, reached for the first mangrove root and drew himself forward across the slime. Once onto the mud he rolled so as to coat his body with a layer of camouflage. Trent slid forward by inches until he was deep into the cover of the swamp – it was always movement that betrayed a man or an animal's presence.

He listened as he shifted deeper into the lattice of intertwined roots and scrub. Ortega could have left sentries along the jungle edge. In the Caribbean or on the coast of Central America they would have been alerted by the hundreds of birds startled off the tidal feeding ground. There were few birds in the Philippines.

He crossed the tracks of a crocodile. Crustaceans resembling outsize scarab beetles were trapped in shallow tidal pools. Crabs scurried out of his path. There were mosquitoes, millions of mosquitoes. Their high pitched whine cut sharp as a carbon blade through the deep rumble of the mountain. The mud protected Trent from insect bites but not from the leeches that were already probing his flesh. Fatigue and disgust at his condition tempted him to surrender but he kept himself going with promises of five hours' sleep once he was safely hidden in the jungle.

10.30 hours – the helicopter flew low overhead and landed midway along the spit. Trent imagined Ortega squatting beside the fake tracks of the inflatable. The marine commander would feel the sand and look out to sea while he pondered the probabilities. More than an hour had gone since Trent had left the two marines tied to the trees. Time enough to have paddled out of earshot before starting a small outboard and to have reached the nearest atoll.

The helicopter rose from the sand and gained height rapidly as it swept away to the south. Trent doubted if Ortega was convinced of their escape; more probably he had begun the search while he planned his next moves. Trent would have done the same.

The heat was intense and the humidity so high that the air felt like damp cotton; the pungent stink of warm mud was overpowering. A snake lifted its head and Trent waited for it to lose interest and move away. His forearm and his thigh throbbed and pain stabbed behind his eyes as he squinted up at the heat-bleached sky. Only twenty yards now to the trees, and he eased forward, searching always for a hidden marine.

Tracks on a tree trunk would have given him away so, having reached the tree line, he scraped the damp mud from his front and from his limbs. Then he squatted in the sun and waited for the remainder to dry so that he could brush it free. He ignored the leeches. Picking at them would leave their suckers to suppurate in his flesh. A lighted match or tip of a cigarette was the only safe way to force them to release their hold.

The fight in the sea had left his forearm swollen and purple with burst blood vessels each side of the almost black crescents made by the shark. The arm would stiffen soon and he exercised the muscles while he waited. Mud brushed away, he sliced the trousers he had taken from the marine into strips, tied the strips into a rope, looped it round the tree, and bound his feet. He caterpillared up to the first fork in a *banas* tree – then clambered bough to bough, up and up, until he felt safe from discovery.

He slept, strapped with trouser strips, in a cradle of branches laid across the narrow V between two thick limbs sixty feet up. Over his years of service in the Department, he had trained himself to catalogue sounds even in his sleep. A footstep on the ground below would have wakened him instantly but his subconscious accepted the increasingly fierce eruptions of the volcano.

The eruptions shook the cave. Jay stirred lethargically. For three days she had lived only for vengeance, her desire fed by torture. Now, with her fantasies unfed, her mind had lost direction. She was at peace. That was all. A peace in which she floated away, further and further from the centre that, had she been able to think, she would have thought of as herself. Her progress was slow but constant, her breathing increasingly shallow as she withdrew – as if her body no longer required fuel.

She was close to death, very close.

The cave shook again and a slab of clay fell from the roof.

Rifle fire spattered the jungle canopy. Trent woke. Men were approaching slowly through the trees. They were a half-mile away to the north and in an angled line that had one end anchored to the river bank and the other advancing on the lip of the cassava fields cleared behind the settlement away to his east. That end would curl round when the marines reached the sea and beat back towards the river so that he would be caught in a purse net. If he could escape, there was a reasonable chance of Ortega accepting the fake tracks on the spit as genuine. Evading the net would be difficult – very difficult, he thought as he tested his left forearm, swollen and purple.

He eased his wounded thigh, exploring its strength, then swung down to the next branch and down one more. He found that he could control the pain in his arm if he operated at half strength but there was nothing broken and full power remained for an emergency. The thigh was bearable.

Once on the lower branch, he looped the trunk with the trouser strips, wound the ends round his wrists and slid the last forty feet down the smooth trunk to the ground. Listening to the marines, he judged that he had half an hour.

First he retreated to the swamp – the tide had washed away all evidence of his landing. Relieved, he squatted between two trees and carefully removed the layer of dead leaves before digging into wet earth underneath. He rubbed the soil over his face and body, then replaced the leaves and stood lightly balanced on the balls of his feet like a gazelle prepared for instant flight. He sniffed at the air, cataloguing the smells so that he would notice the smallest variation: sulphur, rotting vegetation, mouldy wood, mangrove – these were the main ingredients; a trace of sweetness came from a greyish-green bush, gum, a fern that was slightly bitter, the corpse scent of a yellow fungoid.

Wary of traps, the marines beat at the jungle floor. Trent had to remain silent. Landmines, spring traps, pits, these were the dangers. His route was decided by the gap between the trees. The greatest safety lay where the gap was narrow and the root system prominent and extensive so that the ground was hard to dig and the setting of a trap almost impossible to camouflage.

His precautions were constant: first the choice of tree to which he would move, next the inspection of the intervening ground. Certain of where he would place his feet, he sniffed and listened and checked the surrounding walls of greenery. Rather than walk, he seemed to slide from tree trunk to tree trunk; slide and freeze, the balls of his feet alighting, wherever possible, on a root.

Weak links existed in the chain of marines, fear, inexperience, lack of skill. These were hidden from Trent and chance alone governed his choice of where to penetrate the line.

The rifle fire had increased as the marines blitzed anything remotely suspect in the canopy; the wail of a wounded monkey echoed through the trees. The rich perfume of corruption drew Trent left to where a fallen trunk had rotted into the ground. Fungi in pale, creased caps paraded at the base of the barrier and the bark had turned to slime that glistened, faintly phosphorescent. Red ants tip-toed through the slime and a spider's web spread up from amongst the torn roots to a skinny sago palm that had already lost the race for the gap torn in the leaf canopy by the felled giant. A large fern grew at the foot of the sago palm.

The tree trunk remained too wide and high for a man to jump and the extent of its corruption promised hidden horrors – a barrier

146

that few men would touch willingly let alone clamber across – nor did the trunk offer a hiding place; however its length foretold the gap in the chain of hunters at this point.

The closest marines were less than a hundred yards away as Trent circled the open ground to the root end of the tree. He had intended to wait, crouched behind the ferns, distract the marine with a thrown stone, and slip through the cordon. A cobra lay curled half-asleep on the trunk behind the ferns. Frightened, it struck at the source of its awakening. Trent leapt back and the ground collapsed beneath his feet. Pitching forward, he clawed through the leaf mould for solid ground and scrabbled with his bare toes at the side of the pit. The ground was too soft for his weight. Back he slipped, inch by inch towards the waiting stakes. He had one hope, only one hope. He reached behind his neck, grabbed his knife and slammed it into the earth.

He struggled to hold the knife at a reverse angle but the blade cut slowly towards the edge. The pit was ten feet deep and he looked down to his left at the sharpened wood stakes that stuck up eighteen inches from the floor in zigzagged rows with less than a foot between each spike. He heard a Filipino marine strike a bush thirty yards away. For a moment he thought of yelling for help but there wasn't any help, only the possibility of a faster death. Though in all probability the marine would kick the knife out of the ground.

The girl in the cave would die of thirst or of starvation or tumble out of the cave. Li's granddaughter. Trent had never hated any man as much as he hated the Chinese financier.

The crack of a stick under a boot made him look up. He had seconds left, seconds before the knife cut through the last inches of earth that held him from death. He looked down again, this time to his right. At first he didn't see it, then he realised that there was a small gap where one stake had been left out by the man who had hammered the posts in before sharpening them with his machete. The workman had needed that small gap to stand in while sharpening the final spikes.

The gap was two to three feet away from the spot directly below Trent and it was in the shape of a half-lozenge pointed at each end. The square between the points measured 22 inches by 22 inches. Not much of a target.

The marine saw Trent's hands. He didn't shout to the others for fear of having to share the reward for whoever saw Trent first.

Trent clamped his left hand on top of his right and swung on the knife. The extra weight on the blade forced the knife through the last of the earth and he dropped with the knife in his hands. He landed on his left foot close to the point of the lozenge and tipped to his right. His other foot slammed into the centre of the gap. He stumbled and began to fall across the wall of the pit. The stake at the point of the lozenge leapt at his eye as he jammed his right arm down stiff as a window lintel. He began to tip back with the force of the fall but was able to grab the spike with his left hand. He thought the muscles would burst in his damaged forearm but the strength was there and he heaved himself back onto the fulcrum of his right arm, drew in his feet, and pushed himself upright.

For a moment he couldn't breathe but the sound of the marine shuffling in a half run through wet leaves galvanised him and he eased further to his right with the stake between his legs. Recovering his knife, he cleaned it on the inside of his upper arm, then held the blade in his mouth while he wiped the mud from his thumb and first two fingers. Needing a better angle, he slid his left foot round into the second row of stakes.

The marine jabbed the barrel of his M-16 into the pit and leant forward to look over the edge. He saw Trent, naked and unarmed but for a small knife. He saw the reward and beyond into a wondrous new existence of wealth and power in his native village high in the mountains of Luzon. The knife didn't frighten him – it was more toy than weapon. He smiled and began to swing his rifle with practised ease. The traverse was eighty degrees and the distance between the two men was only eleven feet. His target's arm flashed over. There was a fraction of a second in which the marine didn't understand. Then the knife was in his throat. He dropped his rifle and tried to pull the blade out but he was already drowning in his own blood and his strength gave out. He teetered on the edge for a moment, then his knees crumpled and he pitched forward onto the remains of the pit's cover.

The cover split and spilled the Filipino onto the stakes. It seemed to happen very slowly. Trent was shaken by a dry retching spasm and he had to force himself to feel through the blood for the Filipino's pulse. He was already dead and Trent retrieved his knife. A second spasm shook him as he rearranged the marine's head so that a spike pierced the blade wound. Shy of his need, he crossed himself and prayed silently, the words only part remembered from his Catholic schooling.

Facing the wall, he threw his knife hard at a point three feet below the lip. He drew the marine's machete from its sheath and pried the blade deep into the wall, level with his chest. He tied strips of trouser to the handle of the machete and propped the marine's rifle, barrel down, against the wall. Steadying himself on the machete, he clambered up on to the butt end of the rifle. From there he was able to reach his own knife. One foot on the machete, he kicked the rifle away, drew himself up, and peered over the edge of the pit.

Time was against him. The two marines each side of his position had advanced thirty yards. Their orders were to keep the line constant. At any moment they would start searching for the dead man.

Trent drew his knife from the wall, slammed it deep into the ground eighteen inches beyond the pit and heaved himself up over the edge. Lying on the jungle floor, he hung head down into the pit and worked the machete loose with the strips of trouser, cleaned the blade, and tossed the machete onto the broken roof of the trap.

The marine to his left called: 'Tony,' followed by a question in Tagalog – probably asking how he was getting on. Not getting an answer, he shouted louder.

Sheltered by the fallen tree, Trent squatted beside the pit, brushed loose earth into the knife marks, and rearranged dead leaves and leaf mould to hide his tracks.

The marine yelled again, this time calling on the Filipino beyond the dead man. This second Filipino yelled for Tony and, getting no answer, spoke into a radio, then both men turned back. Fifty yards at the most, they would spot the trap in thirty seconds.

Trent remained in the squat position and walked backward on the balls of his feet, fingers brushing lightly across the ground as he covered his path. He reached the first tree and slipped behind it. Crawling would have left a track; if he kept to his feet he would be seen the moment he moved. He scanned the ground ahead, planning each footfall in a route that would leave the least marks.

The marine who had called first, circled the dead tree and saw the pit. He yelled a warning as the other Filipino forced his way noisily through a clump of thick undergrowth. He cursed viciously as he saw the impaled man. The second marine joined him and shouted angrily into his radio.

The marines were heavily armed and fifteen feet from Trent's hiding place. Peering down at the corpse, they had their backs to him. They would hear him if he slipped, see him if they looked round, but it had to be now and he sped like a shadow, his body camouflaged, footfall to footfall. Fifty yards and he was clear of them, hidden within the vast pillared cathedral. He felt weightless as he leapt between the massive trees, the night already signalling its approach with long shadows. He caught a tree one handed and swung round the trunk. *Bang!*

The bullet spat over his right shoulder as he dived and somersaulted. He cursed himself for his stupidity, for not having suspected that the wily Ortega would set backstops behind his main line of search. Those few seconds of acrobatics gave him time to think. He ended on his back with his arms spread, hands open, so that the Filipino could see that he was unarmed and defenceless. He rose to his feet with his hands behind his neck. His chest heaved as he faced the marine. He looked beaten, caked in mud, hair matted, naked except for combat trousers sheared off at the knees, and the wounds, old and new.

'We've got ourselves a real loser,' a mafia heavy had mocked on seeing Trent stripped under a searchlight. Thinking Trent harmless, the gangster had taken too little care. Trent prayed that the marines would make the same mistake.

The marine was young, tough, well-trained, and incredulous at his good fortune. He almost laughed as he inspected the scarecrow. This was their quarry! Ten thousand dollars for the finder and a further ten for the woman. Jesus! That much money and he could set up a short-time hotel and disco in Puerto Galera and sell underage girls to fat Australians. First he had to capture the woman but that wasn't a problem. Making this pathetic creature talk was easy. As a start to the softening-up process, he swung his rifle back and stepped forward to smack Trent across the face with the corner of the butt.

Trent could have killed him but he rode the blow, swaying sideways as if driven by the marine's strength and he whimpered, crumpling to the ground on his knees.

In countries of endemic corruption, police and their kindred develop contempt for those outside their privileged circle. So it was with this marine.

Trent bowed before him, hands covering his head to ward off the next blow. He begged for mercy, snivelling as he drew his hands down flat between the marine's feet, back bowed, face in the mud – an interbreeding of Catholic and Muslim at prayer.

The marine laughed contemptuously and raised his rifle.

Trent's hands swept out and yanked the Filipino's feet, spilling him backwards. Surprise made the Filipino drop his gun. Trent leapt on him but the marine rolled and Trent was underneath. He managed to squirm sideways as the marine tried to ram a knee up between his legs. The marine's fingers clamped on his throat. Trent bucked and twisted his head, forcing his hands up between the marine's arms in a desperate attempt to break the stranglehold.

The marine was well-fed and fresh.

Trent's wounded arm was weak, he was fifteen years older than his antagonist and already close to exhaustion. As he fought, he cursed himself for not having killed the man when he'd had the chance. He used the girl as a goad, thinking of her as he rammed the marine's right arm out. He gasped for air as the marine's fingers slipped from his throat. He tried to butt the Filipino in the face. The Filipino jerked his head back and slashed his elbow into Trent's jaw. Trent's head rolled with the blow. The marine spotted his knife and grabbed at it.

Exultant, the marine held the knife aloft. A ray of sunlight, piercing the canopy, flashed on the blade.

Trent let all the strength go out of his body. The girl was with him and he prayed as he sprawled between the marine's knees as if knocked into semi-consciousness by the elbow blow.

The marine quivered with relief and rocked back onto his heels. He took a deep breath and smiled as he raised his backside, kneeling upright so that he could put all his weight behind the knife.

The angle had to be right. The knife was already plunging down when Trent slammed his right knee up into the marine's crotch. As the Filipino pitched forward, the knife plunged into the earth inches above Trent's head. Trent squirmed free and rolled onto the marine's back, his forearm across the nape of the younger man's neck. He gathered the last of his strength and used all his weight to

151

ram the marine's face into the dirt. At the same time, he dug with his other hand for the artery on the side of the Filipino's throat.

Trent knew that this was his only chance. He had room for nothing else in his mind. He kept his weight on the marine's neck and his fingers on the artery and tried to breathe round the pain that spread out from his wounds.

Slowly the pain eased and the fear ebbed. He knew that he had killed the marine. Rolling onto his back, he lay beside him and watched the sunlight play within the leaf canopy high overhead. Memories of scuba diving came to him, of drifting on a current along the outer side of the reef with the same gentle play of light above. The throbbing cough of the volcano brought him back to the present.

His and the girl's only chance of escape lay in Ortega believing that they had escaped by sea. Back in the pit he had disguised the dead man's wound with the wooden stake. Now he had to build a second scenario. The marine had fired only one shot. There was little chance of it having been noticed amongst the intermittent rifle fire that continued to the south as the searchers flushed the undergrowth.

His hands trembled as he searched the marine for the almost obligatory pocket knife. He found it in the marine's back pocket – a replica of a Swiss army model, two blades, bottle opener, spike, screwdriver, saw.

Trent held the man's trousers tight against his calf and made two tiny punctures with the spike. Slitting the trousers up the seam, he cut two deep crosses into the puncture marks, and squeezed the blood out. There wasn't enough blood. He found the man's cigarettes and lighter in a tin box in his breast pocket. Lighting a cigarette, he held the smouldering point to the leeches on his own legs and torso. As each leech dropped off, he burst the blood out of it over the wound and buried the remains. He had plenty of time. Finally satisfied, he propped the marine forward and bloodied his hands and lips. He let him go, and the Filipino tipped over onto his left side.

Trent spent five minutes meticulously removing evidence of the struggle. The scene looked convincing. How convincing depended on the degree of suspicion. Ortega was as suspicious as a fox raised in hunting country.

18

Separated from the pirates, the corpses of the four Chinese and of the *Ts'ai Yen*'s second officer had been fingerprinted, blooded, and photographed from every angle. Wary of Wong Fu's myriad contacts, Tanaka Kazuko had insisted on flying with the evidence to the police laboratory in Madras.

The marine helicopter dropped out of the dusk and settled in what had been the centre of the pirate village. Manolo Ortega jumped down and strode over to join Sir Philip Li on the river jetty.

The financier had hardly moved since flying in that morning. He stood, hands clasped at his waist. His tie was precisely knotted, shirt collar crisp, grey suit immaculately pressed. Even his brown Oxfords remained clean and polished.

Ortega said, bitterly: 'One of my men fell into a pit.'

'Dead?'

'Very.'

The financier took a slim gold propelling pencil and a small leather-bound notebook with gold corners from his inside pocket. In neat capital letters, he added the man's name to the list of dead whose families he would recompense. Two had been killed in the initial assault. A land mine had killed a corporal. Now this man, four in all, and a fifth had lost his left leg above the knee. Sir Philip slipped the pencil and notebook back into his pocket: 'They've escaped?'

'My man could have been pushed.'

'Is that what you think?'

'I have to consider every possibility.' Ortega shrugged and slapped at a mosquito: 'Trent's the crap sticking to the blanket. Read his CV. You can't find the son of a bitch and he's indestructible.'

'Nobody is indestructible, Commander.'

'That's the theory. With this man there's been a lot of people try over the years. Most of them are dead. I had backstops following up on the main line of searchers – one of them hasn't showed and we can't raise him on the radio.'

Ortega drew a line in the dirt with the pit at one end and the pirate base at the other: 'That's the route the man was on, the man who's missing.' He kicked at the centre of the line as if violence could defeat his worries: 'I've ordered a reverse sweep but we won't find shit in the dark.'

The volcano threw a huge tongue of flame into the sky. The flame gave colour to the financier's face and he looked up, but without interest. Trent and his granddaughter concerned him. Nothing else. He had expected the matter closed the previous morning. Here he was thirty-six hours later with nothing resolved. He had gained face from the massacre, gained more face than he had lost through the piracy. But he had to destroy all evidence of Jay's kidnapping. If he failed, people would consider him pathetic, a spent force. He said: 'That's what you think?'

'That Trent's headed back up this way?'

'Yes.'

Ortega shrugged: 'It's a possibility.'

The volcano was silent for the first time in hours. The silence was disconcerting and curiously more threatening than all the noise that had gone before. Sir Philip Li felt it in the sudden stillness of the air. The volcano as God, he thought. Animate and inanimate, all were frozen, waiting while the mountain held its breath. God of Life and Destruction, which would it choose? The apprehension was obvious in the pilot's face and in the faces of the four marines Ortega had left on duty on the river bank. Even Ortega seemed distracted as he glanced up at the gold-rimmed cone.

Sir Philip said: 'Why would he do that?'

But he had lost Ortega and he smiled, a small bleak smile that hardly moved his lips, but a smile. He touched the marine commander on the forearm lightly, drawing his attention back from the mountain: 'The Englishman, Commander. What reason could he have for coming back this way?'

'His father was Irish. Catholic . . .'

Again the financier smiled: 'Unusual reasons for his return, Commander.'

154

Ortega hadn't followed the financier's thoughts. Then he grinned and gave a quick shake of his head: 'You said he was English. That's all. It was in the CV you had from London, the small print. Irish father, blew his brains out over a cash deficit in the accounts that wasn't his first. The mother put her Jag into a wall a couple of months later.'

Psychology courses were the ones Ortega had most enjoyed – what made a terrorist, or a freedom fighter. Get inside their minds and there was a chance you could outguess them. He'd been successful with the Muslims on Mindanao and Bassalan. He'd understood their aims. He had no hope of outguessing Trent unless he knew what was worth a hundred and seventy grand to Sir Philip Li. Ortega's share was one hundred K which, in the Philippines, was a lot of bread. That Ortega liked Trent was unfortunate but not a problem. Trent had been on the run now for thirty-six hours. Fatigue might make him drop his guard.

Ortega's radio crackled and he held it to his ear. The volcano affected the reception but he understood the gist of his sergeant's report.

'Seems my man died of snake-bite. I'd better go look before they fetch him in.'

He stood for a moment glaring at the massive tree trunks that seemed solid as a wall in the late dusk. 'Only people who like the jungle are the ecologists, Sir Philip. That's how they make their money; grants. Jungle tribes don't have any alternative as to where they live and they don't get grants.' He beckoned one of his men to follow, and strode off into the trees.

Trent sheltered beneath a clump of ferns on the edge of the pirate village. Smoke still trickled from some of the huts and the thick scent of burning wet wood prevailed over the sulphur stench of the volcano. The breeze had dropped and the leaf canopy remained still and silent.

Ortega strode between the charred piles of thatch and vanished into the jungle, one man in his wake. The pilot and three marines remained by the helicopter. Sir Philip Li's bodyguard stood away from the aircraft where he had a clear view of the river and the ruins. Trent couldn't see the financier but presumed that he was on the wooden dock.

Over to his left, the cave in the pale cliff-face looked like a black eye with tears dripping down. Trent watched until the night closed in but didn't spot any guards by the cliff.

He wanted to sleep and he didn't want to cross the open ground between the burnt huts. He had expected the volcano to cover any noise he made and had planned his approach with the light from the eruptions at an angle which protected his night vision. Now the volcano was dark and silent. It was a real pig.

He could hear the marines in the distance. They must have found the man he'd killed. Ortega had gone to inspect the body; he wouldn't be able to tell much, not without a laboratory report – though proof wasn't as important as the feel of a situation. Trent wondered whether Li had told Ortega that the girl they were hunting was his granddaughter. The financier might have stopped short of that detail.

After killing the marine, Trent had collected the length of rope and three tins of stew he'd hidden on the river bank. He hoped the food would give Jay enough strength to cross the mountain.

She had allowed herself to float too far away from reality to notice that it was dark in the cave and she hadn't moved in the past three hours. She lay on her left side, knees drawn up, her hands buried between her thighs. There was as little in her mind as in the mind of a fetus.

In one way she was kin to the volcano, both of them suspended. But the volcano was gathering its energy while Jay's was seeping away.

The wavering beam of a flashlight heralded Manolo Ortega's return to the wooden dock. Sir Philip Li seemed not to have moved and he stood detached and contained as he waited for Ortega's report.

Even the goddamned mosquitoes respeced the son of a bitch, the marine commander thought. There were millions of them, enough to drown a violin with their whining. The helicopter pilot had closed himself up in the aircraft but Ortega could hear him cursing and the three marines Ortega had left with the financier had retreated from the river bank. The mosquitoes had even got to the financier's bodyguard, forcing him to slap and scratch every half-minute or so. The financier stood in protected air-space. As if he were poison, Ortega thought.

'What did you discover?' Sir Philip asked, tone of voice gentle as rosewater.

'Not a lot.'

Having to face the financier made Ortega uncomfortable. Squatting down on the edge of the dock, he looked up at the volcano. He wished the mountain would do something – put up or shut up – but it had shut up. It was this silence which disturbed him. He picked up a couple of pebbles to play with, then found himself distracted by Sir Philip's shoes. The hand-tooled leather was so well polished that they shone even in the dark. He thought that smearing mud over the shoes would be a lot more sport than a round of golf – and a lot more dangerous. Probably fatal.

He said: 'It looked like snake-bite. He'd cut deep crosses in the fang punctures to make the blood flow. He'd even got his mouth to it which couldn't have been easy and he'd spat the blood out on the ground, but mostly he squeezed. Maybe he was too late.'

'You don't appear convinced, Commander.'

Ortega was watching the volcano. He said: 'My guy's dead. That's what I know. For anything else, I need a lab. Trent knows that. It was him, that's what he'd do – which doesn't mean he did it. It means he could have done it. He ambushed the man on the river path, that's certain. And he captured those goddamned idiots on the sand spit. The man in the pit had a stake in his throat which doesn't mean shit except that Trent's CV says he uses a throwing knife and the throat's his preferred target. He knifed the guy, he'd stick a stake in the wound hoping we wouldn't notice.'

He flicked a pebble into the water and shrugged irritably: 'There's nothing I can do in the dark. Come morning I'll take a look at the pit and the ground round about. Maybe that will tell me something but I wouldn't bet on it. If it's him, he's a real pro. Just about the best, or he was. That's what the CV says and I wouldn't argue.'

Sir Philip said quietly: 'You sound defeatist, Commander.'

'Tired. Pissed off. If you told me what this is all about we'd maybe get somewhere,' Ortega said. 'Maybe – but we've left it late.'

'You'd better give me the man's name . . .' Sir Philip had taken out his 22-carat gold propelling pencil and his notebook with the 22-carat gold corners.

Ortega said: 'Money doesn't solve everything.'

'No, but it helps,' Sir Philip said, his smile infinitesimal: 'Disappointing if Trent escapes, Commander.'

There was the threat, no one hundred grand. Or worse, Sir Philip could smash his career. In the Philippines everything was for sale; demotion cost less than promotion – not that cost mattered to the financier. Ortega needed the money. He needed it so that he could marry into the oligarchy that owned and ruled the Philippines, the magic twenty families; even a second or third cousin could assure his promotion to Admiral, or she could get him into politics. Politics was where the serious money lay – Mayor, Governor, Senator. His success in counter-insurgency had already made him a minor hero amongst those who knew. Now he needed the right wife.

He said: 'The volcano's going to blow. I need to get the helicopter out while I can. You should go with it, Sir.'

'I know you'll do your best,' the financier said.

He didn't ask how Ortega knew about the volcano and Ortega couldn't have told him, but he did know. He would have staked money on it. A lot of his training had been concerned with foreseeing danger. There wasn't much difference between foreseeing and sensing and he didn't believe in the pit, nor in the snake-bite. The son of a bitch was out there, close by. If he knew why, he might still catch him but the financier wasn't going to tell him and there was no one else he could ask.

Twenty or so marines had gathered in the village clearing. They had collected firewood and a couple of them squatted over a bunch of twigs, blowing the flames. The helicopter lifted clear of the trees, banked left, and swept away towards Mindanao. Trent had considered using its engines to cover his approach to the cave but it wouldn't have given him enough time. The volcano remained his best shot. He had watched the cone on and off for over an hour, as if watching it would make something happen.

Ortega strode to the fire and spoke with two of his men who nodded, collected equipment, and melted into the trees. Trent wondered where they were going and what Ortega had thought of the snake-bite.

Trent couldn't see the cliff or the cave but he imagined the girl there. He wondered how much Li had promised to pay Ortega on top of the payments to the other ranks. Having a granddaughter killed ought to be expensive.

Trent understood Ortega accepting Li's offer just so long as he didn't know who Jay was. Massacring pirates and their families was no different from massacring insurgents and their families. Trent didn't see himself as part of the equation. He had spent time with Ortega twice and they had a common training, but that didn't make them friends. He was a foreigner and foreigners had a bad track record in the Philippines.

First the Spaniards screwed them for three hundred and fifty years. The Americans screwed them for eighty years, or a hundred counting the Marcos dictatorship, George Bush mumbling support while Ismelda Marcos was already in her bedroom deciding which shoes to pack.

All the Americans left behind was a hamburger culture and the endemic corruption which is a natural byproduct of buying governments.

As for the Japanese, they slaughtered the Filipinos for the fun of it and shipped the women into whorehouses for the troops.

Now there was sex tourism.

Watching the volcano, Trent thought that they should have a woman in charge of tourism and banners at the airport:

PREMATURE EJACULATORS WELCOME

Less work, more pay – and something had to be amiss in those quarters for a man to fly halfway round the world to get laid. They could start a First World promotional campaign:

WHY SUFFER ON THE HOME FRONT?
SHIP YOUR SEXUAL DEVIANTS TO THE PHILIPPINES

Or:

THE PHILIPPINES – A MAN'S WORLD

Trent knew that his anger came from the cave and that it was dangerous. To succeed, he had to remain calm and clear-headed. The last of Ortega's men had come out of the jungle. Now that the fire had caught, they had fed wet branches onto the flames to smoke the mosquitoes away. The men were gathered to windward, crouched shapes heating rations.

Outlined against the flames, the marines reminded Trent of his past and of terrorist encampments, freedom fighters, and always his

159

target somewhere in the group. It was the sense of depression that was similar, men who had suffered too few victories rather than too many defeats. In those days Trent had never considered defeat. Now he looked up at the volcano . . .

19

Every radio station in the Philippines had broadcast pleas to the population to evacuate the east side of the island. The government geophysicists were powerless to enforce evacuation, nor were the scientists responsible for the islanders' distrust of all pronouncements emanating from Manila. They had done their best.

For the past two weeks the volcano had been easing its pressure up through a fault that led into the lava pool within the crater. The lava pool had acted as a safety valve. Now the fault had collapsed and the pressure had only one route of escape, a weakness in the east flank of the cone. The scientists had foreseen the collapse of the fault and they knew of the weakness in structure. They had calculated that a force equivalent to between eighty and one hundred and fifteen tons of TNT would build before the volcano exploded.

In fact the pressure within the volvano was already equivalent to seventy tons of TNT when the fault collapsed.

Over the next hour the pressure rose to one hundred and one tons.

The scientists' instruments gave some indication of what was happening. They called all radio stations to broadcast a final warning to the islanders but the volcano's silence confirmed the islanders' suspicions – no false information could persuade them to abandon their land.

Ortega was reasonably certain that Trent had hidden the *Golden Girl* near the Samal Islands. He was almost certain that Trent remained in the area of the village and, if so, he was one hundred percent certain that Trent would make a break that night. There was only one logical direction for Trent to go and Ortega ordered all but six of his men back to the coast at 19.56 hours. Two men were already in position, one at the base of the cliff while the second had hidden in the machine-gun emplacement up on the crest. The two men were a long shot and one that Ortega didn't have faith in, but he liked to cover himself. The remaining four accompanied him down-river in an inflatable assault craft.

Trent watched the spotlight in the inflatable sweep the banks as the marines cast off. He could follow the progress of the main body of Ortega's men by the slap of their boots in the mud. They had taken the path to the coast.

Now it was easy, but he remained cautious as he ran crouched over, zig-zagging towards the cave.

Smoking was against orders and Commander Ortega was a harsh disciplinarian. The marine he had left on guard at the foot of the cliff cupped a cigarette behind his back. His name was Vicente Ramada; his fellow marines called him Ram.

What light there was came from the stars and from the glow along the rim of the crater. At first all Ram saw was movement and a darker patch of shadow, so he wasn't certain. Then, because Trent ran in such a low crouch, Ram thought that he was probably one of the pirates' dogs. Ram was a country boy and had owned a mongrel that had pined to death when he joined the marines. Putting two fingers to his mouth, he was about to whistle but now the shadow was less than a hundred yards away. It was the wrong shape for a dog; a fellow marine would have signalled him.

Ram was twenty-one years old and about to make his fortune. He began to sweat and excitement pulsed through his entire body. His hands shook slightly as he raised the rifle. He held his breath to steady himself. He couldn't see the foresight well enough in the dark so he fired as if using a shotgun, weight forward on his left foot as he swung six or seven inches ahead of the man. Excitement made him snatch at the trigger and he lost the rhythm of his swing. Then the mountain exploded.

Trent dived flat at the first shot and rolled fast, distancing himself from the shooter's last point of aim. He was angry with himself for having forgotten the two men who had melted into the jungle soon after the helicopter's departure. He had the one marine, the shooter, pinpointed twenty yards to the left of the ladder up to the cave.

He felt the earth shake perhaps a half-second prior to the massive explosion. The pressure had blasted the collapsed pipe clear below the lava pool only seconds before the east flank of the cone fractured.

A vertical spray of lava fountained five hundred feet. Massive rocks, some a ton in weight, speckled the spray. The rocks fell and thundered down the cone, loosening avalanches of ancient pumice that swept down the volcano and across the tiny fields so painstakingly carved and tended by the peasants. Huts were crushed to splinters and buried, their owners squashed like fleas as they tried to escape. As their fields had been smothered, so the thunder smothered their screams.

A slit opened high on the east flank of the volcano, much as if a skirt had been unzipped on the side, a skirt that was too tight on a woman unfashionably plump. Except that it was lava swelling through the slit.

The lava ran surprisingly slowly. It flowed down over the clinker left by previous eruptions and spread along a low ridge that had been the lip of the crater hundreds of years ago. The dip filled and the lava oozed on over the ridge, but divided now into six streams.

The cliff was already weakened by rockets, now great chunks fell loose. Terrified, Ram fled down hill. He ran blind with fear for a hundred yards before remembering the man he'd shot at. He spun round and saw the flames tower over the cliff edge. As the flames leapt, so did the shadows, twisting and turning as they pranced like the demons that had afflicted his childhood nights. It seemed to him in his terror that the end of the world had come and that he was to be punished for the massacre of the women and children – the innocents. He knew that his punishment was deserved because he had been brought up in the truth by Seventh Day Adventist parents – parents who had wept for his soul when he escaped into the marines. He couldn't think properly and he was gabbling prayers as he sprayed the area over to his left where he had last seen the man. His heart was trying to escape from his chest and he wasn't sure that he was firing in the right direction. He spun wildly and emptied the rest of the clip back up the slope then grabbed a fresh clip from his belt. His fingers wouldn't work and he couldn't control the words of his prayers anymore. 'God!' he cried, that was all – over and over again.

Trent's movements were so slow as to be imperceptible and the thunder of the volcano covered any sound he made as he crept to within fifty feet of the young marine. He paused, crouched low in the shadows of a ruined hut, scanning the surroundings for Ortega's second man. The earth shuddered and the landscape seemed to melt and flow in tune to the leaping flames. The barrel of the first marine's M-16 glowed orange in the light and flame spurted from the muzzle as he hosed the slope. Trent watched him fumble as he tried to slap a fresh clip into the breach. The Filipino's panic made him unpredictable and Trent took his chance, running at him out of the hellish backdrop. Bearded and naked but for a coil of rope, Trent must have seemed a devil or a monster and the marine fell to his knees, shaking and gibbering.

Trent struck him once on the neck with the hard edge of his hand and dragged him quickly into deep shadows where he strapped the young man's hands and feet and jammed a gag between his teeth. Ram was small for a marine, light in frame, and Trent took his jacket and his boots for the girl before hiding him beneath a layer of charred thatch.

Fatigue had made Trent careless but now he was alert for the second guard and heard the thin edge of a scream whisper through the rumbling thunder of the eruption.

The massive explosion jerked Jay back from the very edge of disintegration. The ground beneath her trembled and falling clay triggered the instinct to protect her eyes. Instinct goaded her into retreat from the edge and brought with it fear as flame reflections danced across the cave mouth. Then the mouth of the cave collapsed and she was relieved because the flames had gone.

She was awake now in herself and piece by piece the lesser needs of living pressed their demands. Thirst. She recalled that a man had brought her here. Trent. He had opened the iron box, the box in which she had imprisoned Wong Fu. But he was weak and she had watched Wong Fu strangle him.

The earth shook again. Clay and rock broke free of the roof and came to rest close to her feet. She saw suddenly that the box was a dream. She saw through it and saw her own entombment. She saw

Trent as a dark beard and dark eyes. She cursed him for abandoning her, cursed him for his weakness and for being a man. He had even allowed the shooting of her family against the wall when she wanted them alive so that she could punish them and punish them, rather than have them escape into the tranquillity of death.

But that too was a dream and she smacked herself in the face. In doing so, she touched the water bottle that the man had left for her. She drank greedily. Then she fumbled around her in the dark and the terror of entombment returned. She screamed her rage at Trent – weak, stupid, irresponsible. How dared he deny her vengeance? She screamed his name and beat on the floor.

Trent saw, lit by the glow of the molten lava, the mouth of the cave collapse. He could have climbed straight to her but there was the second marine and he searched first along the bottom of the cliff but couldn't find him so he was probably up on the crest. Ortega liked to set backstops.

The pirates had hewn steps up the cliff face to the halfway point above which a series of short ladders connected narrow landings; the ladders had been smashed by falling rock and the landings had collapsed. However Trent had marked a second route the morning of the dawn assault. The way led up a vertical crack in the cliff between three and four feet wide and six feet deep – what mountaineers call a chimney. A few wizened trees and bushes had rooted in the walls of the chimney so there were hand- and footholds but it was a hell of a climb to make with the girl. The marine must have heard the shooting immediately before the eruption and be on guard.

Atmospherics caused by the eruption might have stopped him radioing through to Ortega. Once he made contact, reinforcements would race up-river in the inflatable. Trent imagined being trapped in the beam of the spotlight with the girl on his back. Rifle practice. He might survive the fall if he hadn't climbed too high. He wondered what expression he would see in Ortega's eyes when the commander delivered the *coup de grace*. He realised that he was losing self-control and thought instead of the marine guarding the cliff top. He had to remove him before taking the girl up.

The marine must know that the chimney was the only route. There was an armed man in the vicinity which made looking down the chimney a dumb risk. There was a chance, Trent thought. Not much of a chance, but a chance. He would have to get it exactly right and it depended on the marine not looking down.

The rocks had stopped falling. He brushed the thatch off Ram and dragged him over to the cliff ten feet to one side of the chimney. The marine had to look as if he had fallen out of the chimney and Trent rearranged his bonds to pin his left arm across his chest and his right arm behind his back. Ram was shivering and he kept looking pleadingly at Trent.

Trent patted him on the shoulder: 'Try and relax. You'll be all right.'

The chimney was an easy climb but his arm slowed him. He knew what he had to do. Back when he had worked for the Department, he had done this sort of thing without much thought, part of the job. Now he was self-employed. Since his activation of the radio beacon, there had been a lot of deaths. He didn't mind about the pirates – getting killed was a risk of their profession. He minded about their families, minded very much. The pit and the snake-bite had been *you or me* situations. It was different with the man up above. Trent was the hunter and he felt the familiar emptiness inside him that came with the fear of what he had to do.

Picking his handholds was easy in the light thrown by the eruption. A continuity of minor explosions reminded him of a battery of 88 Howitzers: *Kapwumpff, Kapwumpff* went the shells. One gun was always loaded faster than the others so there was no rhythm to a barrage. Sometimes he had been on the receiving end and sometimes protected by the fire; a few times, when the fire had been ordered to cover his infiltration or homecoming, the shells had hit round him, and he had clung to the ground, cursing and swearing to himself that he would kill the goddamned incompetent son of a bitch of a commander. That was the worst, having what was called friendly fire wipe you out.

Here the air was thick with sulphur rather than cordite. The soil was always particular to a place: he had become expert on both its different perfumes and its texture. This cliff was a friable mix of clay and pumice spread thin on limestone, clean-smelling and dairy-fresh, with a trace of dampness and he could smell, through the earth perfume, the resin of the stunted trees which clung in the clefts of the rock, the slightly bitter scent of their leaves.

Fifteen feet to the top of the chimney and he found a fault in the edge of the chimney wall. A tree a little above the fault and on the opposite side of the chimney seemed solidly rooted. He had about ten feet of rope left. He tied a stirrup in one end and tied the other end at root level to the tree trunk so that he would be able to stand in the stirrup. He needed to be outside of the chimney and he felt along the cliff face for a crack. What he found wasn't big but he forced the tip of the machete into it. He couldn't get much purchase from inside the chimney but he worked the handle up and down, finally anchoring around six inches of the blade into the rock. Six inches of climber's spike would have been ample, but all a climber saw of a piton was the ring or a couple of inches necessary for a foot- or finger-hold. With the machete there were twenty inches sticking out which made it look more precarious than it probably was.

Withdrawing the machete, he rammed the blade deep into the fault along the chimney edge and levered the rock loose. He thought that it would be funny if the blade broke. A death sentence . . .

The chunk of rock was roughly triangular in section and must have weighed a hundred pounds. Trent waited for a quieter moment before yanking back hard on the handle. He yelled in terror as the rock tore loose and plummeted down. Seventy feet to the bottom of the cliff – the rock crashed into an outcrop half way, bounced clear, and shattered well away from the Filipino, Ram, whom Trent had laid out at the cliff foot.

Trent was already moving. He rammed the machete back into the slit outside the chimney and draped the rope behind the blade. One foot in the stirrup, he swung out of the chimney with his left arm wrapped round the rope. The tree supported his weight and the machete held him outside the chimney.

The fear knifed up through his belly into his throat as the tree moved, or perhaps there had been a little slack in one of the knots in the rope. He looked up rather than down. Down only mattered if he was falling – and then only for a few seconds. He imagined the marine up on the clifftop. The marine's first reaction would be to report in over the radio that someone was in the chimney and might have fallen. Ortega would ask which – that much was certain. Checking wasn't easy. The one thing the marine didn't want to do was to stick his head into the chimney and have it blown off.

*

167

The marine had been christened Ernesto Louis. He was twenty-three years old and a first year college drop-out, not from laziness nor from lack of intelligence but because he was the eldest of seven children and the rest of the family would have slowly starved on what his father earned.

Ernesto had heard the climber and had thought of nothing but the reward money while he waited for Trent to reach the top of the chimney. Instead there had been a scuffle and a scream and then the crash of rock down below. Hopefully the climber had fallen, but Ernesto didn't believe in taking unnecessary risks. Nor did he intend sharing the reward, and he would have to share if he summoned help.

The Commander had ordered him to carry a flashlight as well as a rope so he could find his way back down the cliff in the dark. He tied the flashlight to a stick and crawled to the edge. Pushing the stick out over the edge, he weighted the end with a rock and counted to ten. No one shot the light out so he stuck his head over and looked down. A body sprawled faced down a little to the left of the bottom of the chimney. The body wore shorts and a T-shirt. He had one arm up behind his back at a strange angle, probably broken by the fall. His head moved under the light. He wriggled his knees up, tipped over onto his back, and jerked his head back and forth. His other arm lay across his chest at an odd angle. One arm back and one in front was an artistic method of tying a man to look as if he had fallen out of the chimney and broken both arms. Ernesto would have been deceived but for the man's movements. He presumed Ram was the prisoner.

Ernesto switched his thoughts to the climber. The climber was in the chimney and he wasn't going to come out of his own free will – that was for sure. The reward got paid, dead or alive. Ernesto hunted round and found a rock about eighteen inches in diameter. He rolled the rock over and, keeping well back, tipped it into the chimney. The next rock he found was a little bigger.

The first rock shot down the chimney like a pinball. Halfway down it hit a projecting rock, leapt clear of the cliff and crashed to the ground. Trent hoped that it hadn't hit the marine he'd tied up. Trent was less than ten feet down from the head of the chimney. He heard the marine huff and puff as he heaved the next rock towards the edge. The rock bounced against the side of the chimney closest to Trent, bounced across to the other side, then back, and smashed into the root of the tree to which Trent's rope was anchored.

Trent felt the rope shudder as the rock hit the root. The rock shot on down and hit the same projection as the first one. The projection exploded like a shrapnel bomb while the falling rock spun out of the chimney and landed some thirty metres from the cliff foot.

The rope slipped down a little. Trent peered into the chimney and saw that the tree had tilted out five degrees toward the opposing wall. The rope shuddered again as he looked up and the tree bent a further few inches. The next rock would tear the tree out. Trent could hear the marine cursing and panting up above as if he'd found a real monster.

Trent thought of climbing down to the next tree but reaching the nearest one strong enough to support him would take too long. He thought that it was a question of choice, the clean drop down the cliff, or swing back into the chimney and have the rock hit his head. The rock was the marine's weapon while falling seemed to be more his own choice so he stayed out on the rope and felt it give a couple more inches. It was a matter of seconds now and he tried to pray as dirt broke off the chimney lip. He was frightened, not specifically of death or of pain, but frightened and empty inside himself, and angry at himself for letting the girl down. The marine grunted as he heaved the rock a half-roll more. It was a big rock and down it came. It hit the tree and Trent fell.

The volcano thundered as Ernesto heaved the rock over those last inches into the chimney. He knelt, sweat-drenched, and with his chest heaving. It had been one hell of a rock, almost as big as the U into which he'd pushed it. A miracle might have saved the climber from the first two rocks but not from the third. Ernesto watched the lava spew out of the vent in the side of the cone. He thought of the spill oozing toward the fields and felt some pity for the peasants, but they were Muslims and didn't speak Tagalog. He knew that he ought to call in on the radio and report to the commander that the man they'd been hunting was dead but the reward still preyed on his mind. He didn't trust the Chinese, any Chinese. The Chinese and the Jews. Those were the people. They owned everything and you couldn't trust them. Money was all they cared for. They would do anything for money.

Once he had the body he would be absolutely safe. Not even a Chinaman could argue with a dead body. He wondered how the marine down below would tell it. He and Ram came from different islands and weren't close friends, but they weren't enemies. However, Ram might like to get his hands on a share of the reward. Conflicting stories would give the Chinaman an excuse to institute an enquiry. The investigators would demand a share of the reward from whoever they awarded it to – that was certain. In the end there'd be nothing left.

It wasn't fair, he thought as he rolled a rock to the edge of the cliff. The Chinese had everything, the Chinese and the Jews. He tipped the rock down in Ram's direction, but without aiming, and fetched another. He pushed six over in all before focusing the flashlight beam on the foot of the cliff. At least one of the rocks had found its target. He would report that Ram had been killed by a rock fall but he needed to untie him first. Now that the ladders had been destroyed, the cleft in the rock was the only way down – the chimney. He couldn't seen the climber but he wasn't worried. The body had probably got squashed against a tree on the way down.

Ernesto felt confident and pleased with himself as he strolled over to the chimney.

20

The rock was too big for the chimney. It ripped the tree out by the roots, fell a further six feet and jammed with the tree crushed between it and the chimney wall. The rope jerked tight. Trent had accepted death. Now he had been given life. At first he didn't understand. When he did understand, the fear flooded in with greater strength than ever before. He didn't dare move. He thought that the slightest movement might free the rock or tear the rope or the tree free, or the volcano would shake the chimney open. The thunder of each fresh eruption shook him. He forced himself to count slowly, breathing in and out through his nose to the count of ten until his nerves steadied.

The eruptions subsided. From above came the scrape of stone on stone as the marine rolled a fresh boulder towards the edge. Trent nearly let go the rope to have done with it – *it* was the fear, thick and choking in his throat and sharp under the breast bone, sickeningly empty in the stomach. He was tired, desperately tired, and the pain from his wounds came in waves. He wanted done with it.

He had wanted done with it ever since his flight from his father's need. He had been eight years old – that was a reason rather than an excuse. Trent didn't believe in excuses. His thoughts went to Jay and he was ashamed. Think, he told himself. For Christ's sake, think.

The marine heaved the rock over the edge. Trent heard it glance off the cliff before smashing into the ground down to his right. Then came another rock, and another – six in all. The rocks were directed at the marine Trent had left tied up. The reward had to be the reason and disgust drove Trent up over the boulder that blocked his way to the cliff top.

His heart seemed to explode as the boulder shifted under his weight. However it was merely settling deeper into the constriction. He forced himself on and sat cross-legged on the cool stone. His seat had been designed to kill him. He smiled, a dry, wintry smile, and drew his knife.

The marine's footsteps sounded relaxed and easy as he strolled towards the chimney. The loom of his flashlight lit the rim, forcing Trent to protect his night vision with his left hand. The marine's head appeared, a featureless silhouette. Trent threw but knew that he had missed the man's throat.

He clawed the last few feet up the chimney and rolled clear, eyes hunting for his antagonist. The Filipino had staggered a half-dozen steps back from the chimney before his legs collapsed. The knife had entered on an upward slant under his chin. He held it by the hilt in both hands while the blood spouted down his chest. He didn't move his head but his eyes followed Trent.

Trent found the Filipino's battle dressing in his butt-pack. Whipping the knife out of the wound, he held the marine in his arms with the dressing damming the wound. Both men knew that it was a matter of minutes.

Ernesto felt the strength dribble out round the edge of the pad. He wanted to explain about Ram, about the rocks. That the Chinaman was to blame. That it was also the fault of the Jews. That the Jews had crucified Our Lord, Jesus Christ, who is now in Heaven and sits by the right hand of God, His Father.

Ernesto wanted so badly to explain, but then he thought that it didn't matter because God would understand. He relaxed then, and smiled his thanks up at the stranger and floated free into the marble court at the end of which stood the golden throne so brightly lit that he was unable to see His Face but he had no fear at all as he opened himself to judgment. Then he shuddered, but that was only his body and he had no further need of it. Then it became dark and suddenly there was terror in him, terror that God had withdrawn his radiance. He tried to scream but it was too late.

Trent saw the smile. The Filipino shuddered and Trent thought that he was dead. But terror entered suddenly into the man's eyes and his body arched as if he was trying to escape. The strain burst something inside him. Then he was dead and Trent laid him aside.

Searching the clifftop with the flashlight, Trent found the marine's M-16, Colt, and a coil of light rope. He rolled a rock to the chimney and dropped it. The fifth rock finally freed the blockage and he clambered down. Ram was dead and Trent untied his bonds, not because it made a difference to what he had to do, but to disassociate himself from the killing. He hid the body again under burnt thatch so that the girl wouldn't see it.

The yellow light of the volcano dimly painted the trees and the river with jaundice; the stench of sulphur and of burnt huts and of charred flesh was thick as soup; he thought of hell and retched violently; his stomach was empty and nothing came. Cursing himself for giving way, he wiped his mouth on the back of his forearm, picked up Ram's machete and looped the rope over his shoulder before jogging across the clearing to the ladder.

She had dragged at the fallen rock until her hands bled. Two of her nails ripped free of the quick and the pain stopped her. She heard metal pry at the rock from the other side and she flinched and scuttled backwards until her back was against the rear wall.

The fall was of loose rock. Trent levered the rock loose with the machete, manhandling them back left or right of the ladder.

He said: 'It's all right, Miss Li. I'll get you out.'

He repeated himself again and again while he worked. He didn't wonder whether she heard or not. It was more an incantation that kept her alive in his mind and kept at bay the thought that she might be crushed or already dead of thirst or hunger – or dead because she hadn't wanted to live. That was always the greatest danger for those who had been tortured and defiled.

He dug the machete deep behind a rock and almost fell as the blade slipped through into emptiness. She could be buried under the fall so he was careful, easing the rock out, then sliding it over the slippery chicken manure. Another rock came free and he saw the darkness that was inside the cave. He didn't dare shine the flashlight in case he panicked her. He needed to be in the cave and able to hold her.

'It's all right, Miss Li. I'll get you out,' he said. 'Trent. I'm the man who brought you here from the hut. I'll get you out. Remember, I promised. You're going to be all right.'

Three more rocks and he was able to slip through. He spread his fingers over the glass of the flashlight and shone the filtered beam at the roof so that they were both lit gently by indirect light. Covered in chicken dung, crouched and clinging to herself, she looked like a creature in Bedlam.

He said again, 'Trent. Do you remember? I hid you here. We need to move, Miss Li.'

Hate he accepted as natural, but he saw flatness, that was all. Like a wall. That too, was familiar to him from the past. He wasn't to know that she judged him by the kindness in his voice as weak and ineffectual. He held out the combat jacket to her but she hadn't the will to put it on and he had to thread first one arm into a sleeve, then the other.

Dehydration was a danger. He searched for the water bottle and offered it to her but she didn't take it. She was like a window dummy. She didn't even react when he tilted the bottle to her lips and the water trickled down her chin.

The chain added to his difficulties. He looped it over his wrist and tried to guide her forward through the gap in the rock fall. She wouldn't walk.

He held her by the shoulders, wanting to shake her but not doing so: 'Miss Li, please, you have to help.'

She didn't answer and he swore under his breath and said: 'Listen, Miss Li, I'm going to tie your wrists so I can carry you.'

He strapped her wrists with the rope and manoeuvred her through the gap to the edge of the cave. Then he looped her arms round his neck so that she hung down his back. Her weight threatened to pull him over so he lay on the cave floor, easing backward over the edge onto the ladder.

The distance to the ground was less than half the distance he would have to climb in the chimney but already the pain in his neck and across his shoulders was intense. He wasn't sure that he could manage the climb. He thought of the girl and he thought of Manolo Ortega. He wanted Ortega to lose.

The dead marines' radio silence wouldn't worry the commander, not at first. He would blame atmospherics. Eventually he would send a patrol up-river in the inflatable. The patrol might find the corpse Trent had hidden under the thatch. They had to climb the chimney and find the second marine and report back.

Then what?

Helicopters weren't an option; volcanic dust would block the air-

174

filters and chew the gears to bits. No, the chase had to be on foot and there was no point in Ortega ordering the four or five men of the first patrol forward unless he wanted to give Trent target practice. Fifteen men was a minimum and a full complement for the inflatable. Trent had only seen the one boat. Say twenty minutes to get the men ready, another twenty to get them to the base of the cliff, a further twenty minutes before they were ready to move out from the top of the chimney. One hour.

He sat Jay down at the ladder and manoeuvred her feet into Ram's boots. She wouldn't eat from the can he opened and there wasn't time for persuasion. She wouldn't walk so he dragged her to the foot of the chimney, then hoisted her onto his back. The rules said to pick an achievable objective and he never looked beyond the next handhold. He promised himself rest breaks on the way up, not in distance but in counts to a hundred. He counted slowly and used the counting to control his breathing. The pain had to be accepted but separated from what he was doing, part of the background, as was the volcano and the sulphur fumes. He slowed his counting and, on reaching one hundred, urged himself on.

He told himself: 'You can do it! Come on, one more handhold.' Then: 'Push, for Chris' sake! One more. Come on – and again.'

'You said I could rest,' he argued.

'Okay, but one more.'

Fingers tight on a point of rock, he bowed into the chimney at a slight angle to spread the girl's weight off his neck and shoulders and across his back. His right foot rested on a thin ledge four inches long on one side of the chimney; his left foot dug into a hole left by a stone that had come loose on the other side. Most of his weight was on his left leg which was straight and he had drawn his right knee up to gain the new toehold. He searched above and recognised a tree root from his earlier climb, but the root was beyond his reach now that he carried the girl. It had been like that all the way and he was so damned tired. He closed his eyes for a second.

His other self, the driver, said, 'So give up. The girl's not important.'

He swore either back at himself or at the self that had nearly given up. He wasn't sure which. 'At least open your goddamned eyes,' he said.

He sought for a closer purchase and found a small lip of rock about six inches above the cup that held his right foot. He thought that he could get his foot into it, however his right thigh was already horizontal. Lift his knee higher and the muscles lost too much thrust to be able to raise the two of them. It had been so easy the first time. Like climbing a staircase. He cursed again, cursed to stop himself closing his eyes.

A crack in the left corner of the chimney opened some four inches higher than the ridge where his foot rested. The crack rose for eighteen inches and was wide enough for a foothold. He had to move his foot forward and up to get it into the crack and the new position would be more upright.

He gripped hard, lurched to the right, and shot his left foot up and forward into the base of the crack. Feet spread, knees bent, and the girl on his back, he imagined that they must look like a pair of mating frogs. His new position put too much weight on his throat and shoulders. He breathed carefully, getting the oxygen into his lungs, then he shifted his weight again on to his right foot and raised his left foot to the top of the crack. He straightened both legs and shifted one hand to the root, now the other hand, then his left foot back from the crack and up onto a bump of stone. Eighteen inches nearer the summit – that was how the whole climb went.

He said: 'Nearly there. Come on. You can make it.'

Then, in a moment free of volcanic eruption, he heard the purr of an outboard motor. He thought that it wasn't fair.

His other self said: 'No one said it was fair.'

'To hell with you,' he said, and the cynic laughed.

Sweat stung his eyes and made his hand slippery. Mosquitoes circled like Stukas. He hated bugs. He wanted to look up to see how much further he had to climb, but looking up wouldn't speed the climb or make it easier; neither would looking down at the river slow the inflatable.

'Move,' he told himself. 'Move. It's not that far. Ten more handholds.'

He reached the narrows where the big rock had stuck. Fifteen more feet, but he had to rest. No way could he go on. He tried to steady his breathing. The pain had spread from his shoulders and back deep into his lungs, his forearm felt as if it would split open, and the wound in his thigh leaked. He had to ease the girl's weight, if only for a moment. He turned side-on in the chimney and thrust backward so that she was pinned against the upper slope of the narrows. Ten seconds, he promised.

He couldn't help looking down.

The spotlight on the inflatable flashed between the trees close into the bank a half mile below the dock. Looking up the chimney was the first thing one of them would do. Then *BANG!* and it would be over.

Damn them, he thought. He breathed in round the pain, heaved himself round, and dug a foot into the hole left by the tree roots. The next handhold seemed a mile away.

'Up!' he shouted. He swore now in a steady stream that he could hear above the volcano's rumble. Swearing while rivers of sweat spilled over his eyes. He thought that his muscles would burst and of how easy and painless the fall would be.

'Try it once more,' he urged. 'You don't make it, you can let go.'

He could see the edge now and he had lied to himself. Three more changes of hand grip. Three more. He knew that he could do it or that he had to do it. He stopped cursing and fought to clear his head. There went his hands, there, there, and there. The footholds were obvious and easy because of the rocks the marine had hurled down.

'Easy,' he promised. 'Come on, Patrick. Pray to God, you cowardly son of a bitch. Our Father who art in Heaven . . .'

The outboard engine roared then suddenly cut as the helmsman spun the inflatable in against the dock. Trent touched the lip of the chimney but it was too far for a firm grip and he dropped his hands back to a narrow shelf. Left foot up, then the right, and he thrust with his thighs for the last time. Forearms over the edge, he anchored himself with his fingertips and scrabbled with both feet for purchase. The beam of a flashlight spat at him and a man shouted. Then the beam cut out as the man dropped the flashlight and grabbed for his rifle. Shooting up at a steep angle or down are both difficult, especially in the dark. He fired on automatic. Bullets spattered the rock, the whine of ricochets mated with the sharp crackle of the rifle. Trent had one knee up over the lip. He rolled the girl off his back, scrambled after her, and dragged her clear.

He crawled across to the dead marine and found his rifle. For the moment the men below weren't dangerous. If he could disable the inflatable, reinforcements would have to come on foot. Flame from the volcano coloured the river with swirls of faded yellow; the inflatable showed as a darkening of the dock's shadow. Trent fired a long burst in a zigzag pattern.

Ortega might order the four men forward as scouts while he hurried reinforcements up the river bank. Knowing now which direction Trent had taken, he would land fresh forces on the north coast. Trent and the girl could die here on the cliff or make for the other half of the vice. It wasn't much of a choice. Keep moving and something might turn up. Perhaps the Japanese, though Trent had his doubts. He wasn't even sure which or what side Tanaka was on.

Seeking out a large boulder, he eased it down into the chimney. The boulder stuck in the narrows and he added a dozen more rocks. The barrier would delay Ortega's men for a while. They were down there somewhere and he sprayed the clearing as a reminder that Li's money had to be earned.

He took half of the rope, the dead marine's machete and his matches and cigarettes. Slinging the M-16 across his chest, he picked the girl up and draped her over his shoulders. A border of open ground separated the cliff from a thick jungle of bamboo thirty to forty feet in height. Trent followed along the edge of the open ground until he came to a narrow path leading due north. The pirates had dragged down bamboos as camouflage, turning the path into a tunnel, and he had to carry the girl piggyback. Dry fronds rustled and stalks scraped against each other in the breeze. It was a fire trap and Trent began to jog, but the girl's feet kept catching in the bamboo.

With the rocks in the chimney delaying the pursuit, he thought that he had a thirty-minute lead and at least a further hour before reinforcements reached the clifftop.

Resting sixty seconds every ten minutes, he took half an hour to break through to the open mountainside. The ground here was crumbled pumice left by previous eruptions. He set the girl down away from the bamboo. He wished that she would look at him or speak but she sat huddled within her own arms, naked but for the combat jacket and boots – and, of course, the chain. He cut four thick bamboos and a dozen thin ones and laid them beside her. Then he collected a pile of dry fronds and layered them in a loose pile in the edge of the jungle and heaped the pile with slivers of dead bamboo. He had twenty minutes at most.

He bound the thin bamboos that he had cut across the thick ones to make a litter and laid the girl on it. The volcanic ash had started to settle and he dampened a length of undershirt and tied it across her nose and did the same for himself.

'We're going to be all right,' he told her. 'Try not to worry.'

He had made stupider remarks, but not many and he imagined Tanaka making a caustic comment. Thinking of the Japanese investigator was irrationally cheering and Trent grinned to himself as he recalled the detective's Liverpool accent and repartee.

'A little something for them to think about,' he said to the girl as he knelt over the heap of dried fronds and set them alight. As the flames caught, he hefted the M-16 and fired a half clip to remind the pursuit that he was armed.

'We'd better get going,' he said to the girl, and picked up the shafts of the litter. The track led down hill and he could feel the warmth reflected off the nearest lava flow. The convex slope hid the lower reaches of the flow but none of the more distant streams of lava had stretched far enough down the mountain to threaten their escape.

There hadn't been an eruption for half an hour now and the background rumble had muted to a steady spluttering that made Trent think of a drunken giant supping hot soup. Filtered by the fine volcanic dust, the light was a dull sick yellow reflected off the continuously-replenished sulphur cloud that drifted south on the breeze.

There were no trees here; not a bush nor a blade of grass. Only the grey of old lava and the yellow and red streaks of the new flows and, up above, the vast rent in the mountain out of which the lava bubbled so hot that he could smell the heat. Every few minutes there would be a cough from the volcano and it would dribble and wear for a moment a gold feather of flame on its peak.

The bamboo had turned into a blazing wall that bent with the breeze. The fire would hold Ortega's men for a while. The litter ran true in the loose footing and was easy to drag downhill. Sharp pumice spilling into his boots was the only new hardship and he glanced back at the girl and smiled.

Below the foot of the shallow valley, the fresh scar of a massive landfall spread to the coast. He didn't want to think about the climb out of the valley and thought instead of Tanaka.

Trent had relied on people in the past – not during an operation, he had always been a loner – but to get him out. He thought, as he had done earlier, of the Good Ol' Boys. That's what they needed now – a Good Ol' Boy with a chopper. Someone who didn't give a damn for the opposition firepower and, once he'd given his word, wasn't going to wait around for some committee to reach an indecision. That was the British malaise. Terrified of making mistakes, they did nothing and called it acting responsibly. Bosnia had been a shameful example.

But he was drifting now. He had to keep control of himself. The ground dipped sharply and he saw that the valley ahead ended at the cliff edge. A landfall had dammed the foot of the valley. The lava had spread into a narrow lake some twenty metres wide. There was no way round the lava. Ortega's men were closing in behind. The only escape lay directly ahead.

21

The volcano coughed. Flames blossomed like the yellow petals of a lily and a fresh torrent of lava spilled through the rip in the side of the crater. The main river split into six streams of which the one that flowed into the steep valley extended furthest. The stream was three metres wide above the lake. The flow was slow and continual within the stream but intermittent on its surface – as if it were paint from a tube squeezed length by length across a palette.

Trent stood a few feet back from the edge of the flow. The heat dried the last of the moisture from his facecloth and he removed it before looking back at the girl on the litter. He tried to smile but dust, rimming his eyes, had caked in his sweat so that his face was stiff and felt as if it would crack.

There was irony in their being blocked by a narrow stream that he could leap but which was too wide for him to cross when burdened by the girl. He sat beside the litter, arms wrapped round his knees and watched the colours of the stream darken where it cooled at the edges. The side of the valley rose steeply the other side of the stream. It would have been quite a climb dragging the litter. The marines must be less than an hour behind. If he climbed back a hundred yards he could trap them outlined against the sky as they crossed the ridge but there wasn't any point.

He would have to shoot the girl rather than have her fall into their hands. He would do it quickly from the back so that she wouldn't know. And then what? Run for it? He didn't think so. Neither shooting her nor running were very gallant and he smiled at the word, watching her eyes, empty and unfocused.

Hope was a cardinal virtue so presumably despair was a mortal sin; though of less importance to the Pope than the use of contraceptives. Trent didn't have a family but he did have the girl.

Wrapping her foot and lower leg in his combat jacket, he buried it in pumice with the chain snaking out. He spooned lava onto the chain with the machete. The heat faded out of the lava. He brushed it away, adding fresh until the iron glowed dark red. He changed the lava one more time, then positioned himself to shield the girl, raised his left arm to protect his eyes, and emptied the rifle into a glowing link. The bullets sprayed chips of pumice that bit into his arms and legs and into his face where his forearm left it uncovered but the chain flattened and cracked. He piled hot lava again and hammered the machete into the crack. Finally the link opened sufficiently and he levered the chain free. The anklet and six links remained. He showed the freed chain to the girl before flinging it into the stream and he grinned at her:

'We're not beaten yet, Miss Li. Watch.'

Selecting one of the thick bamboo staves from the litter, he jammed the end out into the centre of the lava and vaulted the stream. Flames burst from the stave and he rubbed them out in the pumice before vaulting back.

Squatting, he grinned again and said: 'Easy. You have to do it, Miss Li. That, or have your grandfather's men kill you. Don't give him the satisfaction.'

She laughed at him but she was invisible and he didn't see. He was stupid and he was weak, she thought as she listened to him plead.

'Please,' he begged: 'Please, Miss Li . . .'

She hugged herself with glee at his weakness and put on a *La di da* British accent as she mocked him.

'Please, please, please,' she mocked: 'Please, please, please.'

He didn't hear. There was so much anxiety in his eyes – a dog, she thought, a labrador begging for attention. She patted the top of his head: 'Good boy, good boy.'

He acted deaf and she was tempted to slap his face but she needed him. He would make a good tool. She could tell. She had to reel him in like a fish and slip him into her net. She saw him in the net dying as he struggled for breath and she giggled as she watched his gills fan open. She held the net low over the stream so that he saw and smelt the water. She watched his eyes glaze and his gills flutter. She thought that if she poked him, the dent would stay as it did on fish that had been too long on the fishmonger's slab.

'Not quite fresh,' she said in a mincing voice and she thought what fun that those should be the last words he heard. She spat at him, hoping that he would feel the spittle in his final moments, feel her acid contempt for him, for all men; feel her hatred.

Then she heard her old nurse cough behind her and she suddenly remembered that she needed this man for a little while and she brought him back out of the net, out of the fish.

He touched her forearm.

'We don't have much time,' he said: 'Please, Miss Li. Make this one effort.'

He was already hers but she needed to commit him. She saw her grandfather and Wong Fu and the men in the hut – no, the men in the hut were already dead. But the others . . .

'Promise me,' she ordered.

He thought that something showed in her eyes. Her facecloth was dry and he took it off, sprinkling it with water. Then, holding the bottle to her lips, he dribbled water until she swallowed. She spoke but he had to crouch with his ear close before he understood that she was asking him to promise.

He promised.

He said it twice, so that she could be sure of him: 'I promise, Miss Li. I promise. Now will you try?'

He supported her beneath the arms as she stood shakily beside the lava stream. She had a tough body, however slight in bone structure.

'Try your legs, work them a little so they aren't stiff.'

Kneeling, he chafed her calves.

'You have to be quick,' he warned: 'In with the pole and across before the bamboo burns. It's easy but you have to be quick.'

He stood and handed her a pole. 'Feel it.'

She didn't look at him.

He was unable to sense what was inside her but her fingers gripped well as she hefted the pole. He thought that she would be all right. But he was frightened for her, frightened of the pole slipping and of her falling into the lava.

The pole he had given her was the one he had used. Shortened by fire, it was lighter than the others. There was no need for her to run at the stream – a couple of paces to capture her rhythm, then in with the pole, and swing. He rehearsed her quietly, holding her by the elbow as if he could squeeze into her the way it must be done. Her eyes had gone flat again and he couldn't tell if she understood.

She lifted the pole and he prayed suddenly, deep inside himself . . .

The lava was beautiful, almost white in parts and with flow-curls of yellow and orange, and with dark red and black borders. The smell of its heat filled her with joy. She placed the bamboo stave in Wong Fu's chest and pushed. Toppling back, he floated on the surface. His agony brought her joy. Then she became bored and poked him down. The spurt of flame as his head disappeared made her smile. She turned to the man, Trent, and asked for her grandfather. Instead, he shook her, and took the pole out of her hands.

At first she had put the pole only on the surface of the stream and it was already burning when she thrust it into the lava. She thrust it slowly, as if pushing against an obstruction.

He said, 'You have to do it fast, Miss Li.'

He demonstrated again with a fresh stave. The stream had widened in the twenty minutes they had been on its bank and he held her by the elbow, placing the shortened pole in her hands.

'Don't think, do it,' he said: 'It's absolutely safe, Miss Li. Come on, we'll do it together.' He picked up one of the other poles. 'Ready? Right. Let's go.'

He sailed over and turned to find her watching him. She hadn't moved and he cursed, swinging back across the stream and again stubbed out the flames on the pole.

He said, 'Miss Li, your grandfather's men are getting close. You have to do it, you have to do it now.'

He had to put his ear almost to her lips to hear her whisper: 'Promise me.'

'I promise,' he said. He didn't care what he promised. He had to get her across and up over the next ridge. They would be sitting ducks caught out on the open flank.

'I promise,' he repeated. He said it again to make quite sure that she heard, then he said: 'But promising won't help if I'm dead. And we're both going to be dead if you don't get over the stream. So do it for me. Do it for me now, Miss Li. Come on, we'll do it together. It's easier that way. Ready. Okay, so it's one, two, three, and we go.'

He counted to three and he shouted at her: 'Go!'

Even as he shouted, he saw that there was no need because she had decided to cross. She vaulted easily. He tossed her pole into the stream, vaulted back for the rifle and clipped the water bottle to his belt. He burnt the shortened pole, vaulted over to join the girl and burnt that pole too.

Dampening their facecloths, he tied them in place. The volcano coughed and he looked up to see fresh lava belch from the vent. The marines would have difficulty crossing the stream.

'We've burnt our poles,' he said with a quick grin, and took her hand to lead her up the bank.

She didn't smile and she was looking back. A scuffle of falling pumice came from the ridge. He threw her down and moments later heard the sharp rattle of an M-16. The pursuers were blinded by the light from the stream and the bullets struck high to the right.

If the marines had sense, two of them would come down the slope while the other two remained on the high ground to give covering fire. Killing the first two marines when they reached the lava would be easy but he couldn't kill the other two so there was no sense in it – and he didn't believe that he had the right, not unless it made an awful lot of sense.

The lava spread at about an inch a minute. If he could delay them a little longer, they wouldn't be able to cross. Somehow he had to keep them night blind.

Skimming a couple of bullets out of a clip, he crawled away from the girl. He stuck the bullets in the pumice with their percussion caps pointing to the lava. He placed one bullet a foot from the lava and the other two feet away. He had only crawled a couple of yards when the first bullet exploded. Immediately he was in the middle of a fusillade but he kept crawling. The second one exploded and there was more firing.

He reached the girl. He didn't think that there was much point in explaining his plan but he tried while he thumbed the bullets from three of the last four clips. He arranged the bullets in clumps of five with two inches between each bullet and each clump two to three yards further down stream and a few inches further back from the edge.

The heat fired the first clump of bullets, a few seconds separating each shot. A one hundred and fifty yard climb would bring them to the next crest. He tried to lead the girl but she stuck like a mule so he slung her over his shoulders.

The marines hosed the border of the stream and a ricochet came close. He wondered how many bullets they carried – six magazines plus one loaded and two bandoleers was standard US issue and they were trained according to the US manual. Not much hope of their running dry before he got the girl to the crest.

The loose footing in the pumice added to the strain of the climb and he breathed heavily, staggering to a halt a third of the way up. Tipping the girl down, he flopped beside her as another clump of bullets fireworked. The answering fire was more cautious.

Another clump exploded and he heaved the girl up over his shoulder again. He only gained thirty yards before having to rest. Lying beside her, he said: 'Miss Li, I've about had it. You have to help.'

The extent to which she had been abused held him back from slapping her face, although it was the right thing to do according to books he'd read – they could have been the wrong books.

'Another hundred yards and we're safe,' he said.

He pulled at her arm and she turned those dead eyes on him. For a moment he thought of those who had abused her. A clump of bullets fired and he hefted her again. One hundred paces to the summit.

He told himself to keep going, counting off each step. Fear was ever-present in the background, fear of the bubbling splutter of the lava as it spewed out of the rent. Sweat and volcanic dust set like cement on his face and arms. Dust clogged his nostrils and his wounds throbbed. Sixty, he counted, sixty-one, sixty-two . . .

A wave of lava expanded the stream and a dozen of his clumps fired almost simultaneously. One man couldn't have fired that barrage and now the marines would be searching the slope for movement. Sixty-nine paces, seventy, seventy-one . . .

He told himself that he could do it. Eighty, eighty-one . . .

The slope seemed less steep. Then came shots from the far ridge and he heard one screech off the pumice not far to their left. He dropped, rolled the girl free, and lay on top of her. The marines were firing single shot and knew where to look.

Trent wrapped his combat jacket over the muzzle of his M-16 so that it would hide the first muzzle flashes. He found a shard of pumice the right size, set the M-16 to automatic with the last clip loaded, jammed the shard into the trigger guard and hurled the rifle down and out to his left. Grabbing the girl, he charged at the slope like a tank on loose tracks.

His M-16 drew a hail of return fire. The clip emptied and the marines stopped shooting. He imagined them swinging their binoculars up to quarter the slope.

Line of sight was critical, the line that gave the marksmen on the opposite ridge a clear sight of their quarry against the sky. Trent hadn't been able to see how the ground sloped beyond the crest but there might be fifty or sixty yards to cross. He and the girl would be hard targets to miss and he had run out of ruses.

His father had shot himself at his desk and his mother had driven her Jaguar into a wall at a hundred miles an hour. This girl had been raped and tortured and her grandfather was trying to have her killed which was a lot worse. That was the one truth of life – however messed up your situation was, there was always someone worse off. He was here on the volcano by his own choice, which was a lot better than being at the beck and call of the Department and of a Control who was trying to protect himself by having you killed. No one was going to kill him or kill the girl while she was in his charge.

He said, 'Ten yards to the top, Miss Li. We're going to make it.' He didn't tell her that the top was the real danger zone.

Down by the stream a man screamed – one of the marines must have tried to jump the lava. A single shot echoed up the slope and the screaming stopped.

The volcano coughed and flame blossomed along the crater edge to light a plateau the width of a playing field. They had nowhere to hide. Go for it, Trent told himself. There was another shot, then a burst.

A blow almost spun him round. He fought it and kept charging on because it was too late to do anything else. Everything was the enemy: Li and his cohorts, the heat, the stinking sulphur, the dust, the sweat that stung his eyes, the blood pumping down his back, all the pain.

He saw down to the west a gentle slope swept by the landfall and directly ahead the tail end of a lava stream. A pale narrow line marked the end of the pumice. The line was a track, and fields lay beyond and trees.

22

Bursts of flame lit the landscape and the volcano's coughing vomited lava from the side of the cone. The track was a half-mile away beyond the massive scar of the landslide, downhill and easy. There was no reason for them to be safe when they reached the track, but Trent needed a goal.

Scraps of pumice had tipped into the tops of his boots, grinding the skin away from a band an inch in width. The girl's weight seemed to sink him deeper and deeper into the loose crumble until finally he was forced to his knees. He laid her on the ground and knelt beside her. The bullet had smashed through her shoulder. Ripping his jacket, he made a pad and bound it over the wound, then strapped the upper arm against her side with the remaining strips.

She was unable to feel the pain. It was too far away. Kneeling beside her, the man, with his mumbled sympathies, was pathetic. She had ample strength to destroy him as she had destroyed the others – Wong Fu in the lava – no, that was still to happen. Deep inside her cavern, she shook herself like a dog, and chuckled with delight because the pleasure of Wong Fu's death was in the future, delicious to contemplate.

This man, with his apologies, was hers to order. She examined him from the safety of her retreat and thought that he was weak now in body as well as in spirit and that she must support him. Her servant, she thought, her tool to be kept sharp.

She looked beyond him at the shadow outlined against the flames. The shadow turned into a man with a gun. He crouched as if he were a cat but he was only a man and she giggled at his conceit. 'Kill him,' she ordered Trent.

He was stupid and didn't hear so she had to come almost to the mouth of her cavern where the pain waited. For this need, she would punish him later, but now she had to be quick because the man was close and he had a gun and was very dangerous.

'Kill him,' she ordered again, but her tool continued mumbling his apologies while he fiddled with her arm. Fiddling while Rome burns, she thought, giggling. Then the man raised his gun and hate swept everything else away.

'Kill him,' she screeched: 'Kill the son of a bitch.'

Her eyes had remained dead but he had sensed that she was watching him. Now she had shifted her attention and Trent felt rather than saw a charge of energy shake her.

He said: 'I'm so sorry, Miss Li. It's all my fault.' He said this quietly but he was listening. He stretched his shoulders back as if easing the pain, reaching behind with his right hand to massage his neck.

He groaned and said: 'We've come a long way, Miss Li.'

She looked pathetically vulnerable and he lent a little to his left so as not to shield her.

'About a mile,' he said and glanced back at the ridge they had crossed.

The marine was thirty yards away, outlined against the glow of the vent.

Trent said: 'Oh God,' and to the girl: 'I'm sorry, Miss Li.' He raised his left hand above his head and called to the soldier, 'We're both wounded. We need help.' Then he said, 'Please,' and, 'Oh God,' and, 'Please God.'

Please bring the marine that little bit closer.

The marine advanced as if wanting them to see him clearly. He held his M-16 loosely under his right arm, finger on the trigger, and drew the hand radio out of its pouch.

Twenty yards.

The girl screeched, 'Kill him.'

In that second of distraction Trent's arm flashed over. At thirty feet he could hit a playing card or a man's throat. This was sixty and he sought the larger soft target – the belly. It wasn't a killing hit. He came off the ground and charged like a sprinter off his blocks. He expected the marine to shoot but the surprise had been too great and, dropping his rifle, the marine clutched at the knife hilt.

Trent dived, driving him backwards, away from the rifle. The marine tripped and fell. Trent flipped him over onto his belly and the man screamed.

'Stretch,' Trent ordered: 'Now roll over onto your back.' He stripped the marine of his Colt, his knife, machete, and grenades, then dug the marine's combat dressing out of his butt-pack.

Unbuttoning the marine's combat jacket, Trent loosened the Filipino's belt to take the pressure off the wound: 'I'm going to take my blade back.'

The marine nodded and his lips went white as he gritted his teeth. Trent slapped him left-handed across the face, using that instant of surprise to whip the knife free. He pressed the dressing to the wound and laid the Filipino's right hand on it.

The Filipino tried to speak but Trent said: 'Save it. You need your strength.'

Undoing the lace from one of the marine's boots, he lashed a grenade so that the pin wouldn't withdraw. The marine would need a couple of minutes to undo the knot by which time Trent and the girl would be out of range.

Trent said: 'Your back-up squad comes, throw it well clear so they find you but don't shoot you in the head.'

If the pain got too bad there was the other use for the grenade. They both knew it and the Filipino gave a tired smile.

'It took guts to jump the lava,' Trent said and cursed: 'Li and his blood money . . .'

He emptied half the man's water into his own canteen, sprinkled the marine's facecloth, and placed the Filipino's bottle with the stopper almost unscrewed in the marine's left hand.

'I'm sorry, it's the best I can do,' he said.

The marine repeated his tired smile and Trent turned to the girl.

Desperation had brought her to the surface and she had shrieked. Now pain had trapped her and she couldn't get back. She whimpered and watched the man, Trent, crouched over the killer – she wanted him by her side. At first she was unable to understand what he was doing; then she recognised that he was offering comfort.

The all-male alliance – the image was familiar, men with their backs turned to exclude interruption as they whispered secrets of high finance except that it was always sex that they discussed with a girl's character shredded. All men were untrustworthy. In the past she had pretended otherwise. Never again.

Crawling to the rifle, she grabbed it one handed and sat with her knees supporting the barrel. Finger on the trigger she waited for Trent to turn. She didn't care about the Filipino but Trent was a traitor. She wanted him to read his death in her eyes.

He turned and she smiled as she squeezed the trigger. Then she felt the tears come; she couldn't stop them.

'There's a safety catch,' Trent said. She still had time to kill him but he didn't care. 'Killing is what the other side do.'

He took the rifle and hurled it away down the slope. He squatted facing her and read the pain in her eyes, the misery, the shame. He hated the shame more than anything but it was common in those who had been tortured. He brushed her tears away on the back of his hand. At least she had found her way back so there was hope. He smiled at that – hope on this pig of an exploding mountain.

'Come on, let's see if you can walk,' he said.

He helped her to her feet, supporting her round the waist with her weight on his good shoulder.

'We'll take it slowly,' he said and rolled the bound grenade over to the marine.

The marine raised a finger from the water bottle. It wasn't much of a gesture but its meaning was clear – *this was the way of it and no bad feelings between them.*

Trent thought of repeating that he was sorry but the marine knew this already so he shrugged instead and raised a hand before leading the girl down the slope. He expected to hear the grenade but the man was brave and waited.

The slope was gentle and the head of the next lava stream was well short of the track – ten miles to the flat land at the north end of the island and four more lava streams. The lava would fence the Filipino refugees from the eruption into a narrow corridor above the cliff.

They reached the border of the first landfall. The pumice had lain in drifts three and four feet deep but the landslide had swept it clear of the bedrock. Huge chunks of volcanic rock continued to spill red heat three hours after the main eruption and the bedrock was strewn with warm coals with cores that twinkled like glow-worms through carbon lattice work.

There was no point in Trent attempting to hurry the girl. She did her best but she had been hurt badly inside, the pain a continual reminder of what she had suffered.

They walked in a gossamer mist of volcanic dust, the glow from the approaching lava lighting their path. Always there was the rumble above them, the brooding threat of an avalanche of heat. Stumps of trees smouldered beyond the track and stink of burnt livestock blended with the sulphur.

They reached the track and he held her for a moment, telling her that they had done well, that they were nearly there. He didn't say where. But he promised that they would be safe. It was a lie, of course. Ortega's men were behind them and more of his men were probably already in position at the end of the narrow corridor of agricultural land that was their only route north to where Tanaka Kazuko had said he would wait.

The resort on Mindanao presented a Philippines of picture postcard romance. Lawns hemmed by flower beds. Every rock whitewashed. Ranks of palm trees between cottages of real thatch and real bamboo, though this was only a decorative envelope for the air-conditioned boxes within – boxes with quarry-tiled floors and gleaming bathrooms that sprayed hot water from triple nozzle shower heads, *his* and *hers* handbasins, toilet bowl and bidet. Even the water shone clean from the resort's filter system – imported, of course. Nothing Filipino was good enough for the rich. Except the women . . .

Certain that Trent was on the volcano, Ortega had flown to join Sir Philip Li. His uniform and boots were marked by the jungle. Sidearm and twin grenades on his belt, he looked the real thing, swoon material for two starlets from Dusseldorf's media world flown here by Philippine Airlines to display swimwear from a new collection.

The private dining room had been designed for weddings and the birthday parties of the Filipino oligarchy. A manservant in spotless whites opened the door for Ortega.

Sir Philip sat toying with a plate of fresh fruit perfectly peeled and sliced: mango, pineapple, melon, papaya. He had changed from his daytime grey to a suit of dark blue in a cloth of lightweight wool strengthened with raw silk. White cotton shirt, Old Etonian tie, blue socks, black shoes polished but not over-polished. Pristine but understated . . .

His bodyguard stood to one side from where he could watch both the door and the windows that looked out over the resort's private beach.

This was the lifestyle Ortega wanted. With the reward paid, it would be his, this world of privilege.

'We have them,' he said and laid the map on the table. He pointed to the narrow corridor bounded to the west by the mountain, to the east by the cliffs that plunged to the sea.

A plane had flown over taking photographs. 'There's a vent here,' he said, pointing to the flank of the cone. He told the financier of the six streams of lava and that the southernmost had spilled down a steep valley now dammed by a landslide.

'They crossed that one but they can't get back, he said.'

With Trent and the girl blocked from retreat, he had been able to order all of his men from the south end of the island in pursuit. A further hundred men were disembarking to the north and would cordon off that end of the corridor.

'We have them in a squeeze,' Ortega assured the financier. 'Up the mountain they get fried and there's no way down the cliff unless they want to jump a hundred feet.'

A corner of the map had touched Sir Philip's fruit. As Ortega rolled the map, he saw Sir Philip ease the plate over to a corner of the table. Ortega imagined the refugees, and Trent on the flank of the mountain with the girl. Trent had done well to get so far, very well.

'A lot of times it's mostly reputation but this man's for real,' Ortega said, not by way of excuse for not having caught him, but because he wanted Sir Philip to understand. Like hunting tiger, he thought. Some tiger were easy game. Others were admired by hunters for their courage and cunning.

'We've got him trapped but he's taken another three of my men and a fourth hasn't reported in.' He watched the financier take his little book and the gold propelling pencil from his inside pocket.

He gave the financier the men's names and watched him write in his neat capitals. Sir Philip slipped the notebook and pencil back.

'Let's hope you're right this time, Commander.'

Ortega flushed and looked out across the lawns to the beach. He imagined his men storming the resort. He thought it would be more enjoyable for them than pinning Trent at bay.

'Either way, you'll have fresh names for your book,' he said.

The marine waited where Trent had left him. His name was Rodriguez and he was known as Rocco. At first there had been pain but now there was only a numbness in his belly. He knew that it was full of blood from the knife wound. He thought of his partner, Kip. They had been through boot camp and advanced training together. Kip had jumped short in the lava stream. He had screamed and was already falling backwards when Rocco put a bullet between his eyes.

First there were the two men in the jungle, the man at the bottom of the cliff, and the one they had found dead at the top with the knife wound in the underside of his throat. Then Kip. And now it was his turn.

He pictured the Chinese girl as he had first seen her with the foreigner strapping her arm, then with the rifle. He recalled the foreigner taking the rifle from her and hurling it away. He wondered what the couple had done that was worth the lives of so many men and worth so big a reward. Dead, Rocco was one less at the share-out. However the commander had promised that the Chinese would support the families of the dead so his sister might get to college.

Rocco had seen the Chinese twice. He had helped turn the bodies over for the financier to inspect on the day of the attack and had been one of the guards the next day at the riverside. Always so neat and clean, they were different animals.

The foreigner was more Rocco's type. A man who did his own work and who had treated him as if they were buddies. Rocco supposed that they were buddies, on opposite sides not through their own decisions but because that was the way of it.

He wondered how far the foreigner had got with his girl. Retired from the treasure hunt, Rocco felt a growing sympathy for the couple. He could do nothing but wait. The men were coming now. He heard the rustle of the pumice slithering away beneath their boots. There were a lot of them, perhaps the whole detachment. The commander had always lectured them on making their reports precise.

Forcing himself up into a sitting position, he drew the pin. The blood felt very heavy and he couldn't turn round but that wasn't important. He crossed himself and began praying: *Holy Mary, Mother of God* . . .

He continued praying as he tossed the grenade back over his head at his fellow marines. Seated he made a fine target. It didn't take long and it didn't hurt.

The grenade and the answering fire pinpointed the pursuit at between half and three-quarters of an hour behind. Placing the pursuit was too small an advantage to be worth the pain the marine had suffered while he waited but Trent had expected him to wait. He prayed silently while hustling the girl forward. They had passed the second and third lava streams. Now, midway along the corridor, the mountain steepened and a landslide had gouged out two hundred metres of the track, then torn the carefully-husbanded topsoil loose from the fields, hurling it into the sea.

The remnants of a peasant's hut teetered on the edge of the wound, the rest had vanished over the cliff along with the trees, the few acres of crops, the goats and chickens, possibly a cow, perhaps parents and children. Perhaps it was better that way than starving slowly in a refugee camp; a camp from which even the promises were stolen, let alone the rations; insufficient water, no shade, dysentery, malaria, *dengue* fever.

Trent slid down the side of the scar and turned to take the girl in both arms. She put her good hand on his shoulder to steady herself and looked in wonder at the blood.

He lowered her gently to the bedrock. They were a hundred and fifty feet down stream from the front wave of the lava. Their sweat evaporated in the heat, leaving the dust rimming their eyes and nostrils to set like a death mask. Even the liquid in their eyes dried. As they blinked, the grains of pumice felt like gravel.

The front of the lava was deep red where it touched the ground, white in the middle, deep red again on the surface. The white core moved a little faster because of its greater heat, a vast worm with scarlet lips. But the volcano was quieter.

Trent drew the girl forward across the floor of the wound. The wound was four or five feet deep, its sides perpendicular. They had to pick their way with care through the glowing debris. He told her that she was brave and that they were nearly there.

23

The lava welled from the core of the earth through a fault thousands of feet below the earth's surface. The first eruption had released so much pressure that there was now almost a vacuum deep below and this vacuum enabled a fresh fault to open. The magma rose like water in an artesian well until it met the lava from the older faults.

Trent and the girl were halfway across the wound torn by the landslide and had a further one hundred yards to go. It wasn't far and Trent was more concerned by the pursuit than he was by the lava. The eruption came suddenly and without warning.

First the volcano whistled like a giant pressure cooker. The whistle became the roar of an express train hurtling through a tunnel. Then came the lava. It fountained vertically six hundred feet. At the same time a vast wave of lava vomited out of the new vent and split down the six channels. Most of this new lava took the steeper routes, the first stream and the fourth. Insulated from the ground by the existing flows, it retained its heat and flowed like water.

'Run,' Trent yelled. He grabbed Jay round the waist and raced towards the far wall. As he ran, he watched the wave. It came fast, wider than the old stream, rising in height as its edges dried. Its weight and its greater heat squeezed the existing stream so that the rate of flow doubled. The molten rock hypnotised the girl. She stumbled and would have fallen but for Trent's arm. She tried to run but a crack in the rock had trapped her foot. Her ankle twisted and she cried out. Trent knelt to free her. There was no time now and he thrust his right arm between her legs and, taking her right arm, hoisted her over his shoulders and she screamed with the pain of her shattered arm.

The lava came at them.

The upper wave, three feet in height, raced on down the bed of already-moving lava. It was pale in comparison with the lower stream, pale with heat, and the heat came like a wall. Trent reached the side of the landslip and tipped the girl upright against the vertical rock.

She had one good arm and he knew that it wasn't enough. He shouted into her ear that she must stand on his shoulders. She raised her left foot as he crouched, but her ankle collapsed.

The heat burnt into his left side. He told himself not to look. Grabbing both her feet, he slid his palms under them and rammed her up the rock face. There wasn't time to think of her ankle or of her pain. He pushed and thrust her over the lip. Then he took five paces back, turned, and ran at the wall. He jumped and got his chest over the edge. Swinging his legs up, he rolled away from the drop. He was facing straight into the fresh wave of lava. Its brilliance blinded him. Staggering to his feet, he grabbed the girl by her good arm and dragged her free of the furnace.

He lay beside her on the track. She seemed so vulnerable and so damaged with the bruised flesh round her left eye swollen beneath the grime; bruising on the right underside of her jaw; combat jacket; left arm bandaged and strapped; combat boots that seemed, on her slender legs, like a clown's boots. He wanted to swear to her that he would protect her and get her to safety but he wasn't good with words – agents survived in the field through silence – and he thought that her torment must have made men disgusting to her.

He lay like a pig, filthy in his wallow. Sweat and volcanic dust had mixed to mat his hair and his beard. His dark eyes were dulled by exhaustion and rimmed with baked pumice. A dark stain spread from his shoulder down his back to his belt. The big scab on his thigh was caked with dust, the flesh surrounding it swollen and shiny.

She could feel his weakness but there was strength too, what men called strength, muscle strength – and he was all she had. She thought of aspirin and laughed suddenly inside herself. Vengeance was the only medicament. Even the thought of vengeance helped, but she knew that she musn't run back into her cavern because there was danger there of mislaying her path to the surface. Better the edges of pain where she rested now.

She needed him whole. Knowing his frailty, she reached out with her good arm, touching her fingertips to his lips.

The lava had spilled past them and down over the cliff beyond where the fields and the huts had been. He heard the hiss of it as it hit the sea. Steam drifted above the cliff edge and the scent of hot salt and iodine mixed with the sulphur stench of the volcano.

He thought that they were safe from pursuit but, looking up, saw that the lava spilled through a short gulch high up near the foot of the old crater. It would be hot up there but the crossing was possible for those with courage. The climb followed by an angled descent to the track gave him an hour and half's grace.

The girl reached out and touched his lips with the tips of her fingers. Embarrassed, he said: 'We'd better get moving.'

He scooped her over his shoulders and headed down the track. Six miles was his guess. The footing was smooth but his shoulder and forearm hurt and his thigh. He began counting. Five hundred of his paces made a quarter of a mile, multiplied by four for a mile, and by six to give the total – twenty-four sections. He completed the first five hundred but he thought that he might not be able to pick the girl up again if he put her down so he kept walking, counting until he lost track of the numbers.

The volcano, like a drunk, had vomited and become somnolent, though it snored every now and again and coughed. The track seemed to lead uphill but it was difficult to tell because of the strange light thrown off by the lava and by the flames.

The girl had whimpered at first but she had been silent for a long time now. He thought that she was unconscious. He breasted the slope and stood for a moment awe-struck. The whole side of the cone seemed to have slipped, all the loose fine pumice. It had slipped and spread and buried everything. There was no track, no trees, no fields, no huts. And no people. Nothing but a great flow of pumice that spread from the foot of the mountain to the cliff. Dust hung above it, grey and thick.

Walking through the powdered clinker was as tiring as walking through dry sand, except that the pumice was all sharp edges which wore at the already bare ring of flesh at the top of his boots. He walked very deliberately, lifting his feet so that he didn't trip. He walked with his head up because to let his head sink was to tell the girl that he had surrendered and he didn't want her to lose hope.

For a while he thought of Ortega's men waiting at the end of the corridor and of the men scrambling up the mountain toward the gulch. He understood them. They were mercenaries. They had joined the marines because it was a secure job which carried respect in their community. Now they had been offered more money than they had ever dreamed of. As with Filipino women of pleasure, selling their services was their only escape from subjugation. He had contempt for the buyers rather than for those who sold.

He thought of Tanaka Kazuko, but not much because he didn't want to concern himself with what happened at the end of the corridor. He had to get there. Tanaka had told him forty-eight hours. Trent had tried to lead the marines south, perhaps even trick them into abandoning the chase. Seeing Ortega's men would warn Tanaka that he had failed but that he was alive.

If the Japanese had any sense, he would give up any thought of rescue. He was a successful businessman and needed Sir Philip Li as an enemy like he needed a hole in the head. But he was Japanese and the Japanese were addicted to honour. Trent liked that – walking toward honour. There was less and less of it in Europe and there had never been much of it in the United States, except amongst some of the Good Ol' Boys and they were out of fashion.

It would have been dishonourable to give up so he walked on across the pumice in the dim grimy yellow light that leaked down from the lava through the smog. For a while he counted again and made calculations. The calculations were to occupy his mind. Finally there was only the counting, one step after the other, then he drifted for a while but his head stayed up and his feet plodded on until something dragged at him, making him stumble.

An old man had pulled him by the sleeve. The smog had thinned to a dusty mist. Trent couldn't see the landslip so they were well beyond it. His legs wanted to fold and he had to keep them braced.

The old man pointed at an untidy bundle that lay beside a hand cart that had lost one wheel. Trent made out the face of an old woman at one end of the bundle. She was awake and must have watched him for some time as he stumbled along the track because she wasn't surprised by their appearance. Trent wanted to apologise for not having noticed her but words wouldn't come. He smiled instead and then remembered that a cloth covered his face.

The old man was frightened that Trent would leave. He kept a close hold on Trent's sleeve and repeated the same phrase – something to do with the cart.

Trent let his knees bend and the old man helped him rest the girl on the ground. Untying the cloth from her face, he dripped water on to her lips. She regained consciousness and looked at him while she drank.

He shook the dust from the cloth before damping it and passed the bottle to the old lady but the man took it instead and held it to the woman's lips. She was very weak – perhaps partly paralysed.

The old man tried to return the bottle to Trent but Trent indicated that he should drink first, then he took the bottle. There wasn't a lot of water left in it and he wasn't sure how much further they had to go so he screwed the stopper back on and hooked it back onto his belt.

The old man showed him a flattened iron spike. The spike had held the wheel onto the axle and had fallen out, the wheel had rolled off, tipping the cart. The old man wasn't strong enough to right it. Trent forced his good shoulder under the cart and raised it over onto its side with the axle sticking up. He lifted the wheel on, took the spike from the old man, hammered it in with a rock, and tipped the cart back on to its wheels.

The bed of the cart was of bamboo strip about eight feet long and three feet wide. The twin shafts had been worn silk smooth and there were a couple of hinged legs on the shafts to keep the cart level when it wasn't being pushed. The old man set the legs and they lifted the old lady onto the bed. She weighed less than a sack of flour and didn't occupy much space. She kept smiling at Trent and gave little bobs of her head as if to assure him that he was a good man of whom she approved.

Trent arranged the girl on the cart on her sound side, resting against the old woman so that she wouldn't tip back on to her smashed shoulder. The old man hid the girl's legs under the old woman's rags. He didn't show any surprise at the chain. Trent hefted the shafts and the old man raised the wooden legs, looping them in place with frayed fishing line.

Jay was watching him, but Trent wouldn't meet her eyes. He didn't want to think about her too much. He could think safely about what they had done to her and how much hatred he had for them – but thinking of her was too disturbing and he had to keep what little energy he had.

The track was an avenue of discarded possessions, the tragically humble possessions of a people whose lives had quivered on the edge of subsistence. Clay pots. Old cans with their edges beaten smooth. Threadbare blankets. A palliasse. An unframed square of mirror with the silver peeling from the back. Baskets. A crudely-carpentered chair. But, worse, the tools that had made their subsistence possible: spades, adzes, picks.

A woman in her last days of pregnancy squatted panting amongst the detritus. Two tiny waifs with fear-shuttered eyes clung against her back. The old man lowered the cart's legs while Trent lifted the woman and set her and her children in the cart.

A mile ahead of them a combination of landslip and an old ridge formed a dam for the last two lava flows. The dam was a half-mile long, lava trickling over the top. Below the dam, on the track, were the survivors.

Terrified by the lava, the refugees had tried to escape first through the narrow fields above the cliff but marines had driven them back. Now they shuffled forward in silence beneath the menace of the dam and the guns. There was such sadness to the scratch of their feet on the brittle pumice paving the track. The volcano coughed and burbled. From up ahead came the occasional rifle shot.

Looking back the way they had come, Trent saw a thin line of matchstick men outlined against the downward sweep of the lava below the gulch – Ortega's hounds.

Ortega had flown back from Mindanao to the island. The pilot had landed on the beach eight miles to the north of the volcano. From there, the commander bounced by jeep along a vile track through wetlands, then up the gentle wedge of lava desert bounded to the east and west by the cliffs that encircled all but the two ends of the island. His lieutenant had thrown a cordon round the end of the corridor with men up on the mountainside and in the fields.

The heat of the lava dried Ortega's sweat. Climbing toward the dam, he saw the dead sprawled like half-filled sacks.

The lieutenant saluted and said, 'The only way we could hold them, Commander. They tried to break round the cordon. Same in the fields, but it took longer.'

Given the terrain, it was to be expected. Ortega had no need of the dawn. The lava in the dam and its spillage gave ample light. He had seen film and stills and paintings of refugee columns. Whatever the war, the picture was always the same. This wasn't a war. He wondered whether the dam would hold. He was covered, of course; his men were searching for the pirate chief and his equally vicious concubine. Down at the control posts they had identikits of the two fugitives displayed on a board and photographs of them for their own use.

Glancing up at the summit, Ortega asked how long it had been since the last eruption.

'Ninety minutes, Commander.'

'The damn held . . .'

It wasn't a question but the lieutenant said: 'Yes, Sir.'

Ortega scrambled down to the barrier where a corporal directed the enlisted men sifting the refugees through to three trestle tables. Behind each table sat a sergeant checking identity documents. They had set kerosene pressure lamps on the tables; one of the lamps had a broken mantle. The light was white and harsh on the sergeants' faces; the documents were creased and dirty.

Wary of showing their hate, the refugees kept their faces blank – even the children. Ortega pushed forward amongst them to show that he wasn't afraid, either of them, or of the lava.

They looked away from him, all of them. The stink of their sweat was sour with fear and he smelt the stench of stale garlic and dried fish on their breath. He thought of Sir Philip Li and wondered whether he had gone to bed.

The refugees spilled round an ancient flat-bed truck broken down on the side of the track with its hood lifted and the rump of the driver sticking up. A couple of oil drums were lashed against the back of the cab. Ortega looked up at the dam again with its molten lip. He could hear the pursuit party charge into the tail end of the column. Terrified of losing the reward to the men at the checkpoint, they cursed and clubbed the refugees with their rifle butts.

The old man had seen the marines on the mountain. He glanced at Trent, then began whispering to his fellow islanders. Almost immediately a way opened for the cart. Now they were close to the head of the column. Trent could see the roof of a truck cab ahead.

On the cart, the children sat dry-eyed, one each side of their mother. Trent remembered his father's death; how he had hidden crouched and hugging his knees in a loose box in the stables; that

202

his mother and his guardian had thought him unfeeling because he hadn't wept. He had known that he had to keep hold of himself or disintegrate. He had been so frightened of disintegrating. The edge of an abyss . . .

The marines had no interest in the old man or the old woman, nor in the children and their mother, nor in any of the refugees. Trent looked up at the dribble of lava on the dam's lip. He didn't want to look at the girl but he needed to now. Perhaps the odds had always been too great, but he had done what he could.

He said, 'Jay, you have to get down from the cart.'

He wasn't sure how much she understood or if she understood but she took his hand. He lifted her over the side on to the track and put his shoulder under her good arm.

He said, 'Can you hobble? It's not very far . . .' He was bitterly angry, angry that he had failed her.

The old man protested and Trent heard a murmur spread through the crowd, not words so much as a low but insistent buzz.

He saw Ortega. The marine commander stood leaning against the end of the truck. There were two oil drums lashed to the back of the cab. The driver had his head under the hood. As in a river, there was a small eddy round the rear corner of the flat-bed, a swirl that swept the refugees clear of Ortega. Ortega appeared relaxed and in command of himself. Their eyes met and Ortega smiled as if seeing an old friend.

Trent considered killing him. Instead he held the girl in front of him. He thought of opening her combat jacket so that Ortega could see the scabs on her back. But this meeting was about honour rather than suffering.

'Commander Manolo Ortega, Miss Jay Li . . .' He squeezed the girl's good arm and said: 'The commander is in the employ of your grandfather, Miss Li.' He spoke almost gently: 'I expect he's very proud of himself, Miss Li. His school friend turned insurgent, Ishmael Muhammad, considered him trustworthy in things that mattered. Honour and so on.' Trent nodded at the dam above and the bodies of the dead refugees: 'Strange what people will do for money. But now that he's captured us, perhaps the commander will let the people be.'

Commander Manolo Ortega was very close to his breaking point. He blinked as he fought to control his rage and limit the pain that squeezed his head like a band of red hot iron. He drew his pistol and he looked at the girl, then down at the short length of chain manacled to her left ankle. Then into her eyes again but they were blank. Looking over her shoulder, he faced Trent's cold contempt.

Having a cause had helped Trent, but the Anglo-Irishman had done extraordinarily well. Ortega felt oddly proud of him – they had graduated from the same schools. Further back in the column one of his men clubbed a woman aside with his rifle.

Ortega cocked his pistol, turned, and shouldered his way through the refugees. He shouted at the men at the barrier to let the refugees through.

The lieutenant charged down the mountainside. His pistol was drawn and he screamed countermands. Next he would remind the marines of the reward.

Ortega shot him.

Trent had watched Ortega shoulder his way to the barrier. He heard the shouting and the shot. Behind him, a marine bayed like a hound. The hood of the truck slammed shut and the driver said: 'Dumb Brit, get in the drums – or do you want to walk?'

The crowd swirled round them, the buzz louder now and angry. Hands thrust him onto the flat-bed. He saw a marine drown in the crowd and a drum close on the girl. Then Trent was in darkness and the engine sputtered. The truck jerked forward, the crowd cheering as Tanaka smashed through the abandoned trestle tables toward the beach.

24

Wong Fu's war chief presented a final account of the massacre ten days after the volcano's eruption: four specialist employees dead, no word of the Li granddaughter, nor of the British yachtsman and his catamaran.

The war chief expected his employer to be enraged by the failure of the operation. Sweat dampened his palms as he waited at the marble desk for Wong Fu to finish reading. However he saw only a segment of the picture. There were indirect gains.

Old Man Li had been preoccupied with little else for a critical week and the mice had played, two mice – the Ching niece and the German, Rudi Beckenberg.

The woman had been tempted by Wong Fu's shipping manager with an immediate payment of one hundred thousand dollars. The payment was a relocation bonus – though her move to Singapore as the Fu shipping broker would await the fall of the House of Li.

The German had made his own approach.

Wong Fu had been wise in keeping Timmy Brown in place. The American's skills enabled the two recruits to feed information by computer link from the counting house directly to Wong Fu's penthouse. Wong Fu was already familiar with much of the information but there were invaluable scraps of intelligence that came from private conversations between his new informants and Old Man Li.

Wong Fu knew that victory was within his grasp.

The granddaughter and the British yachtsman were minor irritants – loose ends so to speak. As such, they must be tidied and he wrote on the bottom of the report:

Keep looking for Trent and the girl.

He showed the instruction to his war chief and dropped the report into the shredder.

He had wanted this – a very small part of it – Commander Manuel Ortega thought as he drove his jeep slowly down the long drive between the jacaranda trees and into the courtyard in front of Sir Philip Li's Luzon hacienda. Ortega had made pressure of work his excuse to two previous invitations in the six weeks since the eruption of the volcano. Now the financier was over from Hong Kong again and this third invitation had been passed to Ortega by his Admiral.

'He wishes to thank you personally.'

Pulling up in front of the great doors, Ortega sat for a moment lost in admiration of the courtyard's beauty. Crested with waves of mauve bougainvillea, the stones of the high walls glowed like pale honey in the mid-afternoon sun. White fantail pigeons bobbed and bowed from the arched doorways of a three-storeyed dovecote. The birds' soft cooing delicately complemented the splash of water that trickled from a stone lion's head into a horse trough beyond the triangular mounting block.

A servant coughed for Ortega's attention and requested the keys so that he could park the commander's jeep in the shade of the big plain trees. The tall majordomo led Ortega into the gloom of the vast echoing *entrada* with its row of small, narrow windows cut high in the thick whitewashed wall. The windows were a reminder that the hacienda had served as a fortress as well as a home. The dark paintings and the high-backed chairs and refectory table were other relics of colonial occupation.

The big square drawing room with its minstrel gallery and open side to the patio was in total contrast to the sombre *entrada* but no less forbidding with its overtones of power – the four hand-built sofas cushioned in raw silk, the inch-thick bevelled glass of the centre table, these could be duplicated, but it was the great splashes of colour on the walls which held Ortega's attention.

The majordomo touched Ortega's arm and beckoned to the patio where Sir Philip sat on the tiled edge of the lily pond. The financier wore a grey suit and his hand-made brown brogues sparkled in the shade. He smiled up at Ortega, a rather shy smile. Behind him the entwined bronze lovers kissed. Sir Philip appeared tired in comparison and enfeebled by his age. Even his voice seemed unnaturally quiet and Ortega had to lean close to hear his words through the spatter of falling water.

Sir Philip said: 'I understand you've been very busy since our excursion, Commander. It's a long drive to visit an old man. Most thoughtful of you. Perhaps a cup of tea?' He moved his head a quarter of an inch to the majordomo and waited until he was out of earshot before remarking quietly: 'So they escaped.'

'No, sir.' Ortega produced photographs of the mountain and pointed to the fourth stream of lava: 'They were in this region at the second eruption. My men cmae up the side of the flow to the chasm here and crossed. There was no place else to cross and there was no way back across the first stream. They're dead, sir. Burnt.'

The financier closed his eyes a moment, as if imagining their death, then he sighed, or let the last of his breath out, and eased the cuff of his cream cotton shirt a quarter of an inch below his jacket sleeve. His nails were beautifully manicured but the liver spots were dark on the back of his hands and his eyes seemed old and empty.

'I would like you to be correct, Commander,' he said in his gentle voice: 'Your men believe differently. Some of them believe that you allowed the quarry to escape. You removed the barrier?'

'It was a value judgment.'

'Whose value, Commander?'

'I acted as an officer of the Philippines armed forces.' Ortega accepted that he sounded pompous and artificial but the financier merely nodded.

'Yes, I can see that.' He sighed again. 'It's all so difficult, Commander. Some of your men believe you played me for a fool.'

As if on cue, the majordomo glided through from the drawing room with a lacquered tray. There was one cup on it, faintly blue, the bone china so thin as to be translucent.

'Please,' Sir Philip said, but Ortega was tired of the charade.

He said, 'I'd prefer to leave.'

The financier gave another of his little sighs and signalled the majordomo to retreat.

'At least give me the pleasure of walking you to the door,' he said and took Ortega gently by the elbow.

The financier seemed very small in relation to the massive wooden doors with their iron studs but the hinges were oiled and the doors perfectly balanced.

207

Four men lounged against Ortega's jeep over in the shade of the plane trees. Ortega recognised them from his files. They were Communist terrorists from the NPA, the New People's Army. All four were high on his *most wanted* list and famous for their savagery. They carried AK-47s and wore sidearms and knives.

The financier's bodyguard had appeared out of the shadows and stood at his master's shoulder with a short-barrelled shotgun.

'I'm truly sorry, Commander,' Sir Philip said.

Ortega spat in his face.

Doctor Imai trotted down the wooden steps and across the lawn to the beach. He was a small man, already in his sixties, but without a grey hair, and comfortably rather then dangerously plump. He placed his spectacles in the pocket of his kimono and hung the kimono beneath his beach towel on a wooden spike hammered into the trunk of a coconut palm. Disciplined in his morning exercise, he swam precisely one hundred and fifty strokes out from the shore before turning onto his back to inspect his Philippines domain.

It was a small resort – the main house, and eight cabins. His guests considered it an ashram, a description that embarrassed the Japanese doctor. A heart specialist, he had dropped out of the rat race after suffering his own heart attack and had invested only a loseable part of his savings in building the resort. His intention had been to offer a temporary retreat to fellow cardiac sufferers frightened by near-death into a change of lifestyle. More committed to protecting his heart than his soul, he had determined that the resort should be trouble-free.

The beach faced away from the normal typhoon track and it was further protected by a mountain. Electricity came courtesy of sun and wind. An ample spring on the mountain supplied clean water and all sewage and water pipes were double the standard diameter. Doctor Imai supplied his customers with a diet of locally available fish, rice and fruit. Cooking was over charcoal, all construction was of local materials.

As always delighted with his morning, the doctor swam back to the shore, dried himself, and jogged gently three times round the main lawn. Then he collected two bowls of fruit and two cups of green tea from the breakfast buffet on the terrace of the main house and carried them over to Cabin 5. Seated on the little verandah, he settled back to watch Sam complete his daily routine.

The Englishman had pinned a dozen playing cards in the shrubbery at different heights. Falls, rolls, somersaults – whatever he did, his knife hit one of the cards dead centre.

Doctor Imai found the performance fascinating and he was proud of his patient's recovery: bullet in the left shoulder, badly infected wound in the right thigh, severe bruising of the left forearm, plus considerable wear and tear.

Trent completed his hundred throws with a back flip and came up grinning at the doctor. He plucked his knife out of the tree trunk and collected the cards before sitting down on the steps.

Imai said, 'You could sell tickets, Sam. As a career it would be less dangerous and perhaps more profitable than your present occupation.' He fingered Trent's left shoulder, digging deep into the muscles until he felt his patient wince. 'You can leave if you wish. I will inform your employer when he arrives.'

'Thanks,' Trent said. He sipped the hot tea and thought about Tanaka.

'Marked down on a secondhand car lot in Haiti, you wouldn't sell,' Tanaka had mocked as Trent lay on the doctor's emergency operating table in the main house: 'No partner of mine gets that beat up. You're down-rated to hired hand.'

Haiti was an improvement on Liverpool. Warmer. Nor would Trent have to search back for bright retorts from the Beatles Song Book. He had never been a fan. And he was content with Sam as a cover.

'Me Bogart, you piano player,' had been Tanaka's explanation. 'You prefer Jane, say so. But there's the sex thing.'

Trent looked across the main lawn as the resort's *baslig* glided into the beach. The boat's hull gleamed white, the outrigger poles sky blue to match the stripped awning that shaded the passenger seat forward of the Yamaha diesel. The bow scraped gently on the sand and the boat healed over to rest on the port outrigger. Beyond it the sea stretched into the sun like a field of flowing light.

Tanaka jumped light as a cat six feet up the beach and trotted across the grass. He wore a baggy Hawaii shirt with pineapples printed on it, red and white striped Bermudas, and carried a suitcase.

'How's the patient?' he asked.

'Off the sick list,' Doctor Imai said.

Tanaka rubbed his hands: 'Great.' He sat on the verandah above

Trent. 'Your boat's been collected. Three cops from Kyoto Athletic Club and an Imperial Navy Lieutenant. She'll be at the Kyoto Yacht Club in a couple of weeks.'

Trent said, 'Thanks,' and they sat in silence for a while trying to enjoy the view, the scent of the flowers, the peace and quiet. Quiet was their problem.

Tanaka said: 'No change, huh?'

He was asking for news of the doctor's young Chinese patient.

'None,' the doctor said. Internally Jay Li was recovering and her shoulder was mending well – even the scarring on her back would be minimal. Her mind was the difficulty. She hadn't spoken in the six weeks that she had been his patient.

'It's not shock. Perhaps at first, but not now,' he said.

He had joined his hands as Christians did in prayer, fingertips tapping gently against his pursed lower lip. It was a pose that he had adopted from a Hollywood hospital melodrama early in his career and had used shamelessly during what he now thought of as his bad years as senior consultant at Kyoto Central. Ashamed, he drew his hands apart, but that too was a gesture. Breaking the habit of pretended wisdom was more difficult than he had imagined. Smiling at himself, he said: 'I have no experience of such a case.'

A Japanese of the upper middle class, he had been brought up to avoid any display of emotion and was reluctant to intrude in other people's relationships. Yet he believed that it was important in this case, perhaps the key.

He said: 'Sam, she's dependent on you.'

But that wasn't what he sensed and he corrected himself, searching down into what he had seen of Sam and the girl together.

'Trusting,' he tried, but it still wasn't right because there was anger in her, hate. Carefully hidden but he had smelt it sometimes when Sam's back was turned.

'Waiting,' he finally decided. 'Obviously I don't know why or for what, but that is my feeling of your relationship. The young lady's waiting for you, Sam.' Having had his say, he excused himself and fled across the main lawn.

'The old boy's loosening up in his old age,' Tanaka said – Imai and his father had been colleagues and he had known the doctor from early childhood. 'Maybe you should leave. It's a suggestion, but you can't stay here the rest of your life. You rescued her, that was crazy enough. Now you have to get on with the next project and you haven't seen your new office.'

Trent looked at him and Tanaka grinned: 'Abbey Road, Nassau. Think I'm going to let you go? No way, my friend. All my life I've been looking for someone dumb enough to stand in the way of the bullets. What else are you going to do? Sail round the world the rest of your life? Do it, but at least have a purpose or you'll take to drink or drugs like the rest of the drop-outs.'

He tossed a passport, a driving licence, and three credit cards into Trent's lap.

'Sammi Samuelson,' he said with one of his big grins. 'Argentine police officer who made a mistake, politics not crime. Ricardo Acciapatti in the Buenos Aires SIB put us in touch. I gave you a job setting up the new branch. The suitcase has all the papers and clothes and enough background to fool Immigration.'

From over the far side of the lawn came the snip of the doctor's secateurs as he began his morning's pruning of the flower beds.

Trent said: 'Why don't you give me the bad news?' and Tanaka dropped an envelope of press clippings on the step:

Commander Manuel 'Manolo' Ortega had been captured by marxist terrorists of the NPA. Having tortured him, the terrorists left him nailed to a tree on the roadside. Hero of the counter-insurgency campaign, the commander was a close friend of the Hong Kong financier and philanthropist, Sir Philip Li, and was abducted when driving home from Sir Philip's Luzon hacienda. Though Sir Philip was unavailable for interviews, sources close to the financier reported that he was devastated by the tragedy.

'Pretty,' Tanaka said. 'You want more, there's two contracts out on you. A hundred and fifty grand each, so Li and Wong Fu agree on something. A couple of the major *triads* are in competition – keep clear of Chinatowns or you'll end up as a take-away chop suey.'

He looked beyond Trent. Jay stood on the veranda of Cabin 2. Despite the warmth of the morning, she wore a terry towel bathrobe and held the collar with crossed hands gripped to her throat. She glanced at the two men, then walked down to the beach. Seated on a flat rock with her feet in the water, she watched the sea play with her toes.

Imai had said that she was waiting and Trent wondered whether Tanaka understood.

He said, 'You're going back today?'

'Tomorrow morning,' Tanaka told him.

'I'll come with you.'

Trent strolled over to the main house, poured two cups of tea, and carried them to the beach. He needed to be very casual. He put the second cup on the rock beside the girl and sat a little behind her on the sand. She drank the tea in neat sips and he waited for her to put the cup down. A hornbill called from the lower branch of a screw pine on the edge of the lawn and she looked round.

'Jay, I'm leaving in the morning,' he said.

Their eyes met. She didn't bother to hide her anger and hate. He thought of the pain that caused it, the calculated sadism she had suffered. The scars would be there till she died, companions of her nights, perhaps every night.

Looking away, out to sea, he thought of the diplomat he had brought out from the Lebanon. He remembered the sunshine, the scent of fresh mown grass, of roses and honeysuckle, how beautiful England had been that summer morning as he breakfasted on the lawn outside his cottage on the Hamble while the diplomat's body floated by and out to sea. A different sea . . .

A dark red butterfly fluttered close to the edge of the water. He said: 'Your grandfather had Ortega killed – the man who let us escape? You should stay here a couple of weeks while I try to work things out.'

The patterns drawn by the swirl of the sea round her toes was more interesting. Or perhaps she was remembering the night of their escape, the thunder of the eruptions, lava, the stink of sulphur. Which side he had been on didn't matter to her. A segment of her wanted him dead for having been part of it. She wanted them all dead.

The tide had washed a mitre shell up on the sand at the foot of the rocks and he picked it up, running his thumb over the silky surface. He wished that he was better with words – or with emotions – but he had been trained in subterfuge and never to reveal himself.

She had turned away and he read contempt in her hunched shoulders. He knew very well what she chiefly remembered from their escape. Doctor Imai had been wise in his conclusion.

A tiny crab inched a feeler out of the shell. A servant had cut open a durian fruit on the verandah outside the kitchen in the main house and the soft breeze drifted the stench across the lawn.

Trent breathed in the cloying scent of putrefaction. The crab touched his thumb. 'I know – I promised,' he said.

She stood and turned and looked down at him. The bulk of the robe made her seem even smaller than she was, as if in a cocoon. She touched the tips of her fingers to his lips for perhaps a second, not more.

She had rewarded him with the same disdain after they had escaped from the lava of the second eruption and her touch burnt like acid. He said quietly: 'That wasn't necessary.'

She didn't hear him.

It was all jumbled and she mustn't remember, not yet, not until it was finished.

When it was finished, she would be clean and she would remember all of it. She would set it in order and fold it and put it away in the drawer with her photograph album that had the pictures of her parents, pictures that stopped after the first three pages.

She didn't mind about that album any more. She could look at it now and think about it, about the first three pages. But not about the new album. Not yet. It had to be cleaned first. Trent had promised to clean it, then he forgot. She had punished him with her silence until he had remembered. He deserved punishment. Men deserved punishment. But he made a good tool when he remembered. Soon she would be safe and clean. She looked down at him. He looked funny to her – shaggy, like an old dog – but she was pleased with him. She gave him the tips of her fingers to lick. Watching the pain come into his soft brown doggy eyes, she giggled and spoke for the first time since arriving at the resort. The few words came quietly and without inflection:

'I want to be there. I want to watch.'

Trent walked back to his cabin. Tanaka was waiting for him on the veranda. Trent picked up the passport and checked the photograph. With a little work he could make it fit.

25

Trent had lived undercover for eighteen years. He believed that disguise was far more dependent on acting in character than on the paraphernalia of the make-up artist.

Age and colour of eyes, carriage and mannerisms, clothes and haircut, these were the foundation. Next came the details: how a man knotted his tie; would he carry coins loose or in a change purse? the way he laced his shoes; the ambience in which he felt comfortable – where he lived, shopped, car, hotels, restaurants. Did he exercise? What did he watch on television? Cinema. Newspapers and magazines. Books? Music . . .

Sammi Samuelson was easy.

Resident in the Dominican Republic, he had obtained a United Kingdom visitor's visa at the British High Commission in Nassau and had spent an hour at a Nassau bank before flying into Miami with American Eagle from where he flew AA to London. He looked to be in his mid-fifties but hoping to look younger, black hair swept straight back with a little grey at the edges and bifocals, but these were to be expected at his age. He had kept himself fit and carried himself almost too well given that the military are out of fashion.

His tweed suit was a little lightweight for the climate but obviously made to measure and reasonably cut and he carried one of those cashmere overcoats that look good in the store but begin to sag over the shoulders when they've been worn a few times. His shoes were the same, brown brogues made in Mexico to look British but not quite pulling off the act, and he wore one of those striped ties that pretend to belong to something but don't – or not to anything that anyone would want to belong to. The flight attendants had picked him as a possible grabber but he'd behaved well and had drunk nothing but club soda or coffee so perhaps he was an alcoholic in recovery. He didn't smoke.

Argentina and Britain had been friends for many more years than they had been enemies and Sammi Samuelson had a white skin, so the immigration officer was polite and asked him only a couple of questions before stamping his passport. He collected a fake leather suitcase from the carousel and passed through the green exit from Customs without being stopped.

The courtesy bus took him to the Post Hotel where he reserved a room for a week, giving Reception his American Express card, the ordinary green colour. Not bothering to unpack, he rode the underground into central London, getting off at Green Park. It is a small station and he crossed the park and walked past Buckingham Palace into the Mall, then turned up past St James's Palace where he waited to the left of the pedestrians' arch long enough to light a cigarette with a temperamental lighter.

Nobody followed him through the arch.

Dropping the cigarette down a drain cover, he walked along Jermyn Street window-shopping the bespoke shirt-makers. At five minutes to one, he turned down towards the Hunt Club, haven of British upper-class Catholicism. A speck of something blew in his eye halfway down the block. Sheltering in the doorway, he tried to get it out with the point of his handkerchief. He couldn't see much without his spectacles. While fitting them over his ears, he cannoned into a typical English gentleman in a good grey flannel suit heading, as he did every week day, from his office to his club for lunch.

Sammi Samuelson begged pardon in Spanish and, in English, said, 'The Criterion restaurant, fifteen minutes.'

On the south side of Piccadilly circus, the Criterion is art nouveau at its best, marble walls and floors and a domed ceiling mosaiced in mirror. Sammi asked for a table midway down the first section behind a buttress. He had given a young woman lunch here once and hadn't heard a word because of the echo. The echo made it a great place for a meet.

The Englishman came in right on time. The Criterion wasn't quite his kind of place, his clothes were a little too gentlemanly, and the friendliness of a six-foot waitress in Doc Martens and with a crewcut scared him more than anything had during the Cold War. His name was Charles Benson – medium height, brown eyes, brown hair, slim face, slight of figure. A forelock with a wave in it threatened to fall forward over his eyes, giving him a boyish look at variance with his age. Though a civilian, his pay scale was military and equivalent to that of a brigadier. Last time they had met there had been rein calluses on the sides of his fingers but losses at Lloyd's had put paid to polo. Now he jogged. He would have been Sammi's control, had Sammi stayed with the Department.

'Sammi Samuelson,' Sammi said and they shook hands while the waitress hovered.

'Beer? Or would you prefer wine?'

'Mineral water,' Benson said without looking at the waitress. The two men sat at ninety degrees to each other, secure within the echo, heads perhaps a little closer together than is normal in England but Sammi was obviously a foreigner.

He said, 'Nice to see you Charles, thanks for coming.'

'It's against regulations,' Benson said. He wasn't nervous. It was a reminder that they needed to be careful. And perhaps that he would prefer the meeting to be important because his salary was necessary to him now that Lloyd's had decimated his capital – but everything was nuance with Benson and reading him could be like using your eyes to read Braille.

Benson said:'There was word that you were in trouble.' He had a smile that promised greater humour than he liked to display: 'More than usual?'

'A little . . .'

Sammi told him about the contracts.

'*Triads* are nasty.' Benson said. He ordered from the menu without looking at the waitress, then came straight to the point: 'What can I do for you?'

Sammi said: 'Someone's touting my history round the Far East. Too obvious to be in the Department so he's an ex. He'll have done you a favour recently – you know how it works. Probably commercial information, maybe with a Chinese background to it, shipping, construction, finance.'

'Selling you?' Their food hadn't come but he wiped his fingertips on his napkin. 'Not very pleasant.'

'A name's all I want, not the information he gave you,' Sammi said.

Information belonged to the Department and Benson nodded his gratitude. 'Give me till the end of the week, Mr Samuelson. You should jog, good for you. How about Richmond Park? Saturday morning. Robin Hood Gate.' The waitress brought their food and Benson moved a sliver of perfectly cooked lamb's liver from one side of the plate to the other: 'I think I'd like his source in the department.'

'However high up?'

Benson gave a quick nod: 'Yes, however high up. You might be more effective at that, or more speedy – you know? Difficult for us. Too many rules on deportment. I'll need a statement from him so I'd like him back alive, if that's all right?'

'A letter?'

Benson thought a moment, then touched his napkin to a spot of gravy on his lower lip: 'Yes, perhaps a letter might be better. Less fuss, Mr Samuelson.'

The wind blew cold off the mountains and across the slate grey waters of Lake Geneva. Sammi Samuelson walked along the shore road with the collar of his overcoat turned up, hands deep in his pockets. He had bought a tweed cap with a button on the crown at Geneva airport. Peak pulled down, it kept most of the wind out of his eyes and his spectacles helped.

He had been walking for two hours now and there hadn't been even the smallest break in the thick grey cloud cover. One hour out of town and the return was enough. Sure that he was clean, he strolled up from the lake between the grey Swiss granite buildings and turned in at the side entrance to the bank. A security guard inquired whether he had an appointment. An elevator took him to the fourth floor where a middle-aged secretary in a heather-grey twin set showed him through two sets of doors thick with sound-proofing. The banker was as grey as the building and looked older than he probably was – grey eyes, grey hair, grey suit, grey tie, grey spectacle frames. Filtered through windows secure against electronic surveillance, even the light seemed grey.

Fourth floor was serious wealth. The banker was too experienced to show surprise at the Argentinian's clothes – Sammi Samuelson had been recommended by a colleague in Nassau.

He said, 'We'll have coffee, Señor Samuelson. I have this new machine.'

The machine had been designed to hiss a lot, all very secure and useful so long as you weren't a coffee drinker.

'Wonderful,' the banker said. 'Modern technology. Now what can we do for you?'

'Take delivery of gold to the value of fifteen million Swiss francs,' Sammi said.

The banker closed his eyes a moment: 'One ton thirteen and three-quarter ounces – opening prices in Zurich.' He almost smiled: 'A trick of mental arithmetic, Señor Samuelson. It impresses old ladies and gangsters.' It was the most polite of warnings and he leaned back in his leather chair, fingertips touching beneath his chin, manicured nails.

Sammi said: 'There is no question of illegality, however there may be irresistible pressure for disclosure of the transaction. My clients would be agreeable to disclosure but they would wish first to negotiate a substantial loan.'

Hissing contentedly, the gleaming coffee machine seemed more emotional than either negotiator. The banker looked at it, as if for reassurance, then asked quietly: 'With urgency?'

'Great urgency,' Sammi conceded. 'The issuing bank will supply a certificate of weight signed by their chairman but you will naturally require to verify personally the cargo. It would be convenient if verification took place during loading. You and I will be alone in knowing that you represent the accepting bank. Delivery instructions will be issued to the driver by telephone during the drive. Delivery will take twenty minutes at which time details of the transaction can be made public.'

The banker raised his fingertips to his lips and tapped gently on his front teeth. Only the most boring of people fail to delight in intelligent larceny and the banker chuckled softly: 'I rather like that, Señor Samuelson. Most original. In fact probably unique. And a very personal service. Shall we say ten percent? And, Señor Samuelson, do advise your clients to enjoy their profit rather than bewail our fee.'

'My clients will be most satisfied,' Sammi assured him.

The banker conducted Sammi to the elevator, remarkable evidence of respect. 'Cold wind today,' he said and Sammi said:

'It will be a lot worse in Moscow.'

Sammi's destination was a scrap for the banker to throw to whatever wolves came hunting and the banker smiled his understanding.

'A pleasure doing business with you, Señor Samuelson.'

*

Those who were once hidden behind an impenetrable wall of secrecy and security guards now advertised their wares like street vendors. Sammi found Doctor Dimitri Ignosiev listed under four separate numbers in the directory of officials: his office at KGB Headquarters in Levitno Street, the clinic, the apartment in the KGB condominium for senior grades on Veratnigoi, and his *dacha* out at Melnshiv.

Sammi described himself over the telephone as a journalist and gave the name of a KGB expert on Latin America as his reference – a major who had saved Sammi's life. The reference allied to a suitable consultation fee to be paid in US dollars earned him an invitation to the doctor's *dacha* and Sammi hired a pirate cab outside the Beliztny Hotel. The driver grumbled incessantly about the execrable state of the road and refused to take his car down the last quarter-mile of rutted driveway.

Midges and mosquitoes were the only wild game left alive in the birch woods. Sammi fastened the cuffs and collar of his shirt and pulled his Geneva airport cap over his ears before hurrying through the trees, jacket on his arm and a nylon hold-all slung over his shoulder.

Three sheep kept a half-acre of grass cropped round the large log cabin. A Lada of indeterminate age and colour stood under a tree with the hood up. A backside in a tight blue skirt bent over the radiator. The skirt was short, the legs white and strong and barefoot. Their owner had scratched a mosquito bite behind her left knee with an oily fingernail. A spanner clattered and there were choice Russian curses accompanied by the appearance of a young woman with black hands. Her eyes were a brilliant blue.

Seeing Sammi, she said: 'You're Daddy's foreign something or other.'

'Journalist,' Sammi said.

'Something or other,' she corrected and shouted for her father before crawling under the Lada to retrieve the spanner.

Tall and lean, Doctor Ignosiev had been collegiate high jump champion in the fifties and remained fit. Sammi presented him first with the promised envelope.

'If he can fix a carburettor, he can stay the night,' the daughter called as Doctor Ignosiev shepherded Sammi up the steps to the wide porch and through into a book-lined study.

There were two armchairs and a desk with a writer's chair behind it, two coarsely-woven Turkoman rugs in rich earth colours, and a wood-burning stove. Outside there were the three sheep and the blonde daughter with her head in the Lada, some rose bushes in bloom, the birch trees and a lone pine. The mosquitoes didn't show through the dust on the window panes. Nor was the doctor's service with the KGB visible. Doctor Dimitri Ignosiev was the world authority on torture-induced trauma.

He faced Sammi, nervous, even frightened: 'For an Argentinian, you speak exceptional Russian, Mr Samuelson. I would have judged that you came from the Caucasus. Who are you?'

'A storyteller,' Sammi said. 'I'm not out to disclose you to the world's press. I want to tell you a story about a young woman and answer any questions you put to me. Then I will examine your daughter's carburettor while you consider. And we might have a drink. Once you've given me your advice, your daughter can drive me back.'

Delving into his hold-all, he produced a bottle of fifteen-year-old Springbank single malt whisky that was as dry and as clean on the palate as any XO Cognac.

The two men relaxed opposite each other in the deep, comfortably-worn leather armchairs and Sammi related all he knew of Jay Li. The psychologist listened without taking notes nor did his expression ever change. The story ended with Sammi quoting Jay as she stood over him on the beach: 'I want to be there. I want to watch.'

The doctor had been holding his breath for the last seconds and he let it out, nodding to himself:

'Oh yes, yes indeed, *I want to watch*. I can definitely see that, can't you, Mr Samuelson? You'll have to tell me a little about yourself. You are not a journalist of course. I can tell what you've been in your past. However, it's the present that interests us, you and me, Mr Samuelson.'

He smiled suddenly: 'You might consider your reply while assisting my daughter, Mr Samuelson. She doesn't approve of me – understandable given even the little she knows. But my wife died last year and she considers me rather the way someone who is reluctant to do the housework might consider a bad-tempered and smelly old dog they have inherited. Shooting would be the obvious answer, but then what? No one left to blame for the state of the home. I tell you this, Mr Samuelson, because she is seldom tolerant of my visitors and I wouldn't like you to take her attitude personally and be offended.'

Sammi found her sitting beside the Lada on the grass. She had dragged the back of a hand across her face to wipe away the sweat and had left a streak of black grease which further accentuated the blue of her eyes. Her cheekbones were high, her nose short and broad above generous lips. There was a freshness to her that matched the sun slanting through the branches and the hum of bees and the tangy scent of the birch trees. Not much of her father in her, Sammi thought. The new Russia. A smile would have been nice.

'No luck?' he asked.

She said: 'There's a piece missing.'

He thought back through all the things that he had taken to pieces when he was a boy that had ended up with a piece missing or a piece too many. He counted twenty American single dollar bills from his billfold.

'I'll hunt while you pay off my cab,' he said: 'The fare's agreed including waiting time. Don't tell me it's too much. Cabs are always too much – anywhere in the world. It's one of those rules like which way the planet turns and the tides and your parents turning stupid immediately you get into your teens.'

He found the missing part in the grass, stripped and reassembled the carburettor, and adjusted both the jets and timing. Fixing Ladas was a skill taught by the Department – they were the only cars a field agent could steal within the Soviet sphere back in the Cold War. Now there were stretch Mercedes and BMWs belonging to disorganised crime.

The daughter had returned and was watching him. Perhaps he had looked depressed because she said: 'If you are going to kill yourself, do it somewhere else.'

'I hadn't thought of it,' he said.

He washed at the kitchen sink before going back into the study. The doctor had helped himself to a second glass of Springbank. He patted his lips on a folded handkerchief and smiled a dead smile. Then raised the glass: 'To the brave Mr Samuelson. Not the innocent. We were none of us innocent. However guilt remains a matter of degree and I never once pulled a trigger nor administered medication beyond the discipline of my calling.'

He sipped abstemiously, then rolled the whisky round the glass.

'Excellent, quite extraordinarily excellent. Did they tell you that, Mr Samuelson? those who told you to seek my counsel? That I never did the dirty work?'

He was too intelligent and too understanding of men to expect sympathy or forgiveness. He was setting the record straight, perhaps for his daughter listening outside. 'No, Mr Samuelson, none of us were innocent. And what now? Have you escaped your cocoon and become a knight errant? Or are you merely a butterfly flitting round the world?'

He sipped again, a few drops, while studying Sammi over the rim of his glass. 'Oh yes, I can still be cruel – that much is left to me. And my experience, of course. So which is it? Knight or butterfly? Is there a difference, Mr Samuelson? But I forget that you have come for a clinical judgment on the young lady rather than on your own condition.

'Consider a woman raped in Bosnia, Mr Samuelson. Imagine her humiliation as she watches television and, night after night, sees those who instituted rape as a policy given substance and legitimacy by television interviewers and by the negotiators at Geneva.

'The case of your young woman is similar. That is the terrible humiliation she suffered – that she was abused, not even out of desire, but as an implement of policy, a spectacle. And you, Mr Samuelson, whatever your role, are one of the spectators. The butterfly must fly away, Mr Samuelson – or is it the knight errant who must ride off across the steppes? Yes, Mr Samuelson, do your duty, then be gone out of her life.'

He paused to refill his glass, then slouched in thought for a while. A mosquito wined by the window. Sammi watched it settle on the curtains. Footsteps crossed the verandah and he watched the girl drag a deckchair into the sun. He was envious of her youth, her lack of involvement in the past.

The doctor tapped a long bony finger on the arm of his chair to draw Sammi's attention back from the outside world of sunlight and summer perfume. His thoughts were ordered. He sat very upright, shoulders back, and looked straight at Sammi. He spoke quickly but with precision: 'My experience as a clinical psychologist leads me to believe, Mr Samuelson, that the only absolution for the humiliated lies in the public humiliation of their persecutors.

'There is no time limit on trauma, Mr Samuelson, so there can be no, *It all happened so long ago.*

'The Galtieris and Stroessners and Pinochets, Mr Samuelson; and our ones; Heshner, Degariov, oh yes, and myself amongst millions; old men hiding in the jungle, in monasteries. They must be brought, not to justice, but to the footlights. Yes, first the stocks, not the birch – and then? Two eyes for an eye, Mr Samuelson. That's the cure.'

Rising from his chair abruptly, he blundered through the swing door to the garden and disappeared amongst the trees. Sammi came out onto the porch and the daughter asked: 'What did you do to the pig?'

'He told the truth – it upset him,' Sammi said. 'I'd prefer not to spend the night. Perhaps you'd drive me back into Moscow now that your car's fixed.'

26

Fifteen miles from London's West End, Richmond Park is just under three thousand acres of Royal parkland studded with clumps of oak trees and beaches. There used to be elms but the Dutch bugs murdered them. Some five hundred deer graze the park. Saturday was one of those beautiful summer mornings that English expatriates long for when they have difficulties at the office.

Charles Benson had run cross-country at school and at university and Sammi Samuelson had his work cut out keeping him in sight. Benson turned up into the oaks above the polo ground. He stopped amongst the trees to retie his trainers and left a thin tube of onion-skin paper in the V of a big root. He had written the name, George Ross, on the paper and a brief outline of his career and habits.

George Ross had worked for thirty years in that part of Military Intelligence concerned with internal security. In a commercial environment he would have been called a filing clerk. However, handling of certain files was restricted to senior administrative grades. Head of Records, this regulation enabled him to take early retirement with a pension equivalent to that of an army colonel.

He then transferred with departmental protection and approval to a major security organisation in the private sector, where his presence was convenient to his old employers who suffered, with the demise of the Cold War, from restricted funds and were keen to develop outside sources of intelligence.

George Ross soon widened his role to encompass other branches of the SIS and the armed forces and became a trader, bartering security intelligence to his private clients in return for financial information useful to his old masters and to his surviving Cold War friends at Langley.

The financial rewards were considerable and he now revelled in bespoke suits and cigars, and a pied-à-terre in London as well as a country house. He had also joined the Royal Automobile Club, not prestigious in social terms but far more opulent than such haunts of the aristocracy as Whites and Boodles and the Hunt.

He preferred London at the weekend. Waiters were more attentive and there was pleasure in driving his Daimler through empty streets. It was his habit to dine and play bridge at his club on Sunday nights.

He was eighty-six pounds to the good when he left the bridge table. Strolling through to the cloakroom, he dressed himself against the night air in a field officer's grey overcoat and a silk scarf.

George Ross had swelled with affluence and was inclined to sweat easily. The purchase of the field officer's greatcoat had fostered his tendency to strut and give abrupt nods of recognition to acquaintances. He nodded to the duty porter in the hall as he set his hat straight and eased on his gloves.

His Daimler was parked round the corner of the block and he took off his hat and undid his overcoat buttons before settling himself into the seat. He loved the car. Its perfume of Connolly leather, Cuban cigars and Trumper's after-shave was the essence of his new position. The engine started easily and he signalled correctly before easing the big car from the curb.

'Drive to Heathrow, the short-term car park at Terminal Three,' a voice said and George Ross felt something cold and thin tighten round his throat. 'It's called a garrotte,' the voice said.

Sammi didn't want George Ross shouting for help. In warning, he tightened the wire as George lowered the window to take the ticket from the machine at the airport car park.

The barrier lifted and Sammi told him to reverse into a parking space so that he could watch for intruders.

'Do you know who I am?' Sammi asked.

George shook his head and sweat sprayed from his face.

'Trent,' Sammi said. 'Remember? You sold me? You're going to tell me who to; you're going to tell me who gave you the information; you're going to tell me the other names, the names other than Trent that your source told me I use. Is that clear? Of course you don't have to tell me anything, George. This is a free country. But if you don't tell me, I'll kill you.'

Sammi grabbed George by the side of the neck and dug his fingers in, cutting off the blood to George's brain for long enough to leave him dizzy for a minute.

'Understood?' he asked.

George nodded.

'Splendid. Let's begin at the beginning,' Sammi said: 'Who did you sell me to?'

George Ross told his story with many pauses to mop his face. He was paid a retainer by a score of commercial clients in the Far East. Two of these clients, Cairns Oliver and a subsidiary of the Wong Fu Group, had asked for a search on a British yachtsman, Trent. George had played the name through his normal sources and had struck gold at Trent's old Department. He hadn't known there were any other aliases so hadn't asked his source – there had been no further enquiries.

'I swear,' he said.

He demurred at giving the name of his source so Sammi tweaked his ear. A sadistic teacher had tweaked George's ear in the first form at his preparatory school and the tweaking worked.

Tossing George a writing pad and pen, Sammi told him to write down every piece of information that his source at the Department had given him over the years. Sammi wanted a similar letter concerning George's contacts in Washington.

When George had finished, Sammi took the letters, folded them, and slipped them into his pocket. Then he explained to George a little of the background to what had happened: that he wanted the girl to be safe and about the gold he wanted paid by Sir Philip Li and how Sir Philip was to pay it.

'Li is going to do all this, George, because if he doesn't, the newspapers are going to learn that he paid to have his own granddaughter murdered. All I want is the girl's safety. To be safe, she has to cease to exist.'

He detailed the funeral carefully: 'Tell Sir Philip to have his men find a corpse of a girl the same age as his granddaughter. The funeral has to be next Friday and it has to be midday and I want Wong Fu standing beside Sir Philip at the grave. If Wong Fu doesn't agree, tell him the same thing, George, that I want the girl safe. He comes to the funeral or the newspapers learn that he sponsors piracy.'

Sammi gave his instructions in great detail and, once George had

226

written them down, read them through to make sure there was no mistake.

'They'll kill me,' George said.

'Not necessarily, George. You're not that important.'

Sammi Samuelson instructed him to leave the keys in the car and get out. George Ross had difficulty standing.

Sammi said: 'There's no need to be scared. I need you, George. I'm going to borrow your hat and coat and I'm going to lock you in the trunk for a while. You'll be quite comfortable and I'll drive carefully.'

Driving the Daimler back to London, Trent turned down into a pretty Regency crescent off the Holland Park Avenue end of the Ladbroke Grove. He parked the car and walked up the steps to the front door of a house in the middle of the crescent.

There was a Director General of Trent's old department, a Deputy Director General and eight heads of section. The house belonged to one of the eight, Marcus Richworth. Trent leant on the bell until a curtain cracked in a window above the door. George's car was outside and Sammi was wearing the right hat and coat. A light went on and footsteps came down the hallway. There followed the usual modern-day rattle of security locks and chains.

Jean Richworth opened the door. She was a comfortable-looking woman, big-breasted and broadening in her middle age. She had been brought up on a farm and had never seemed quite at home in the city. She said, 'Oh, my husband thought it was George Ross.'

'He's in the car,' Sammi said.

She could see the car so he added, 'In the trunk. He's all right.'

She said: 'It's gone wrong.'

'Yes,' Sammi said.

She said: 'I always thought it would.'

Sammi had always liked her and he said: 'I'm sorry. It won't take long but I do need to speak to your husband.

'Yes,' she said. 'Yes, of course. I'll fetch him. Would you like a cup of tea, or coffee, or a drink?'

'Coffee would be nice,' Sammi said.

She showed him into a pleasant chintzy drawing room perfumed by a cut-glass bowl of iceberg roses. Bow windows opened onto a cast iron terrace from which steps descended to communal gardens. There should have been dogs and children but the Richworths had never had either. Sammi had often wondered about the lack of children. Now he realised that she had lived for years with the fear of scandal and of its effect on the young.

She called up the stairs and her husband came down dressed in an expensive dressing gown, silk pyjamas, horn-rimmed spectacles. He had been putting in his teeth and smelt of toothpaste. He was older than his wife. Though younger than Trent's old control, the two men had been great friends and allies, supporters of the special relationship with the US, with the cousins. To the europhiles the special relationship was better called servitude.

'Where's George?' he barked: 'Who the devil are you?'

His wife said, 'Don't be silly, dear, you remember Pat Mahoney.'

'Mahoney? Nonsense the damn fellow's dead. Years ago. In Ireland.'

'Sammi Samuelson,' Sammi said. He didn't offer his hand. 'We need to talk,' he said and Jean Richworth nodded and said:

'Yes, yes of course – of course you do. I'll make the coffee. Sugar, milk?'

'A little milk,' Sammi said.

She gave her husband a light pat as she went out: 'Try to be sensible, dear. Brave. It doesn't really matter.'

But Richworth was full of bluster: 'Damned impertinence, charging into my house in the middle of the night. How dare you? Scaring my wife.'

'You sold me to George Ross. Charles Benson knows and I have a letter from George to the Director General,' Sammi said. 'Who else did you sell me to? And under what aliases?'

'Trent, that's all, and only to George. And I didn't sell you. It was an exchange of information beneficial to the Department.'

'Perhaps you should read the letter.' Sammi took it from his coat. It was a long letter, ten pages or more.

Shocked by its length, Richworth accepted it reluctantly. Taking off the horn-rims, he patted his pockets for his reading spectacles. 'Damn, left them by the bed,' he said: 'There's a spare pair in my study.'

'Benson will be here in half an hour. He's bringing a couple of men from Special Branch,' Sammi said.

Richworth went out. Sammi heard the study door shut and thought that he heard the key turn. He thought that he ought to do something but there wasn't anything to do.

Jean Richworth hesitated outside the study on her way back from the kitchen and Sammi heard her ask through the door, 'Are you going to be all right, dear?'

Richworth said, 'Yes, yes of course I am. Don't worry, old thing.'

She came in and, setting the tray on the low table, sat beside Sammi on the sofa. She poured the coffee. Then she said, 'Would you mind awfully if I held your hand?'

Sammi said, 'Of course not.'

She was crying and she apologised for being silly.

Sammi said: 'It's all right.' He wanted to leave or be angry but he was tired and the image was there of his father sitting at his desk. He shuddered and she said:

'It must be difficult for you.'

The shot came and almost immediately the sound of feet climbing the front steps followed by a single ring of the doorbell.

'I'll let them in,' Sammi said.

Seven o'clock in the morning and Sammi Samuelson played with a cup of bad coffee and a sad croissant at a corner table in the cafeteria at Paddington Station. He faced towards the door, airline ticket protruding from his breast pocket.

The American was five minutes late. He bought himself a coffee and a cup cake and carried the tray over.

'Sammi Samuelson,' Sammi said.

The American said, 'So I heard.' Early forties, he was a neat compact man, ears flat against his skull, grey eyes, square hands. He had dressed for a day in the country, corduroys, flannel shirt, tweed jacket, and good shoes – one of the professions, but not from the city, and with inherited wealth – that was the image. He turned his cup round in the saucer. 'I have to tell you, Sammi, there's a lot of people back in Washington who think you're poison. First there's the body bags you filled for the Cold War dinosaurs. Then they believe you saved Castro's arse a while back. What happened? Did you fall out of a helicopter on the way to Damascus? The vision thing?'

He was about to sip at his coffee but the smell saved him and he gave Sammi a smile that touched only one side of his face and, like his voice, was casually self-mocking:

'All that's so you know that I checked you out. If I'm here it's because there are a couple of people I know personally, people for whom I have a lot of respect, who say I should trust you with everything except my career.'

He smiled at Sammi again: 'Senior people, so you didn't do them any harm. I thought I'd risk getting my feet wet . . .'

Sammi took out George Ross's account of his American operation and handed the American the top two pages.

The American read fast. He blew air through pursed lips and looked up: 'Hell of a breakfast present. What do you want, Mr Samuelson?'

Sammi told him about Jay Li. 'She's a US citizen. I want her to feel safe and have a chance at building a new life.'

'She'll have money?'

'Enough,' Sammi said.

'Then I'll need to speak with an acquaintance at IRS.'

The American thought a while: 'You planning a switch?'

'Tokyo,' Sammi said: 'That's near enough to where I have my boat.'

The American busied himself with the logistics. 'The documentation needs to be done inside the US,' he said: 'American Airlines flies into Dallas from Tokyo. I'll pick the lady up at the gate.'

'Thanks,' Sammi said. He passed the remaining pages across the table.

The American read them through, then folded them and slipped them into his jacket. His smile was back as he thanked Sammi:

'I'd like to believe that I'd have done the new identity without the payment, but that would be self-deception.'

'Don't worry about it,' Sammi said.

Trent was Sammi Samuelson when he went through immigration at Sydney and rented a Ford at the Budget desk. He was Sammi Samuelson when he called a theatrical agency for an appointment. Driving into the city, he bought a couple of pairs of Chinos and two sports shirts, socks, and a pair of trainers, all at David Jones, and a pair of Fry boots over on Conner Street.

Sammi Samuelson's suits looked better in Australia than they had in Europe and the receptionist at the theatrical agency was reasonably polite. The director of the agency was in her early forties with bright black intelligent eyes in a clear-skinned oval face framed in auburn hair cut to her shoulders. A silver chain held a single opal in the hollow of her throat. A cream shirt with French cuffs and opal links, beige linen skirt, a body that was worth the daily maintenance and the gym fees – Chloe Isaacs. Her slim long well-kept hands, no wedding ring but a square-cut diamond, went to sleep each side of a legal pad while she listened.

'The girl has to be young and she has to be small,' Sammi said: 'Five one or two, and she has to be Chinese. Not Vietnam pretending, but real Chinese, Miss Isaacs. It's not a career but it's legal, it's good money and there's no danger.'

Sammi wrote the name and telephone number of a Special Branch Inspector with the Australian Federal Police on the back of a Sammi Samuelson visiting card and under it, another name: Cefyn Evans.

'Check if you want.'

She read the card: 'Cefyn Evans – that's you, Mr Samuelson . . .'

'Sometimes,' Sammi said.

She swore and said, 'One of them.'

Sammi shrugged. 'It's better than being a child molester or shooting porno movies, Miss Isaacs.'

'Chloe,' she said.

'Chloe . . .'

Sammi drove up the coast and stopped the night in a motel. He left the motel at five in the morning and headed inland. A thirty-mile drive took him to the sign pointing to Glengar Stud and he turned in at the gate. The private road was well-maintained and ran between clean, well-watered paddocks fenced in split logs. There were enough shade trees to keep the horses comfortable on a hot day. The horses looked good at a distance. Trent counted twenty mares and a dozen foals before giving up. The stables were at the top of a slight rise with an all-weather track below and an extra strip climbing straight up the steepest part of the hill. The house stood a quarter-mile off to the left in a stand of blue gums. The house was white wood with a wide verandah and a tin roof, big enough for a couple with two kids. Below the house a dozen sprinklers played over five acres of emerald green alfalfa. The breeze blew cool off the alfalfa as Sammi carried his suitcase and the bag of new clothes and the boots up the steps.

The sound of the car had brought a tall woman out onto the verandah. She had a good look at Sammi before saying, 'Shit.' But she gave him a cheek to kiss and a hug. 'You'll find Charley down by the track.'

'I have to talk with you first, Marce,' he said. They had known

231

each other for fifteen years and losing her friendship would have hurt. He watched her grey eyes and strong hands as he told her a little about the girl over a cup of coffee in the kitchen.

She sat hunched over the scrubbed-pine kitchen table, a big-boned competent woman with a lot of love in her that two fast-moving kids and a husband in a difficult line of work hadn't used up. She had always been a good listener and she waited for him to finish but there was a lot of anger in her eyes and her lips whitened into a hard line. Her hands worked on each other toward the end. There'd been no washing machine on the sheep station where she grew up and they were big-knuckled muscular hands that could chop a log into kindling without getting tired.

She said: 'Jesus, shit,' when he'd done. She covered his hands with hers and stroked their backs with her thumbs as if she was trying to knead out the pain. She wanted to be sure that he knew that she understood and that she was on his side not because he was family from way back but because she wanted it done the same way he wanted it done. She gave his hands a final squeeze and said: 'You'd better get down to the track. Tell Charley I said it was all right.'

Sammi changed into chinos, sports shirt and the Fry boots. The man he had come to see was studying the way a mare moved as a young Aboriginal woman eased her round the track. He was in his early sixties, five foot one inches in height, slim and straight as a bamboo. A wide-brimmed hat shaded his face and he was chewing a straw.

The scent of horse sweat, saddle soap and the dust scent of the track were like old home week. After a while Sammi said, 'Left hind. What was it, a strain?'

'Bump,' Charley said. 'Horsebox got in a shunt with a Mac truck.' He spat the straw out: 'What do you want Paddy? If it's a job, say so.'

'A job,' Paddy said. He was tired of being Sammi.

'I retired,' Charley said.

'And I'm out of the Department. This is personal, Charley, and it pays two hundred.'

Charley flagged the girl, had a word with her, and watched as she led the horse up to the stables. Afer a while, he said: 'Where?'

'Hong Kong.'

'Marce'll do her nut.'

'I talked to Marce already,' Paddy said: 'It's something she understands.'

Charley had told him to take the bay. The horse was a comfortable ride and didn't mind the midday heat that bleached the colour out of the grassland and made the blue trunks of the gum trees quiver against the flanks of the hills. They covered four miles before Paddy dismounted in the shade of a tarity tree. He'd brought a spade and he dug down two feet before hitting the box. It was made of Kevlar rather than steel. A metal detector wouldn't have helped a search party.

The box contained six waterproof packages, each neatly marked in black ink. Richard O'Neill was an Australian tax lawyer with a home in Normandy and an office in Liechtenstein. His financial stuff was all Swiss.

Sammi Samuelson disappeared into the wood stove back at the house.

There had been a trace of brashness in Sammi Samuelson more suitable to a mid-range motel. Richard O'Neill was first class air tickets and the Connaught or the Meurice in Paris, five-star, but conservative. His hair was grey and short and he had startlingly blue eyes behind a pair of gold-rimmed spectacles. He wore a lightweight navy suit bought off the peg at Vince Moloney's, a cotton shirt with double cuffs, and a cricket club tie.

Chloe Isaacs said, 'I could get you a part in a mid-market soap.'

He smiled.

The Chinese Australian waited in the next room. She'd studied for four years at drama school and had a few small parts but nothing that was going anywhere. Chloe Isaacs introduced her as Laura Sing. She had a firm handshake and swimmer's shoulders.

'I don't photograph well,' she explained with a nice shrug that said it wasn't anyone's fault: 'I'm okay on the stage but that doesn't pay bills.'

He turned to Chloe Isaacs: 'I'd prefer having this interview out at the beach.'

The girl looked surprised but Chloe said: 'Doesn't a bathroom with the tap running do? Or is that old hat?'

'The beach is more pleasant.'

He drove Laura Sing out to Bondi where they walked for an

233

hour, rehearsing the details. He had to tell her enough of the background so she would understand the risks, but no mention of Charley. She asked if he had a thing with the girl in Hong Kong. He said he didn't.

'So you're doing this because you think you ought to?'

He didn't answer.

'I like that,' she said, tucking a hand through his arm as they turned back toward the car.

He dropped her downtown and drove back to the office to finalise payments. He paid cash and said he didn't need a receipt but Chloe wrote one anyway.

All the travelling and the name changes and Richworth's suicide had left him tired and out of balance. He said, 'Chloe, I don't suppose you'd like to have dinner?'

'I'd like to a lot,' she said.

He should have left it at that but he asked anyway, 'Is that a yes?'

'It's a yes, I want to – but I'm the wrong age to be that stupid.'

She was right and he didn't argue.

27

Richard O'Neill hired a Hertz Nissan at Ninoy Aquino airport and drove into Metro Manila. The multi-level car park was a block down from the Paseo de Roxas in Makati. Richard found a back slot on the sixth level and locked the car. Tanaka had instructed him to look for a silver and gold Toyota Landcruiser with smoked glass windows parked on the fourth level. The electricity supply was dead so he walked down and found the Landcruiser backed up against a pillar. Tanaka shoved the door open. Richard climbed in and dropped his bag in the back.

Tanaka had acquired a Philippine passport in the name of Miss Angelica Chu. The photograph of Jay Li in the passport had been shot with excess flash to flatten her features and could have been any of ten million young Chinese women. Richard thought it was perfect.

The two men didn't talk much as they drove out of town and down the southern highway. Luzon is the largest island in the Philippines. The town of Sorsogon is near the south tip, eleven hours by car from Manila. The two men shared the driving. The Toyota's headlights cut through trees as they turned off the highway down a dirt road a few miles out of town and then down a track to the beach where Doctor Imai's *baslig* waited. Richard O'Neill left his blue contact lenses in the car and put on his spectacles.

The water was smooth as an ice rink in the hour before dawn and the narrow hull sped over the water at fifteen knots with only the after tips of the bamboo outriggers touching the surface. The sky was extraordinarily clear, the stars bright as halogen lamps, and the islands rose at them out of the sea, black and softly shaped.

Dawn brought a light mist that spread like smoke on the water. The island they headed for floated on the mist. As the sun rose, the mist broke up into threads that trailed up the mountain. The resort beach shone like a sliver of pale gold.

The boatman cut power one hundred yards out and the *baslig* ghosted in over coral heads plainly visible in the clear still water. A shoal of tiny fish flashed like polished copper under the starboard outrigger and a frigate bird sailed overhead. Then came the sudden clatter of a pan in the kitchen and Doctor Imai appeared from the house.

Tanaka and the doctor competed in Japanese etiquette for a couple of minutes. Jay Li came out onto her cabin's tiny verandah. Her hair was wet from the shower. She wore a patterned silk sarong and a white cotton top with long sleeves loose at the wrist. Richard walked up to the cabin and said: 'Good morning, Miss Li. I hope you're better.'

She looked at him but she didn't smile or offer him her hand so he sat with his back to her on the bottom of the three wooden steps that led down from the verandah to the lawn. The two Japanese had finished bowing and were on their way up to the main house. The doctor had acquired a tame mouse deer in Richard's absence. The deer wore a collar and was tethered to a post to keep it out of the flower beds. Richard watched the tiny animal nibble at a jackfruit one of the gardeners had split open on the edge of the grass.

Doctor Imai reappeared with a black teapot and three cups on a tray. He walked over to Jay Li's cabin, set the tray down on the verandah, and filled the cups. He called Trent Sam instead of Richard O'Neill, and hoped that his journey had been fruitful.

'Very,' Richard said.

Having drunk their tea, the two men strolled along the beach and the doctor gave his appraisal of Jay Li's condition. Her wounds were healed, she was fit to travel. 'We are discussing the young lady's physical state,' he said.

Richard O'Neill returned to his seat on the step. He said, 'Miss Li, we have to discuss your future. I've arranged to have you buried in Hong Kong on Friday morning and I need to be there. You'll have more freedom once you're officially dead. I'm arranging funds for you – you'll be well off.'

She walked down the steps and stood on the lawn facing him. She stood very erect inside some kind of cloak that was invisible but tough and impenetrable. The silence continued for what seemed a long time.

Finally he said, 'What you wanted – it's all fixed.'

She accepted his assurance with a brief nod that reminded him of her grandfather.

She hadn't spoken to him yet but he said: 'My name's changed to Richard O'Neill. If you come with me, that's something you have to remember. Flying into Hong Kong you'll be Angelica Chu.' He handed her the Philippine passport: 'You'll change names again after the funeral and that gets you to Dallas. You'll be met off the flight by a friend of mine. He'll take you through customs and immigration and issue you a new US passport in the name of your choice. You'll need to rest a couple of days, but you have to go to Nassau. That's where your bank is and another friend of mine is expecting you. Once you've done the bank you can go anywhere you want. Perhaps somewhere quiet for a while. Maybe back to school?'

She leafed through the Philippine passport and for a moment he thought that she might comment.

Richard O'Neill and Miss Angelica Chu had connecting rooms at the Mandarin in Hong Kong. Richard telephoned Braemar Lodge at seven in the evening, gave his name and asked to speak to Sir Euan Wiley. He was told that Sir Euan was busy so he gave the date and place of their meeting in the Philippines.

Sir Euan must have been listening on an extension – he came on the line in seconds. Who was O'Neill? What did he want?

Richard said he was a lawyer specialising in insurance claims where piracy was involved. The Philippines was an area of particular interest. He asked for a brief meeting. A meeting would be to Sir Euan's advantage. He would be free at eleven if that was convenient?'

'Eleven – eleven at night?' The chairman of Cairns Oliver was out of his depth but he didn't bluster. 'Where do you want to meet?'

Braemar Lodge suited Richard – the fewer people who knew of the meeting the better.

He had rented a Budget Honda at the airport and a cellular phone. He left the hotel at nine, drove up the Peak, and parked fifty yards from Braemar Lodge under a street lamp between a

Rover Stirling and a big BMW. He watched the house and garden for an hour before telephoning. Wiley answered. Richard apologised profusely but he was running forty minutes behind schedule.

A short while later a car phone buzzed a couple of times up ahead. A man got out, put his hands on his hips and arched backwards to stretch his spine as if he had been waiting a while. A few bending exercises, then he lit a cigarette and finished it before getting back into the car.

Richard wondered whether he had a partner in the car – a non-smoker.

He had expected the tap on Wiley's phone and wondered which of the two financiers had employed the surveillance team or whether one of the *triads* had traced him. He folded the gold-rimmed lawyer's spectacles into their case and squeezed out the blue contact lenses. Sliding out onto the sidewalk, he approached the car on his belly. He had to stand to see in but he was safe because any occupant of the car would be watching Braemar Lodge or the road. There were two men, one in the front, one in the back. Chinese, they wore dark slacks and dark shirts.

The car was a stick shift. The smoker had curled round the stick with his elbows on the driver's seat. Chin cupped in his hands, he was watching Braemar Lodge through a peephole in the door handle. He might have a handgun on the floor but he would need time to get unentangled from the stick. The second man was off-duty and had stretched out on the back seat with his head and shoulders against the curbside door. The lock button was up.

Richard jerked the door open. The man fell back and Richard slammed his head on the sidewalk. The smoker tried to twist round. Richard grabbed him by the hair with his free hand, dragged him halfway over the seat and chopped him on the side of the neck.

Blood dripped from the first man's scalp and he groaned as Richard heaved him up against the rear wheel. Richard relieved him of the 9 mm Browning in his belt, took the belt too, looped it round the man's neck and tied it tight to the rear doorhandle. That was one man safe for the moment.

Getting into the front of the car, Richard jerked the smoker flat across the front seats, and hit him with the Browning across the side of the jaw. Two of them safe. The smoker's handgun was on the floor by the drive pedals and Richard found a roll of heavy duty parcel tape in the glove compartment. The tape suggested that whoever had sent the two men wanted Richard alive. He taped and gagged both men. Neither of them carried identification, so they weren't police which would have been embarrassing. He hoped that he hadn't cracked the first man's skull.

He eased the man's pants down, lifted him carefully into the boot of the car, and used the pants as a pillow. The smoker he locked in the hire car's boot. Fifty minutes remained until his meeting. Less than a dozen cars drove by. None of the cars did so more than once so they weren't circling the block. Nor did any of the cars park.

Satisfied that there had been no reinforcements for the surveillance team, he crossed the road quickly and let himself in at the side gate to Braemar Lodge at precisely eleven thirty. He carried a yellow plastic file cover.

Sir Euan Wiley answered the doorbell – perhaps the servants had been sent to bed. He wore a striped city shirt, blue cotton slacks, and monogrammed velvet slippers that Trent presumed to have been a gift. Unsure of himself, the *taipan* seemed less tall than in Sir Philip Li's company at the hacienda.

'O'Neill?'

'Correct,' Richard said. He didn't offer to shake Wiley's hand.

The dimly-lit hall was Scots *Schloss* Gothic, twin sets of armour on guard either side of the door, flagstones, and a stuffed grisly bear at the foot of the plum-carpeted stairs. A breakfast room opened off the hall. The wall-panelling and furniture were french-polished mahogany, dark and heavy. A small cut-glass chandelier supplied the only light. Wiley closed the door carefully before facing O'Neill: 'You're a lawyer? Australian, by the sound of you? What's this about a meeting in the Philippines?'

'I represent Miss Mai'sin Jasmine Li's estate, Sir Euan.' Richard O'Neill tapped the file cover: 'I have here an exact account of the events following on the piracy of the *Ts'ai Yen*.'

He dropped the file on the table.

At first Wiley didn't touch it, then he riffled a corner as if interested in the quality of paper. Finally he picked it up.

There were twelve pages, double spaced. The lines marking Wiley's face deepened as he turned the pages. Finally he came to the three signatures:

John Patrick Trent, Tanaka Kazuko, M. Jay Li

The signatures had been witnessed by a Judge in Manila and a half-dozen stamps in various inks made it official.

'M. Jay Li . . .'

'My client,' Richard said.

Wiley had begun a second reading: 'And the girl – the one we're burying tomorrow?'

'Does it matter?'

Wiley looked up at Richard as if he were the criminal: 'Good God, man, don't you see? They may have murdered a girl for the corpse.'

'They won't have done that,' Richard said. 'There's a professional in charge and it's always simpler and cheaper buying from a local morgue or a funeral parlour.'

Wiley fiddled with the file as he worked it out: 'George Ross?'

'Under my instructions,' Richard said.

Wiley looked at Richard, prying at his disguise, but sure now: 'What do you want?'

'I want my client left in peace,' Richard said.

It wasn't enough and Wiley waited patiently. After a while Richard said: 'I don't have much faith in the good intentions of the immensely rich. They exercise too much power . . .' But it was obvious and he was tired of playing games and living behind different skins. 'Just do it,' he said in Trent's voice, or Patrick Mahoney's voice.

Wiley looked across the garden at the intricate wrought iron gates to Braemar Lodge – Wiley, the chief clerk, prestige without power. He recalled Philip leading him by the elbow out of the meeting at the hacienda and he wondered how he would have acted had he known Philip's intentions. Would he have put a stop to it? Or protested?

Trent had promised to return to the hotel by midnight. Jay tried to watch the film on TV but found herself concentrating on the minutes as they ticked by on the TV alarm.

A young maid let herself into Trent's room to ready the rooms for the night. She came through the connecting door and said: 'Good evening, Miss.'

Jay watched her strip the cover from the king-sized bed, turn down the sheet, and plump the pillows.

Finished, the girl gave Jay a little smile. There was no mistaking her presumption that Jay and Trent were lovers.

Jay wanted to scream at her. Her legs began to shiver and she

240

had to fight hard to keep still. Then she couldn't move, not until the maid had said good night and let herself out.

She knew that she was losing control but there wasn't any way of saving herself. She double-locked her own door. She didn't have the key to Trent's. The best she could do was drag an armchair against it. She returned to her own room and sat facing away from the bed.

She knew that she had locked her door. The key was on the dressing table. It had a brass tag. She tried not to look at it but she couldn't stop herself. She grabbed it and ran to the door, fumbling as she tried to fit it into the lock and dropping it on the carpet.

She knelt to pick the key up. Someone was out in the corridor, listening. She shuffled backward on her knees to the telephone. The concierge answered. He was Chinese. So was the maid. Jay slammed the receiver down.

Trent had brought her here. Her hate for him was suddenly so strong that it drove the fear out. She searched his luggage for a weapon but he had out-guessed her and taken it with him. She didn't panic. There was a paper-knife on the desk. She felt its point – it was sharp enough.

Trent was clever in getting Uncle Euan to act as his negotiator. Her grandfather trusted Euan. Everyone did. She wondered how much her grandfather would pay Trent. She knew she couldn't escape. They were watching. The look on the maid's face should have warned her. She didn't mind dying. It would all stop once she was dead, all the pain of it, the shame, the fear. But first she must kill Trent. Confident in his deception, he would be off-guard.

Everything had to be normal so she dragged the armchair back from his door. Then she took the upright chair from her desk and put it in the doorway between the two rooms. She dug the tip of the paper-knife into the ball of her thumb to be quite sure of its point. The opening words were important. As she rehearsed the scene, she bore in mind Trent's background and determined to be very English so that he would feel at home and safe.

Abandoning the Honda with the smoker locked in the boot, Richard drove the surveillance team's car down from the peak. Headlights flashed at him at the second intersection below Braemar Lodge – that would be the surveillance team's back-up. He returned the flash and accelerated hard, backtracking at the next corner, then a left and a right and left again as he checked his rear view mirror.

Certain that he was clear of them, he headed directly to the Central Hospital. He parked the car in a No Parking zone close to the casualty entrance and found a phone booth in the reception area. Dialling EMERGENCY, he reported the injured man in the boot. The operator tried to interrupt, wanting his particulars. He told her to shut up and listen. He gave the registration number of the car, its make and colour, the keys were under the front seat. He waited five minutes for a team with a stretcher to come running to the car. A police car raced by as he flagged down a cab out on the main road.

Richard paid off the cab a hundred yards beyond the hotel and walked back. He had told Jay that he would return by midnight and he was late. He took his key out of his pocket in the elevator to save time and strode quickly down the corridor. He opened his door and Jay smiled at him. She had been sitting between the two rooms in an upright chair but she got up and tripped towards him as if she was wearing a long gown.

She said: 'God, I've missed you. You've been so *long*. I thought I'd die, Darling, absolutely *die*.'

English literature hadn't been his strong suit but it sounded like Noël Coward. She lunged at him and he sidestepped, plucking the paper-knife from her hand. She began to cry. He said: 'I'm sorry, Miss Li. I got delayed.'

She had cut the ball of her thumb. He led her through to the bathroom and made her hold the wound under the cold tap. The Russian had said that there must be no emotional involvement.

Richard said: 'The meeting with Wiley went well, Miss Li. Now there's only the funeral and you can get on with your new life.'

He didn't expect her to answer but she said: 'Hand me a tissue.'

They were the first proper words she had said to him and he remembered holding a young woman in his arms on his last operation with the Department. They had come through a hurricane on the *Golden Girl* and he had just killed two gunmen. She had asked for a tissue. He had searched his pockets but all he had was a knife, handgun, and a lot of bullets. The young woman had smiled at him and said that it didn't matter.

Later they were caught in an ambush and it got bloody.

The SAS had flown in to pick him up. He had been sitting on the

242

step of a truck. She had stood beside him and he had wanted to touch her, just touch her, but his hands were stiff with dry blood. The SAS officer had nodded to him that it was time to leave. He had felt awkward with the soldiers watching so he hadn't said goodbye. Mariana was her name – like Miss Li, still in her early twenties. She had written to him care of the British Embassy. He had written back, trying to explain that emotions that grew from shared dangers could seem more then they were and that he was too old for her. Her reply had been brief: *Why are you such a bloody coward, Trent?*

He took an elastoplast from his wash bag and bandaged Jay's thumb. She said, 'Thank you, Trent.'

'Richard,' he said: 'Richard O'Neill. You've got a long day tomorrow, Miss Li. You should get to bed. I'll sit up for a while.'

Sir Euan Wiley was awake and caught the bedside telephone on its second ring. Philip was on the line with a request that he come down to the Li compound right away. No, it couldn't wait.

Wiley had spent the past hour in thought without coming to a decision as to what action he should take over the report on Jay Li. The summons was most untimely. One o'clock in the morning always sounded a much more reasonable hour than it was. He dragged on a polo shirt and lightweight slacks, shoved his feet into black leather loafers, and took the back stairs down to the garage.

The nanny's Mini was less noticeable than their other cars and he had his hand on the door when he changed his mind. With a nod to the guard, he went back upstairs to the library and called Philip Li's private number.

He said: 'Philip, forgive me, but I had some damned lawyer from Australia here late and frankly I've had it. I'm sixty, for God's sake and we've all got a dreadful day to get through. We'll meet at church.'

Replacing the receiver, he looked up and saw his wife watching him from the doorway. He said, 'Philip wanted a word. I told him I hadn't the energy.'

'That's a change,' she said. 'I thought it was only me that you hadn't the energy for.'

In the months of their illicit courtship he had never noticed the cruelty in her mouth. Nor, in those days, had he ever thought of himself as a good catch. Now there were children to be considered.

The children had to come first. He said, 'This piracy thing has upset us all. You'll see, things will get better after the funeral.'

'They couldn't get much worse.'

'No, I suppose not,' he said.

28

There were people of importance in the financial world who spoke of Sir Euan Wiley as Li's poodle. They were in error. Sir Philip didn't like dogs. He had picked and groomed Euan because they shared a sense of humour and because the Scotsman's shyness hid his intelligence from the unwary. Euan was also stubborn and honourable. But most of all he was a poor cousin, and cousins fought the hardest to prove themselves to the family.

Robert had flown in for the funeral. They were to meet Timothy Brown at one o'clock in the morning at the counting house. Philip Li had wanted Euan present but his absence wasn't important. Li wondered what lawyer had called so late. Euan had never learnt to compartmentalise his business life. Sir Philip thought of his own glass collection, his rugs and paintings. He said to his son: 'We're fortunate in having outside interests, Robert.'

Hong Kong's harbour never slept. The two men stood for a moment admiring the lights that lanced from the big ships anchored out in the roads and from the launches and junks scurrying about their late-night business. The thickness and heat of the salt air were foreign to Robert, as were the oppressive scents that rose from the polluted waters. He dabbed a lawn handkerchief to his lips as if to protect himself.

Sir Philip smiled in recollection of his own homecoming so many years ago. 'You'll soon get used to it,' he said, and led his son along the wharf to the counting house.

All staff, however senior, were let in and out after normal office hours by the night security guards. Using his own key to the big doors was one of the many small pleasures Sir Philip drew from ownership. The guard, educated to Sir Philip's ways, saluted and stepped aside.

The financier sniffed with enjoyment at the cool dry atmosphere, so familiar to him as was the stirring of the overhead fans. In earlier days he would have been greeted by the chatter of teleprinters but now there was only the hiss of paper as it slid from a laser printer. As always, the half-dozen market-watchers had shed their jackets. One of them even had his feet on his desk and, spotting Sir Philip, nearly tipped backwards.

Sir Philip's smile seemed conspiratorial as he nodded to those of his employees who looked up from their terminals. He knew that this was a night that each one of them would remember and recount in detail long after his departure to another world.

Riding the elevator to his office, he told his son to take the leather captain's chair at the partner's desk: 'Get accustomed to it, Robert.'

Robert switched on his father's Compaq laptop and Sir Philip led him through the access codes.

'We'll get this wretched Brown business out of the way first,' he said.

Timmy Brown took a cab across town to the meeting with Sir Philip. It was over now but he recalled the beginning: how he had lain with his eyes shut beneath the giant Chinese and felt the trickle of the man's finger on the back of his neck, so gentle for one so muscular. He had wanted to cry with the gentleness because it was so cruel, as were the promises of love and fidelity the Chinese whispered in his ear. The door opened. Cameras flashed. The weight of the Chinese lifted from his back.

Timmy had clutched the sheet to his breast while one of the intruders adjusted the television. The screen flickered, then came pictures of the bed and of Timmy Brown with the Chinese who had approached him with such delicacy at the bar.

'You will do us a service,' one of them said.

Timmy Brown had dipped his head in obedience – he had known that they were Wong Fu's men.

There were few who knew him of old who would have considered him a brave man but he had grown with his illness. Only when connecting the final wire to the telephone in Sir Philip's study had he almost given way to his fear. He had already bugged the conference room and Sir Philip's office and wired Sir Philip's office telephone. This last connection would end his usefulness and he had wiped the sweat from his forehead on his sleeve, knowing that the connection was his death warrant.

He had been saved by the defections of the Ching girl and Rudi Beckenberg. From then on Wong Fu had needed him to install and service the links between the counting house and Wong Fu's own computers.

Timmy was one of the best in the business. He had done a good job but it was finished now with his summons to the counting house. He had reported the summons to his contact within the Wong Fu organisation. Then he had slipped out of his apartment and lost himself in the crowd.

Withdrawing a small but powerful transmitter from his nylon backpack, he directed the cab driver down Connaught Road. He opened the cab window as they passed the Wong Fu building. Peering up at the glass pyramid, he imagined the financier at his desk, and he smiled as he pressed the transmitter's send button.

He paid off the cab at the entrance to the Li compound, nodded to the security guard, and entered the counting house for the last time. A couple of the market-watchers looked up and he grinned at them sheepishly. Scurrying across to the elevator, he rode up to the second floor. He knocked before entering Sir Philip's office and he thought of Wong Fu listening.

Sir Philip took Timmy's hands in his and held them warmly as he inspected the young Californian: 'How are you?'

Timmy said that he was all right.

'Good. Splendid . . .' Turning to his son, the financier said: 'Meet our secret weapon. Timothy Brown, my son, Robert.'

Sir Philip turned Timmy toward the side table on which Miss James had left a bottle of champagne on ice and three Lalique flutes: 'It's your victory, Timothy. Do the honours.'

Wong Fu had ordered two of his men to pick up an Australian lawyer who had called Wiley for an urgent meeting connected to the funeral. One of the men was in hospital with concussion and a lightly fractured skull. Not even the police were to be allowed to interview him for the next twenty-four hours. The second of Wong Fu's men had disappeared and Wong Fu was already enraged as Timmy Brown eased the cork free. He had been in a rage ever since George Ross had flown in from London with his blackmailing demands that Wong Fu attend the pretended interment of the Li girl.

True, these irritations were merely temporary, and inconsequential when compared with the impending destruction of the House of Li. Wong Fu had decided to spring the trap immediately after the funeral.

He was puzzled rather than anxious as he listened to the pop of the cork which sounded as clearly in his penthouse as it did in Sir Philip Li's office.

'Veuve Cliquot. Good year, 1982,' Sir Philip said: 'Timothy, sit yourself down and tell Robert how you did it.'

Rage darkened Wong Fu's face, his scar pulsed, and the muscles in his shoulders swelled, hands crushing each other as he listened to the American detail each step in the surveillance – all the transmitters and the wire taps and the recorders he had set up at the instructions of Wong Fu's men.

'Tell him the last bit, that's the best,' Sir Philip said with an almost childish chuckle.

It was twenty-five minutes past two and Wong Fu listened to Timothy giggle: 'I rigged his computers. If he touches a key he'll trigger a virus that wipes his progammes and his disks. He has back-up but even a top man will need a couple of days straightening things out.'

Frozen at his desk, Wong Fu listened as Old Man Li listed for his son all the false information he had fed into Wong Fu's system over the past months. Most disastrous were the falsehoods he had fed to Beckenberg and Shirley Ching. These had been the base for Wong Fu's final attack. He turned in furious despair to his keyboards but his fingers froze. He had nothing without his computers. Not one single record existed on paper. Not one.

Grabbing a pad, he began to list from memory his many holdings. His handwriting was slow and ugly and even a beginning would take all night. There was no point. The rage exploded in him and he smashed both fists down on the nearest keyboard. The plastic split and he turned on the next. Smash, smash, smash, smash – four in all. Kicking his chair over, he stormed across to the window facing out across the city to the Li compound. He should have killed Old Man Li right at the beginning. Instead he had waited and plotted for the deeper and lasting pleasure that came with vengeance.

*

'The second million,' Sir Philip said and handed Timmy the envelope containing the draft.

The first million was held in trust at a Li bank for Timmy's parents and his brother and sister. This million was for himself and his partner back in San Francisco. At least they would be as comfortable as their illness permitted.

'I've put some suggestions in with it and an introduction to a friendly banker in Bermuda,' Sir Philip said: 'I only wish there was something else I could do.'

There wasn't anything that anyone could do. Timmy gave a wry grin and ducked his shoulders so that he looked sideways at the financier: 'Mostly it's been fun. Okay if I take the bugs out?'

The ring of the telephone exploded into the silence of the penthouse office. Wong Fu snarled as he grabbed up the receiver. It was the son rather than Old Man Li.

'I will be taking control of the House of Li tomorrow,' Robert said with the same courtesy that his father exercised: 'There are matters we must discuss. Perhaps you would be so kind as to drop by our counting house after the funeral?'

Sir Philip Li was satisfied as he watched his son. The breaking of Wong Fu would be Robert's first task on taking command. They had planned it well and once it was done there would be no doubts in the financial world as to Robert's strength. True, Trent and the child remained but the pair would relax once this ridiculous charade of a funeral was done with. His men would find them. It wasn't Robert's concern. Sir Philip would deal with it himself as he would with that weak fool, George Ross – that was something better done in England where it would draw little attention. A mugging or perhaps a traffic accident.

Consulting his watch, he calculated the time difference. The gold would be loaded soon and his manager in Geneva would follow it to the bank of receipt. They were such innocents, Trent and the girl, not to understand the power of the House of Li.

The driver reversed the security firm's truck into the bank's loading bay. Four of the bank's employees loaded the gold and three men from the security firm stacked it. The banker who had agreed the details of the bank-to-bank transfer with Sammi Samuelson was the fourth man in the truck. He and the men from the security firm wore identical green boilersuits and crash hats. Two hours in the back of a truck checking gold ingots was pleasurable when it paid ten percent of fifteen million Swiss francs.

Fifteen million demanded a great many signatures. Finally it was done. The steel door to the street lifted and the truck eased out into the well-behaved Geneva traffic. Once outside, the banker called his bank on his mobile telephone and gave the code that authorised the loan and immediate transfer to the account of a private trust at a bank in Nassau.

The transaction took one minute and fourteen seconds. Arrival of the money in the trust account triggered a computer programme that randomly transferred the money every forty-two seconds through a series of numbered accounts in five different countries.

The driver of the armoured truck had instructions as to which route to take through the Geneva traffic but not his destination; this he received by radio telephone ten minutes into his journey.

The truck reversed into the accepting bank's loading bay twenty-two minutes after leaving the bank of origin. The money had already been transferred twenty-five times, the programme had posted a coded message on a public bill board, then wiped itself.

Eight minutes later an emissary of the House of Li entered the office of the receiving bank's president. They bowed to each other and shook hands but the Li representative was in a hurry and they didn't take coffee. The House of Li had paid fifteen million in gold bullion and wished to have its destination traced. There was no need for threats or persuasion – the House of Li was too important a potential client. The president summoned the vice-president in command of the transaction.

The vice-resident was most apologetic. Had he only known that the House of Li was an interested party – but of course he hadn't – and he was most sorry but the bulk of the funds had been transferred to Nassau. He had checked the gold in the truck.

Yes, it was unusual and, yes, most unfortunate.

A Mr Samuelson had made the arrangements – a Latin American gentleman according to his passport, but with a Moscow connection. The details of the transfer were in the banker's office on the fourth floor. Though against banking regulations, the House of Li was

250

such a valued and respected institution. If the gentleman would be so good as to accompany him upstairs . . .

In Nassau the House of Li's representative spent ten minutes with the accountants at the Nassau bank of first receipt. A realist, he knew when he was beaten and didn't bother asking the name of the private trust that had triggered the computer programme. The money could be in one account or a thousand accounts spread through fifty different countries.

Miss Jasmine Li's grave had been dug midway up the gently sloping cemetery. Hong Kong's elite of all races and religious persuasions attended the funeral, and there were as many police and private security personnel and bodyguards as mourners.

The Australian lawyer, Richard O'Neill, intercepted Sir Philip's secretary as she followed the financier up from the limousines toward the grave. Obsequious so close to power, he whispered to Miss James that he had been retained to represent the deceased's estate by a Mr Trent. He handed her a business card, engraved of course, giving his law firm's Liechtenstein address and begged if he might have the very briefest of words with Sir Philip.

A combination of diligence and his years in Europe had tempered the lawyer's Australian accent but it remained painfully noticeable when compared with the old Etonian English spoken by Sir Philip.

He apologised profusely for intruding on Sir Philip's grief but he accompanied a great aunt on the maternal side of the deceased's family who was reluctant to attend at the grave without Sir Philip's leave.

He did so hope that Sir Philip would understand but there was one further matter . . .

Embarrassed, the lawyer blinked in the harsh sunlight. He had been put in a most difficult position that was not of his own making. However there seemed to have been an attempt to trace the deceased's estate, unsuccessful of course, but never the less unsuitable. He did so hope that Sir Philip would ensure that there was no repetition of such conduct.

A slight whitening of Sir Philip's lips was the only visible sign of his rage. He took a slim gold-cornered notebook from the pocket of his dark blue suit and slipped the Australian's business card inside the cover.

'I'm glad you've been so understanding,' Richard said.

Jay Li's great aunt was short and a little dumpy in her black suit, and wore an out-of-fashion black hat and veil. As apologetic as he had been to the grandfather, so Richard O'Neill was now solicitous for the welfare of the elderly lady as he escorted her up the slope through the crowd of mourners to the graveside.

Deeply respectful of Sir Philip's desire for privacy in his grief, the lawyer steered the great aunt to the opposite side of the grave from Sir Philip's little group. He bowed to Robert Li who stood beside his father, Miss James and Sir Euan Wiley a pace to the rear. Forever-watchful, Richard took note of the ancient hearse abandoned on the grass. Near the top of the hill a Chinese woman knelt at a grave, her motor scooter parked at the curb.

Wong Fu's Cadillac glided in through the cemetery gates. Three of his men escorted the tall Chinese. There was a hush amongst security personnel and mourners as the bitter rivals confronted each other. The two men hesitated before shaking hands, but finally it was done and they turned to face the grave as the six pall-bearers lowered the coffin onto the electrically operated straps.

There came a moment of awkwardness as, short-sighted, the bishop sought amongst the plastic grass for earth with which to fill his miniature silver shovel. The director of the funeral parlour coughed for his attention and proffered a matching bucket of a dry topsoil most suitable to the granddaughter of one of the good and great.

Charley Smith watched the bishop sprinkle earth on the coffin. The sun sparkled on the shovel as the prelate passed it to Sir Philip Li. The director of the funeral parlour scurried in attendance. Next it was Wong Fu's turn.

Charley watched the tall Chinese dig into the little bucket. Charley understood about Paddy's Chinese girl and young Paddy had explained how he wanted it done. There was plenty of time. Charley waited calmly and without a trace of nerves.

There were few amongst the Chinese at the funeral unsuspecting of Wong Fu's part in the piracy and kidnap. The hush deepened as he stepped to the grave. The patter of earth falling from the tiny shovel seemed shockingly loud.

Charley squeezed gently. The rifle was a Manlicher, the bullet hollowed and refilled with Mercury. Charley didn't bother to look, he had never missed a target in a quarter century of wet work. *Sin* was his nickname in the profession, short for *sin error*. He was rumoured to be a Spaniard or a Latin American. He rolled left through the hinged side of the coffin plinth in the ancient hearse and hit the grass in an athlete's squat. The hearse hid him from the funeral party.

The Chinese woman who had been praying near the top of the cemetery touched her brakes as she rode her motor scooter past the hearse. Charley sprang astride the pillion. The scooter's speedometer registered a sedate 15 mph as they cleared the cemetery gates. Charley kept his face buried against the woman's back. He wore a boy scout's uniform. They looked like a mother and son on the way to a scout meeting.

The bullet hit Wong Fu precisely in the centre of his forehead, smashing his head back. His knees buckled forward and he fell quite slowly into Miss Jasmine Li's grave.

There were shouts from the police and bodyguards as the mourners fled. Whistles shrilled and sirens screeched. There were even a few unseemly screams as the sedate event turned to chaos.

At first Sir Philip Li seemed bemused, as if age had finally conquered him. However his mind worked with its usual speed. He looked up from the corpse of his rival and across the grave at the Australian lawyer and Jay's dumpy great aunt from San Francisco.

The aunt raised her veil. His granddaughter stood there. She laughed at him. *Laughed* at him. His rage was like fire, growing in intensity with every second. He couldn't break their eye contact. Not even as the fire exploded back out of his heart into his brain.

'We can go now,' Jay said quietly. She rested a gloved hand lightly on Richard O'Neill's arm as they walked down to their limousine.

'The hotel first,' Richard told the driver. They were booked on the 19.46 flight to Tokyo so there was no hurry.

Ahead of them, Charley Smith glanced at his watch. The woman rode the scooter with skill, weaving through Hong Kong's traffic. He would be back at the hotel in time to watch the three o'clock on TV. Charley only bet on his own horses, but he loved to watch.

EPILOGUE

Third-generation Australian, Laura Sing was about as Chinese in her psychological make up as an elephant. She had enjoyed every moment of her three days in Hong Kong. She had also spent a good deal of time thinking about Richard O'Neill. Most of her friends and acquaintances were in her profession. They tended to lack confidence – perhaps because there were so few parts available. For the same reason, loyalty wasn't always their strongest suit. Added to which most of the men were narcissistic as well as self-absorbed.

Laura had sensed a strength and certainty of purpose in Richard O'Neill that was very different. She wouldn't have accepted the job if she hadn't wanted something to happen. That wasn't in her character. The circumstances were ideal. But she wasn't at all sure as to how it would turn out.

Her airline ticket said that she was flying first class to Dallas via Tokyo, which gave her access to the Monarch Lounge. She had picked up that month's issue of *Vanity Fair* at the kiosk in the hotel lobby and sat with it now, seeming to read as she would have on the stage while in fact watching for her cue.

Richard O'Neill and a young Chinese woman entered the lounge. Richard presented their tickets at the reception desk. The Chinese wore a beige cotton and silk mix travelling suit and a wide brimmed hat that shadowed her face. She carried a blue tapestry Gladstone bag and a matching shoulder bag in a rabbit design sufficiently unusual to mark the owner. She and Laura were about the same age and build. Laura supposed that they must look much alike to anyone who wasn't Chinese.

Jay stood beside Trent at the reception desk and looked round the Monarch Lounge. There were a half-dozen Chinese women of

254

about her age and she wondered which one was her double. She was surprised to find that she could care a little. She touched Trent on the arm. He looked down but all she did was nod and turn away to the restroom.

Their clothes exchanged, the two young women inspected each other in the cramped cubicle. They weren't sure of the protocol but Jay whispered her thanks and Laura said that it was fine and she was looking forward to it.

Richard had said that they should leave the restroom together. Laura swung the tapestry shoulder bag as she crossed the lounge and asked at the bar for a glass of orange juice. She looked over at Richard and he said, 'A coffee, please, Jay.'

Robert Li, Euan Wiley, and Miss James sat in a private waiting room at the hospital. Robert had been dictating a statement to the banks. He spoke in the same quiet courteous manner as his father:

Recent rumours concerning the House of Li were a product of the enmity between Sir Philip Li and Mr Wong Fu. Mr Robert Li has taken control of the House of Li and to allay any uncertainty as to the House of Li's future, has decided to break with tradition in declaring the value of the House of Li's realisable holdings. These stood at eleven billion dollars as of the first of the month and certificates of valuation will be made available to those with legitimate concern. The House of Li also holds eleven million dollars in bank deposits.

Mr Robert Li intends returning to the House of Li's tradition of expanding only through use of its own funds and all present bank loans will be repaid within thirty days. It is also the intention of Mr Robert Li to assist in steadying the market by taking control of those companies associated with Mr Wong Fu, many of which are heavily indebted to the House of Li.

The cardiac specialist returned and Euan Wiley watched Robert talk to him in a hushed voice.

The specialist withdrew and Robert continued quietly: 'Have Beckenberg and Shirley Ching's desks sealed. Get men round at their apartments. All papers and their computers go to the top floor. They won't argue. Inform everyone we trade with that we'll look askance at either of them being employed. I want the banks notified and I want their accounts closed, credit cards withdrawn, everything.

'Now that lawyer, O'Neill . . .'

'He doesn't exist,' Euan said. There was more of Philip in the son than he had suspected. He felt a little uncomfortable as he turned to Miss James but he knew his duty:

'The letter to the banks should be in my name, Miss James. I'll sign it as soon as it's typed.'

'Murder, attempted murder, conspiracy to defraud – it's all there, Robert. Trent brought it to me last night. It will have to go to the authorities if you don't see sense. I suggest the bulk of the estate be divided between a series of charitable trusts.'

Trent watched the real Jay Li disembark at Tokyo's airport. An American Airlines attendant waited to guide her through to AA's Dallas flight. Jay strolled up the ramp, seemingly very much in command of herself. He had wanted to warn her of the dangers of remaining imprisoned and of not trusting but he wasn't good with words. They hadn't even said goodbye.

Tanaka's police friends were there, bowing, shaking hands, telling Trent that the *Golden Girl* was ready for sea. They had a car waiting for the drive to Kyoto. One of them had crewed the catamaran from the Philippines and wanted to discuss technicalities and what course Trent would take to Sydney. Trent had allowed six weeks for the voyage. Six weeks for the real Jay Li to adapt to her new persona.

Laura slipped her hand through his arm. He looked down at her for a moment, then up again along the moving sidewalk in time to see Jay look round. Jay smiled and gave a little shrug and was gone. Bloody girl, taking such a damn fool risk. He'd told her not to look back.